BLOOD,
SALT,
WATER

BLOOD, SALT, WATER

A NOVEL

denise mina

LITTLE, BROWN AND COMPANY

NEW YORK   BOSTON   LONDON

For Luke, Liam and Wolfie

Little, Brown and Company
Hachette Book Group
1290 Avenue of the Americas, New York, NY 10104
littlebrown.com

First United States Edition, December 2015
Originally published in Great Britain by the Orion Publishing Group, July 2015

Little, Brown and Company is a division of Hachette Book Group, Inc. The Little, Brown name and logo are trademarks of Hachette Book Group, Inc.

The publisher is not responsible for websites (or their content) that are not owned by the publisher.

The Hachette Speakers Bureau provides a wide range of authors for speaking events. To find out more, go to hachettespeakersbureau.com or call (866) 376-6591.

ISBN 978-0-316-38054-6
Library of Congress Control Number: 2015949262

10 9 8 7 6 5 4 3 2 1

RRD-C

Printed in the United States of America

BLOOD,
SALT,
WATER

All of us have in our veins the exact same percentage of salt in our blood that exists in the ocean, and, therefore, we have salt in our blood, in our sweat, in our tears. We are tied to the ocean. And when we go back to the sea – whether it is to sail or to watch it – we are going back from whence we came.

John F. Kennedy

I

She'd been as biddable as a heifer for the two days they had her. She came willingly when they picked her up in the van. She asked no favours, made no appeals for mercy while they waited for Wee Paul to give the final word: kill her or let her go.

At first Iain was pleased that she was passive. He'd never had to muscle a woman before. Then he began to wonder why. She didn't seem frightened at all, she even smiled sometimes. She only spoke once, to ask a question: *How much longer will it be?* Slowly they began to realise that she had completely misunderstood what was going on.

Tommy smirked when he worked it out, nodding at Iain behind her back, laughing at her. It wasn't funny to Iain. The longer it went on the worse he felt about it. It was dishonourable, but he couldn't very well warn her or let her go. The deception made him so uncomfortable that a couple of times, in the long last night, he was tempted to just get up and leave. He couldn't. He had to see the job through to pay the debt. Screw the nut and see it through.

After Wee Paul called this morning and gave Tommy the decision, Iain couldn't look at her any more. They put her back in the van and drove from Helensburgh to Loch Lomond.

Out of the van under a rain-threatening sky, low grey clouds muting all the colours on the mountains. They marched in single file through high sand dunes, Tommy leading, her in the middle, Iain behind, following a zigzag path through to the lochside.

The sand dunes were industrial dumps, destined for a golf course, neon yellow and very high. She turned to look at the glinting sand and Iain saw the apple of her cheek swell in a small smile. What was she thinking about? About warm holidays on yellow beaches, maybe. Blue seas. Suntans. She still had no idea. Iain put his hand in his pocket and touched the cosh. He wouldn't hurt her face, she had a nice face. He'd make it as quick as possible.

She flinched at a bitter wind off the water as she stepped out onto the lochside. Then she looked up. Her step faltered at the sight of the boat. She sagged at the knees, lifted her face and screamed a rasping animal shriek, sore on the ear because it was so close.

Tommy spun back, reaching for her mouth to shut her up but she flailed her arms, squawking 'NO!' in little breathy bursts. They were astonished by the fight in her. She turned, shoulder-shoving Tommy until she knocked him off balance, trying to get past. Tommy wheeled on his heels, grabbing at her even as he fell. His hand slipped down her hip, he was on his knees and she made it past him.

She got two long steps around him, heading down the dock, running for the thick line of trees.

Iain was a big man with a long reach. He grabbed her upper arm, pulled the cosh from his pocket and turned her to him. He hit her on the jaw as hard as he could.

Her head snapped back on her neck. Her eyes rolled. She slithered to the ground as if filled with sand herself. Then she lay on the dock, gracelessly folded over one of her legs.

An old prison trick. You might hit someone hard, but hit wrong and a man could just turn back to you, angry and ready. For a knockout, the head had to whip around fast. It made the brain bang against the inside of the skull. Make the head move fast enough and you could almost guarantee a drop.

Iain and Tommy stood looking down at her. Tommy was panting, scared. Iain was surprised he didn't hide it better. They didn't really know each other, hadn't worked together before. They were still laying out their stalls. Tommy was doing a TV baddie, swearing, growling. Iain was being the most frightening men in prison: expressionless hard nuts who gave no warning before they went for you.

Looking down at the unconscious woman, he thought of those men. He'd envied them. They never seemed to feel anything. He wondered now if their blank eyes hid a despair so profound it squeezed the air from their lungs. If self-disgust weighed like a brick in their guts. Probably not.

They watched an egg-shaped lump rise on her jaw. The movement of her chest was faltering. Her eyes flickered behind the lids. Unconscious but not dead. The plan had been to get here, drove her to the boat, maybe even get her quite far out on the water before they killed her.

Tommy growled, 'Don't just leave her there. Fucking finish.'

He was right. She could wake up and that would be beyond cruel because it would still need to be done, but she'd know.

Iain bent down fast. It was a mistake born of compassion. A burning-hot needle stab in his lower vertebrae made him groan. Embarrassed, he straightened up. He tried again, keeping his spine straight, lowering himself down on one knee as if he was being knighted. He got all the way down and settled into the pose, shifting his pelvis in tiny movements, forward and back, testing the limits. His sore back was new, the pains random, not yet mapped.

He ground his teeth as he lifted the cosh over his head and brought it down again and again, the way he used to cull fish when he was a boy. He did it on the top of her head, going in through the hair so that he didn't damage her face. It was the only mercy he could afford her. Whatever she had done, however much Iain needed the job, she deserved to keep her face.

Tommy looked away, affecting disinterest, staring at the boat. He pointed over at the peeling twelve-footer slapping against the dockside on the choppy grey loch. The *Sea Jay II* didn't look like much.

'Check the fucking state of it,' he said, overplaying his interest in the state of the boat because he couldn't watch. 'The paint's all fucking peely.'

Tommy didn't know shit about boats. The boat was sound.

It was done. A halo of scarlet bloomed around her head. Iain found he was panting and his knee hurt terribly. His whole body weight was pressing through it onto the rippled concrete.

He leaned over the woman's body to push himself up, forming a windbreak over her. In the vacuum he glanced at her face, close enough to see her without the swollen jaw or the bloody wound on her head. Quite suddenly he saw her as a woman, maybe a woman he knew once, or loved, he couldn't place her, but it made her a person and she hadn't been until now. Until now she had been an awkward chore. One of those things you had to do but couldn't bring yourself to think about.

Leaning on his hand and bending his elbow to lever himself up brought him closer yet. He felt warmth radiate from her cheek. Motherly dew from her breath settled on his eyelids. His ear was just inches from her mouth. He wouldn't have heard her otherwise. From deep inside her came a sound: *Sheila*. His mother's name.

Shocked, he reeled back. As his mouth aligned with hers he gasped and sucked in her warm, wet last breath. He sucked it deep down into his lungs.

Iain scrambled to his feet. He stepped away, hands up, surrendering. No. That was stupid. *Shee-lah*. Not his mother's name. Just sounds. From a body. Not Sheila. *Shee-lah*. Not real. But his lips were damp with her, his airways full of the screaming of her.

The loch clawed at the dockside. Gulls skirled an indignant dirge high overhead. A handful of sand pattered on her face, lifted by the lamenting wind.

'You finished?' Tommy was keeping his eyes on the boat. 'Is that you done?'

Iain opened his mouth to speak but shut it again. He didn't want to speak because he didn't know what would come out of him. All the fight she'd had left in her, all her everything, had gone into him. It had risen up, leaving her body, and he had sucked it in. Her soul.

Now she was trapped inside him. She was writhing and angry and flailing and she would burn her way out through his guts.

2

Alex Morrow's work phone rang loud and shrill on the passenger seat.

'Roxanna's missing, ma'am,' said McGrain, one of her DCs. 'We lost visual at school drop-off yesterday and didn't find her again. She's just been reported missing by an anonymous caller.'

'What? Who called?'

'We don't know. It was a child's voice. English accent.'

'One of her kids?' Morrow was holding the phone on the steering wheel and shouting at it. She was breaking the law, but that wasn't why she was shouting. She was personally invested in the fate of Roxanna Fuentecilla. 'He's done it, hasn't he? Shit. The fucking boyfriend.'

'Well, we don't know who called. Sounds like one of the children.'

'I'll be there in ten minutes.' She hung up and hurried through the mid-morning traffic to London Road Police Station.

The car park was full but she had a reserved space. She got out and locked the car, walking quickly to the back door, giving herself a talking-to. She should calm down. She'd never even met Fuentecilla. Whatever Morrow admired about her was just conjecture. She'd watched a lot of footage but that didn't give a fully rounded picture at all. She was a crim. Remember that. Us and them.

Through the back bar and the entrance to the holding cells, Morrow gave the desk sergeant a quick nod and a hello. She hurried through the locker rooms and cut across the lobby. Opening her office door, she bowled her bag to the leg of her desk, doubled back across the corridor to the incident room and found McGrain. He was leaning on a desk sipping a mug of tea and listening to DC Thankless, a bald, muscled man with an aggravating manner. Morrow didn't like him.

'Jees-ho.' McGrain stood up straight when he saw her. 'That was quick.'

'Come in here.'

McGrain followed her into her office and closed the door after himself.

'This is not a canteen.' She was looking at the mug of tea in his hand.

Embarrassed, he ducked back out, left it on the nearest table in the incident room and slipped back into her office. 'Sorry, ma'am.'

'Sit down.' She pointed to the chair. 'Now, tell me.'

So he told her: they lost visual contact with Roxanna Fuentecilla yesterday after she'd dropped her kids at school. She always came home from her office at the same time but last night she hadn't been seen going into the house. Nothing suspicious though: the lights went on as usual in the front room, the kitchen, her bedroom. Her car wasn't there either but she was known to park in another street sometimes when it was busy.

They had been following her for three weeks; they lost her sometimes and hadn't thought much of it. It would be too expensive to physically follow her, budget cuts had reduced them to doing their own filing and rationing biros, so they'd been relying on CCTV. They watched a lot of street-cam footage. Fuentecilla was not considered a flight risk because of her kids. They were fourteen and twelve, at a good school, clean and fed and thriving. She clearly adored them.

Overnight the CCTV from all the usual sources had been checked. There wasn't a single frame of Fuentecilla yesterday. Then at seven this morning, a call, anonymous, from a phone box in Central Station. A voice, small and young, reported Roxanna

Fuentecilla missing since yesterday. When the operator asked if the caller had any idea where she might be, they said they didn't know 'where they've taken her', which suggested more than one person, so, not the boyfriend in a blind rage. Then the phone cut out abruptly.

'One of her kids,' said Morrow.

'Yeah. The English accent sounded posh, kind of drawly. Can't be that common up here.'

'CCTV of the phone box in Central Station?'

'Asked for it and it's on its way.'

'Good. Send me the audio of the call. Notify the chief's office. They'll set a meeting.'

'Yes, ma'am.' And then McGrain was gone.

She shut the door and turned on her computer. It booted up slowly. She felt her customary cheerful serotonin spark, as she did every morning now, at the thought of following Roxanna Fuentecilla, but corrected her chemical self: there was no footage today. Roxanna was missing. She felt as if her favourite show had been cancelled.

The case had become a soap opera for her, a story with a lot of money and super-good-looking people doing fun things and having arguments. Fuentecilla herself was hilariously argumentative. She was from Madrid, from a rich family who'd squandered a fortune. For a number of reasons, not all of them her fault, Fuentecilla had been left penniless and seemed to be trying to set up some sort of mysterious criminal scam involving seven million pounds of someone else's money. She was supposed to be keeping a low profile but was always smashing jars in shops that incurred her wrath, shouting at her boyfriend in the supermarket or bawling in Spanish at other parents outside the school for parking irresponsibly. Her relationship with her live-in boyfriend was stormy; though not actually known to be violent, it seemed inevitable that it would be. Fuentecilla had issues in the area of dispute resolution. Still, seven million was serious money, suggesting she was working with serious people. Morrow shouldn't have warm feelings about her.

The desktop resolved onscreen. Doleful, she glanced at the fresh files of CCTV. She usually clicked on them first but there was no point today. Opening her email instead, she found the emergency call file already there. She plugged in her earphones, clicked and listened.

It was a child's voice, a posh English accent. They spoke calmly at first, the sound almost drowned out by the background hum of the station. When the operator asked them to spell 'Roxanna Fuentecilla' they did so fluently and gave her home address and postcode without hesitation.

'She's been missing since yesterday morning,' the caller said. 'I'm worried she's been killed or something.' At the word 'killed' they faltered and were breathless for the rest of the call.

The operator asked if the caller knew where Fuentecilla might have gone. 'I don't know ... I don't know where they've taken her.'

The operator asked again, 'Can you give me your name and address?' But this time the caller hung up.

Morrow felt sure it was one of the kids. She remembered the bakery incident. Not the boy, please not that wee boy.

Police Scotland only went into the bakery to find out what had happened because Fuentecilla was taken from there to Accident and Emergency in an ambulance. Suspected broken ankle, really just a very bad sprain. Morrow and her team had watched the CCTV from behind the counter over and over, just for entertainment: mother and son coming in, boy cowed, mother furious, he must have done something very bad. Roxanna bought and paid for a Victoria sponge cake, pulled it out of the box and hit him in the face with it. Mother and son stood laughing at each other in the shop, bits of cake dropping off his cheeks onto the tiled floor. Then the boy wiped a big lump off his cheek and hit her back and she laughed so hard that she slipped on the cream-splattered tiles, fell over and hurt herself. Morrow thought of his cream-and-jam-smeared face, of laughter tears rolling down his cheeks. Not that wee boy, please.

McGrain was at her office door. 'We've got the film from Central. I can't send it to you without compressing it, d'you want to just come and see?'

'Of course.'

Like a lot of technical things Morrow didn't really know what 'compressing' meant. She worried it might undermine her authority to keep on admitting it so she just followed him to his desk.

3

Boyd Fraser was chopping fresh mint leaves with a large twin-bladed mezzaluna. In Italy, mezzalunas were the tool of under-chefs with no knife skills but no one here knew that. In Helensburgh, a twee Scottish seaside town, the mezzaluna was a sophisticated novelty.

Feeling himself watched by one particular customer in the café, Boyd chopped for longer than the mint needed, getting into the rolling rhythm, working the green mint oil into a large olive-wood board. He wanted to look up and make sure the customer was really watching, but he didn't. They might not be watching, might just have their face pointed in his direction. Anyway, he didn't need their fucking approval to chuck a bowl of tabbouleh together.

He knew a lot of people came to eat here, paid the high prices, because of what was implied by eating in the Paddle Café. Organic, local, farmers' market. Nose-to-tail. Seasonal. All the hollow pro-words he used to give a fuck about. It was an underground movement when Boyd got into it. At one time he'd cared with the same fevered certainty his minister father had for his faith. Past heresy, his father used to say, was the present orthodoxy: the food revolutionaries now found themselves unwilling high priests of a bland new consensus.

His wife, Lucy, got very drunk at a friend's wedding once. Just before she threw up into a rhododendron bush that was older than her grandmother, she said that a café with a mission statement was utter bollocks. Boyd liked her that night. Not just loved her, he always loved her, but he really liked her. If they'd met for the first time that night he would have fallen in love with her, right there and then.

The mission statement was printed on the Paddle menus. Even the takeaway menu had a mission statement on it. *Bringing organic eggs blah blah blah. Supporting our local blah blah blah.* He knew that the blah blah was their profit margin. Customers only paid five fifty for six eggs because of the blah blah.

Boyd chanced a glance up. The watchful customer still had her eyes trained on him through the glass display case. An older woman, but everyone in this town was old. Sharp greying bob, cornflower-blue eyes, expensive sweater in mustard cashmere. She had a very long straight nose, pinched at the end. Her blue neck scarf was pinned with a Victorian brooch, opals and diamonds, inherited. She was smiling at him, her eyebrows raised in recognition. He didn't know her.

Taking their brief eye contact as a prompt, she stood up and sidled around a display crate of organic local seasonal tomatoes.

'Boyd. It's Susan Grierson.'

He reeled at the sound of her voice. 'Miss Grierson? For goodness …' He stumbled around the counter to her, a boy again, thrilled to see his old Akela from Scouts, his very first sailing instructor. He sandwiched her hand in both of his, wanted to hug her but knowing it would be too much. 'You're back!'

'I am,' she said, the warmth of her smile meeting his. 'My mother died.' Boyd hadn't heard that and he usually knew these things: the café was a hub of local news.

'Oh, I'm sorry,' he said. 'Me too. My father.'

'Your father? Well, that must have been a well-attended funeral.' She meant his father's congregation, not friends, certainly not family. In fact, the turn-out was poor. Most of them were very old. 'My mother's funeral was pitiful.'

Miss Grierson looked tearfully at the floor, shaking a little, as if she had forced her mother to be old and lonely by going out into the world. Lots of people came back here after a death.

Grief and dislocation took them all differently but everyone felt guilty. Sad and guilty. There was no use in it.

Boyd tried to help her out of it. 'So, where have you been living?'

'US. I was in the Hamptons for twenty years.'

'What's that like?'

'Quite like Helensburgh, in fact. Lovely, gentle people. Changed a lot now, though.' She looked sad but lilted her voice, as if trying to lever her mood. 'Then London for a while.' The sadness lingered, joined by what looked like wet-eyed anxiety. 'So . . .'

'Well, I was in London too,' said Boyd kindly. 'Fifteen years. Glad to get out in the end?' He was leaving it open for her to denounce London, as people who left it often did. It usually cheered them up but she didn't take the bait.

'Where were you living in London, Boyd?'

'Crouch End.'

'I knew it!' She smiled and looked around the Paddle's interior. 'Hamble and Hamble?'

'Ah.' Boyd gave a cheeky grin. 'You've found me out.'

'I knew it! I lived right next door in Highgate. When I walked in here I knew it was a copy. Because of the local produce oath on the menus.'

'I can picture you in Hambles'.'

'You even used the same colour of Farrow and Ball paint.' She nodded at the walls. 'Don't they mind?'

'Well . . .' He looked at the wooden shelving displaying retro-style olive oil drums, the tumbling basket of sourdough bread and the string of brown paper bags hanging from a bare nail hammered into the wall. 'They don't know. They would know if they came in but they won't come in.' Because no one came here – at least, no one Boyd was very interested in.

'I'm so glad to be back now, in time for the independence referendum . . .'

Boyd knew then that she was *just* back. With three weeks until the vote no one else was glad. Those in favour of independence could hardly wait another minute, and the other side just wanted it to be over. Miss Grierson raised her eyebrows, waiting for him to say whether he was pro or anti. Boyd didn't. He ran a business, for fuck's sake. He couldn't afford to take a public position and alienate customers on the other side. He raised his eyebrows back at her and she changed the subject:

'And I was so pleased when I saw you did gluten-free bread . . .' Miss Grierson got that look in her eye then, a look of mild martyrdom Boyd recognised as the presage to the biography of an allergy. He zoned out on the details but she seemed to be hitting all the narrative points.

'. . . found I wasn't *actually* coeliac but certainly had a very strong reaction . . .'

Boyd's mind wandered again. He was thinking about giving up the gluten-free range. A big Waitrose had opened nearby and they did it cheaper. He didn't want to have to listen to this story three times a day any more. 'Allergy bastards', he called them, in his head and to Lucy. 'Allergy bastards bought all the bread today,' he'd say while they were watching telly. Or, 'Had to chuck all the gluten-free out because not enough allergy bastards came in.' They didn't seem able to buy the stuff without telling him about their Damascene journey. He'd spotted a gap in the market. It didn't mean he wanted to keep a chart of their colon function.

Miss Grierson had stopped talking. She looked at him quizzically, sensing his disengagement.

'So,' he said, 'how long have you been back, Miss Grierson?'

She hesitated, probably meaning to tell him to call her Susan, but decided not to, for some reason. 'Recently – going through her things.'

'Sad?'

She looked sad. 'No. She was very old. A lot to do in the house, though. Garden's a mess.'

The Griersons' garden was a huge lot in the middle of town, three quarters of an acre. A small estate really. He used to pass it on adolescent runs in the summer. Giant Scots pines with trunks the colour of ginger snaps. A hundred-foot lawn and a big walled vegetable garden at the back. He had been passing again recently, out running or walking Jimbo, but the walls were high and even the hedge breaks were overgrown. He couldn't see in any more.

'Well,' he said, 'you'll know that most of those big gardens have been sectioned and sold off for new builds. Bear that in mind when you're selling—'

'Oh, I'm not selling. I'm moving back.'

Boyd smiled. '*I've* moved back.'

'We're all moving back, aren't we? The old pack.'

'Seems that way. I see a lot of old faces in here.'

She touched his elbow in a comradely manner – 'Our *age* . . .' Though he was only thirty-five, younger than her by a good fifteen years.

Suddenly conscious of all that needed to be done before lunch, Boyd let his weight shift to his back foot, moving behind the counter. 'Do you still sail?'

'No, our boathouse is empty now. Mother sold them when I left for the States.'

'We have a boat, if you'd like to go out?' The offer was no sooner out of his mouth than he wished it back. He saw her eyes widen, wonder, file the invitation away for possible use later. Boyd didn't sail for company. He was dreading his boys being old enough to go out with him.

'Maybe, another time,' she said. 'Thanks, Boyd, it's kind of you.'

He wanted to change the subject. 'Were you an Akela out in the States?'

'No,' she said. 'I gave it up when I moved. I loved it, though, while I did it. Gave me real confidence.'

'Leader of the pack?'

15

'I'm not much of a leader, but, you know.' She warmed at the memory. 'It gave me such courage just to go off and *do* things. Super thing for a young woman to have, that confidence. Good for me. My mother made me do it because I didn't go to uni with my friends, you know, "Do something, Susan!"' Miss Grierson launched into a dull reminiscence about her mother giving her advice and how it was good advice or something, but Boyd wasn't listening any more. He picked up the mezzaluna again, holding it loosely with one hand. It was a prompt to her, to say goodbye, but she was talking without heeding the listener, rolling through a story to please herself, the way old people did.

Boyd raised the mezzaluna slowly, waiting until the end of the story. She got there, looked at the knife and then around the shop.

'So,' she said vaguely, 'd'you have a job for me?'

Very American. Forthright and unembarrassed. Quite unattractive.

'You can't need the money?' He looked at the teenage wait-resses on the floor and dropped his voice to a murmur. 'Miss Grierson, the money I pay is crap.'

She smiled. 'Call me Susan, please. No, but I need to do some-thing. I can't bear the thought of working in a charity shop. The people in them are all my age. I like a mix.'

Boyd grinned at her: every second shop in the town was a charity shop. They were staffed by retired people volunteering for a few hours a week. Most of their stock came from post-mortem house clearances and the ring of old folk's homes that circled the town, ornaments and personal effects the families didn't want back, after.

He leaned in and whispered, 'It's the half-dead selling the knick-knacks of the dead to the almost dead.'

They both tittered, she with shock at his maliciousness, he with discomfort. He'd said it often but he wished he hadn't said it now. It was quite nasty, and she was decent, so it mattered.

'That's what people call it here, anyway.' He was lying. The line was his.

She looked uncomfortable. 'It's a bit mean!'

Boyd pretended to think about it for the first time. 'Actually, it *is* a bit mean. I could do with a hand tomorrow evening, if you're free?'

She seemed disconcerted by that and looked around the café. 'Are you open in the evenings?'

'No. We're catering a dinner dance at the Victoria Halls. Charity. Raising money for a children's hospice. I need someone to stand with a clipboard and mark off the tables as they get served, time it so that no one is waiting too long between courses. Think you can do that?'

He saw her fingers close over the edge of an imaginary clipboard. 'Yes,' she said. 'I think I can manage that, yes.'

'Righto, Miss Grierson. Be here at five thirty, then. And wear black.'

'Please, Boyd, call me Susan.'

'No,' he said firmly, 'I like "Miss Grierson".'

4

In the van, driving back.

Tommy and Iain were heading out of the wild, back to Helens-burgh on a road that cut through chocolate-box Scotland. On high, rugged hills mist clung to the lochans and rain blackened the stone cliffs.

Iain had a barb in his throat. The lassie, the dead lassie, her breath was stuck in there, a cough about to happen. Why did she go with them? What did she think was going to happen? Iain felt the catch in his throat throb and tighten, as if she was trying to explain to him. He tried to reason himself out of the mood. This is a good thing, he told himself. It was done now and the debt paid. But it didn't shift the contamination deep in the core of him.

'You're very quiet.' Tommy accelerated on a sharp turn, making the chassis of the old van groan. 'Did that do your head in?' A smile was tugging at the corner of his mouth.

Tommy got a wild buzz from acting like a gangster but he wasn't one. He'd never been in prison. Iain knew what he would have been like: cowering in his cell at association, hand-washing some thug's underpants in return for protection.

Iain had done long time. He was always weight for a bigger man and had done his time with dignity. He'd been out for eight months now but he still had the head of a passman. *Passman*: a prisoner trusted to dole out cleaning products and pens. The passman was halfway between screws and prisoners. They were the moral compromise that kept the whole system working, the vilified keepers of order. Everyone felt superior to them, Iain knew that, but everyone colluded in the compromise because everyone wanted something.

Keeping order didn't include killing a woman. That was a different thing.

'Did it?' said Tommy. 'Do your nut in?'

Iain shook his head.

'Here, she won't just wash up on the beach outside the kiddie rides at Loch Lomond Shores, will she?'

She wouldn't. Loch Lomond was a mile deep in some places. There was nowhere to go but down. Sailors without life-vests, swimmers and weekend canoeists got sucked under by the eddies and were paralysed by the cold from the deep water. They didn't come up for weeks. Sometimes they never came up.

Iain looked at his hands. Her blood was watery on his cuffs, under his nails. It was one of the few bits of concrete advice Sheila ever gave him and he'd forgotten it when it mattered. Salt water lifts blood, only salt water. It was a fresh-water loch.

After they dropped her over the side of the boat, Iain looked at his bloody hands. He wanted to be clean and plunged his hands into the water. He had expected warmth, the sensation of putting his hands under a duvet on a cold winter morning, but the water was scaldingly cold. He yanked his burning hands back out, contracted into claws, and stood, panting with shock, bloody water running down his forearms. His hands looked unfamiliar, like someone else's. And now his cuffs were drying in the heat of the van, turning crusty.

They drove on, passing a Waitrose lorry.

'I was in that Waitrose. Don't know what all the fuss is about.' Tommy was determined to chat. 'You coming to the dinner dance?'

Iain looked at him.

'Tomorrow night?' Tommy licked the corner of his mouth, keeping his eyes on the road. 'Got your ticket?'

Iain nodded.

The Children's Hospice Dinner Dance. Iain had forgotten. He did have a ticket. Everyone had a ticket. Mark Barratt made it clear everyone had to go. He wanted everyone to attend because his niece wasn't well and it was a good cause. Wee Paul, Mark's second, nagged and nagged until everyone could prove they'd bought a ticket. They did whatever Mark wanted. Mark wasn't going. He was away in Barcelona while the deed with the woman got done. Alibi. Privilege of management, he said.

'Hey, you thought about "Yes" yet? "Bairns not Bombs", eh? Thought about that?' Tommy was forever trying to bring up the independence referendum, pushing 'Yes'. The naval base nearby meant there were nuclear bombs barely a mile down the coast. The independence camp had vowed to get rid of them and spend all the money on nurseries or something.

'That's what we're about. The future. Hope, yeah?'

Iain nodded. He just agreed with everyone. He'd never voted. He wasn't registered. Mark said they were all to vote against it. He said independence would interfere with his business in Europe.

'Ye not talking, buddy?'

Iain didn't say anything. He was so low he wasn't sure he could speak.

'Ach, well, you're maybe just tired.'

Just tired. It was weird that Tommy chose that phrase, said it the way Sheila used to. Iain wasn't thinking about her, exactly, but he felt as if he'd just been about to. It was stupid, what he'd thought the woman said, but it was as if Sheila was determined to come back into his head and this time she did it through Tommy.

Just tired.

When Iain was young, if he came in with bloody fists, or a sore face, or a bag of something he had no business having and he didn't want to tell her what or why, she always said maybe he was 'just tired' and made him a wee cup of tea.

Sheila died so young he didn't have the time to think of her as anything but his mother. The only time he ever thought of her as a person in her own right, as having anything that wasn't him or about him, was as he stood in the pew at her cremation. Some guy was talking about Jesus. Not a priest, though that's what she would have wanted. Behind closed red curtains a squeaky wheel signalled the lowering of her coffin. Iain wondered what would happen to the metal plates in her head. What temperature would they cremate her body at? Would it melt the metal or would it just burn everything else around it? He imagined the skull they were attached to melting like butter in a pan and the plates collapsing towards each other, tired sides on a house. Just tired.

Metal plates in her head and jaw. The guy who hit her wasn't Iain's dad, he was just some guy. Early in her life, Sheila declared herself unlucky in love and then went on to pick arsehole after arsehole.

Every time Iain met a new one, even if the guy seemed nice or gave him sweets, he knew that they would turn out to be an arsehole. There was one guy who tried to touch him, and Iain didn't have the words to tell but Sheila worked it out somehow. She told the local heavies and they broke the man's arms and ankles. He never came back to the town. Heavies were heroes to Iain. They were order and justice to him. They were the Passmen of Outside.

Iain was allowed to visit her in hospital after the plates were fitted. Her head was bandaged, her jaws wired. She sat up in the bed, unable to speak. Iain was exactly seven years and three months old. He knew that for sure because, much later, a lawyer in some case brought it up as a plea in mitigation – 'severe head injury'. Seven years and three months when the social worker brought him to the intensive care ward and stood at the door to the room, watching to make sure he was OK, not too frightened by the machines or Sheila's bandages and her wired-up jaw. Iain was fine with it. He was only there to show off to the other foster kids. He had a parent who wanted to see him and they didn't need social work supervision for visits. His mum didn't want to hit him. His mum really liked him and could make food and dinners and clean his clothes and everything. The other kids in the foster home were spitting with envy.

Sheila's eyes brimmed with joy at the sight of him, and Iain ran over to her bedside. She couldn't talk. She held up a hand, warning him not to touch her face or head. She rolled her eyes to show him it was sore: Oooof! She made the noise with her throat because she couldn't move her lips or tongue. Then she smiled with her eyes to show it was OK. Iain hugged her toes, staying as far away from her head as he could. He squeezed her toes and kissed them through the rough hospital blankets and Sheila watched him and crinkled her eyes to show him that she liked it. Then her eyes invited him to sit on the bed with her and cuddle in and watch the telly and he did. He lay his head on her belly and she stroked his hair with lazy fingers and he listened, half to the giggle of her guts, half to the news on the telly.

After, when the wires were taken out, Sheila stayed not talking much. She shrugged, what is there to say? She had a point.

Iain looked out of the van window at the massive hills, the snowcaps and the veils of mist, hearing Sheila's guts giggling in one ear and Tommy's nasal breathing in the other.

'I'll bang some tunes on, then,' said Tommy, a bit huffy that Iain wasn't for talking. He touched the play button and Fiddy's 'I'm Supposed to Die Tonight' filled the cabin. The bass made the ill-fitting windows buzz. Tommy bobbed his head to the beat.

Iain recognised that this wasn't new. He had felt this before, this distance from the world. It reminded him of Andrew Cole, because he'd been there, then. Iain and Andrew were in prison together and had nothing in common. Andrew was posh and read all the time but he said a nice thing to Iain at a time when it mattered. You'll be all right. Just try and act normal. A kindness in a time of despair. The words and the tenderness stayed with Iain, a prison tattoo, ink in a ragged cut.

Just act normal. He heard the music and tried to follow the

sequence of the melody, but he was off the beat, jerking his head out of time, as if he was rehearsing smashing his face on the dashboard. He stopped, distracted by a tiny shift: the barb was gone from his throat. She had moved down, deep down into the dark. There was nowhere to go but down. But she wasn't paralysed by the cold. He felt her move, uncoiling in the dark spaces.

Face to the window so Tommy couldn't see, Iain shut his brimming eyes and shrugged a shoulder, resigned. She was going to bite her way out through his chest. She would be the death of him but he didn't care. The debt was paid and he was spent. Save him the bother of doing it himself.

5

Central Station had sent two footage files, both an hour and a half long. McGrain had scrolled through both to 7:03:32 a.m., ten seconds before the call came through. He pulled up the first. A very wide shot of the concourse and five platforms, with the bank of phone boxes in the bottom right-hand corner of the screen. Obscuring the view of the phones was an out-of-focus forest of what looked like erect grey pipe cleaners. Morrow squinted at them.

'What is that?'

McGrain touched the screen. 'Unfortunate. Anti-pigeon spikes. Stop them landing. They're all furry with dust from the station.'

'Is the other one a better shot?'

'Pointing in the wrong direction.'

'I'm so hoping this isn't the wee cake-guy,' she said quietly.

McGrain nodded heavily. 'God, me too.'

They stood still for a moment, smiling sadly at the screen as they each remembered the mother and the child and the cake and the contagious silent laughter. Morrow was the first to pull herself out of it. She pointed at the screen. 'Come on, then.'

McGrain clicked play.

A grainy smear of movement, people walking, standing facing the giant information screen. The image was grey but for orange beacon lights flashing on a mobility cart in the distance. The camera was pinned above the entrance to a shop.

A small figure in a dark green parka, fur-trimmed hood up, walked in from the bottom right. They went straight to a phone box, picked up the handset and dropped a coin in. The person they were looking for had dialled the free emergency number so Morrow wasn't sure it was their caller, but then the hooded figure reached into the slot for a returned coin. They were talking into the handset.

'Teenager,' said Morrow, looking at the skinny-leg grey jeans under the baggy parka.

'Teenage boy,' said McGrain, pointing at the back pockets sagging halfway down his legs.

The caller was getting agitated, looking left, stepping from foot to foot. They hung up suddenly, at 07:04:09, exact to the second for the audio time. They hesitated, hand resting on the receiver, and then scurried off, head down under the hood as if they were crying.

McGrain pressed pause and they both looked at the screen. It was hard to tell if it was the boy. They didn't really know how tall he was and they'd never heard his voice. It sounded more like a girl but the jeans seemed boyish.

The second file of footage showed the same action but was less in focus.

'Did you ask for other cam views?' said Morrow. 'Maybe we can get the face?'

'I know one of the guys over there, he checked the three exits in that direction. Found them leaving, hood still up. Got in a waiting taxi but we can't read the reg.'

'Why not?'

'Camera hood's broken. It's hanging in front of the lens.'

Morrow nodded. 'Typical.'

It had to be the cake-boy. They couldn't see his face but Roxanna had a teenage boy and a teenage boy had called them. They should go speak to the kids immediately but they couldn't. They couldn't do anything. They needed permission.

'PINAD,' said McGrain.

Morrow nodded. 'Fucking PINAD.'

She went back to her office to await instructions, pending the chief superintendent's office getting in and bothering to call her. She felt miserable and wanted to check the CCTV anyway, even though she knew Roxanna wasn't on it. She wondered why she was so involved with this woman, wondered if Roxanna was filling a space in her head that Danny usually filled.

Danny McGrath was Morrow's half-brother. He was a well-known and feared Glasgow gangster until he was sentenced to eight years for conspiracy to commit murder. Morrow didn't think he was funny or sweet or strangely admirable, not the way she thought about Fuentecilla, but he did preoccupy her to the same degree. Once or twice a day Danny came into her mind and Fuentecilla had started to fill those spaces. One big similarity, she realised, was her feeling of impotence about both of them. She wasn't even allowed to brief the PINAD team on the woman's disappearance until she had word from on high. She busied herself with duty forms and background files for other cases, waiting.

The PINAD case began six months ago and four hundred miles away with a fishing exercise. The Met were monitoring a boozy Park Lane charity auction for money-laundering activities. It was a good place to look for ostentatious spending: rich people showing off to other rich people in a drinking environment. The Met's curiosity was piqued when a barman and his unemployed girlfriend paid sixty-four thousand pounds for *Cabinet – a Larkin & Son's Design Icon*. The PINAD incident room had a picture of it on the wall. According to the description in the auction catalogue it was handcrafted rosewood, inlaid with walnut and ebony marquetry, made by master craftsmen. Sixty-four grand's worth of ugly wall unit, as far as Morrow was concerned.

The Met began a minimal investigation into the couple. They found that the boyfriend, Robin Walker, worked as a barman in a private dining club in Belgravia. Roxanna Fuentecilla had no income. She had no inheritance. She had never worked.

Robin Walker was not the children's father. He had moved in

with Roxanna Fuentecilla just over a year ago, following a whirl-wind romance. Their natural father, Miguel Vicente, came from an absurdly wealthy Ecuadorian family. Three years ago he left the family home with an overnight bag and flew back home to Ecuador. A month later he married a fellow absurdly rich Ecuadorian: she had a plastic surgery ski-jump nose and a zoo in her garden. Pictured in an online society magazine, the couple were a bizarre sight for Scottish eyes: their teeth looked as if they had stolen them from a child, both had their eyebrows plucked, both had shiny, line-free skin. Vicente stopped supporting Roxanna and the kids a month after he left.

Robin Walker was handsome, directionless and in his late twenties. He lived with his new family in a serviced flat in Belgravia. Despite their straitened circumstances, they wintered in St Lucia. Roxanna continued to educate her children alongside ambassadors' kids at an exclusive central London Spanish-speaking school. Sensing money, the Met investigation grew.

The incomeless couple were seen in the company of a Colombian attaché and his wife. Checking back, Maria and Juan Pinzón Arias had paid for the table of ten at the charity auction, Robin and Roxanna had been their guests, but the wealthy couple bid on none of the items themselves.

The Arias children were at the same Spanish school as Roxanna's. The four kids weren't known to be friends, they were in different years, but Maria and Roxanna became very close very suddenly. Roxanna travelled often with Maria Arias, usually on overnight stays to Barcelona, a known distribution point for cocaine. Smuggling was suspected. On their third trip the Met investigators compared the airline's weight of Roxanna's luggage on the way out (twenty-three kilos) and on the way back (thirty-three kilos). The differential was suspiciously precise.

Maria Arias was using a diplomatic bag which could be neither searched nor weighed. The investigation grew again, serious now because of the diplomatic implications.

Like Roxanna, Juan Pinzón Arias also had money that could not be explained. He bought cars with cash. He bought three flats in central London in his mother's name, all in the same block of foreign investment flats. The Met were moving in, swift and hungry for a proceeds-of-crime bonanza. They'd get to keep a percentage of whatever they found. Every police force needed that sort of money. It looked like fifty or sixty million net, estimated from the iceberg tip they could see above the waterline.

Then, abruptly, in the middle of a school term, Robin and Roxanna packed up and moved to Glasgow. With no capital, Roxanna Fuentecilla bought a viable insurance business for a peppercorn sum. The nominal amount suggested an off-the-books payment. She arrived with seven million pounds of investment money, transferred from a string of Cayman Island companies. It would take months of document recovery and tracing to prove legally, but the original account was in Maria Arias's name.

Police Scotland took over the surveillance and began to covet the Fuentecilla slice of the case.

Met investigators speculated that the insurance company was engaged in fraudulent claims but Morrow couldn't see Fuentecilla going from suspected cocaine smuggling in London to insurance fraud in an unfamiliar city. That was a career-criminal move and she certainly wasn't that. The Met had a theory that Arias and his wife were trying to distance Roxanna, something had gone wrong. That explanation seemed wrong to Morrow as well, but no one wanted her input.

Paul Tailor, the brand new chief constable of the brand new Scotland-wide police service was an ex-Met man. He had taken a personal interest in the case. All developments were to be reported directly to his second in command, Deputy Chief Constable Hughes. DCC Hughes channelled the chief's voice as surely as a soundboard and he had made it very clear to everyone involved that, whatever happened, he did not want them to cock up in front of his old comrades. Her chief inspector had taken this to heart: no one would be using their initiative on this but they might well take the blame. They understood the implication: Police Scotland were the chief constable's stagehands but not his audience. Among themselves officers began to refer to the investigation as P.I.N.A.D. 'Are you on that PINAD case?' 'Pass that onto the PINAD team'. The acronym stood for 'Prove I'm Not A Dick'.

A month after Walker and Fuentecilla moved to Glasgow, Morrow's instincts were proved right: the Arias couple weren't trying to distance themselves. Juan Pinzón Arias, short, lumpish, and his wife Maria, tiny and as elegant as a dragonfly, flew into Glasgow International on a private charter plane and spent a night at an exclusive Loch Lomond hotel, fifteen miles north of the city. Walker and Fuentecilla drove up to meet them, dressed in full regalia. The local cops kept an eye and reported a meal for four in a private dining room. The drinks bill came to almost three grand. Someone liked their whisky old and overpriced.

Looking at the bill for the meal, Morrow knew she was right: the Colombians weren't sidelining Fuentecilla and Walker. Roxanna had been sent here to do a job. The question was, what.

Her desk phone rang. She watched it for a moment, thinking swear words in a long unbroken stream.

The deputy chief constable's PA ordered her to come into Pitt Street right now. The deputy head of the entire country's police force was holding a meeting about a missing woman.

PINAD.

6

Tommy stopped the van on the esplanade and pulled on the handbrake. 'So, I'll see you at the do tomorrow?'

Iain was staring over the choppy grey estuary to a low peninsula rising out of the water. A brigade of uniform trees stood to attention, same height and shape, planted at the same time and subject to the same conditions. The Dark Wood, it was called. The foliage was a deep, warm green, a welcoming green.

'Iain? Bud? You getting out or what?'

Move. Iain opened the cab door, pushing hard against the wind. He dropped down to the pavement, flat-footed, every part of him heavy and worn.

'Bud? You all righ—' Iain slammed the door before Tommy finished his sentence and stood still, his back to the van, until it moved off behind him, following the long shore road to Rhu.

He felt dead. The breeze salted his lips. He was nothing but a heavy husk standing there, hypnotised by the Dark Wood across the water, the trees outlined against a brightening sky. It looked clean, soft as a bed. Iain took a step towards the sea.

No.

That was her thought. He couldn't walk through the water to get to the Dark Wood. If he was going to die he should still be careful. He'd draw attention to himself, walking off into the sea. He might undo the payment of the debt and that was the one good thing he had to cling to. Anyway, between the paved esplanade and the water there was a ten foot drop to a shale beach and then fifty yards to the water's edge. Somebody would see him. It would cause a fuss and Mark would be angry.

He stood anyway, looking at the water, wondering. Maybe she wanted him to walk into the salted sea to clean the blood off.

'Iain Fraser?'

He only half heard the woman's voice.

'Iain Fraser? Is that you?'

He looked. A tall woman. The wind whipped strands of wild white from her bob, hairs wiggling up like cartoon electricity. She had rich-people skin. Soft cheeks and a long, straight nose.

He looked her in the eye and saw that she was scared. Was she scared of him? She blinked it away and her face broke into a warm, masking smile. 'Iain, you're so tall! It's me, Susan Grierson. Don't you remember me?'

Susan Grierson had been an Adventure Scout. He didn't want to make her frightened. She was nice. She had tried to get him to join the Scouts but there was too much going on. She had taken him sailing.

Sitting in a boat in Loch Long, Susan Grierson and the other cub scouts doing all the work. Iain sat in the middle, holding the sides, watching the water. It was very early in the morning. Why were they out so early? It was dark still. A chill was radiating from the deep grey. A small boat, low enough to hear the sibilant rustle of the water breaking on the bow. She excused Iain from the work of sailing because something bad had happened and it was a shame. He couldn't recall what particular thing it was that time.

He had watched the wash from the boat breaking, soft and rhythmic. Over and again the water bulged, splitting at its peak, a knife slit in a bag of sand. It rose and split and fell back again and again as they sailed down the soft grassy coast. Iain had found hope and comfort in the rhythm of that. A swell breaks and another swell arises, everything passes. It seemed a different image to him today: something about death. Death was rhythmic, an endless pattern. Every death looked identical as long as you were far enough away.

Susan Grierson smiled warmly up at him. The last time they met she'd been taller than him. 'Do you remember me?'

He took a deep breath and tried to speak, because it was her and she was nice: 'I'd remembered, you then, in a boat?'

She gave a small, confused frown, her eyes focusing on a space between his nose and mouth.

'Sorry?'

Iain shook his head. No. He shouldn't say that again. It didn't make sense.

'Iain? Are you all right?' Head tilt, concern, but another thing in there. Something else too. Something glad in there. She liked helping people. Moneyed people often did. 'Are you all right?'

It was a big question. Iain looked back at the water, letting the wind sting his eyes. He was twice as tall as he had been when last he saw Susan Grierson. They left, all of the townspeople from then, left and came back, some to stay, some to bury, some to brag and gloat. In and out, sea water in the estuary. And, like the sea, they looked the same when they came back but they weren't. Iain wasn't the same when he came back from prison. They all acted as if they were the same, as if nothing had changed, as if they could all trust each other.

Susan liked helping. She stayed next to him, pulling her cardigan tight around herself. They stood still for a long time.

'Beautiful, isn't it?' she said, filling the space between them. 'So, so beautiful . . .' She talked on, stringing bland clichés together into observations. She could just fuck off and leave him alone. He didn't need help.

He wanted a cigarette.

He hadn't smoked for six years. He couldn't remember when he last craved one but he dearly wanted one now. He'd go and buy tobacco in a minute. He would smoke it out, this thing, this woman.

'When you take the time to stand and watch the water,' Susan was saying, 'it's mesmerising, isn't it? Like a fire.'

Her accent was odd. He recalled some information about her from somewhere. 'Didn't you move to America?'

'Yes.' She looked away, down the water. 'I lived in the States for a long time.' Her voice was gentle and calming.

'Chicago?' He didn't think it was Chicago but he wanted her to speak again.

She glanced at him. 'No, not Chicago. Nassau County, in fact ...'

'That near Chicago?' He was slurring.

'It's on Long Island.'

They stood for a moment, but he missed her caressing voice. 'On Long Island?' he said. 'In America?'

Her face twitched and she stepped away very slightly. Iain wasn't offended. His delivery was wrong, he knew that, but he felt quite proud of himself. However strange he seemed on the outside, it was nothing compared to how baffled he was on the inside.

'Long Island,' she spoke carefully, 'is near Manhattan. Near to New York City. Do you know the Hamptons?'

It seemed like an abrupt change of topic. 'D'they live here?'

Now they were both confused. Iain sensed that it wasn't just him. The conversation had become bewildering.

Their voices overlapped: 'I want baccy,' he said, and Susan said, 'Come to my house.'

She looked very keen.

Iain ran back through what had been said so far. Was there a build-up to that? He didn't think so.

Susan was looking at him, desperation shining out of her. She really wanted him to come to her house. Was she religious? But then her smile widened and warmed. Did she want to have sex with him? Iain found that slightly frightening. The scariness didn't make it entirely uninviting though. It kind of added to it. She wasn't a stranger, but like a teacher from when he was young, maybe he'd imagined her naked, back then, and owed it to his old self. But maybe not, maybe not safe. His head was already messed after this morning.

'Uch, I don't—'

'Come on!' She waved an arm uphill. 'I'm not far at all! Just up there on Sutherland Crescent.'

Iain had never been in a Sutherland Crescent house. They were the originals, where the town plan began, the earliest of the Helensburgh houses. Plain, but something to see. He'd been hearing about them all his life.

No. He should be careful. Something shifted inside him. Something behind his ribs, precursor to a stitch. If he was indoors, alone with a woman, he thought maybe something bad would happen.

'I's just going to buy tobacco.' He thumbed up the seafront, resisting.

She held his eye and stepped towards him. 'There's a newsagent's on the way. We can get whatever you want.'

Somehow, then, they were crossing from the esplanade together, heading to the far pavement, the town's shore. They kept quite far away from each other in the empty road and she was smiling. Iain didn't know why she was smiling. Maybe she thought Iain and Tommy were going to let her go, or she was thinking about suntans and beaches and maybe she would make it to the trees. No. He shook his head at the tarmac. No, that wasn't Susan Grierson.

But Susan was as passive as a heifer too. He was worried for her, worried that she trusted him.

Turning into a quiet street, the wind dropped suddenly and they could hear each other walking, breathing, the scuff of their clothes. It was intimate without a chaperoning wind. She moved close to him, falling in step. Iain felt he could have held her hand, exchanging warmth skin to skin, and it would be all right. There was something in her. A familiar sadness, maybe a bond. She was a bit lost too.

They walked on until she stopped at a shop window.

Handwritten adverts behind the glass. Dogs needing homes, events, Zumba classes, buy stamps here. Iain read, looking for answers to questions he couldn't quite formulate.

She was staring at him. He searched her face for clues. Finally, she nodded at the shop. 'Cigarettes?'

He remembered then. He pushed the door open, setting off a loud 'beep', and stepped in.

He'd never been in here before. It was half empty. A shelf by the door held three long-life loaves. The teabags came in small packets, the bags of sugar were mini. It was a place for forgetful shoppers, old ladies, people with no car to get to out-of-town superstores.

Behind the counter a shopkeeper was absent-mindedly arranging jars of penny sweeties as he chatted foreign words into the mobile clamped between his shoulder and his ear.

He raised his eyebrows in hello, letting Iain know he could still serve, even though he was talking on the phone.

Iain walked to the back of the shop. He needed a moment. He hadn't felt this numb in a long time. Had he just pulled? She was handsome. Nice women had often wanted to save him and she was not a mental junkie. She didn't even seem to have weans because she made and held eye contact. The eyes of mothers flitted over your shoulder all the time. They were always watching out.

Had he just pulled? Iain looked into an open chill cabinet, blue light flickering over milk, and caught his reflection on the steel back. He looked like a sad fisherman. Broad shoulders, thick blond hair. But dirty. His trackie top was smeared brown at the cuffs and down the front. Susan Grierson wouldn't pull a man this dirty, but then, she'd been in America for a long time. People change. Some women were attracted to mental guys. Sheila was. If he had sex with Susan Grierson would she expect him to be rough? Iain didn't like that sort of thing.

He walked over to the counter, nodding at the tobacco packets behind the shopkeeper. 'Golden Virginia. And green papers and give us one of your lighters as well.'

The shopkeeper picked up some yellow plastic lighters and showed them to Iain. Clear yellow neon yellow sandy yellow. 'Three for a quid?'

Iain didn't need three but it seemed like less effort to say yes. 'Aye.'

Three yellow lighters.

Other coloured lighters in the box, green and blue, red ones, purple ones, but the guy chose all yellow for him.

'Nine quid.'

Iain looked at the tobacco pouch, glinting in a cellophane envelope. Last time he smoked was with her in Glasgow, a thin woman.

The man smiled and said, 'You haven't smoked for a while, pal? Dear now, innit?'

But Iain was with the thin woman a long time ago, in Glasgow, who asked him to hold her throat and pretend to strangle her while they were having sex. Iain was scared of her and what she might make him do. Her hair smelled stale. She had a stain on her blouse, green, washed-in, like she'd vomited bile and washed it and it hadn't come out. He tried to get away from her but she followed him to the pub. *You look like a movie star.*

'Pal? Nine quid.'

Iain was staring at the counter, thinking about a bloody curlicue vessel snaking across the white of her eye. The memory brought a bubble of sadness up from deep in his gut. Why did she go with them to the boat? If she'd screamed in the house someone might have called the cops and stopped it. But then the debt wouldn't be paid, so he didn't know what to hope for—

'Buddy?' The shopkeeper had seen his confusion and reached out tenderly. 'You OK?'

Iain was ashamed. He slapped a hand over his eyes, rubbing hard. He put a tenner down on the counter and picked up the things, tucking them into different pockets, the pouch and papers and yellow yellow yellow lighters.

Holding the change so tight that the coins dug into his palm, Iain reached for the door. Susan Grierson was still there, waiting on the pavement, hopeful as a wayward teenager outside an off-sales. She watched his face as he came out and she sighed.

'Gosh, Iain,' she said, 'you looked so much like your mother just then.'

He stepped heavily down into the street. He wasn't getting his hole off her then. His mistake. He was half relieved. Too much had happened today already. His chest tightened.

They walked up the road, she a half-step ahead, leading him.

'So, Sheila died?' She was nodding. 'Mum told me.'

Sheila. Sheila Sheila Sheila Sheila Sheila Sheila. Today was a wall of Sheila.

'While ago, aye,' he said. 'Eight, maybe nine year ago?'

'Gosh.' She let off a huff of dismay, politeness. 'I'm so sorry. It was a brain haemorrhage, of course. It was a danger she lived with every day.' Susan was talking in a sort of churchy voice, like she was reading at Sheila's funeral or something. 'She was astonishingly brave, leading an independent life with that degree of brain damage. I think the doctors were amazed she could even walk.'

Iain stopped walking. *Brain* damage? The words clattered around his mind. Sheila had brain damage?

Susan Grierson was looking at him as if everyone in the world knew. Iain didn't know. It was obvious, now he thought about it. Sheila had a home help and a social worker to manage her money for her. He always thought she got support because he was so much trouble. He thought her respite weekends were giving her a break from him.

He looked at Susan. 'Sheila had brain damage?'

She nodded. She seemed to understand that he didn't know. 'Didn't they tell you?'

Did they? Her reluctance to talk and angry-for-no-reason moods. No one ever told him. Did they tell him? He might have been told in a couched way, in a kind way, and misunderstood.

Miss Grierson talked on about Sheila at school and what a good sailor she was and the dances they went to, in all the great houses, when they were girls.

They were walking along by a tall hedge when she arrived at Sheila having Iain: '. . . *young* when she had you. I never had children.' She gave him a glancing blow of a look, a demand for pity.

It wasn't a pity. She wouldn't have thought it was if she had stayed and knew what Iain had put Sheila through. The shame and the worry. Prison visits and court dates. Little 'hiya' waves to her from the dock.

He looked at Susan, saw the self-pity in her eyes and found her disgusting. He felt a scaly tail flick inside his chest wall.

'Look.' He stopped suddenly. She overshot him, had to turn back to listen. 'Eh, Susan, I'm just going home.'

'Please! No!' Her hand flew out, reaching for his forearm. The plea was too intense. She held his eye. 'I can't go home alone.'

'How? Is there somebody in the house?'

'I don't know.' She looked around the pavement, blinking hard.

Not a boyfriend who wanted to hit her. She would have told him if it was that. What wouldn't she tell him? The figure of her mother? A voice in her head? She couldn't say but she was begging him not to leave her. Her need was craven. He knew that feeling. He didn't have the strength to leave her now.

Stepping towards her, he draped his arm over her shoulders, telling her that she wouldn't have to beg again, that he understood. She melted towards him for a moment, grateful, and then drew away.

"S OK,' he said softly, as if she was Sheila. 'It's all right. I'm coming with you.'

Susan Grierson smiled at the pavement, nodded them uphill and they walked on together towards her house.

7

Morrow sat with her back against the wall, calm observer in a blizzard of clammy panic. Three of the most highly paid, powerful men in Police Scotland had been called in. Heavy personnel. As if to justify their places, each took turns monologuing about mistakes others should avoid, things they should be afraid of. A day's wage from each of them would have paid to keep one of the rural stations they were shutting open for a week. The power differential between Morrow and the rest of the room was so steep she felt that she could be sitting in her pants and no one would notice. Most DIs would give half their pensions to be here. Morrow was astute enough to know that she barely was.

She kept her own counsel, as she watched Deputy Chief Constable Hughes ask questions of Nolly Dent, her chief inspector. Nolly had a silly name but was a good guy, handsome, small and smart. She saw Hughes half listening to Nolly's answers, half imagining his chief constable's reaction. She watched him conduct the meeting calmly, lay out his jurisdictional argument for Police Scotland getting a slice of the seven million when it was found. It was a Scottish case. The investigation predated the move here but the takeover of the firm was a cut-off, a fresh start for a criminal action. It wasn't his argument. It was the chief constable's and it was really smart. She had thought of him as vain and petty because of PINAD, but her conviction wavered now.

When her turn came to speak, Morrow insisted that they should not be blinded by the proceeds money but follow normal protocol in the circumstances. By far the most likely explanation was that Fuentecilla had been killed by her partner during a domestic argument. However, they could use this as an opportunity to access the firm's files and find out more about what was going on.

Fuentecilla was argumentative, she told them. She argued with everyone. It was unlikely that her domestic set-up was peaceful. Plus the caller seemed to be her kid. If she had run away she would have taken the children with her.

Chief Superintendent Saunders smirked at her. 'Don't you think you're being a bit soft on her? What is this, the mother's union?'

Morrow wished she had a Victoria sponge cake with her. She didn't speak but her face was saying something very eloquent.

DCC Hughes moved the meeting on. The perils of Roxanna Fuentecilla were obliterated by stats and jurisdictional issues, by suggested strategies for questioning hostile witnesses and legal issues over the proceeds. Morrow would never have noticed, normally. Their job was to police the city, not save the damsel, but she was listening like a member of the victim's family. The more she thought about it, the more she knew that it was all about her brother. Roxanna was Danny without the shame and resentment. Her defences were down because Danny and Roxanna were so unalike: Roxanna was female, Spanish, wealthy, but she had Danny's audacity, his same shameless sense of entitlement. Secretly, Morrow realised, she admired that.

The pointless meeting burbled on. Even the DCC seemed to think the monologues were too long. He got up to leave before the meeting was concluded, nodding at his PA to shepherd them through that last boring bit. He didn't need to stay because the course of action had been decided: Morrow and a hand-picked DC would attend the missing woman's domicile, posing as everyday cops on a Missing Persons call.

They would follow normal procedure, voice record everything for transcript. They would insist on access to the insurance firm's offices on the pretext of hidden debts. They would get all the info on the firm that they could.

Three of the most highly paid men in Police Scotland had gathered together to arrive at this complex strategic decision: go and see.

The energy went out of the meeting after Hughes left. The final statement was rounded up as everyone packed away their papers. The meeting ended in jig time.

Out on the landing, waiting for the lift down, Morrow stood with CS Saunders. He was a fat man, an important man, but she didn't really know him. He knew he had offended her and was sorry. He stood next to her, catching her eye, nodding, smiling, seemed to want her to say something. Morrow would have said whatever he wanted her to say, but she couldn't guess what it was. She smiled back. She nodded back. She was on the brink of giving a thumbs up when he said,

'It's been chaos out there since your brother went away.'

Morrow dropped her smile. The lift arrived and they got in. The door shut behind them.

'Yep. He kept it all quiet,' CS Saunders told her, 'is what I'm saying, while he was running things. These people . . .'

He smiled at her, saw it was going down badly and awkwardly turned his bared teeth to the door. Morrow felt herself go very stiff, as if a spider, too big to swat, was running across her back. Accommodation. No one in the force ever vocalised it but they all knew that the black economy was essential. Men like Danny were responsible for twenty per cent of global GDP. If justice was done and they were all imprisoned, the world economy would collapse. Civilisations would fall.

'Yes, sir,' she said, hoping that sounding agreeable might be an end to it.

'Yes, indeed.' He took that as encouragement. 'They're tearing each other to bits over territories now. Little more than a few streets, most of them. The stab stats for last quarter read as if a civil war has broken out.'

The lift alighted and the doors opened. She should have let

him go first, out of respect, but she slipped past him.

'Been quiet for years because of your brother . . .' he called after her.

'He's my half-brother,' said Morrow quietly. 'Just my half-brother, sir.' She walked away without being dismissed: an underling's revenge.

McGrain was waiting for her in the lobby. They walked to the car park in silence. McGrain was wary of her mood. As they got into the car, he asked what the chief was really like. He was guessing she'd been shouted at. Morrow said the chief was professional and climbed into the passenger seat. McGrain got in and started the car.

Danny was carrying on his business vicariously from prison. Not much had changed for him but he had stopped power-broking between factions in the city. It meant chaos on the streets. Keeping the peace was in his interests as much as anyone else's, but Danny wouldn't do it any more, just to show them what they had brought on themselves. People were dying because Danny McGrath was in a huff.

8

Iain and Susan stepped carefully on the overgrown path to the pale green front door. The garden was wild and smelled mulchy. The house itself looked well preserved. It was a miniature villa with windows on either side. Little pillars and an open porch over shallow steps.

Susan stepped up to the door. She turned the key in the lock but waited until Iain was flanking her before she pushed it open. The heavy old door swung into a wide hall, carpeted and papered in faded blue and yellow. Light filtered in from the far kitchen at the end of the corridor. It looked misty but Iain realised that it was a fog of dust, stirred up by the suck of the front door opening.

Susan looking around as if she'd never been there before. She stepped in and waved Iain over the threshold, shut the front door quietly and tiptoed through an open door on the left, into what seemed to be a dining room.

The house was incredibly fusty. A dresser just inside the door had a thick layer of dust on it, so thick it looked sticky, as if time had compressed it.

Iain followed her in. A dirty whisky glass was sitting on the varnished dining-room table in a clear smear in the dust coating. It must have been Susan's, from earlier, because she didn't look at it twice. Iain noticed she was tiptoeing.

'Is there someone in here, Susan?'

She ignored him, checked the hall again and then turned to whisper to him, 'I need to see Mark Barratt.'

Iain looked at her mouth. *Mark Barratt?* How could she know about Mark Barratt? 'Mark's in Barcelona.'

'Will you call him?'

'Can't.'

She clearly didn't know Mark. He never took calls when he was away. Everyone who knew him knew that. Left the mobile at home when he was in Barcelona. Sometimes, when he came back he had to go away again almost immediately.

Iain suddenly wondered if Susan was a cop. She looked like a cop. She was fit and slim, but she was emotional and she was bringing him home, which was not-cop.

'Why d'you want to see Mark?'

'D'you know who would have his number?' She began walking down the corridor to the kitchen, careful scanning for someone as she went.

Iain followed. He was about to ask if she had been broken into, what was going on, but he was startled by the state of the kitchen.

The kitchen was massive and almost derelict. Big windows to the garden were netted with ragged cobwebs. Part of the ceiling had fallen in and lay crumbled on the worktop. At the far end of the room an archway opened onto a filthy windowed conservatory, filling the room with reproachful sunlight.

She went into a pantry cupboard, checking it out.

'Have you been living in here, Susan?'

'No. Just got back a day or so ago. My mum died.'

Iain thought old Mrs Grierson had died two years ago. He thought he'd heard about it on a day release. The house was messy enough to have been left for years. But Susan had just come back now. She stepped back into the kitchen, saw him again and seemed relieved.

'Tea!' she announced, her mood abruptly lighter. Looking through cupboards, she found an electric kettle under the sink and took it out. She blew the dust off. Iain was not a fastidious man but he didn't think he'd be drinking anything out of that. She filled it with water from rattly pipes and plugged it in, watching with surprise as it went on.

'I'll go and find some cups,' she said, and left the room.

Iain couldn't fathom what was going on. He wanted a smoke. That was all he wanted and then he'd leave. He dropped down into an armchair and a puff of dust rose around him. The chair was in the mouth of the archway to the conservatory, draughty because a hole had been dug in the conservatory floor under the outside wall, but at least it was blowing the dust away from him.

He took out a cigarette paper, opened the tobacco pouch and teased out a pinch. Engulfed by the scent of chocolate, he laid it along the paper valley. It was harder to do than he remembered, his fingertips clumsy, but the smell and sounds, the cleanness of it filled his eye, batting away memories of his midnight qualms and the bloody dock and sailing with Susan. His mouth watered with anticipation as he licked the gum. Even though it had been a long time since he smoked, he remembered everything about the ritual of this. He remembered too all that it used to mean to him: a mood change, a cogent plan, a reward or compensation. Now he wasn't hoping for any of those things. He just wanted to flood his lungs and smother her breath in him.

Sitting the cigarette between his lips, he felt in his pocket and took out a sand-yellow lighter. He lit it, heard the crackle of the paper, tasted the warm toxins flood his mouth.

He inhaled. A sharp, pebbled wave scratched down his throat. The tide of nicotine coursed across his inward ocean. Up it foamed, on, up estuaries and rivers, burns and rivulets, until every inland shore and bank was tainted and trilling.

The smoke kick-started his heart in an irregular bossa nova rhythm. It throbbed in his throat, as if the fat fist of an organ had shifted to make room for the squatter in his chest.

He felt her ebb. It was working. He tried to hold the breath but his diaphragm convulsed, expelled the smoke in wild, wet, spluttered coughs.

'Here we go,' sing-songed Susan as she came back and sat a

tray of tea things on a dusty side table. She pulled a kitchen chair over and sat down next to him.

Side by side, Iain and Susan looked out into the conservatory. Light filtering through dirty green glass. It wasn't a modern conservatory full of sofas or anything, but an old greenhouse attached to the back of the house. A crack on one of the panels was mended with time-yellowed masking tape. Empty glass shelves lined the walls. A seedlings table, the wood bleached grey with light exposure, had been shoved to the side of the room, making way for the hole dug next to the ventilation grate.

'Shall I pour?' Susan Grierson smiled fondly at him. The tea things were tacky with dirt.

'OK,' he said, because she was holding the teapot and waiting for an answer. Iain wondered if she could see the dirt.

He hadn't heard the kettle boil. He wanted to ask her what was going on but she didn't seem much more together than he was. It was a mistake, coming here. They weren't going to help each other. He'd leave in a minute.

She poured two small, prissy cups of weak tea and added a sprinkle of powdered milk. Iain said he took three sugars and she put them in as well, stirred with a little spoon and handed him a cup and saucer. He took it and put it on the arm of his chair.

'What happened in there, then?' He pointed to the freshly dug dirt floor on the conservatory.

'Lead pipes,' she said. 'Had to be replaced. They replaced all the piping in the house years ago but that offshoot serviced the garden and the conservatory. Worrying, actually, because Mother was growing her own tomatoes and lettuce and watering them with leaded water.'

'Worrying, actually,' he echoed, glad they were talking normally.

'Lead poisoning is cumulative. I mean, she didn't die of lead poisoning, she had a heart attack. But it's terribly bad for you.'

The shape of the hole, long and deep and tucked away in a corner, it made him think of bad things.

'The pipes were right deep down there ...' She touched her hair and looked harried. 'There's so much to do to this house. A lot of it fundamental.'

'Dusty.'

'Hmm, it is dusty. There are damp spots in all the bathrooms, leaky pipes, and the decoration – dreadful. So old-fashioned. Oh – biscuits!' She leapt up and went back to the counter again.

Iain heard her moving about behind him. He was hoping she wouldn't bring a dead rat over and say it was biscuits, she was a bit Baby Jane, but suddenly something sharp stabbed him in the back, from the inside. She was feeling for a way out.

He took another tremulous draw on his cigarette. The pain cowered deep. He held his breath, held it, held it, his eyes shut, concentrating. He held fast, though his lungs were begging and his eyes throbbed.

He felt her wither. He felt her gone.

Iain let his breath out and found he couldn't stop. He began to cry. He hadn't cried properly for a long time. His tear ducts yawned, aching, as salt water dropped from his cheeks down the front of his top.

'Jaffa cakes?'

Eyes flicked open. Susan was holding a blue freezer bag inches from his nose. It had Jaffa biscuits in it, most of them broken. Iain slapped it away just as she let go and the bag slithered into his lap. He picked it up and shoved it at her. 'GET THE FUCK—'

But Susan didn't mean any harm, he reminded himself, and she was in a state too. 'Look, no thanks, OK? I just ... I don't like biscuits.'

The blurred bag retreated. She walked away.

Iain wilted forwards over his lap, his hands in his hair. He heard the cigarette singe, smelled the sulphurous tang of burning.

'... upset?' She was saying something, he wasn't sure what she was saying, but she was saying something new. Now she had

47

stopped talking. She was sitting. A warm palm came out and drew a circle on his back.

The paralysing sadness was lifting. He wiped the wet from his face, pinched drips off his nose. He dried his hand on his trouser leg. The cigarette had burned out. Another cigarette maybe.

'More tea? Oh, you haven't drunk that one yet.'

Iain glanced over. Her hands were folded in her lap. She smiled, politely, determined to keep to the script of tea, whatever he did. It was annoying how fucking insistent she was about the tea and biscuits and a fucking saucer. For all she knew his best friend might have died. He might not be crying because he was guilty of a terrible thing. She didn't know. He was angry at her and he looked at the hole in the conservatory floor again.

Susan was smiling, an awkward moment at a minister's tea party. They looked out into the smoke swirling in the empty conservatory.

'Why did you ask me to come here? How d'you know Mark?'

'Well, Iain,' she spoke confidingly, 'frankly, I wanted to ask a small favour. I don't know anyone here, but I'd like a pinch and I heard Mark Barratt is the person to see about that?'

'You want a what?'

'A deal. Of white. Coke. Charlie. Prince? I want to buy. Can you help me?'

9

Robin Walker was furious when he opened the front door. He chewed his cheek as Morrow and McGrain showed their ID. They spoke to him on the phone? Half an hour ago, about the call this morning? They asked to come in to talk about his missing partner, Roxanna Fuentecilla?

'Yes. Come in.' He karate-chopped a hand at the hall carpet, ordering them to move, snorting with annoyance as Morrow and McGrain sidled into a narrow hallway.

Policing meant spending a lot of time with angry people, not all of them members of the public. Morrow knew anger well, its moods and its nuances. She found that anger was usually just fear with its make-up on, so her question was this: was Robin Walker frightened because his partner was missing, or was he frightened because someone had called the police?

'You said it was an anonymous call?' He was tall and lean and loomed over them, avoiding eye contact, giving sharp, rhythmic pissed-off little nods.

'Yes,' said Morrow, taking in his thick dark hair and pale blue eyes. Smeary footage from distant cameras didn't do him justice. 'Yes, is Ms Fuentecilla missing?'

Walker caught his breath, dropped his chin to his chest and looked back up. When he spoke his voice was thick with emotion: Yes, she is missing.

'And you are . . . ?'

'Robin Walker. I'm her partner. Boyfriend.'

'Can we go through? Talk to you there?'

49

He waved an impatient hand at the living room door and stormed off through it.

Morrow let McGrain go ahead of her, glancing down the narrow corridor to a rack of coats and saw a green parka with a fur-trimmed hood.

Heading into the living room, Morrow's eye was drawn to the carpet. It was new and white. She glanced at the skirting board, checking for carpet worms, telltale strands of wool that worked their way out as a carpet settled. She couldn't see any and found that reassuring: Robin hadn't beaten Roxanna to death and replaced the carpet. Probably.

Compared to the narrow hall, the living room was dazzlingly grand. A chandelier the size of a shopping trolley hung from the ceiling. Two enormous floor-length windows framed heavy-boughed trees nodding gently in the street. Robin and Roxanna's furniture was designed for a small London flat and the couch and coffee table, the dining table and chairs were dwarfed to doll-size in the high Victorian room. It looked as if the family were squatting in the lower third of a fish tank. Morrow was so distracted by the clash of scale that she didn't notice the children at first.

They were on the couch, watching her come in, sitting completely still. Martina and Hector Vicente. Their ankles were crossed, hands folded in laps, backs poker-straight, one a mirror to the other. They looked at Morrow and McGrain with the composed disinterest of Gainsborough portraits. Blonde like their mother, long-limbed and lush-lipped. Neither had a flicker in their expression. She looked at Hector and wanted to smile, remembering him with his mum in the bakery, but he dropped his gaze to the floor and she remembered herself. He was wearing the grey skinny-leg jeans.

She told them her name, that she was here about their mother, and stood near them. She wanted them to speak. She had a voice recorder running in her pocket so that the bosses and the bosses' bosses could read every word once it was transcribed. The audio would be useful too though: they could compare their voices to the call file.

'Don't you have school today?'

'Our mother is missing,' said Martina. 'We thought it would be best if we remained at home.'

'I see.' She wanted a sample of Hector's voice too. She nodded at him. 'Don't you have school, son?'

'I do also but my sister' – he gestured to Martina very formally, it was clear he was talking in his second language – 'thought it would be best if I stayed home today.'

Morrow nodded. 'I see. Thank you.'

He was still on the child side of twelve, his voice high. The caller could have been either one of them but Martina's jeans were blue.

Morrow felt she had to respond to the strained situation. 'Sorry, Robin, were you having a chat in here, before we arrived?'

Walker glowered at the children. Hector opened his mouth but his eyes flicked to Martina and she gave him a stare that told him to shut up. No one spoke. It had taken twenty seconds to reach deadlock.

'OK.' McGrain clapped his hands with synthetic cheer, making everyone jump. 'Here's a plan: how about you kids go and have kick-about next door and let us chat to your dad for a minute?'

Everyone panicked in the silence. Then Hector spoke. 'Robin's not our—'

'Shut up, Hector.' Martina stood up, her eyes firmly on McGrain. 'That man said for us to go.'

She stood, gestured for Hector to get up and led him out. They moved like despondent dancers making the long walk off stage after a bad performance. Walker scowled and followed them, slamming the door, and came back, sitting in their place.

'Were you talking to the kids before we arrived, Mr Walker?'

'Yes. After you called I asked them and they told me Hector phoned you. About their mum.'

McGrain smiled gently, 'You don't seem very pleased about that.'

Suddenly animated, Walker looked up. 'I'm fucking furious. Why did they think they *had* to go behind my back? I've been up all night, worried sick. Just *tell* me – that's what I'm angry about.' He raised his voice reproachfully at the door, continuing the interrupted argument. '*That's* what I mean. I'm not an ogre.'

His eyes reddened suddenly, but not with the slow grind of worry, not with sadness, something more intense than fear. It looked like panic. He wasn't behaving like someone who had murdered his girlfriend the day before and then let the police into his house. He wasn't trying to act innocent at all.

Morrow looked away, giving him a private moment. She found herself staring straight at the sixty-four thousand quid display cabinet. It looked smaller than it did in the photographs, but just as ugly.

'That's a one-off. A Larkin and Sons.' Walker took a deep breath. 'A design icon, actually. Handcrafted.'

'Nice,' said McGrain politely.

Morrow nodded and hummed as if she agreed. 'What is "a design icon"? I've never really understood that.'

Walker struggled to explain. It was a special design. Sort of a very good one? One that other people copied, he thought. He attempted a charming smile. The mouth managed it but his eyes stayed sad and angry. Walker was out of his depth. He was young. Being so handsome wasn't making him less sympathetic.

Morrow remembered who she was pretending to be. She opened her briefcase, took out the missing person form and a pen.

'So, Mr Walker. Let's see if we can find her, put an end to your worry. When did you last see Roxanna?'

Robin Walker looked into the near distance, clutched his hands together and told them that Roxanna had left for work yesterday morning, dropping the kids off at school. He hadn't seen or heard from her since. It was very out of character.

McGrain nodded encouragingly as Morrow wrote.

'You've just moved here?' she asked.

'From London. Two months ago.'

'And how are you enjoying Glasgow?'

'Great,' he said, but a twitch in his jaw suggested otherwise. Morrow tried not to smile. Glasgow was strong cheese: not to everyone's taste.

How did Roxanna seem yesterday morning? Fine, normal. She took the kids to school at the normal time but then didn't go into work, didn't call anyone, had not been back to the house. None of her clothes were missing and her passport was still here: he'd found it in a drawer in the bedroom.

She asked him: Had they argued? Most couples argue sometimes. He smiled. We argue *all* the time. But no. Nothing special. Do your arguments ever become physical? She hit me with a pizza once ... He hurried to correct himself: but it was funny, she was trying to be funny because we got, sort of, you know, stuck, fighting about something. He refreshed his smile, wrung his hands.

McGrain echoed the smile.

Walker was giving a very bad account of himself. If Morrow had no previous knowledge she would be suspicious. The pizza story rang true. If Walker had killed his girlfriend he would be trying to misdirect them. He'd say they didn't fight, theorise that she had run away. He would have hidden her passport.

'Why didn't you call us?'

He looked her straight in the eye and, unblinking, said he didn't know, he just didn't know. That part wasn't true: he did know. He hadn't called because they were doing something illegal. Morrow noted his tell: the long, unblinking stare. He had the grace to wring his hands as he lied.

She began to work her way through the set questions on the missing persons form: did he have a recent photograph of her?

Walker stepped over to the mantelpiece and lifted a silver-framed photo of Roxanna. He handed it to Morrow. Roxanna, head and shoulders, grinning lovingly into the camera lens, a soft spring light behind her. She was gorgeous: high cheekbones, olive skin, scarlet lips. Her thick blonde hair was pulled up loosely, pinned with a feathered fascinator.

'Is this your wedding?'

'No. We're not married. We were just at a wedding.'

'We might do better with a more workaday one.' As she handed it back, Walker's eye fell on the image and yearning, un-bidden, overwhelmed him. He turned away and laid the picture face down on the mantel. 'I'll get you another one.'

He left the room. They heard him walk down the hall and then return, hesitating behind the living room door. He came in hold-ing an original iPad, round-edged and lumpy. He sat down next to Morrow, turning it on and opening the iPhoto file.

McGrain craned to see it: a checkerboard of pictures, most of Roxanna alone but some with her children, all from the past year. It must have been Walker's iPad because they were nearly all of her: Roxanna on a white beach, Roxanna in a dark London street and, in all of them, Roxanna craning into Walker's gaze, radiating love. In the manner of digital photography the same view had been captured several times, less an attempt at bettering the image than an articulation of the photographer's enthusiasm for the moment.

One or two were of the couple together. Robin and Roxanna standing together in a park, stiff-smiling for whichever kindly stranger took the snap. Some were of Robin and Roxanna with either Martina or Hector, the other child presumably behind the lens. In the group photos where Martina was the photographer Robin's head was invariably cut off by the top of the frame. She had some of her mother's pugnaciousness.

Morrow scrolled down to the more recent ones, taken since they had arrived in Glasgow. Roxanna in the orchid house at the

Botanical Gardens. She was standing in the foreground, the light dusky and yellow. Behind her, at opposite ends of a long bench, were Martina and a man Morrow knew as Mr Y.

Mr Y was an unidentified but recurrent character in the CCTV of the Glasgow PINAD investigation. He was one of the first people Roxanna made contact with when she arrived. He'd been seen going into the office, the house, sitting in cars, always with Roxanna. He was slim, around sixty, dressed carefully and had a neatly trimmed moustache. They'd been trying to put a name to him for weeks.

In the photo Martina sat as far away from everyone as she could, hard up against the arm of the bench.

Morrow asked Robin to print that picture. He took the iPad from her, tapped the screen a couple of times and a printer snapped awake out in the hall.

Morrow referred back to her list of missing persons questions: friends and relatives?

He told her, only being somewhat cagey: Roxanna's parents were from Madrid but had died some time ago. She had a sister who lived in Boston. They called each other once a week. They were close. Morrow had listened to the Met's recordings of the stilted calls. The sister was a snide bitch and Roxanna was warm. 'Close' was overplaying it but that didn't make it a lie: most families were held together with myths. He said Roxanna hadn't made any friends in Glasgow yet but she hadn't been in touch with friends in London since she disappeared, he'd called everyone the night before.

Morrow asked the next question on the form: Did Roxanna have any medical conditions they should know about?

No, she was healthy. She had a heart murmur but it was being monitored and she exercised around it. It was a stable underlying condition, he said, using an insurance-form phrase.

She was thinking about the recorder in her pocket, really, imagining herself heard by her bosses, so she read out the next question without thinking: Could they have a DNA sample for Roxanna?

Walker froze.

If Morrow had been a real missing persons cop she would have been aware of the emotional impact of the question. She would have tiptoed into it, dropped the tone of her voice or something. She back-pedalled: Only so that they could rule out anyone who happened to be found, not because they had any reason to think anything, you know . . .

Walker's voice was husky: Where would he even get a DNA sample? McGrain suggested a hairbrush. Walker stood up slowly and left the room. He came back, his eyes smarting, holding a heated hairbrush reverently in two hands. Morrow took it and thanked him. It was completely useless, heat killed DNA, but she hadn't the heart to say that to him. If necessary she could ask for something else later.

She bagged the pointless item and slipped it into her briefcase, asking as she did so for Roxanna's bank account details and her mobile number, his mobile number and the kids' numbers too, if they had mobiles.

He baulked. 'What do you need her bank account number for?'

'To see if she's taken any money out. That'll tell us where she is and if she's safe. We need her mobile number too.'

He chewed his lip, thinking, and then flashed a cagey smile. 'Honestly, Rox hasn't called me.'

McGrain explained that it wouldn't just help them check her calls. If the phone was turned on they could track her movements from it. It would really help.

Walker agreed to give them all of the information but seemed to change his mind when Morrow handed him the form. There was a deal of fumbling with the pen, an overly elaborate writing-out of names. He was reluctant, but in the end he gave them every-one's numbers: his, Roxanna's, the kids'. It made Morrow think he was concerned enough about her to give them information he thought potentially damning.

She asked if Roxanna had ever gone missing before and Walker looked shifty. 'Not that I'm aware of. We've only been together for a year and a bit. She may have. You'd have to ask the kids.'

'The kids aren't your kids?'

'No, their father lives in Ecuador.'

'Do you know his name?'

'Miguel Vicente.' He spelled it for her and watched her write it down. She asked for Vicente's address and was told that he had two: one in Quito and a beachfront house in Guayaquil. Both in Ecuador.

'Would Roxanna have contacted him?'

Walker snorted at that. 'Not bloody likely.'

'Why "not bloody likely"?'

The story came out in a messy jumble. Her ex, he, well, he was a total bastard, sort of, you see, left without telling her where he was going and married someone else a week later (Morrow knew it was a month) and he wanted the kids now, but only because his wife was infertile (she had two kids) but he'd never bothered about the kids before (he had). Morrow could hear Roxanna's voice in the bitter rant. She'd heard divorce talk before. Vicente didn't pay a penny in maintenance, either (true). Rox'd seen a lawyer but it made no difference . . .

'Of course,' said Morrow, trying to impress the voice recorder audience with the breadth of her knowledge, 'Ecuador doesn't have a reciprocal maintenance agreement. We see this a lot in missing persons. It's not uncommon for children to be taken abroad by an ex.'

She imagined the DCC Hughes reading that, surprised and impressed by her erudition.

Walker looked puzzled, 'No. The kids aren't gone. *She's* gone.'

He was right. RMAs were irrelevant. Hughes would read that too. Morrow's smugness curdled to mild embarrassment. She was addressing the wrong audience. 'Are the kids in touch with their dad?'

They weren't, as far as he knew. Rox got upset at the mention of her ex, he said, and gave a little cringe. Morrow felt that maybe it was Robin who got upset at the mention of her ex. It was the downside of utterly condemning an ex to a new partner: it left no room for mitigation when the bitterness receded.

She asked him about the business.

'Injury Claims 4 U,' he said. The tacky posters were everywhere, on the underground, on bus stops, jarring red on yellow. The I of 'Injury' was represented by a silhouette of a ladder with a tiny red man falling off it. 'Those posters aren't hers. The owner was retiring, he was building up the goodwill. I don't really know anything about her business.'

Morrow said casually that they would have a look at the books, to check for debts undisclosed at the time of sale, railroading him by segueing straight into: 'If you could go and find contact details for the children's father while we speak to them.'

She stood up and McGrain did too.

Robin got up and block her way. 'This isn't about custody.' He said it very carefully. 'As I said: the kids are still here.'

'I didn't say it was about custody, Mr Walker. She may have tried to contact Mr Vicente—'

'No, she hasn't. It's not that . . .'

They looked at each other, Morrow soft, Walker frightened.

'Is there something you want to tell me, Mr Walker?'

'No.'

'Are you sure? Because I feel like you're worried about something but not being completely open with me.'

'No.'

'OK.' She nodded McGrain to the door, 'We'll speak to the children.'

Through the dark hallway and down the back corridor, they stopped at a printer on a table and Robin handed her a B5-sized print of the Botanics picture. It was still damp. They came to two bedroom doors facing each other.

Martina and Hector were at their respective desks in their respective rooms, both playing dull platform games on their laptops with the sound turned off. They had been listening but now affected surprise that there was anyone there. Martina stood up. 'May I help you?'

Robin stepped between them. 'They want you to tell them about Mummy.'

Martina spat viciously at Walker, 'What *about* her?'

He took a threatening step into the room, pointing at the girl as if he'd like to slap her. '*Has she phoned you?*'

Martina pointed back at him and shouted, 'Would we have called the police if she had phoned us?'

'*Since* you called the police? Has she phoned you *since* then?'

Evidently it was a high-volume household. Morrow raised her voice. 'I'll talk to the kids alone, please, Mr Walker.'

'Marty! Has she?'

'ALONE, Mr Walker.'

Malevolent joy rippled across Martina's face as Walker backed away. Hector was watching from his bedroom door, still as a hunted rabbit.

Morrow decided to start with Hector. Gesturing for McGrain to follow, she walked into the boy's room. Martina followed them.

'Go back to your own room.'

Martina tried to catch her brother's eye. Morrow stepped in and blocked her view. 'We'll come and see you in a minute.' She pulled the door over, not closing it, knowing Martina would listen. They heard the girl step away and shut her own door but felt her vigilance radiating across the corridor.

Hector sat down on the side of his bed, holding his stomach as if it ached, rocking softly back and forth.

'OK, son, we're just going to ask a few questions—'

'In the car!' he hissed in a whisper, watching the door. 'They had a big fight. Going to school. Yesterday.'

'Yesterday morning?'

He kept his eyes on the door. '*Yesterday*. Mummy went crazy because Daddy phoned Martina.'

'Doesn't he phone, normally?'

'Sometimes. She was furious, though.'

'Why?'

'Something he said about Auntie Maria. It made Mummy really furious.'

'Who is Auntie Maria?'

'Maria Arias. Mummy's friend in London.'

'What was it?'

'I don't know. I thought, maybe ... Daddy had a lot of affairs. Mummy and Daddy don't get on.' Hector shrugged. 'I don't know. Marty said it was bullshit.'

'Hector,' Morrow whispered, 'did you report her missing this morning? Did you call us?'

He nodded. 'Marty waited in the taxi. She said there would be cameras and two of us was ... you know. Obvious.'

'Why didn't you just call from here?'

He looked at the door.

'Is it because of Robin?'

He frowned at his bed.

'Do you think Robin would hurt your mum?'

He shrugged again. 'I don't really know him. What's he doing here?'

'Isn't he your mum's boyfriend?'

Hector nodded. Morrow thought he meant that he didn't want Robin to be there, rather than his presence was confusingly pointless.

'On the phone this morning you said, "We don't know where they've taken her." What did you mean?'

'I don't know.'

'Why do you think someone's taken her? Why not that she's just run off?'

He found it hard to articulate but eventually held his hands up at the room. 'Why are we here, in Glasgow? What are we *doing* here?'

It was an astute question. Long-serving police officers were wondering the same thing. He was rocking back and forth, nearly crying. He couldn't talk any more, could hardly catch his breath. Morrow patted his hand, felt a strong urge to lie and tell him everything would be all right. 'I'm going to ask your sister about the argument in the car, OK?'

He hummed warily at the door, steeling himself.

Morrow got up and went across the hall, knocking and opening the door simultaneously. She found Martina standing by her bed, waiting. Her manner was imperial.

'Martina. Can you tell me what your dad said on the phone that made your mum so angry?'

'Nothing.' Martina's voice was flat. 'He didn't say anything.'

They looked at each other for a while. Finally, Morrow broke the silence. 'Why did you call us if you don't want help?'

'Get us away from Walker . . .' Martina was crying a little now, not like Hector though. It was controlled, as if she was squeezing it out.

'Are you afraid of Robin?'

'No!'

'Do you think he had anything to do with your mum—'

'No!'

'You don't think he hurt your mum?'

She couldn't bring herself to say that. She slumped down on the bed, defeated. 'No.'

'What do you think has happened?'

'She calls at four fifteen, when we get in from school, normally. We were worried when she didn't call, but maybe she was driving?'

'Why would she be driving?'

'I think she drove to London to see Auntie Maria. I think she gave her a fucking ear-bleed.'

Morrow took a moment to navigate her way through the teen-speak. 'Was she angry with her?'

Martina shook her head. 'She was angry about nothing. Literally *nothing*. She went crazy: "What did he say? What *exactly*." But he hadn't said anything. "Auntie Maria said you're doing geometry." Literally that boring.'

She was a child whose mother was missing and she'd been dumped on an unloved stepfather but still, Martina didn't evoke sympathy, not like Hector. She was beautiful, privileged, but bitter and angry, as if she had everything but couldn't fucking believe she wasn't getting more.

'You got your brother to call us, why not call yourself?'

She shrugged carelessly, as if she just couldn't be bothered, but Hector had been listening and called out from his room, 'She was crying so much she couldn't speak.'

Martina glowered at the door.

'Has your mum ever left you before?'

'*Never!*' She spat the word. 'She has never, ever left us before. Mummy is *fierce* about us, so I know there's something wrong, otherwise she would have phoned.'

'Well, she has left and she hasn't phoned. What do you think could cause that to happen?'

Martina, chewed her cheek, looked tired. 'I think she's in trouble,' she whispered.

'What sort of trouble?'

But Martina's chin trembled and she dropped her face to hide it. Morrow saw then that she wasn't mean or haughty, she was just a child who didn't know where her mum was and she was scared. Fear with its make-up on.

'Money trouble?'

She gave her lap a tiny nod and then glanced up at McGrain, pleading with them not to press it.

Morrow didn't want to ask. Incriminating evidence from children looked bad, especially if they had been questioned without an adult present. They could ask her to elaborate eventually, if they needed to.

Morrow held up the photograph from the Botanics and pointed out the mysterious Mr Y. 'Who's this man?'

'Frank Delahunt. He's the lawyer for Mummy's business up here. He's a creepy wanker.'

Back in the car with McGrain, Morrow puzzled the dynamics in the family.

'What do you think? Martina seems desperate to get away from Walker. Is it a child protection issue?'

'Nah,' said McGrain, knowing exactly what she was talking about. 'Bosses wouldn't let you anyway. They've spent too much on it.'

He was right. Abusing stepfathers with an eye on a child often picked chaotic families, but usually with a mother they could control. Roxanna wasn't that. Both the Met and Police Scotland had spent too much money on the case already to let Morrow blow it with a speculative social-work intervention. A request for a home visit wouldn't make it off her desk.

'She hates him,' said McGrain. 'He's her stepdad. The problem is that he's a child himself and he hates her back.' He started the engine. 'I'm a stepdad to three.'

'Do they hate you?'

He pulled up at the lights on the busy Great Western Road. 'They did. At first. Their mum thought it would never pass. Your job is just not to react. It was easy for me. Mine are diamonds.'

Morrow looked out of the window as the lights changed and they drove on.

She didn't think Roxanna Fuentecilla would walk away from her kids. But Morrow had to face the possibility: maybe she didn't know her at all. Maybe all the good stuff was just projected hope.

IO

Iain tripped downhill along streets of high hedges around big houses. He felt conspicuous, imagined householders spotting him through their windows and stopping to neighbourhood-watch him. He knew a lot of the town, but nobody from up here. The big-house people were often incomers. They kept themselves separate, above, geographically, socially, even in the elevated seating positions of their high-up cars. Iain's only contact with them was through their cleaners, or childminders, or if he met their gardeners in the pub. Or if they approached him for a deal. Susan Grierson made sense now. She'd probably ask him to recommend a cleaner when he got back.

He turned eastward, heading for Tommy's mum's. It was helping his mood, having a thing to do. Even walking was helping him keep focus, the slap of his feet on the pavement drowning out the physical sensations of the morning. He stopped at a kerb, heard a seagull in the distance and remembered the rough dock pressing hard on his knee, the warm wet of her breath on his lips. He hurried across the empty road without really looking, eager to get moving again.

Five blocks down he arrived at Tommy's mum's tenement. The window frames were peeling. Someone had emptied an ashtray from their car into the gutter just outside. The entry door was propped open with a broken brick. He walked into the concrete close and the familiar smell of damp and sea and air.

Tommy lived with his mum, Elaine Farmer, in a disabled-access flat on the ground floor. Lainey had bad knees. Iain had known her for a long time. He flicked the letter box a couple of times, the metallic clack ricocheting back from the stone walls of the close.

He listened. A footfall. A door creak. He could imagine Elaine standing still inside, wondering.

Finally, she called out, 'Who's it?'

Iain leaned into the joist where the door would open. 'Me, Lainey.'

Pause.

'Iain Fraser,' he said.

She shuffled across the hall and opened the door a crack, peering out with one eye. 'Keep hearing you're back.' She opened the door to let him in.

God, she was old. And heavy. One good thing about prison food: it was hard to get fat. She had a purple T-shirt on, too small. It was gathered around her middle. Her thin blonde hair was tangled at one side.

Lainey had not grown into her looks. If anything she'd grown out of them and she wasn't looking after herself. Her grey skirt was ripped at the hem where it had caught on something. Her legs were bare and her calves bulged with black veins, as if she was already full of worms. She wore slippers shaped like black and white footballs. Iain stared at them to spare himself the sight of her.

'Footballs. Like 'em? Tommy got me these for Christmas. Comfortable.' She dropped her voice to a sensual murmur. 'What you doing here, Iain?'

Iain and Lainey had a night a long time ago; a high point for her, a low point for him. Iain wouldn't let her know he felt that way though. She'd never been very attractive but she was nice.

'Kind of looking for Tommy, Lainey, looking to buy.'

She tutted reprovingly. 'Not for yourself?' Iain was known for his abstemiousness. It made him stand out.

'No,' he gave a sheepish smile, 'just for a friend.'

'Oh.' She looked down the close. 'Tommy's out just now. But seeing as it's you. Much you after?'

'Three gram?' He held up the money. It was more than a pinch but Susan had given him the price plus half again to get it.

'Come on in, well.'

Iain didn't want to be alone with Lainey in an empty house. He wanted to keep on walking, actually. Stay moving, stay outside, but he couldn't think of a good excuse so he slipped sideways into the hall, flattening himself against the wall by the door as she shut it.

'Well, my God, Iain Fraser.' She stepped back to look him over. 'You get better-looking every time I see ye.'

She reached forward to touch his chest and Iain flinched away. He couldn't be touched today, not by her and not there. She was hurt. He mumbled an apology.

'Nuh nuh.' She dropped her hand. 'You're entitled.' She glanced down at her slippers, lifted a hand to touch her messy hair. He could see that she was blaming herself, finding the fault in her appearance.

'Lainey, I'm . . . it's been a hell of a day . . .'

'Fair enough, Iain. Just saying.' She tried to smile warmly but dropped it and turned away, casting a saucy look behind her. 'Just . . . wouldn't kick ye out, if you know what I mean.'

Iain stayed where he was and watched her shuffle down the hall. The ridiculous slippers made her look as if she was dribbling two footballs. He pressed his hands to the wall behind him and waited. He could hear her rifling through a drawer.

He remembered the hallway being bigger than it was. He slid across it in his socks before dawn, trying not to make a noise as he left. Tommy was at his dad's, the house was empty, but Iain had started at the sound of a pipe clanging as it came to life. He hurried across to the door, saw Tommy's school bag and trainers in a pile by the cupboard, thought they were his own for some reason, and stopped. Lainey was at the bedroom door before he got moving again and she took him back to bed. They tried again, and again he couldn't. She was too raw. Even when he shut his eyes all he could see was her face, her broken veins, her drunken smile. The second time he came out of the room into the hall Lainey called after him that she wouldn't tell anyone, it was their private business, he shouldn't be ashamed. Iain wasn't ashamed. He'd have been more ashamed if he had been able to. It would have meant he was blind to the smog of need and lies around her. She didn't want it either. They called it sex because they didn't have the words for what they needed. They were both looking for a hand to hold in the dark, a friend, a makeshift mooring.

In the back room now Elaine slammed the drawer shut. She came back out, cellophane wraps in her hand. 'Tommy's already bagged them into grams.'

Iain gave her two thirds of the money. 'Very efficient.'

'Aye, small businessman of the year, all that shite.'

Iain opened the door. She knew he wanted to get away. He'd hurt her and wished he hadn't but he couldn't think how to make it OK so he just walked away.

'Iain,' she called after him down the close. Iain turned back. 'Not want to stay for your tea? I'm making Tommy's anyway.'

He didn't want to see Tommy.

'Shepherd's pie?' she said, as if that was what was worrying him.

'Nah, you're all right, Lainey, but thanks, love.' He stepped away.

'Iain?'

He turned back once more to look at her, keeping his body to the door.

'Iain, I can see . . .' Lainey drew a line down her cheek. She knew he'd been crying. She blinked slow. Sympathy. The vain hope of connection. That's why he went with her before.

Iain shook his head. 'Please, don't tell Tommy.'

She shrugged a shoulder. 'I won't say.'

Grateful, Iain lifted a hand to wave. Puzzled, Lainey squinted at his fingers.

'What?' Iain looked at his own hand.

'What's that?' She looked at his hand and touched her own fingertips.

Stained brown with blood. He hid his hands behind his back. She shouldn't be looking at that. She was nice, Elaine, she was a nice person. 'Nothing.' He backed out of the close.

'Iain,' she called, 'anything. Just phone me, OK?'

'Will do, Lainey. You're a star.'

Iain didn't have a phone. He was ashamed of that. Not that he couldn't afford one but every time he got out of prison the technology had moved on so much he couldn't catch up.

He hurried away from her, into the west, slowing to a panting walk because of the weight of the smoking on his lungs. It was a deceptively steep climb to the posh bit. He stopped to catch his breath.

Too much had happened to fit into one day. The day before had been so calm. She sat where they put her, in Iain's room, calm on the low-down stool. They bought in a curry. She chose butter chicken and ate it with a plastic spoon. Sometimes, when Tommy spoke, Iain saw her looking at them, smiling as if she was part of the conversation. She saw no threat in them. Right up to when they were walking through the yellow sand when he saw the apple of her cheek, tight and round, smiling as they led her to the dock. As if she didn't mind. She was like a holy martyr.

He leaned over his knees, breathing deep. Maybe she didn't mind. He stood up, hands on hips; he looked out over the sea. If someone was going to kill him right now he didn't think he'd mind. Maybe that was how she'd felt. The thought cheered him until he remembered her screaming and fighting and almost making it to the trees. He headed back up to Susan's dirty house.

Stepping through the overgrown hedge around the front garden he saw her watching for him through an arrow-slit window at the side of the front door. Iain dropped his head as he walked up to the opening door, wondering what the fuck it was with Susan and realising that he didn't care. These women weren't his problem. He should get away and be alone.

She let him in, not even looking at his face. 'Put it down there,' she said to the dresser. Iain put the wraps on the sideboard. Susan stayed at the door, waiting for him to leave.

The coke was what she wanted and it was all she wanted. She nodded the way out. 'Sorry you're upset today. Was it because I mentioned Sheila?'

Iain looked at his feet. 'Yeah,' he said. 'Sheila.'

She reached out and squeezed his upper arm like a witch testing him for the pot.

'So brave,' she said, cold now that she had what she wanted.

Iain looked at her. She didn't care about anything but getting him out of there. 'Why's this house so dirty?'

'I beg your pardon?'

'You weren't here, were ye? She died on her own.'

'Sorry?'

He looked back into the dirty kitchen. 'Fucking look at this place. She died in here, didn't she? And you've just got back.'

Susan was surprised, amused even, as if she'd been walking a dog and then it looked up and spoke to her. 'Oh. But my mother died. I'm sorting through her affairs—'

'Alone,' he said, his lips tight with the effort of being so vicious. 'She died alone in here so don't think you can talk to me as if I'm some kind of arsehole. At least Sheila knew I wanted to be there.'

Susan's eyes were narrowed now. 'But you weren't there, were you? You were in prison.'

She was goading him, chin out, eyes slits, and Iain wondered out loud, 'How the fuck would you know that?'

Suddenly embarrassed, she tried to herd him out of the door. 'Just get out.'

Iain didn't move. 'How do you know I was in prison?'

'Mum told me.' It was possible. Her mother might have told her that. But she looked caught out. As though she had given something away.

'Have you been following me or something?'

'Just go.'

Did she have a crush on him? No, it wasn't that. But why would she know that then? 'Are you a cop?' She didn't react so it wasn't that. He looked down to the kitchen. She was definitely hiding something in the house. 'Is there someone in there?'

She pushed at him. 'Get out.'

Iain half called out because she didn't want him to, 'Who's in there?'

It was so sudden. Her foot shot out in a judo move, curling around his calf, throwing him off balance and she shoved at the same time. Iain tumbled out of the front door and into the garden. The door slammed shut in his face.

Through the dirty window at the side of the door he saw her shadow hurry down the passageway to the back of the house.

He stood for a minute, waiting for the surprise to subside, and then he asked the peeling front door: 'Who the fuck are you now?'

II

They were assembled around the same table in the same sterile meeting room.

Morrow gave her report in bullet points: a transcript of the entire Walker interview would be available tomorrow morning.

- The Fuentecilla kids made the missing persons call this a.m.
- The bank had been contacted and were checking RF's account for withdrawals.
- Traces were being conducted for the mobile phones.
- Mr Y is Frank Delahunt. Family report that he is the company lawyer. They were tracing him right now.
- Walker had consented to allow them access to the office. They were currently looking for officers with forensic accounting diplomas who were available tomorrow morning. They'd get them into the Injury Claims 4 U office and gather as much intel as possible.

She continued:

- Martina Fuentecilla suggested that Roxanna might have driven to London to confront Maria Arias. There had been some suggestion of a possible romantic connection between Maria and their father, Manuel Vicente.

In conclusion:

- Still missing, still no reason to suspect foul play.

She looked up. That was about it.

Somewhat glassy-eyed after listening to her report, CS

Saunders pushed a sheet of paper over to her. It had a photo on it. A security shot of Roxanna from inside a cash machine. The bank had sent the jpeg as Morrow was driving here.

Fuentecilla had withdrawn cash from an ATM yesterday at twenty past two in the afternoon. It was in Stone, Staffordshire, four hours south of Glasgow down the M6. She took out fifty quid and there had been no charges to the card since then. Her normal pattern was fifty quid a day.

So, concluded DCC Hughes, Martina is correct: Roxanna was on her way south. The car GPS had been traced, all the way down to the M1. Just after the cash withdrawal, Fuentecilla had pulled into a car park in Luton and the tracker was turned off manually.

Morrow looked at the cash point picture. It was taken from an unflatteringly low angle with a fisheye lens. Her mouth was slack as she punched in her PIN. Her hair was in disarray, her eyes puffy.

Morrow was disappointed in her. Even if Roxanna had only gone to London to shout at a love rival, she hadn't phoned the kids at four fifteen to reassure them. She could have rung. She hadn't called last night either. Morrow looked at the picture again. Roxanna looked frightened.

Saunders and Hughes were still talking. CI Nolly Dent was doing his customary obsequious nod. Morrow had to turn the picture of Roxanna on its face to stop her eyes straying to it. She tried hard to listen and pay attention but was aware of her hand resting on the cheap, porous paper, of the moisture from her palm warping it.

The bosses were telling each other that Fuentecilla didn't know anyone in Staffordshire or Manchester or Birmingham, the major cities nearby, so they could conclude that she was heading straight for London. Morrow should be ready to fly down in the morning to question Maria Arias, before the Met heard that Roxanna had been there. The Met and the Serious Fraud Office were closing in on Juan Pinzón Arias's money. A freeze on his accounts was imminent. The chief didn't want the seven million in the Fuentecilla case being requisitioned into the Met's proceeds pot. The chief got up as he finished talking and gave them all a stern, warning look: find the money before the Met do.

Outside, Morrow gave McGrain his orders for the morning. Get this ready, trace that, bring your passport because you and I will probably have to fly to London. McGrain listened but was shaking his head, a gesture so small it seemed almost to himself.

'I've got tomorrow late off.'

'Can't you change it?'

'Kid's hospital appointment. Wonky hip.'

She didn't like that. 'We'll be back on time,' she said, knowing they probably wouldn't be.

'Can't take the chance, ma'am.' He held his breath, not at all comfortable about standing up to her. 'We've been waiting for three months for an appointment . . .'

She could insist. She wanted to. She saw herself suddenly as one of those old bastard bosses who were in charge when she was coming up, throwing their weight around because they could.

'Right. Tell Thankless to bring his passport. I'll take him instead.'

But she was pissed off about it: she didn't like Thankless.

12

Boyd Fraser was in a terrible mood. He wanted to go for a pint or something, have a minute to himself. That was the problem with living somewhere small; he had no sooner finished work than he was at his own front door. He'd got used to the rhythm of London, having an hour or so commute after work, time to decompress, read or listen to music. Here, his life felt unremittingly dutiful and tedious.

He crossed the steep road home and took the long way, circling the block to his house. The sky was bruised pink, the day drawing to a lazy end and a soft breeze blowing in from the sea. The warmth of the café lifted from him like the odour of fresh bread.

Really, he was under a hell of a lot of pressure, new business, young family. He needed a break but Lucy didn't see it that way. She wanted him home, always. He circled the neighbours' grounds and arrived at his own garden gate eight minutes after locking up the café.

He climbed the six steps to the lawn. Pretty bungalow, lovely garden. The lights were on in the front rooms.

It was a modest house by the standards of the town, but not spectacularly modest. A bungalow with four reception rooms, four bedrooms, a small kitchen with the original larder and a butler's pantry. The garden was well established. The roof was in good repair. It was picturesque: the front had a panoramic view of the sea from a covered wooden porch.

The Reverend Robert Fraser kept the house well until he died. Too old to undertake improvements, he had not stapled an ugly conservatory to the front porch or had plastic windows installed.

No work needed doing, no ugly dissonant changes needed reversing, which was just as well. Boyd arrived back in the town with nothing but two sons and a wife. They had remortgaged to start the business.

Hameau de la Reine.

Fuck. It pissed Boyd off how often that came to his mind when he looked at the house. It was spreading too. He thought about it in the café the other day, when someone, a middle-aged woman, naturally, bought organic local free-range eggs. It was the look she had on her face when she asked if they were 'local?'.

Hameau de la fucking Reine. It wasn't even part of their holiday itinerary. They might have strolled through, none the wiser, but the tour guide happened to be giving a talk in English.

Lucy and Boyd made a trip around Europe the year before William arrived, in a VW van with a brand new engine. They visited the Venice Biennale, stopped in the Alps, ate and drank and fucked and danced all over Europe. The weather was perfect, the reconditioned van admired wherever they stopped. The trip was beautiful. They were beautiful. They were so full of each other that Lucy's pregnancy felt inevitable, a comma in a long, fluid sentence. But here, in Helensburgh, what lingered in his mind was that ridiculous Hameau.

Marie Antoinette had it built in the grounds of Versailles. A grotesque. She commissioned it to escape the pressures of courtly life. It was a phony peasant village, a place where she could play the part of a country maid. She would come here, the tour guide said, and milk freshly washed and perfumed sheep into Sèvres porcelain pails commissioned for the purpose. But the Hameau wasn't just for her to play the peasant in. It also allowed the residents of Versailles to feel as if they were in the wild French countryside, instead of a fenced-in enclosure surrounded by starving, angry Frenchmen.

Pretty bungalow. Lovely garden. He tramped across the dewy lawn to the side door.

Boyd looked up, saw the soft lights spill from the windows onto the damp grass. It looked idyllic. He thought of taking a picture and sending it to Sanjay. But he was always sending photos to Sanjay. Jumpers and wellies and rosy-cheeked kids, sea-spray-tousled Lucy, pictures of the dog. Sanjay's texted responses were getting shorter and shorter as he lost interest. *You lucky fucker, man, I'm stuck on the Circle line* became *Looks great* became *Great*. Last time he even replied in text speak – *gr8* – something they both disapproved of. It was as if he didn't care whether Boyd thought he was a prick any more, because Boyd was a ghost to him. Sanjay would have visited if they'd moved to Cornwall. All their friends would have visited if they'd been in Norwich. It only took two fucking hours to get from Heathrow to Helensburgh, but no one came.

Angry now, instead of snaking around the edge, Boyd stomped across the lawn. Halfway over he felt his heel sinking into the immaculate grass. Lucy had taken on the garden and she'd be bitching about that for a month now.

He walked around the back to the kitchen door, tripping the pensioner-paranoid sensor lights his father had fitted. They felt like a perpetual reproach from a frightened father to his absent son. Boyd would have pulled them down if they weren't so far up the wall.

Opening the back door, he let it bang off the wall, heard the kitchen noise of the kids die abruptly. Even the dog was quiet for a moment. The household was reading his entrance to gauge his mood. Annoyed by that, he kicked his shoes off, hitting the door with one of them.

A sniff and a scratch on the inside door and Boyd leaned over and opened it. Jimbo, the black Cairn terrier, looked up at him with worried old-lady eyes, his pink tongue frozen on his lips.

He wilfully misunderstood the dog's concern: 'Well, go on then,' he motioned for him to go out to the garden, 'get out and do it, you incontinent little shit.'

In the kitchen the boys laughed uproariously because their dad had said 'shit' and because Jimbo was in trouble and not them.

Jimbo scurried past him to the dark rockery.

'Don't let him go in the rockery, Boyd.' Lucy was standing in the doorway, a blackened oven glove on her right hand. Isabel Marant joggies hung from her yoga-perfect hips. She wore a white T-shirt, good French cotton. A wedge of skin was exposed at her waist. Boyd wanted to kiss it.

Lucy saw his lascivious ogle and smirked. 'Seriously – don't let him poo in there. I'll have to pick it up.'

Boyd kept his eyes on her hips. 'Give me ten minutes.'

Lucy looked back at the oven, then at Boyd. She knew what he was thinking.

'I've got a moussaka coming out of the oven, it's the boys' supper. I've spent hours—'

'*No,*' he said, refusing her refusal.

A look of sadness flickered in her eyes but she blinked it into a wry smile. 'Fuck off, Boyd.'

She went back to her oven.

Jimbo was at the door, waiting for permission to come back into the house. Boyd swung his foot behind the little dog and booted him gently indoors, shutting the door to the porch.

He walked into the kitchen. She'd brought the little flat-screen TV in from the bedroom, stood it on the counter top and they were watching a Loony Tunes DVD. She was keeping the boys' eyes busy. It was far too exciting for early evening. Larry was watching and throwing his weight back and forth, banging the feet of his chair dangerously on the floor.

'Daddy,' William observed absently, keeping his eyes on the screen.

Lucy had her back to him, her shoulders defensive as she lifted the steaming dish onto the hob. They had talked about using the TV as a babysitter. She knew it was wrong.

Boyd stomped over to the counter. 'Put the fucking telly off,

Lucy!' He pressed the switch too hard, nearly knocking the flat-screen over.

The boys chorused their objections. Jimbo joined in, huffing loud yips, and Lucy swore at him. Boyd walked away.

'IT'S BAD FOR THEM,' he shouted and went into the bedroom to take a shower, slamming the door.

He could hear Lucy out there, screaming down the corridor, calling him a FUCKING wanker. Then the boys started crying because they were arguing again.

Boyd wasn't sorry. He was angry and wanted her to be angry too.

He shed his work clothes on the bed, hating the spindly legged furniture in here, the heavy padded headboard, the three-mirrored dressing table. His mother's choice. Everything old and brown and so well made that they couldn't justify spending money, even Ikea money, to replace it.

He went into the en suite and turned the shower on, waiting for it to get hot. First thing he'd do when they made some money: have a proper walk-in shower installed instead of an afterthought over the bath.

He had to huddle under the flow to get more than one shoulder wet at a time. His mood warmed as he realised what he had decided. He smiled down at the floor, letting the water run over him.

He was going to have a blowout. Tomorrow, after the dinner dance, he was going to have a mental night, get wrecked, dance, whatever the fuck he wanted. And then the day after he'd be sorry and start again.

13

Alex and Brian were slumped on the settee in a living room scattered with damp towels and small toys, nappy bags tied at the neck, toast-crumbed plates. They were half watching the news. Mostly, though, they were listening for the twins on the baby monitor.

With the insight unique to those who have known otherwise, Morrow was aware of her profound contentment in this moment. She felt the warmth of the nice man next to her, savoured the health of her children. She even had a cup of tea and a biscuit. She found happiness hard to recall most of the time – misery was stickier, puzzling, more intense – but she could be happy in the moment.

The twins were thirteen months old and now, from the moment she walked through the front door until she left, she was lifting, wiping, changing or dressing them. She measured every task in the distinct number of hand movements it required. Brian and Alex were almost ambidextrous now. Out of necessity, they could both feed a baby and make a sandwich at the same time. But now her hands were empty. And she was sitting down. Celebrating the moment, she reached lazily across the settee, not quite reaching Brian. 'Your day all right?'

'Usual,' said Brian. 'You?'

'Same as ever. Liars and politics.'

'Oh, aye.' Brian kept his eyes on the telly. 'Spent forty minutes this morning answering emails while the boss lectured me about how men can't multitask.'

The baby monitor crackled, glowing green. It sounded as if

the twins were asleep but that didn't mean they were. They were conspiracy incarnate.

On the TV a smiley man was forecasting a change in the weather. Heavy rain, danger of landslides. A debate show started, angry audience and suited panel, talking about the independence referendum. Both Alex and Brian lurched for the remote.

Brian got it first and flicked over.

'God,' he said, 'I hate this. Next office down's handing out literature and holding lunchtime rallies in the canteen. They look at your lapel before they look at your face.'

The fervent had taken to wearing badges declaring their allegiances, putting stickers and signs in their windows and cars. It made the vote an incessant background thrum, impossible to forget.

'It's getting mental,' said Morrow.

'This must be what the Reformation was like,' said Brian cheerfully. 'At the beginning. When it was all bright hopes of the Resurrection.'

She huffed, 'I can't wait for it to be over, anyway.'

'The Reformation?'

Alex snorted a laugh. 'That too.'

Brian grinned at her. 'It's the Reformendum.'

'Bit of a mouthful,' said Alex as her phone lit up on the side table. Unknown caller. She frowned and answered it.

Alexandra Morrow? This was Shotts Prison. They had her number listed as Daniel McGrath's family contact.

The officer apologised for phoning so late but her brother had been stabbed and was in hospital. He had been operated on. He was in a stable condition. If she wanted to visit him she needed to contact this person in that department of the Scottish Prison Service. Thank you, sorry, and good night. They hung up.

Brian watched her hand drop to her lap, still clutching the phone.

'What?'

'Danny. Stabbed. In hospital.'

'He OK?'

'Stable.'

Brian's hand found hers across the settee.

'Are you all right?'

'Aye,' she said, but too high, too fast.

He squeezed her hand. 'Want to call the hospital?'

'Tomorrow.'

They lay shoulder to shoulder in bed. Lazy tears oiled from Alex's eyes, running into her hair at the temples.

The light on the baby monitor lit the room kelp-green. An undulating ocean of sound filled the room, an ebb and swell of little boys' breathing. Brian waited for a wave to crash before he spoke.

'You crying?'

She waited for the next back draught and whispered, 'A bit.'

'I'm sure he's OK.'

She wasn't crying because she was worried about him. She was crying because, again, Danny had robbed her of the delusion of nobility.

In the moment after she hung up, before Brian squeezed her hand, Alex had wished her brother dead with a fervour that was almost sexual. Not because he was a bad man. She wasn't wishing him dead for the good of the world. She wished her brother dead because he was an obligation she did not want to meet. He made her uncomfortable. It was mealy, malevolent, and she didn't want to know it about herself.

Brian whispered in the green dark, 'Never going to be over, is it?'

She didn't answer.

They shouldn't even have her number. Danny must have given it to them. She tried to believe that he'd done it to shame her but that was a lie. Danny gave them her number because Alex was all he had. She had all of this: Brian, the twins, her job, everything.

But she was all that Danny really had and she didn't want him.

She lay still, listening to the wash of the twins' breathing. They were trying to synchronise: one would snuffle, the other stumble over an exhalation, correcting themselves, trying to meet as completely as they had in the womb, but failing. Always failing.

14

It was a fraught morning. Paranoid about Danny, afraid someone would phone at an inopportune time if his condition worsened, Morrow gave in and called the prison service. They told her Danny was in the Southern General acute post-surgical ward. They couldn't tell her anything about his current condition, she'd have to phone the hospital. That probably meant he wasn't dead.

She turned to her work for comfort but found none. The first item in her email was the trace that had been run on Fuentecilla's mobile. It was preliminary, covering the last forty-eight hours only.

The phone had taken the motorway south, stopped at Stone in Staffs, in the Luton car park, and then went on to Mayfair in central London, arriving yesterday in the early evening. Maria and Juan Pinzón Arias lived in Mayfair. Four hours later, through the night, the phone was tracked coming back up the M1, making its way to Scotland. It was a six hour drive each way to London. It was a long time to stay angry, thought Morrow, even for Roxanna. She didn't look angry in the ATM photo.

Fuentecilla arrived in Glasgow and, avoiding her house, passed the airport and took the Erskine Bridge across the Clyde Estuary to Argyle. At five o'clock this morning she made a call from a hillside outside Helensburgh. The call was to the landline of a Mr Frank Delahunt out in Helensburgh. Then the phone went dark.

Morrow mapped the site of the phone call. It was from a bare field on the coast road, a mile outside the town.

The second email was from DS Saunders, warning her that

the Met had been notified about the missing persons call. They'd been cc'd on Fuentecilla's phone trace, had decided to handle the Arias angle themselves. She wasn't getting a jolly to London.

Met officers would visit Maria Pinzón Arias and her husband in their Mayfair home this morning. Met officers would be offered fancy-dan tea and, doubtless, biscuits. Meanwhile, Morrow was charged with checking out the site of the phone call. She was to stand on a rainy hillside, wading through the rain and the cow shit, looking for bodies and/or bits of telephone, and then visit Frank Delahunt.

She phoned the farmer who owned the field. David Halliday sounded old and gruff. He lived next to the field, worked the farm alone, he said. And he'd heard something: he had woken up at five o'clock yesterday morning to his dogs barking. That meant someone was there, which was rare enough because the road was a dead end. He went back to sleep but they kept barking on and off. He'd seen headlights on his ceiling. Two cars, he thought. The dogs kept on barking though. Morrow asked what that meant and he said he didn't know, the dogs never said. Mr Halliday sounded like a bit of a laugh. Going to visit him might take the tinge off the melancholy morning.

She hung up and went into the incident room to ask McGrain about his kid's hospital appointment. She was feeling low enough without scheduling in a morning listening to Thankless talk shit. As she walked in the room she scanned for anyone else who had been fully briefed but Thankless was all there was. He looked up hopefully at her, not yet aware that he wasn't being flown to London for the day. He watched with open-mouthed anticipation as she spoke to McGrain across the room.

McGrain said he had to be back here by two fifteen. She was only going to Helensburgh now, she could still take McGrain but it would be a tight turnaround.

'There's a call, ma'am.' DC Kerrigan, a blond woman with very jaggy teeth, handed her the phone. 'Mr Halliday from Lurbrax Farm calling you back.'

Mr Halliday sounded out of breath. Listen, pet, he said, he'd just been out and followed one of the dogs around the back of the big shed. He found a car. It was black and big and it wasn't his and there was no one in it.

Roxanna's car was black.

Morrow told him to touch nothing, please keep the dogs in and she'd be there in half an hour. Scene of Crime might be called if they found a body. McGrain was out of the question. She motioned to Thankless to come. He stood up, smirking, and pulled his passport out of a drawer.

'No, we're not flying to London,' she called across to him, 'we're driving to Helensburgh.'

The incident room enjoyed that.

It took her fifteen minutes in the car to remember why she disliked him so much: Thankless was aggravatingly declamatory. Sometimes he was right, she couldn't insist that he wasn't, but it was the way he said things.

She filled him in on the morning's developments as they drove out to Helensburgh.

'The Met'll get the proceeds,' he announced as they passed the Erskine Bridge. 'Our chief hasn't got the pull.'

She ignored that. Fuentecilla had been traced to London—

'She's run off with a boyfriend.'

She tried to denote her annoyance by leaving a pause, but he was undeterred.

'Spanish woman are diff—'

'*Fucking shut up.* You're just *burbling*. It's bad police work. Wait for the facts, let things become clear. Keep an open mind, for fuck's sake.'

Thankless's eyebrows rose high and stayed there.

Alex looked out of the side window. She'd done it again: another stranger met, another friend made. She had a bit of an anger problem. It was her problem, she reminded herself, not his problem. People were allowed to be annoying.

They drove on in silence until the sharp turn-off to Lurbrax Farm. It was on the side of a steep hill a mile before Helensburgh, overlooking the broad Clyde Estuary.

'Here,' said Morrow, and they took the turn.

Hedged on either side, the bumpy road led up to a cluster of run-down farm buildings set around a house. The farmhouse had 'Yes' referendum campaign signs in each of the high windows, white on a pale blue, propped against the inside of the glass.

Thankless nodded at them. 'He's got guts,' he proclaimed. 'It's pretty much solid "No" voters out here.'

The problem was hers, not his. She grunted and Thankless took it to mean – really? Do elaborate, you interesting and knowledgeable man. So he did:

'"Yes" want to shut the nuclear sub base. They're saying the housing market'll collapse out here. Prices are frozen now.'

A Ford Fiesta, a city car, was parked up ahead; Morrow had been told the forensic photographer would visit the scene and guessed it was hers. The fact that she was here at all was down to PINAD. Fuentecilla's body hadn't been found, just her car, she shouldn't really be here at all. Thankless parked behind it and Morrow was shocked to see a 'No thanks' campaign sticker in her back window. It was a contentious issue. The photographer might as well have turned up wearing a football strip.

Morrow got out into a fresh shower of warm rain and pulled her coat around her, stomping up to the farmhouse.

Two dogs heralded their arrival with a chorus of unthreatening barks. An older dog, grey haired with a cataract in one eye, looked out of the open-sided barn and disappeared back into the dark. Mr Halliday came out, flanked by his milk-eyed companion. He shouted at the noisy young dogs, 'Shut it!'

He looked older than he sounded on the phone. A weather-beaten man in his sixties or seventies, the curvature of his belly accentuated by the ribbed jumper straining over it. He looked at Morrow with a cheeky twinkle in his eye. 'Is it you?'

'Aye,' smiled Morrow. 'It that you?'

'I suppose it is.' He turned his attention to Thankless. 'And who's this one?'

Thankless smiled beneficently and held his hand out. 'I'm DC Thankless of Police Scotland.'

Halliday showed his brown teeth, a little bit aggressively, and shook Thankless's hand. 'Well, son, I'm Me of Here.'

They uncoupled their hands and Halliday turned to Morrow.

'So, I'm saying: I was asleep yesterday morning, that's my bedroom up there' – he pointed to a small window at the top right of the farmhouse – 'until about five o'clock. Dogs woke me up, barking. They did it another couple of times.'

'You didn't get up, though?'

His hand strayed to the dog's head. 'The dogs always get up afore me. I was up late, watching *Breaking Bad*, have you seen it?'

'No.'

'I'll tell ye what,' he nodded solemnly, 'certainly make ye circumspect about what ye stick your nose into.'

Argyle and Bute was one of the safest areas in the country but she could imagine Mr Halliday cowering under his covers, watching headlights stroke the artex on his ceiling: Mr Fear of Crime.

'Not that I've got anything worth robbing, mind.'

'I thought all farmers were millionaires.'

Mr Halliday huffed at that. 'Did ye, indeed? Ye've been listening to *The Archers*, mibbi. I never used to worry but, you know, ye get old, you get scared.'

'I'm not old,' said Morrow, 'and I'm scared all the time.'

He liked that. He pointed up to his 'Yes' window signs and confided, 'There's people about here would burn ye out for that.'

Tempers were running high, she knew that, but there was a

lot of paranoia, and both sides were vying for gold in the coveted victim stakes.

'I thought it was a blanket "No" out here.'

'Oh, it is. It is indeed.' He looked over her shoulder, as if 'No' assassins might be hiding in the hedgerows. 'Because of the property prices.'

'You not worried?'

He looked at her defiantly. 'Nah! I'm not scared. Lots of them out here are though. Protecting themselves. You wouldn't believe it. And they're nasty. The council are a bunch of masons. They've let the "No" mob set up a campaign gazebo in the square. No planning permission. Nothing.'

It seemed an oddly comedic thing to object to. 'Have you been threatened by anyone in particular?'

'No, just in general.' He shrugged and smiled. 'I'm retiring. I'll say what I like. And I don't care if I lose out personally. If Scotland can finally—'

'No!' Morrow held her hand up. 'Please! No!' She couldn't live through another monologue about politics. Everyone in Scotland had one ready.

Mr Halliday misunderstood and nodded. 'I know. 'Cause you're the police. You can't get involved.'

She let him believe that and showed him the picture of Roxanna's face from the orchid house picture, singled out and enlarged. He didn't recognise her.

'What sort of car did you see pulling out?'

He stepped down into the road and pointed at the photographer's car. 'See that red one there? That kind. But silver.'

Hoping he couldn't see the window sticker, she stepped back and looked. It had a distinctive indent in the side panel, like a shadow under a cheekbone. 'You didn't happen to get the registration number?'

''Fraid not.'

'Where's the black car you found?'

Mr Halliday led them to a field and lifted the chain off the gate, walking the gate back into the yard to let them in. He led them along the fence to the back of the shed. The black Alfa Romeo 4C Morrow had been watching footage of for three weeks was blocking the entire lane by the field. It was hidden from the road and the farmhouse. She could see why Mr Halliday hadn't found it for a day. It was in a space so small Roxanna would have had trouble climbing out of the driver's door. They walked over to the fence to look in.

'I'll leave you to it,' said Halliday, and went back to his dogs.

No blood, no handbag, nothing out of the ordinary. Morrow pulled on a plastic glove and tried the back passenger door. It was unlocked.

The photographer was stepping cautiously over the muddy field towards them. She had already photographed inside the car, she said, and then gone uphill for wider shots of the situ, but she was on the clock and had to leave. Everything was about the numbers these days.

'Was the car unlocked when you found it?'

'Yeah. You might want to look in the glovebox as well.'

'OK.' Morrow watched her walk away before she remembered: 'Hey – lose the "No" sticker. You're on police business.'

The photographer rolled her eyes. 'I'm so sorry. My car broke down, it's my dad's car.'

'Well, cover the sticker up if you're using it.'

'I'm a "Yes" anyway,' she said.

'Yeah, well, I don't want to know your private business. Just cover the sticker up.'

The photographer nodded and backed away.

Morrow turned her attention to the car. For a Londoner to leave their car door unlocked probably meant Roxanna had stayed nearby. It meant she intended to get back in.

Feeling suddenly very cold, Morrow told Thankless to go and check the field for phones or anything at all. He went off and she lifted her coat, stepping over the wire fence. She opened the car door, reached in and let the glovebox fall open.

A blue freezer bag with *Waitrose* printed on it. It was secured with a white wire, a bulge of white powder in the corner. The contents box hadn't been filled out but she could guess. She bagged it up as evidence and looked at the floor for anything else. It was strange: Roxanna had driven for twelve hours, through the night, but the floor was almost sterile. There were no stray blond hairs, no pastry flakes, no single blade of grass dragged in on the sole of a shoe. It had been vacuumed.

Morrow looked at the door and the steering wheel closely, checking for fingerprints or palm smudges. Both had been wiped clean. She squinted at a residue on the door handle: alcohol wipes. She knew the sort of marks they left because they used them on the fingerprint machine at the station after someone had been brought in and charged, always aware of the danger of hep. C transmission. They had to use alcohol sanitiser a lot in their uniform days and it was rough on the hands. Morrow could still remember the raw-fingertip feel.

She shut the door carefully and phoned the station: Get a forensic tow truck out here right now and send McGrain and Kerrigan. She needed bodies to escort evidence into the station. Airtight cases fell on the basis of faulty chains of evidence. She could already hear a lawyer cross-examining Mr Halliday: And the car was left unlocked by a field for how long?

Thankless was in the field, slowly walking away from her as he scanned the ground beneath him. She walked over to him. 'Find anything?'

'No, thank God.' He was relieved not to have stumbled across anything gruesome. But Morrow felt that maybe she had: the alcohol wipes suggested premeditation. They were ominous. Most people would use the sleeve of their jacket to wipe prints off.

She straightened up and suddenly saw the spectacular view. A lush green run of fields dropped down to meet the glinting water.

The hills rose, green again, on the far bank. Smiling, she looked down the coast to her right and saw Helensburgh laid out in a neat grid, the rain-drizzled roads silvered by sunshine.

'I actually know Helensburgh really quite well.'

He was telling her he was an asset. She didn't want to encourage him so she just looked away. 'Yeah, it's old.'

'Actually, no. It's only three hundred years old. It was built as a luxury holiday town. The founder named it after his wife—'

'I know.' She didn't know that, but he was interrupting her train of thought.

He tried to impress again. 'Did you know: a quarter of all the millionaires in Britain lived there at one time?'

That was quite interesting, if irrelevant. Morrow stayed silent. She looked over to where the street grid ran out and big trees and lawns intermingled up the early slopes of the surrounding hills.

'I know it well because I was in the Sea Cadets. We went sailing over there at the outdoor centre.' He pointed to a distant coppice of masts.

Morrow nodded in the right direction, thinking about the alcohol wipes. Buoyed by her lack of hostility Thankless asked, 'Were you in Cadets?'

'No,' said Morrow.

'It was great. I loved it.'

She wondered why they were talking like this, exchanging personal information as if they were friends. It was the setting. Being near the water made the trip feel like a holiday.

'D'you know that area of Helensburgh up by the—'

'Never been.' She cut the comradely thread abruptly with, 'We were Largs people,' and headed for the car. She glanced back and saw Thankless looking sheepishly across the water to Largs.

The two towns were on opposite banks of the wide estuary, each looking diffidently away. Helensburgh was three hundred years old, pretty and stood on its dignity. Largs was a thousand years old and didn't care what anyone thought. It had seen Viking battles and German bombers, the Black Death and the EU. It was a place of ice cream parlours, vulgar amusement arcades, chips and sweets and pocket-money toys. It was a working-class day out. Helensburgh was aspirational.

He caught her up at the car. 'Well, if I win the lottery I'd live out here. All that fresh air—'

'I don't like the country,' said Morrow.

'Why?' He was smiling at her, surprised and patronising, about to explain why she was so very wrong and 'the country' was a great thing.

'The shops are shit,' she said. 'Anyway, cut the chat. You phone the station and make sure Kerrigan's bringing the forensic team.' Kerrigan was, Morrow knew she was. She was just giving Thankless a job to do to remind him she was in charge.

She walked away, glad to have shut him up but disappointed in herself. It was her problem. She'd hated bosses for behaving like this to her. She hated them for doing it now. She thought of DCC Hughes walking out of the meeting before people had finished speaking.

Back at the gate Morrow glanced once more at the beguiling view. Wind rolling up from the water swept a soft Mexican wave across a rapeseed field.

Morrow felt in her gut that Roxanna was probably dead. Alcohol wipes and a handheld vacuum for the floor of the car. It was professional and it was serious. There were no professional hit men in Helensburgh, just fat men in tracksuits stabbing rivals for a fist of fifty quid notes. A professional would have been conspicuous in such a small community.

She took out her phone and called CI Nolly Dent.

15

Leaving the lunch time rush in the café behind him, Boyd Fraser began to run, heavy-footed. He had forty minutes before he had to begin preparations for the charity dinner. He blamed his trainers at first, then remembered that he always blamed the trainers, that he didn't actually like running.

He ran straight west, staying away from the unbroken shore road to give himself an excuse to stop at the crossroads and catch his breath. The black asphalt glistened and an electric car startled him as it ghosted past, wheels hissing the rain from the road.

He wasn't enjoying the run. The wind annoyed him. Cars and pedestrians got in his way, everything hurt. He had been very fit once, running the London Marathon. He even beat his training partner's time by three minutes, something Sanjay never really forgave him for. Now Boyd was always comparing himself to that never-again peak of fitness. But he ploughed on, passing rustic houses, sailing houses, the entry gate to a Neo-Gothic castle. He felt his shoulders rounded from leaning over work surfaces and account books, from picking up kids and crates of milk.

Meeting Miss Grierson yesterday had disturbed him. It created in his mind an unbroken timeline between then and now, as if he had never been to UCL or spent fifteen years in London or camper-vanned or surfed in Cornwall, as if he'd always been here and Lucy and the kids had magically appeared in the town of his birth.

While he was away, at university, on his travels, he'd cast himself unhappy in Helensburgh, trapped by the oppressive propriety of his home life, the coldness of his father. The dry Sunday School days, crayoned pictures of Jesus, the smog of family history and the weight of expectation. They were the good Frasers, the righteous elect. His mother thought that everything that went her way was part of God's plan. Everything else was the work of Catholics and Anglicans.

But meeting Miss Grierson took his mood back to that time, reminded him of what growing up here was really like: it was quite pleasant. His parents were kind and gentle people, bigoted, a little rigid, but well meaning. The desire to rip things up, the bitterness, the sneering, those were Boyd's own. He wished he hadn't given Miss Grierson a job tonight. He didn't want to see her again.

Boyd puffed on, troubled by the realisation that he had never really suffered terribly much and should be happy. But he wasn't. Whoever's fault it was, the fact remained: he wasn't. He felt sorry for himself. He felt cheated of something vital and he didn't know what it was.

He shook his head as he approached a road, shrugging off the thought. Why did he feel so sorry for himself? He couldn't remember.

He stopped at the kerb: Lucy. Lucy was pissed off all the time. It was the pressure of work, starting a business, sleeplessness because of the kids. It was one of those. Feeling relieved, as if he made sense again, he ran on. It was the pressure of court life. Marie Antoinette.

He was back to the fucking Hameau again. Annoyed at the intrusive thought, at his weak legs and his weight gain, he turned and ran downhill towards the water, stopping to let a Waitrose van pass. Fucking Waitrose stealing customers and allergy bastards, Waitrose turning the whole town into a retirement village for bank managers.

Fuelled by anger, he was going quite fast now. He thought back to Sanjay and the jagged competitive edge between them.

That's what he missed. A spur to get him to his personal best. A peer group. That's what he needed.

As if the universe had heard him, he looked up and saw, almost half a mile away down the shore front, a man he vaguely recognised. The man was facing Boyd, leaning against an electricity substation. His head was shaved, he wore a tracksuit zipped up over his belly, a cheap gangster, and he was smoking in a louche, cowboyish manner. Boyd knew him but not from the café, just from seeing him around the town. He couldn't fit a name.

Boyd found he was sprinting towards the man. He could get some sniff from him, or at least he'd know someone. A chemical adventure. Maybe that would do it. A little blowout.

He slowed as he approached and caught the gangster's eye, stopped to catch his breath and nurse a stitch. The two men stood parallel but apart, nodding hellos.

'Right?' panted Boyd.

The cowboy nodded and pushed himself off the wall, hips first, then back and shoulders, finally pushing himself upright by the base of his neck.

'I know you, do I?' asked Boyd.

The man dropped his cigarette, grinding it into the ground with a twist of his toe. 'Who're you?'

'Boyd Fraser.' Boyd needed a breath then, and by the time he'd caught it the moment for asking the cowboy's name was past.

'*Fraser?*' The cowboy was smirking, as if he couldn't quite believe it. Fraser was a well-known name in the town.

'Aye.' Boyd didn't usually say 'aye'. His mother wouldn't stand for that sort of language.

'I know a Fraser.' He walked over to Boyd. For the briefest moment Boyd thought he was about to hit him. Instead he stopped, tilted his head and said, 'Who's your da?'

Boyd turned square to him. He was taller than the man, wider on the shoulders and fitter. 'Reverend Robert Fraser.'

'Those ones? You own that café? That Puddle place up at Sinclair Street?'

'Paddle. Aye.'

The cowboy looked serious and held out his hand. 'Tommy Farmer.' English name, cross-border accent but chubby Scottish build: a navy kid.

Boyd shook it. 'All right, man?' He didn't quite know how to broach the subject of where to get a deal. 'Hey, I don't suppose you'd know—'

But Tommy had spun away. 'Murray! Murray Ray! 'Magine bumping into you!'

Boyd had been only vaguely aware of two people ambling towards them down the shore road but the man and the child must have changed pace, hurrying while he wasn't looking. Now they were standing near and the man had stopped and he looked scared. He held his daughter's hand tightly. He wore a small 'Aye' badge on his lapel but was trying to cover it with his free hand while keeping a frightened eye on Tommy.

Boyd understood that Tommy Farmer was the cause of the fear. He found it exciting. He shifted his weight towards Tommy, sliding behind his shoulder, implying that they were together, though they weren't.

'Hiya, Murray.'

'Hiya, Tommy.' Murray dropped his gaze, cowed. 'The badge – I know Mark doesn't—'

'Never mind that,' said Tommy, 'I'm a "Yes" myself.'

But the badge was not the problem, apparently, because the atmosphere between them didn't improve.

'Are you a "Yes", Boyd?' Tommy looked at him. Boyd was an emphatic 'No' but he could hardly say so. He kind of nodded and the men went back to looking at each other.

Boyd was impatient for the father and child to move along because he had decided on his gambit: *Tommy, you don't happen to know where I could get a bit of sniff, do you?* He was rehearsing it in his head. He was waiting for a break.

But Tommy and Murray were eyeballing an acrimonious private conversation. They wouldn't argue in front of the child because it was a small town, small enough for the children to feel like a collective resource. Grown-ups disguised their enmity to protect the kids and festered threateningly instead. But if Boyd spoke to the girl, kept her busy, the men could talk and Murray would move on.

Boyd looked at her. About ten or eleven, thick specs, a pink puffa and matching woolly hat that seemed itchy. She kept scratching her head through it.

'What's your name?' he said.

'Lea-Anne Ray. What's yours?'

'Boyd Fraser.'

'Oh, aye. You one of the Lawnmore Frasers or the Colquin crowd?'

It was a staggeringly astute comment on his family history. Generations back the family had split into those who lived in Lawnmore and the other side who hadn't done so well and ended up in the council flats at Colquin.

'Lawnmore,' he said.

'Oh, aye. Very good.' She pursed her lips and looked away. She didn't seem to entirely approve.

Murray intervened. 'Our Lea-Anne's a right wee Granny Grey Hips, aren't ye, pet? She's brought up by her grannies.'

The men were just watching him talk to her, not taking the opportunity Boyd was giving them. He realised it was futile and stopped trying.

Tommy gestured to Murray who was near to tears. 'Boyd and Murray, you don't know each other, do yees?'

Boyd, still panting a little, shook his head.

'Well, fellow proprietors,' Tommy was smiling but he looked a bit mean, 'this is Murray Ray. He owns the Sailors' Rest down there.'

Looking down the seafront, past the man and child, Boyd saw the squat little pub. The windows were boarded up. Outside, parked like a fleet of company cars around the back, sat three large skips.

'Doing it up, aren't you, Murray? Must be costing ye.' Tommy wasn't really asking and Murray didn't seem to have the breath to answer. He was trembling, his head bobbing on his neck.

'Arm and a leg,' said Lea-Anne. 'Remortgaged the house.'

'Is that right, wee hen?' Tommy was talking to her now, not nasty, not threatening the way he was to her father. 'Boyd here,' he said, continuing the introduction as if they were old pals, 'has that Puddle café up there on Sinclair.'

Lea-Anne nodded, politely feigning interest.

Suddenly finding his voice, Murray said loudly, 'You're taking a hell of a chance! Starting a business in this economy! You don't know what's going to happen! Don't know who you'll offend—'

'Calm yourself down, Murray,' Tommy warned but he was enjoying this, Boyd could tell. He realised that Tommy had been hiding behind the electricity substation, watching the pub, waiting for Murray Ray.

'You don't know WHO you're going to offend!' Murray wasn't even pretending to talk to Boyd now, he was just shouting it to the wind. 'Or what'll FUCKING HAPPEN TO YOU.'

Hearing the curse word, Lea-Anne looked at her father, her mouth a tight little 'o'. He muttered an apology and squeezed her hand. She accepted the apology with a small nod but looked away and muttered '*Dizz*graceful' to herself.

'And when's Mark back anyway?' Murray said, wild-eyed and reckless. 'Is he on his *holidays* again?' He barked a desperate half-laugh at Boyd, implicating him.

Tommy leaned in, warning Murray to shut up but the desperate man burbled on, 'Hey, Boyd Fraser, were you at the *bonfire* up at the golf course?' Lea-Anne tried to pull her hand away from her father's. He was holding it too tight and hurting her. Murray nodded at Boyd, his face a rictus grin. 'Up it went and everyone's like that: "Mark Barratt must be on holiday!"'

It didn't make a lot of sense. Boyd didn't know who Mark Barratt was. Lea-Anne looked confused too and scratched her head again through her hat. Boyd was only half listening. His mind was on a warm remembered night in London, dancing at five in the morning, feeling tall and alert and on it. Fifty nights conflated in his mind to one moment of total confident certainty.

'You're doing the food at the dinner dance tonight, aren't ye?' Tommy was talking to Boyd.

'Yeah,' he said, 'we're catering the hospice dinner.'

'Great.' Tommy rubbed his hands together. 'I'm coming.'

Boyd was more than pleased at that. Relieved. Tommy would be there. Tommy would probably have a little baggie on him, at the dinner, or he'd know someone who did.

Tommy nodded at the father and daughter. 'You're coming, aren't ye, Murray?'

'Aye,' Murray said, calmer now, distracted.

'And who's babysitting you, Lea-Anne?'

'Granny Eunice.'

'Not your Granny Annie?'

'Nut. Eunice's leg's giving her gyp. Knee's all swole. Annie's got a ticket.' She shrugged. 'Giving the dancing a by, though, with *her* bladder.' It was a little freakish, hearing the words of an old person from such a small child. They all looked at her for a moment.

'Great,' said Tommy, enunciating the 't' so sharply it sounded like a spiteful finger-flick to the ear.

The sky was darkening. Lights were coming on across the water, throbbing uncertainly. Boyd's break time was running out and the men were arguing about something he didn't understand or care about. He should go.

'So, yeah,' said Boyd, 'see you later, anyway.' He nodded at Tommy as if they had a date.

Murray and Lea-Anne shuffled out of his way and he jogged past, gathering speed on his tired legs, regulating his breathing.

He ran on, past the boarded-up pub. It looked like a bit of a dive but the navy base nearby meant that dives could make enough at the weekends to tide them over an empty week.

Boyd ran on for five or so minutes, as far as the edge of town, and then turned back. He wasn't sure of the time. He found it hard to put a time on the strange conversation with the old/ young girl and the two angry men.

He ran up Sinclair Street towards Lawnmore, a steep incline straight uphill from the water, a final push.

Opening the garden gate, he stepped in and climbed the little steps. He stood for a moment, looked around the garden like a visiting stranger.

The Lawnmore Frasers. It occurred to him that in London he had had anonymity and liked it. Here, in cosy, rosy Helensburgh, he was a young business owner from an old family, part of the fabric of the town. He didn't like knowing who he was so exactly. He didn't like other people having the measure of him.

16

'Alcohol wipes?'

McGrain looked through the closed window at the inside of the car. He sniffed the outside of the car door. His hand, hanging loose at his side, reflexively came forward, stopped and dropped back. He'd been about to touch the handle. He looked at Kerrigan who was watching him and grinned, shocked at himself. She grinned back, showing off her pointy little teeth.

McGrain turned his eyes back to the marks on the dashboard. 'I can't catch the smell but it does look like the sort of marks they leave.'

'OK,' said Morrow, who had been hoping for something a bit more insightful, 'let's get it on the truck anyway. You due at the hospital at two?'

'Cancelled,' said McGrain. 'Emergency case. Sent us a text.'

'That's annoying.'

'Well, probably not for the emergency case. Some poor old dear took a tumble or something.'

'You come to Helensburgh with me then. I've got some evidence that needs taken in. Thankless?'

He came over when he heard his name.

'I want you to take this into evidence.' She gave him the evidence bag with the Waitrose freezer bag inside it. 'Have it tested and logged. OK?'

Procedurally, the fewer officers who handled a production before it was logged the better, but she could see that Thankless felt he was being sent off for a misdemeanour.

'You were great today,' she lied. 'Thanks for that.'

Torn between confused and chuffed, Thankless took the evidence bag and went off to the car.

She told McGrain, 'Before we set off, find out if Frank Delahunt's got a silver Ford Fiesta.'

Mr Halliday was hanging about in the yard with the dogs. He was craning to watch them load the car onto the truck but keen to give them space.

'Mr Halliday,' she said, walking over to him. 'Just to be clear: how many cars do you think were here? Was it two?'

His eyes glazed over and he thought about it. 'Mibbi three.'

'Why three?'

He looked at the ground. 'I didn't see the tracks to that yesterday morning.' He pointed to the Alfa Romeo. He waved at a muddy patch where the dirt yard overlapped the tarmac on the road. 'Three-point turns. Two lots. So I was thinking "There's two cars come, turned and gone." But that was wrong. There was three.'

They looked together at the indistinct mud, both ruing the overnight rain.

'Thanks, Mr Halliday.' She held out her hand and he shook it warmly. He walked with her back to the car. 'And where's this you're off to, now?'

'Helensburgh. Know of anywhere we can get lunch?'

'Chips or soup or what?'

'Wee roll?'

'Greggs. Can't go wrong.'

McGrain was in the car waiting for her. Frank Delahunt didn't have a silver Ford Fiesta. He had a Jaguar.

She filled him in on Halliday: three cars, good guy. McGrain commented on the 'Yes' campaign sign in the window, said he thought it was bad out here and Morrow told him about the furiously contested gazebo.

McGrain grinned. 'God, everyone's going mad. And the man's wrong, there's going to be ructions after.'

The chief had announced to the press that there was no overtime scheduled for officers. The campaigns had been peaceful and they expected it would continue to be so. No one knew if he was hopeful or stupid.

'He's from down south, though, isn't he?' observed McGrain.

'Aye.'

'Doesn't know how far some of them'll go for a fight up here.'

It occurred to her that McGrain was probably against independence, judging from the phrases 'down south' and 'up here', instead of 'England' and 'Scotland'. Even within the police force the referendum had heightened the atmosphere of paranoia and mistrust, reducing them all to hyper-vigilant readings of their neighbour's microsignals.

They drove on towards the town, passing through pretty coastal villages with signs for tearooms and conservation areas, past mini delis and newsagents advertising broadsheet newspapers. Looking across the car park to a large Waitrose, Morrow thought of the bag in the glovebox. Waitrose was incongruously posh for a baggie. She wondered if it might be worth tracing freezer bag purchases from the supermarket but realised it would be pointless. They must sell loads of them.

McGrain told her what the forensic accountant had found at the Injury Claims 4 U office. Nothing much. Potentially fraudulent claims were minimal. As soon as Fuentecilla arrived she started laying off staff and winding the office down. Everyone had been laid off. The bills had all been paid and the lights were going out next Friday. It was completely unexpected. 'Is she changing the business?'

'There's no sign of that on the books,' said McGrain. 'It looks like she's just shutting down the office. We can't find anything else she's moving into, she's just leaving it dormant.'

'Is she asset-stripping?'

'They didn't find any assets. The office is rented, the furniture's worth nothing.'

'Where's the seven million gone?'

'Gone from the bank account but they haven't found it yet.'

They had no excuse to stay in. She called the office and gave them a message for the accountant: photograph everything and get out quickly, don't draw attention.

She hung up, paused for a moment with her eyes shut, thinking about alcohol wipes. She rubbed her fingertips along her thumb, remembering stickiness and a fine grain. It was a professional job, done by a fairly competent trained party. They were trying to get away. She opened her eyes and sat up and found she was smiling.

They were coming into Helensburgh on an inauspicious dual carriageway, passing old tenements, new builds and factory-style nursing homes. They passed forecourts to petrol stations, a gas storage tank and then, abruptly, entered the town of Helensburgh.

A long parade of Georgian houses and shops faced the water. Morrow saw then what Mr Halliday was talking about: every street lamp had a purple 'No thanks' sign on it. Many of the shops had the sign propped in their windows.

The esplanade along the shoreline was perfectly paved but devoid of people. There were only three buildings on the waterside, all tucked away around the ferry dock: a small council swimming pool, an unattractive concrete box of a pub, boarded up, and a small ticket office for the ferry.

'Take a right here,' said Morrow.

McGrain turned uphill into a suddenly busy street. They passed a chemist's and a newsagent's, a train station and a big church. A block away they saw a big, wide square with a white tent covered in 'Better Together' signs.

McGrain pointed at it and shouted, 'Gazebo!' joyfully, as if it was a driving game.

Morrow got him to park outside a café.

It was warm inside and old-fashioned, pale cream walls and a dusky blue counter. They had ordered before Morrow noticed that it wasn't a nice old café. It was a café that was made to look nice and old. The customers were mostly women of a certain age wearing jumpers of a certain price. Their bacon rolls arrived: six quid each.

Out in the car with the bag of hot rolls, they ate in a stunned silence.

'*Six* quid,' said Morrow. 'That's the price of two packets of bacon.'

McGrain looked accusingly at his lunch. 'We'd just passed a Greggs as well.'

Morrow rolled the bacon around her mouth, waiting for the extra-special flavour to kick in. It didn't. It was just bacon. Maybe her palate wasn't sophisticated enough. She put the last bite in her mouth, brushed her hands clean and pointed him onto Delahunt's.

All of the houses were built looking out to sea, like football fans on a stand, each handsome villa staring at its downhill neighbour's backside. Uphill, well-kept front lawns ran towards them. Downhill was an ugly composition of garages and wheelie bins and back walls. The streets had no pavements, just grass verges with occasional paths walked through them.

They took a street overhung with heavy trees, chainsawed into geometric voids at lorry clearance height.

'Christ,' said McGrain, 'it's swanky out here.'

She shared his analysis more than Thankless's.

They parked on a grass verge and got out. Delahunt's house was uphill, through a locked metal gate. Morrow pressed the button on an intercom, quite new and sleek, and waited. Stone steps curved up to the lawn beyond the wrought-iron gate.

A pause.

Frank Delahunt was in and wanted to know who was there.

'Hello, Mr Delahunt, we're from Police Scotland. Can we come in and have a word, please, sir?'

He hesitated. 'What is this concerning?'

'Can we come in, please, sir?'

Another pause and then the gate dropped open. Morrow pushed it and climbed the four steps. A long stretch of immaculately striped grass led up to a yellow sandstone house.

A set of slim French windows looking onto the garden opened and Mr Y, familiar from the photographs, stepped out to greet them.

Delahunt always dressed in red or pink trousers and a dress shirt. Sometimes he wore a yellow tweed jacket, sometimes a mossy green cardigan with brown elbow patches. Today he wore neither but had folded his shirtsleeves up carefully, as if he was working.

Looking up at him Morrow realised that she had always assumed he was gay because he wore so many colours but seeing him now, his legs-apart stance in the doorway, his slightly pissed-off rugby player glare, she wondered if he could have been having an affair with Roxanna. It would make sense of the five a.m. phone call in a moment of crisis.

Delahunt watched them walk towards him, raising his hand in a tentative greeting, dropping it before they got halfway up to him.

'Hello, Mr Delahunt. I'm DI Alex—'

'I'd much rather you had come around the other entrance,' he said, his accent clipped and rounded. '*This* is not the actual entrance to the property.'

Morrow followed his eyeline back to the lawn and saw their twin sets of footprints through the wet grass. It was for looking at, apparently, not for walking on.

'Well, I'm sorry about that but this is the address we got for you.' She pointed back to the street where they had parked, saw the sweeping view of the sea from the house, marred only by the roofs of the houses downhill.

'Well, the damage is done now,' he said magnanimously. 'Do come in, DI Alex, won't you?'

It didn't seem like the time to correct him.

He ushered them through the double doors into a study lined with books. In the middle of the room stood a big square desk, dark wood with a green leather top. The desk had workstations on each of its four sides: open books and papers ready for attention. The chair had been pulled back to a neutral position near the door but Morrow followed the furrows through the ornamental rug to a position at the desk that faced straight out onto the lawn. It was where he had been until a minute ago, she could tell, because his mobile phone was sitting on a book, weighting it open.

It was a gorgeous room, high yellow walls and a crisp white cornice but Delahunt didn't want them to linger in there. He stood by the door, arms out, like a militant guide in a stately home, shepherding them into the hall. His insistence made Morrow suspicious. McGrain followed the path drawn out by Delahunt's arms but Morrow nipped right and skirted the long way around the desk.

'Good heavens!' said McGrain with uncharacteristic enthusiasm. 'What an amazing house!' He had stopped, apparently mesmerised by the segmented plasterwork on the ceiling, drawing Delahunt's attention away from Morrow. He was quite good, McGrain. 'What date is this house?'

Delahunt kept his hands out to usher but still seemed pleased to have been asked. He followed McGrain's eye to the ceiling. 'Eighteen twenty-two. My family have lived her for four generations. This street was laid out as part of a development . . .' He talked on, telling McGrain about the street and the building. McGrain was doing a good job of acting interested, or maybe he really was, Morrow didn't know him well, but she took the chance to glance at the book under the mobile phone. A heading caught her eye:

The body–

'Would you,' Delahunt was asking her, 'come through?'

She looked up. McGrain had run out of moves and Delahunt wasn't taking his eyes off her.

'Of course,' she said and followed him.

Delahunt led on and she glanced down to the main heading at the top of the page: *Succession: General Issues.*

The hall was dominated by a wooden stairwell that had been stripped and then glossily over-varnished.

'We could sit here.' He waved them to a seating area under the stairs.

McGrain and Morrow sat next to each other on a padded bench that was slightly too small. Delahunt pulled over a chair. They were sitting in the void under the stairwell, a small cubby-hole in a massive, apparently empty house. It felt strange. It felt suspicious. Roxanna could be tied up or hiding. Morrow found herself listening intently.

Delahunt raised his eyebrows expectantly, reaching into his trouser pocket to take out a cigarette case and a slim gold lighter.

'You're not local police officers. Are you from Glasgow?'

Morrow nodded.

'Hm. Not a spate of break-ins then?'

'No.' Morrow watched him flick the lighter, waiting until he was touching the flame to the tip of his cigarette. 'Roxanna Fuentecilla.'

Delahunt's hand shook, but only a fraction. He exhaled and raised an eyebrow. 'So sorry. What is it you're asking me?'

'You know her.'

He gave a little nod.

'She's disappeared.' Morrow met his eye. 'No one knows where she is. We know that she phoned you yesterday.'

She waited for him to speak. It took longer than she expected. He leaned carefully over to a small table, picked up an ashtray and set it on his knee. He looked up at her, as if surprised she was still there. 'I don't know what you want.'

'When did you last see her?'

He mumbled, 'Thursday. In Glasgow.'

They had been seen together in Byres Road. It was at least partly true.

'Mr Delahunt, as far as we know, you're the last person to have contact with her before she disappeared. What happened yesterday morning?'

Delahunt tapped his cigarette into the ashtray, blinking in time as he did. 'Phone call,' he muttered.

'Speak up, please.'

'I got a phone call. From her.'

'What time?'

'Fiveish.'

'And?'

'She asked me to come and pick her up.'

Morrow waited again. Delahunt waited. McGrain shifted in his seat. If Delahunt was a practiced conman he would have known how to fill the space, but he didn't. He tried smoking and tapping non-existent ash before he blurted, 'I went. But she wasn't there. Then I came home.'

'What did she say on the phone, *exactly*?'

'"I'm in Halliday's Field. Come and get me."'

'And you said . . . ?'

He held her eye as he raised a hand to the ceiling. '"I'll come and get you." And then I went and she wasn't there and I came home.'

'What sort of car do you have?'

'Jaguar SX.'

'What colour is it?'

'Burgundy.'

Morrow was conscious that she had taken quite an intense dislike to Frank Delahunt. She had a chip on her shoulder, was more comfortable interviewing working-class people. She was frightened about Danny. She'd just paid six quid for a bacon roll.

But over and above all of that there was something about the precision of Delahunt's mannerisms and his dress, about the smallness of his physical gestures that made her slightly furious.

She tried to read him carefully. It wasn't just class resentment that made her angry. It was his disdain. She saw him take in her cheap coat and patent leather shoes, rimmed with mud. She saw him glance towards McGrain's bitten nails and iron-shiny trousers. She saw him think they were cheap and stupid. She wanted to prove him wrong.

'Halliday's Field, where is that?'

'It's up the coast road, towards Glasgow.'

'What was she doing there?'

'I don't know.'

'You didn't ask?'

'No.'

'But you knew where she was talking about when she used the expression "Halliday's Field"? Why?'

'It's just . . . it's a known place.'

'She's Spanish. She moved to Glasgow from London a couple of months ago. It must be very well known.'

He shrugged and smoked, legs and arms crossed in a posture so defensive she felt certain she'd be back here with a warrant.

'Did you ask why she was phoning at five a.m.?'

'No.'

'Was it an expected call?'

'No.'

Morrow looked around the hall: everything was tidy, symmetrical. A bowl of tiger lilies on a table by the front door had the orange stamens pulled off so that they couldn't brush against a sleeve and stain a shirt. Everything was precisely placed in here, no piles of coats, shoes, nothing by accident. Frank Delahunt wasn't the guy you phoned when something unexpected happened at five in the morning.

'Were you having an affair with her?'

'No.' Calm at the suggestion. Not even suppressed desire simmering there.

'After the phone call, what did you do?'

'I got dressed.' Pause for a draw on the cigarette. 'I came downstairs.' Exhale. 'I put my shoes on.' Tap on the ashtray. 'I got in my car and I went there.' His eyes came back to hers and narrowed.

'This was at five in the morning?'

He nodded. 'Five thirty. I got there and she'd left. I called and she'd switched her phone off.'

'Was there another car there?'

That made his right eye twitch. 'No.'

'Sure?'

'Absolutely, there was no one there. She'd just driven away.'

He hadn't seen Roxanna's car.

'Where did you think she'd gone?' An awful stillness had come over Delahunt. 'Mr Delahunt?'

'I thought she'd run off.'

'Why would she do that?'

'I don't know. I don't know her personal affairs. I work for her company.'

'Doing what?'

'General legal advice.'

'Her car was found near the field this morning. She must have left with someone else, in another car. Do you know who that would be?'

'Robin? Her partner could have come and collected her. He has a car, I believe.'

'She wouldn't leave her own car, hidden behind a shed and wiped for fingerprints, though, would she?'

He was shocked by that. 'It might have ...' He broke off and she saw that his forehead was suddenly a little damp.

'What were you going to say?'

'Her car might have broken down? But that doesn't explain ...'

'Yeah,' said Morrow as if confiding. 'It doesn't *explain*. You can see why we're worried. Does she know anyone else in Helensburgh?'

'No.' He seemed very sure.

'How did you come to be her lawyer?'

'Bob Ashe recommended me.'

'He owned Injury Claims 4 U before Roxanna?'

'Yes.'

'Where's Mr Ashe now?'

'He retired to Miami. *Grandchildren.*' His lip curled in a sneer.

Morrow didn't think Frank Delahunt hated grandchildren. He was shocked and a little bit frightened for Roxanna and it was making him behave strangely. 'Where is she, Frank?'

He looked out over the lawn to the sea, sucked hard on his cigarette, so hard that his eyes narrowed. 'I don't know.'

Morrow pointed back to the study door. 'In there. There's a textbook. Can I look at it?'

He huffed a nervous laugh. 'Textbooks are in the public domain, aren't they?'

Pre-empting any objections, she got up and walked quickly into the study. Delahunt followed swiftly behind.

The section headed 'The body' outlined the legal requirements for disposal of a dead person but the mobile phone was not placed to let him read that. It was balanced precariously over the top of the page, clearing the paragraph below. She put her finger on the section and looked at him.

'That's,' he was flustered, 'that's not about her . . . I'm not . . .'

Delahunt ran out of bullshit.

Morrow read it out to McGrain standing in the doorway: '*If a person simply disappears, so that there is no body . . .*'

Delahunt couldn't look at her.

'Where is she, Frank?'

He mustered all of his disdain to look at her through half-shut eyes. 'As I said: I'm legal advisor to the firm she owns. It's my job to be aware of the legal implications of any developments and anticipate them.'

'She wasn't there when you went to meet her and that prompted you to look up the legal conditions for the property of a dead and missing person? You're all heart, Mr Delahunt.'

He looked at the floor.

'As a matter of interest, Mr Delahunt, what are the legal implications of a person "simply disappearing"?'

He shrugged as if he wasn't really all that interested. 'Well, it tells you there.'

'What does it tell me?'

He didn't want to say it. But then he did. 'If they're still missing after seven years they can be declared legally dead.'

'This book is about succession. What happens to her property?'

'Just – normal. Her family inherit her property. Just normal stuff.' He smiled miserably. 'You can buy the book yourself, if you're that interested. It's widely available.' He smiled at McGrain, looking for an ally. McGrain looked away.

'But you're not the family lawyer, Mr Delahunt. You're the company lawyer. What happens to the property in the company?'

They both knew the answer. It reverted to the investors. And if it took seven years to declare Roxanna dead the money would be held for seven years, her property, untouchable, unconfiscatable, until there was a declaration of death. Seven years was a long time in the memory of the criminal justice system. Arias might have everything but the filings in his mouth confiscated, but they wouldn't get that seven million because, wherever it was, it wasn't his. Yet.

'I'm afraid I have a client arriving shortly. I'll have to ask you to leave, officers.'

17

The fly-zapping electric buzz from the intercom startled Iain
so much he almost threw up. He wasn't used to the sound, had
few visitors, and he was feeling fairly seasick anyway. Marooned
on his bed after a long night of broken sleep and unaccustomed
smoking, he had been up since four watching house improve-
ment programmes, drinking pint after pint of tap-water and
wishing he could stop smoking. He was looking forward to the
tobacco running out.

The buzzer sounded again. *Zzzb zzzb* double buzz. Two dead
flies and Iain thought *shit* as he edged himself to the end of his
unmade bed. He used the remote to shut the telly off and stood
up.

His flat was on the attic floor of an old tenement block. The
ceiling was head-skimming. It hadn't been a flat before the
housing service renovated the building. It had been empty roof
space but dormer windows and insulation meant that they had
no reason to ignore the hollow corridor above the proper flats.
Plastered and partitioned, it had been developed into a tiny, easy-
to-manage studio flat. The dormer windows were unforgiving
though, the daylight relentless. Iain stood up into a viscous swirl
of suffocating smoke.

He shut his smarting eyes against it, felt himself drowning and
swooned forward, catching himself before he fell.

Zzzzzzzzzb

Shit shit shit.

Hands out in front of him like a B-movie mummy, he waded
to the window and opened it. Wind from the hills stormed the

room, chasing smoke into corners, sucking it out of the window. Iain backed up to the intercom by the front door.

'Who is that?'

'Iain? 'S that you? It's Murray.'

'Murray who?'

A moment's hesitation. '*"Murray who?"* What fucking Murray do you think it is, ya dick?'

Aye, right enough. Iain pressed the buzzer and let him in. He waited at the door to save himself coming all the way back over here again.

Murray. Nice one.

He was glad that it wasn't yesterday when Murray came up, glad it was today. Murray wouldn't like the smoking, that was for sure, but Iain would be able to look him in the eye today because overnight, in the long hours of smoking, Iain had come to a truth about yesterday: he killed that woman. There were no softening justification, no narrative antecedents. When he saw her scream and run he gave her a massive head injury.

Massive head injury. Iain understood his place in the story, this circular story, and knew he had found it overwhelming because of Sheila. He was the bad man who hit women's heads, and the pity of his background didn't fix any of that today. His sad childhood and what he did, they were bits of two different jigsaws. Plenty came from worse than him. Murray came from worse than him. And the pain in his chest, that wasn't her. It was himself struggling not to admit it all. He admitted it now though, and there was a peace in that. He might be a piece of shit, but he wasn't a lying piece of shit.

Iain answered a flurry of knocks on the door. Damp and breathless from the six-flight climb, Murray fell into the room, swiping and cursing at the stinking air. He went over to the window and opened it wide to the heavens.

'Fucking hell. 'S absolutely fucking honking in here!'

Iain couldn't really move very well, stiff from the bed and

smoking and lack of sleep, but he smiled as he watched Murray slapping at air.

Murray was Iain's lifelong friend and here is the story of Murray: Murray went with a girl and she had a baby and that baby was Lea-Anne. Lea-Anne's mother went to Bristol to live with a man that she met on the internet. She left the baby with Murray.

Lea-Anne was the making of all of them.

Murray brought her to visit Iain in prison when she was a baby, when she was a chubby toddler chewing the edge off the table, when she was a girl dressed in the pink puffs and frills of prettier girls. Iain was a doting ne'er-do-well, her cautionary-tale uncle. The mother's mother, Eunice, and Murray's mother, Annie, became the best of pals. From these discarded bits and unravelled scraps Murray pulled a family together to form a wall around the child. Lea-Anne was growing up with never a cause to doubt that she was the absolute fulcrum of every life around her. They were all performing the same miracle: repairing the insult of their own childhoods by making it all right for her.

Murray was looking at him: 'The fuck you doing smoking?'

Iain shrugged. 'Just smoking . . .'

'Well, don't,' ordered Murray.

Iain couldn't think what to say to that. Murray was right so he said, 'OK. I'll stop now.'

That settled, Murray waved at the air in front of him again, but it wasn't that smoky in the room any more, just windy. He just did it for something to do. 'Where were you yesterday?'

Iain didn't want to talk about the morning. ''Member Susan Grierson?'

'No.' Murray kicked at a dirty plate on the floor. 'State of this place.'

'Her that took the Scouts years ago. Went to America?'

'No.'

'Well, she's back. I met her.'

'Well, I still don't remember who the fuck she is so I don't know why you're telling me about meeting her.' He wasn't in a very good mood.

'What's the matter?'

Murray slumped down on the edge of the bed. 'Tommy fucking Farmer came to see us there. Hanging about, waiting on us coming out the Sailors'.' He looked up at Iain, red eyed, and Iain felt as though his lungs were turning to stone. 'D'you know?'

Iain was looking for disgust in Murray's face, he'd be furious if Tommy had told or hinted, but all he saw was fear.

'Mark's away.' Murray's chin convulsed. '*He's in Barcelona.*'

'No.' Iain sat down next to him. 'No, man, that doesn't mean that. Murray, it's clear. That won't happen.'

'Tommy's as good as said it's happening—'

'Murray!' Iain touched him on the hand, skin to skin, uncomfortably intimate. They both winced away. Iain curled his fingers into his palm. 'No, no, no.' Soothing, calming. 'It's . . . I've cleared the debt with Mark. It's good. It's sorted out.'

Murray owed Mark five grand. He should have paid it back by now. He planned to remortgage the pub once it was open but the building work had dragged on and on. Murray got a last warning but Iain had cleared it. Murray was in the clear.

Knowing Mark, knowing Iain, Murray looked scared. '*What?*'

Iain sucked a click through his teeth. 'Nothing, man, nothing.'

'Iain, what have ye done?'

High voice, guilty face. 'I've did nothing.'

But Murray wasn't stupid and five grand was a fuck of a lot of money. He knew Iain had done something, five grand's worth of something. Murray was overwhelmed, frightened for Iain, teary and spluttering, 'Iain? Man, what've ye fucking done?'

'I've did *nothing*.' Iain's voice came out so strangle-high he sounded like the small scared boys they had been, hiding in muddy ditches from bigger boys, boys with dads and brothers, boys with dinners on tables and sheets on their beds.

They cowered under the pitiless wind from the hills reeling above their heads.

Murray bit his lip hard to stop himself crying. Iain had sorted it out for him, made it safe for him and he didn't have the words to express what he felt. Iain understood. He'd always understood Murray. Iain had the brawn and the courage but Murray was the warm heart of their ramshackle family. Iain knew what he was feeling.

Iain nodded, encouraging. 'Ye OK?'

'Oh, man . . .'

'Know? For the wee hen.'

Murray shook his head. He was sad, he didn't want it this way, financial security for Lea-Anne, riding lessons for Lea-Anne, maybe a private school when she got to secondary. He whispered, 'D'ye set a fire for him, Iain? *Don't do that.* They'll Carstairs ye for that, man.'

Iain got up quickly, his back pain stabbing him, making him bend sideways and shut one eye. 'Whoah, fuckinghell. No. No fires, bud. Just . . . Fuck that's sore.'

Murray stood up. 'Hurt your back?'

'Don't know how I did it.' He pointed Murray to the door. 'Go on and fuck off, OK? I'll go and check it's clear with Wee Paul.'

Murray opened the door to the close and stood, looking at Iain. He meant to say something, thanks or something, but none of the words he could think of were big enough.

'I was wearing a "Yes" badge when Tommy saw me.'

'Don't worry about that. Tommy's a "Yes".'

Murray nodded. 'I know, but would he grass us to Mark?'

'No,' said Iain. 'He's para about Mark finding out about him.'

'You registered?'

'Aye.' Iain wasn't.

'You "Yes"?'

'Course.'

'It's for the weans. For their future.'

'OK.'

'OK.' Murray pointed a finger up at Iain's nose as he shuffled out of the door. 'Don't smoke.'

'I'll not smoke any more.'

'You're a good man, Iain,' said Murray. He had never said anything like that to Iain and it made Iain want to cry.

'No, I'm not. Go on away with ye.'

He closed the door after Murray and listened to his fading steps. The pain throbbed in his back. He shut his eyes and saw Murray standing in a pew at Sheila's funeral, two rows behind, little wave. Iain was not a good man. He deserved nothing in this life.

They rolled her body over the side. The water folded in softly around her and they stood, looking, unable to see deeper than half a foot down. Iain imagined her falling, falling through the black to the deep bed of the loch, to keep company with bits of thousand-year-old boats and beer cans and langoustine.

The skin on his hand was tight and dry, stained with brown bloody water. How to get blood out of material: salt, cold water and soak. Advice from Sheila during his baffling tumble into adulthood: When a girl becomes a woman, she said, as if Iain was a girl, the very first thing you learn is how to get blood out of clothes.

A basin of water on their old bathroom floor. Green tiled floor, the same dirty green as the sea after a storm. The basin had a scum on the surface, salt crystals clinging together in drifting clouds, blindly feeling for the edge. Sheila's underpants, fibres swollen from being left to soak. Salt lifts blood. It made him flinch away from the basin. He didn't understand why she had blood on her pants. He knew later, of course, but not at that time. He wondered now: if she had a brain injury would she be able to remember how to get blood out of pants? He didn't know. But giving her son advice about periods, that sort of suggested that she did have a brain injury. The trail of thoughts took him back to Susan Grierson.

When Susan Grierson taught him to sail he didn't even try. She squeezed his arm: Don't worry about it, you've got a lot on your mind, just enjoy the water. Susan wanted him to think her kind and good. Iain refused to think that because she was pushing it so hard. It was the only power he had back then, refusal.

Now he thought of Susan Grierson, across the sea for twenty years, washed back up here like salt-dried wood. Where had she been all this time? Not Chicago, they'd established that much. Iain didn't care who she was then and he didn't know who she was now but he knew that she was different. The Susan Grierson then wouldn't buy three grams of cocaine at once. She wouldn't live in a dust-dirty house or wait outside a newsagent or show you a plastic bag full of biscuits. Everything about her was off. Maybe everything about him was too. Maybe that's just what time did to people, time in the water.

He opened his eyes and felt lighter, physically weakened, but clear. He'd go to Mark Barratt's house and ask Wee Paul about Murray and the Sailors'. Just to be sure.

18

Morrow and McGrain had trouble getting in to see the local cops. The station was locked up. They banged on the door to get access but no one heard them. The number for it went straight through to an answerphone. Eventually, they called London Road Station, got them to call direct and tell them to let them in. Stations were shutting everywhere to save money. Points of contact were fewer and fewer. Police cubicles had been set up in A&E wards, in twenty-four-hour supermarkets, mobile units were parked near streets of drinkers at closing time but, for Morrow, that wasn't real policing. Real policing meant being part of a community.

A surly uniform opened the door to let them in, warming up when they showed him their badges and asked to see the officer in charge. He told them to wait at the old front bar.

It was a small cop shop, old-fashioned and, typical of the town, was partly functional, partly museum piece. A high, dark-wood counter formed a barrier between the back office and the waiting room. Displayed around the walls were the same posters they had up in the London Road Station. Alcoholism. Burglary. Be Theft Aware! Crimestoppers. No photofits here though, no appeals for public help or participation, because the public weren't allowed in.

Morrow had been warned that Argyle and Bute were spread thin. They had a rota of six staff covering a very wide geographical area, one DI and two cars.

The uniformed young man came back out. He led them into the back office and sat them down while he went to look for his boss, DI Simmons.

Inside, the office was small and cluttered. Three desks were piled high with papers and forms and leave slips and case files. Boxes of papers were stacked up on top of one another against the wall under the window. There was no one else there. A computer at the back of the room showed a game of solitaire in mid commission; right next to it was a pile of paperwork. Bad discipline.

The uniformed officer came back and his boss came around the corner.

DI Simmons was a nippy-faced woman. Her hair was short and sternly set, her lips pursed. The skirt and blouse she wore were so functional they made her look as if she craved a uniform. She gave a stage sigh and stomped towards them.

Morrow stood up, using her height for once, and held her hand out. Simmons shook it, squeezing too hard.

'And what can I do for you today?' she snipped, as if they'd wasted a grotesque amount of her time already.

'We'd like to ask you about the local vicinity, wondered if you might help us with a missing persons inquiry.'

'Why?'

'The missing person phoned a local from Halliday's Field.'

Simmons frowned. 'Where's that?'

'Can we talk in your office?'

A tidy room, small, stacks of boxes in a neat brick-like arrangement against the wall. She explained to Morrow that a pipe had burst upstairs and they were only using half of their accommodation, presently. She spoke like a rookie on their first time in court: precise, wordy, jarringly immellifluous.

Morrow dropped her open handbag to the floor, half spilling the contents, knowing that Simmons would disapprove – Be Theft Aware! – and stepped over to a map of the local area on the wall.

'So, we're looking for this missing woman.' She handed over the photo of Roxanna at the Botanics. 'The last time her phone was picked up it was on this hill, by Lurbrax Farm. A Silver Ford

Fiesta was spotted nearby.' She pointed to the map. 'The chief's office are involved and we need a bit of background on this area. Do you know a man called Frank Delahunt?'

Simmons gave a slow blink at the map. '*The* chief?'

Morrow didn't have time for this. The chief of Police Scotland was now everyone's chief but old habits of divisions and factions and geographical resentments would take longer to shuck. No one was happy, no one liked change. Some good people got their books, some bad people got promoted and everyone blamed the chief, especially people who had never met him.

Morrow leaned forward aggressively. 'Can we get on with this?'

Simmons was a big fish here and annoyed at being stood up to. She sat back, defensive. '"Police Glasgow", they call it.'

'Aye, well, I just call it my work, Simmons, and I'm at it now. Can we get a move on?'

Simmons sat down and Morrow caught a waft of smell, a sour something, coming from a white mark on the side of her skirt. Simmons smelled it too and covered the mark with her hand. Her face hardened. 'Chief's an *arsehole*.'

Morrow was genuinely shocked. 'Whoa! Mind your fucking language there.'

Simmons was surprised at the challenge. 'Well, it's what we're all thinking, isn't it?'

'It's not what I'm thinking.'

'Have you met him?'

'Yes.'

'And you didn't think he was an arsehole?'

'I've just met *you* and I think you're a fucking arsehole.'

They stared at each other.

Intermittently, officers were sent on training courses about particular topics. Often, they would be shown videos of actors in scenarios illustrating how not to do things. Morrow was very much aware that, if this was a training video about establishing inter-departmental co-operation, she was the bad officer. Having run up a steep hill and taken the moral high ground, she had then thrown herself off, face first. Looking into Simmons' eyes, as she was now, she could see the woman formulating ways to fill out the complaint form.

'I'm sorry for saying that.'

A tiny movement on Simmons' lap caught her eye. She was tapping the tip of her forefinger on her knee, a slow rhythmical tap. Morrow smiled inadvertently. Finger taps to distance the anger from the heart. It was an exercise from an anger management course officers were sent on if they'd had a certain type of incident.

'What's so fucking funny?' demanded Simmons.

Morrow nodded at her hand. '"Mindfulness At Work". Does it help?'

Simmons looked accusingly at her now still hand. 'Sometimes. How do you know about it?'

'Been sent on that course, twice.'

Simmons looked at Morrow's hand. 'You don't do the finger taps?'

'No. It makes me angry. I'm sorry. I have an anger problem. It is my problem—'

'—*not yours and I apologise for my behaviour towards you.*' Simmons finished the anger management course mantra for her.

They both relaxed.

Simmons gestured to the sour-smelling stain on her skirt. 'My mother . . .'

'Not well?'

Simmons half shrugged.

'I've got twins,' confessed Morrow. 'Thirteen months.'

Simmons looked her over for signs and couldn't see any. Morrow slipped her coat off her shoulders and turned to show a slash mark of milky vomit down her shoulder.

Simmons smiled and softened. 'What do you need here?'

Morrow pointed at the map. 'What information do you have about that area?'

'Nothing.'

'It's not known locally as "Halliday's Field"?'

'Not as far as I know.'

'And you've been here, how long?'

'Eight years. What else d'you want?'

'A lawyer called Delahunt—'

Simmons rolled her head away. 'Frank Delahunt. Lawyer, retired from practice. Old-town money. He's a front for the criminal element out here. Sets up phony companies and winds them up.'

'"Winds them up"?'

'You know, to muddy where the money's coming from.'

'I see.' Morrow made a note to check Delahunt's MO later. 'And who is the "criminal element" out here?'

'Mark Barratt. Used to be an upholsterer, suddenly he's mega money, but he's *quiet*. It's as much as you can ask, isn't it?'

Morrow thought about Danny for the first time in hours. She realised that he might have died in the interim and felt a spark of hope. She hated herself for it.

'How does Barratt keep it quiet?'

'He makes it pay for everyone. No real trouble. If anything's kicking off he goes away— Oh.' Something had occurred to her.

'What?'

'Barratt's away just now.'

'So his mob could be involved?'

'Could be.'

Morrow pointed to the map again. 'She's from Madrid, lives in London and she's suspected of cocaine importation from Barcelona—'

'That's ...' Simmons held a hand up and nodded. 'Barratt. That's the connection. He's over there all the time. Lots of money. We know it's coming from him but we can't prove anything yet.'

'OK. Might be how they know each other. She moves up here

and seems to know this field as "Halliday's Field" but no one else has heard of it. What about the Ford Fiesta?'

Simmons looked sceptical, 'Silver? No reg number?'

'No, I know,' said Morrow hopelessly, 'there's a million of them. Keep an eye out anyway.'

Simmons' phone rang and she looked at Morrow before picking it up. She said hello, listened, nodded and paled. She said she'd be there in twenty minutes and hung up.

'DI Morrow.' She stood up and spoke formally, as if she was giving a report. 'We have a female body coming out of Loch Lomond. She's not been in there for long.'

19

Iain walked along the street, keeping close to the back wall of the houses, his face down. His chest felt heavy. He was breathing as if he had stones in there. He could almost hear his ribs straining apart to inflate his lungs. A car drove past him slowly, a 4x4, black, old and boxy. He scratched his forehead, covering his face. Mark didn't like them coming to the house but Iain had no option.

He saw Mark's gate up ahead. High steel gates with a door cut in one. Iain knew he was being watched. Two bulbous cameras were placed high on the garden walls, each giving a 180-degree view of the street. He'd been inside a couple of times and Mark made a deal of showing how impenetrable the house was. Iain thought Mark probably showed the camera room and security sensors to everyone so they'd tell each other and word would get about.

As he approached the gates, the inset door sagged on its hinges. He pushed it open and stepped through.

A bricked forecourt with a triple garage to the left, small outbuildings to the right. One of the buildings was full of weight-lifting equipment. Mark didn't lift weights. Maybe he had meant to when he had the room designed and built, Iain didn't know, but he liked to show the guys the room and the en suite sauna. It was a big sauna, for eight people. Mark had it built but he never seemed to have used it. The bench still looked a bit skelfy.

Wee Paul stepped out of the far-away outhouse. 'What you doing here?' His voice was comically high but no one laughed about it because he was a good guy and reportedly quite handy. Iain had never seen him hit anyone but that was his rep.

Iain walked over and glanced at Paul's 'Yes' wristband. 'What you doing wearing that?'

Paul shrugged and smiled. 'Not here, is he?'

They went back in. It was a small room, freshly plastered and floored, but bare. The only things in it were a chair and a table with a large computer monitor on it, showing feeds from all the cameras around the property. A separate monitor showed the sensor net as an abstract of red lines, all unbroken.

It was very cold. The walls on these old building could be a foot thick. Cold seeped in through the plasterboard and varnished black floor tiles.

Paul shut the door firmly and turned to looked at Iain. He nodded at Iain's chest, asking if he had a microphone on him.

Reluctant and annoyed, Iain took his jumper and T-shirt off, dropped them on the table and undid his belt and zip, letting his jeans slide to his ankles. He held his hands up so Paul could give him a good look-over.

'Mobile?'

'Left it at home.'

Paul looked at him, sceptical. There was something a bit gay about standing there in his Ys while Paul examined him. Maybe it was because the room was small and they were quite close together. Maybe it was that Wee Paul only came to Iain's nipples, or that they were alone, but it felt a bit gay and they were both glad when it was over. Paul gave him the nod and Iain pulled his trousers up. He picked his T-shirt and jumper up and put them back on, enjoying the residual warmth clinging to his clothes.

'So?' said Paul.

Iain pinched his nose. 'Sorted that thing out.'

'*We know*,' said Paul. 'You don't need to come here and tell me that.'

'Listen,' said Iain, '*I* sorted that thing out.' He thumbed to the house. 'Said Murray Ray's clear if I did. And I did.'

Paul, assuming they were being taped by someone, somewhere, held his hands out and shrugged, humming a prompt at him to continue.

'Murray met a friend of ours yesterday. He's *concerned*. But it's clear.'

Paul nodded at the floor. He nodded at the screen. He looked at Iain. 'We'll sort this out ...' and he thumbed at the house, meaning when Mark gets back.

'Sort it out' meant Mark would have to intervene. 'Sort it out' meant it wasn't yet decided whether Murray was in the clear.

'T.' Iain looked paranoically around the room. He shouldn't have said that and Paul eyed him a warning. Iain nodded. He knew he'd broken a rule. He held his hands out in front of him, as if measuring a yard of Tommy. 'Was outside the Sailors'.'

Paul pretended not to understand the significance of that. 'It's a wee town. People go places.'

'*Deliberate*.' Iain was getting desperate.

Paul shrugged. 'Well ...' He wasn't going to discuss it any more. Iain knew he could see how desperate he was, how tired and fucked up he was. Paul nearly smiled and that sealed it.

In defiance of the unseen audience Iain grabbed the neck of Paul's hoodie, twisting it into a knot to get traction, and pulled him onto his tiptoes so that his ear was touching Iain's lips. 'I cleared it. I did it and cleared it.' And then he let go, slowly lowering Wee Paul back to his feet.

Now, Wee Paul relished being a hard man. In truth he had nothing else going for him. He didn't have Iain's looks or Tommy's brains or Mark's skills in upholstery. He was small and his voice was high and he wasn't even good at football or snooker. He had nothing to give him status but his status so the slight of being picked up by a big scary man stung in a way it wouldn't have hurt a bigger man and this made him reckless.

He raised himself to his tiptoes, aware of the diminishing nature of the stance, and whispered in Iain's ear: 'T's saying *he* done the thing.'

He stood back down and watched Iain for a reaction. Iain shook his head. 'No.'

Paul raised his arms and tipped his head to the side. It was out of his hands. They'd just have to wait until Mark got back and sorted it all out.

'*No,*' insisted Iain.

Paul shrugged again, hands out, asking Iain what he expected him to do about it? One man's word against the other. Who the fuck knew?

Iain pointed to an empty bit of floor, indicating a third party.

'Lying.' He touched his chest. ''S clear.' He made a fist and showed the flat knuckles on the outside to Wee Paul. 'Anything happens before . . .'

Wee Paul looked at the wall of knuckles and Iain could see he was scared. Paul looked at Iain and nodded.

'Sort it out.'

Paul thumbed the house. They'd sort it out when Mark got back. '*Day after tomorrow.*'

'Seven fifteen?'

'Course. Only one flight a day. Still going tonight?'

'Going where?'

'Dinner dance. Vicky halls.'

Mark had ordered them to go. Paul was asking Iain if he was in or out of Mark's team. 'I'm going. Of course I'm going.'

'Ye better go home and wash. Starts in a couple of hours.'

'Aye.' Iain was breathing heavily again. He should say something back. 'You getting?'

'Aye,' said Wee Paul. 'I'm getting to go. I'll see ye there.'

'Paul, bud, I'd lose the wristband.'

Paul glanced down. 'Everyone knows I am anyway.'

'Except Mark.'

Paul shrugged and waved him out.

Iain stepped out of the small door in the gate and walked back along the way he had come. Tommy must have met Paul, maybe in the street, more likely at the Snooker Q. He must have met him and told him straight to his face that he, Tommy, did the thing. Or else he'd done it more subtly. Implied it. Let it be implied. Either way it was a fucking outrage.

Iain had suspected that Tommy might be a bit of a prick but he didn't honestly think he would take credit for another man's work. It was contemptible. He'd chin him about it at the dance, in front of Wee Paul, and then everyone would know. Arsehole.

20

It looked like the entrance to a high security prison in *Brigadoon*. The golf course gates, cast as the cross of St Andrew, were hung on sandstone gateposts topped with giant carved thistles. Next to the gate was a sentry box, small and grey, flanked by a free-standing intercom. Cameras were posted everywhere.

Beyond the security measures though, hidden from casual view, were pretty cottages, columned and cute, peeking out from behind perfectly manicured trees.

The sun was going down over Loch Lomond, a soft pink light settling over snow-capped mountains. Morrow was a city child, most familiar with Scottish mountain views from toffee tins, and looking up at the hills still gave her a hankering for caramels.

McGrain drew up their car behind Simmons'. Simmons lowered her window, spoke into the intercom and showed it her ID. Her hand withdrew and the gates barring their way whirred open. Both cars drew into a straight driveway framed by big trees

A blazered usher stood at the far end, blocking the way to a car park outside a club house. He flagged down Simmons's car, spoke to her, directing her away with an angry chopping hand. The window rolled up, the car pulled to the right and Morrow's phone rang. It was Simmons.

'Follow me. It's down here.'

The usher glared in at Morrow and McGrain, jabbing a finger after Simmons' car.

Morrow told Simmons on the phone, 'This gentleman doesn't seem particularly grateful for our assistance.'

But Simmons blanked the collegiate undertone: 'He doesn't

want anyone to see us. They've had to shut the course.' She hung up. She had other calls to take.

An immaculate tarmac road led them past back roads. It was a world-famous golf course, even Morrow had heard of it. There was certainly a lot of money here. The grass was of uniform height and colour, the trees pruned and symmetrical. Even the bins had manicured hedges around them. Simmons' car took a turn-off to a wood. Morrow and McGrain followed it down into a clearing with ten foot high hills of yellow sand blocking the view of the loch side.

Simmons was out of her car, standing and waiting for them. Morrow nodded to her. 'What's the story?'

Simmons was anxious to get home, Morrow recognised the agitated look. She gave the briefing in truncated phrases, as if that would get either of them home faster. Estate worker, out on a boat to clear crap out of the loch near the course. Saw a pair of feet stuck in a branch. Local cops went out in a RIB. Secured area. Estate worker brought back. That's his house. There. She pointed at a cottage peeking coyly out from behind a magnolia tree. Scene of Crime and the path lab are on the way from Glasgow.

'How long ago did the estate worker call it in?'

Simmons checked her watch. 'About an hour. He's in shock. He tried to hook it, thinking it was a shop dummy. The head's badly damaged. Cops said face is over here.' She slid her hand down over one shoulder and then, as if shocked by the thought, turned and walked away.

Morrow followed her through a well-trodden zigzagging path between the sand dunes until they came to a small dock. It seemed little used.

'What's all the sand for?' she asked.

'Bunkers. On the golf course. And the grey stuff behind it's for building works. They're always building crap for the tourists out here. Heard now they're doing some blackhouses with steam

showers and jacuzzis. Blackhouses are what they used to keep
pigs in.' Simmons pointed to the far end of the dock. 'That's his
boat there.'

An old boat bobbed on the water. A small crane gibbeting
hung off the back, a metal crab claw hanging on a chain. The
wheelhouse was as narrow as an upright coffin. Old and worn
and nifty, the *Sea Jay II* looked like the inspiration for a kids'
cartoon.

A grey police rigid inflatable boat was docked behind it, ready
to take Morrow and Simmons out. An officer on the dock handed
each of them an orange life jacket. Morrow copied Simmons,
slipping it on, doing the clips and mirroring her moves as they
stepped into the boat.

They sat down next to each other on a bench at the back, the
two officers standing up front to counterbalance their weight. The
boat took off out of the dock, skimming gently into the middle of
Loch Lomond before taking a left.

Morrow had never been on a boat before. She'd been on a ferry
but never a proper on-the-water boat. The RIB took the middle
lane, moving at a regal pace, making its way slowly up the loch
to minimise any wash from the engine. They wouldn't want to
dislodge any evidence around the body.

Mountains in the distance were shrouded in the dusk, receding
and misty, flats on a theatre set. Passing a cluster of small islands
near the shore, each of an almost magical roundness, they reach
the open loch and a wide expanse of water. As they pulled gently
to the left, the boat tipped slightly and Morrow steadied herself,
laying a hand on the side, a queen taking a solid rubberised cour-
tier's arm. It was so pretty and Victorian, she could almost hear a
faint crinoline-crinkle hanging in the air.

They slowed as they turned at a small island. Through trees,
she saw a dirty-feathered swan settled on its nest. The waterline
was a black rim, built of peat bricks. Surprised, she realised that
the island was a landscaped feature.

'Is that not a real island?' she asked Simmons.

'Nothing out here is real,' Simmons said. 'There's too much money out here for any of it to be left real.'

Slowly circumventing the island, Morrow saw what it had been built to shield. Loch Lomond golf course was laid out ahead of them on a long, immaculate peninsula. Acres of perfectly undulating green velvet, pockmarked with yellow sandy craters. The trees by the water were pollarded to uniform height.

The RIB engine was switched off and they floated towards the tree-lined shore on its waning momentum. The RIB officers used their paddles, turning the boat side-on to the shore.

Simmons stood, a hand on Morrow's shoulder to indicate that she should stay down. They both looked over to the base of the trees.

The dead woman was almost completely obscured, tangled in an underwater root system, the underground branches creeping out into the clear cold water. She was on her back, arms out, legs splayed, in a relaxed pose, as if she was in a hot bath. Blunt trauma to the head. Her face had slipped sideways but the water allowed the viewer to believe the distortion was refracted light. No blood in the water. It could have been washed away but she had probably been killed elsewhere, which was annoying. It meant they had no scene of crime to examine, which meant they had a lot less to go on.

Simmons' hand was shaking. Her knee buckled slightly and she sat down next to Morrow to disguise her distress. She clasped her hands together and turned her face so that no one would see how hard she found it to look. Morrow liked her for that, visceral compassion was rare at their level.

Morrow took a turn at standing. The dead woman was chubby. She had mum-jeans on. Her feet were bare but Morrow saw the seams of tights over her toes. A white cotton T-shirt had turned grey and transparent in the water. Underneath she wore a heavy-duty white bra with industrial straps. Too short, too dumpy. It wasn't Roxanna.

'Not mine,' she said.

Simmons touched her on the back, telling her to sit down then and let her get back up, but just then the tail of the boat slipped past the body. It was peeking out of the front pocket of the jeans. A ribbon loop. Yellow with red writing on it.

'No,' said Morrow, shoving Simmons' insistent hand away. She told the RIB officers, 'Bring me back around.'

The officers paddled conservatively, holding the flat of the paddle so that the water moved around them. The boat bobbed a full circle.

The ribbon in her pocket was a lanyard, worn around the neck to hold an ID badge. A yellow ribbon with tiny red ladders printed on it. Injury Claims 4 U.

'Is it her?' asked Simmons at her hip.

'No,' said Morrow, 'but I think it's connected.' She nodded to the RIB operator. 'Could you say where she went in?'

'It depends how long she's been in there.'

Morrow looked at the colour of her skin. She wasn't even bloated yet and her knees were articulated. 'Say, not much more than a day?'

He looked back at the body, at the tangle of roots under the water. He turned and looked out onto the water.

'Well, it's a quiet day, not much wash coming in from vessels. At a guess,' he pointed out to the flat plain of water, 'I'd say just there.'

'Not far then?'

'Yeah,' he said. 'Really not far. Different if it was a weekend or the ferry was out. The water would be moving a lot more. It's very deep in parts but not until you get right out over there.' He pointed across to the distant mountains. 'Not around here.'

Whoever had done it had left her in just the wrong place. It looked more like a mistake than an attempt at displaying a body. It was a pretty obscure place.

She asked, 'Who did you say found her in here?'

'Estate worker.' Simmons sat back down and dropped her voice. 'He's just done a sentence.'

'What for?'

'Possession. Still on parole. But he's a nice man. His mother's well known and liked in the town. She's on the flower festival committee. Lady Cole.'

Morrow suspected that 'nice man' was Helensburgh short-hand for middle class.

The RIB retraced its path, moving again with excruciating slowness. They turned the corner around the swan's nesting island and gathered a little more speed, approaching the dock they had come from.

One of the RIB officers was waiting in a clearing of trees with the estate worker who had found the body. The worker was about forty, wearing a red baseball cap, rubberised yellow dungarees and a green knitted jumper.

McGrain was standing at the other end of the dock, by the sand dunes, watching for her.

'Ma'am,' he shouted, pointing further up the dock to the sand dunes. 'Found the scene!'

'Thank fuck for that,' muttered Morrow. 'Simmons, can you wait here and direct the forensic and pathology people? I want to talk to the estate guy.'

'Of course.'

'And get photos of everything.'

The boat drew up and Morrow stepped out fluently, unclipping her life jacket and chucking it back in the boat. She waved to McGrain to join her.

Andrew Cole, estate worker, was devastated. Shock manifested in odd ways and Morrow noted him looking at her with glazed, languid eyes. He raised a hand to scratch his cheek, moving with the tantric slowness of a man who cannot assimilate what he has just seen.

'Mr Cole,' said Morrow gently, as she approached, 'can we go to your house? I'd like to ask you some questions.'

'Sure,' he whispered, looking at his feet, his eyes obscured by the peak of his cap. 'Yeah.'

Morrow and McGrain walked him carefully along the dock to his house around the corner. He walked slowly, dragging his feet, his shoulders slumped.

Around a tree they came to a tiny Georgian villa, painted yellow, the door framed by stumpy Doric columns and a low overhanging roof. He reached deep into the dungarees, to the pocket of the trousers he was wearing underneath, and took out a lone key to unlock it. It seemed odd to Morrow that he would lock his front door, but she didn't know the area.

Cole shuffled down a low hallway to the living room, fell into the only armchair and lit a cigarette. Without looking for it, he reached out for an empty ashtray on the fireplace and sat it in his lap. He inhaled deeply, blowing the smoke out through his nose.

'Choking for a smoke?' asked McGrain.

Cole started slightly, as though he'd forgotten they were there. 'Oh.' He spoke softly. 'Can't smoke on the grounds. Sacking offence.'

'How long have you lived here, Mr Cole?'

He blinked several times before answering, 'Five months?'

'Is the cottage a perk of your job, or do you own it?'

'With the job.' He took his hat off, the rim of it scorched red on his forehead, and ran his fingers through his thinning ginger hair. He set the hat on his knee and drew on his cigarette again. Even from the little he had said so far, Morrow could tell that Mr Cole, the estate worker, was much, much posher than she was.

He smoked in silence for a moment and she let him, looking around at the small room. It was long-term messy. He hadn't brought much with him by way of furniture, one armchair, a telly, a side table and ashtrays.

She could read Mr Cole's route through his day from the room: a half-drunk mug of milky tea was on the floor by his chair, a creamy cloud coagulating on the surface: it had been there for a while. Also on the floor were two plates, stacked on top of each other, separated by a half slice of toast on the bottom. The top plate had a single bite of a coleslaw sandwich left on it. The mayo was still opaque and the house was warm. Morrow guessed it had been there since lunchtime.

The armchair seemed to be the centre of operations for Mr Cole. His laptop, clunky and inexpensive, within reach on the floor. The chair itself faced a small supermarket flat-screen television.

From these facts DI Morrow deduced that Mr Cole was a single gentleman. He seemed to spend his leisure time sitting in his chair, watching telly, smoking and eating, not for pleasure, but to appease his hunger. A normal day, until he went out onto the water and found a dead woman.

'Did you phone from the boat, Mr Cole?'

'Phone?'

'Call us, when you found the woman?'

'In boat? I work for the course.' He pointed vaguely up the shore. 'Called.'

He wasn't making any sense. He blinked hard at the floor and she thought suddenly – heavy smoker, bad diet, terrible shock: he could be having a stroke. Her mind sped up: young man but it might be a congenital. She ran through the diagnostic check list: facial drooping: none. Clawed hand: none. Rubbing painful shoulder . . .

Cole gave a great sigh and bent forwards over his knees, a potential sign of pain. Morrow's hand was on her phone in her pocket, thinking ambulance, but he sat up straight, shut his eyes and took another languorous draw on his cigarette.

139

'Mr Cole, are you on any medication?'

He shook his head.

'Statins or anything?'

'No. Pills, no.' He gave a puzzled smile at the wall behind her.

Morrow understood suddenly. Mr Cole had done a sentence for possession. She barked a laugh at the sudden realisation and McGrain laughed along with her. Mr Cole looked up at them and his face cracked into a please-like-me smile.

'I thought he was having a stroke,' said Morrow.

But Mr Cole was neither suffering from shock nor was he having a stroke. It seemed that Mr Cole had smoked an Olympic amount of marijuana this morning.

McGrain stepped towards him and bent down as if he was addressing a lost child. 'Mr Cole?' He smiled pleasantly. 'You're still on parole, aren't you? Would we be correct in assuming that you've been smoking certain substances today?'

Mr Cole looked indignant. 'What you would say that to me . . . ?'

They chuckled to each other. Aware that they were laughing at him, Mr Cole stood up. Swaying, he held onto the fireplace to steady himself and touched his chest, inadvertently assuming the pose of a Victorian actor in a melodrama.

'Officers? From my point of view? I think to say, that I'm, frankly, quite *hurt* of the suggestion.'

Morrow and McGrain stood and laughed a joyous gale at him. It wasn't just the timeless joke of an inebriate in denial, it was funny because he was posh and sincere. It was sweet how sincere he was.

'Let's bring him in,' she told McGrain. 'Speak to him later.'

'Never gets old, does it?' chuckled McGrain.

Mr Cole confided sadly to the carpet: 'I'm very offended right now.'

McGrain stepped forward, took a firm hold on Cole's arm and turned him to the front door. 'We're going to take you to the station, Mr Cole, see if we can have a better chat there.'

'No.' Cole addressed McGrain's grip on him. 'That's . . . but I'm upset of this laughing.'

'Well, that's a very great shame, sir.'

Mr Cole stopped, his mood shifted and he smiled beatifically at them both. 'D'you know what? Don't worry about it.'

'Oh,' McGrain grinned, 'you're very kind.'

Cole asked, 'Where we going?'

'We, sir, are offski.' McGrain opened the door. 'To the station. Where you will be held, pending a five minute interval when you're no longer off your tits.'

They left and Morrow found herself on her own in the room. Cole wasn't allowed to smoke in the grounds. He must have smoked the hash before he went out. She looked at the floor and realised that there was no hash lying around. There were no pipes or torn papers on the floor, no papers at all. No roaches in the ashtray.

The detritus of his wasted day was lying around the room, but before he went out on the boat Mr Cole had the foresight to hide the evidence of a parole violation.

Silly, sweet, harmless Mr Cole had known that the police were coming.

21

All of the tables in the Paddle Café were arranged into three stations: starters, desserts and two types of mains. Small plates of cold poached salmon were laid out on big catering trays and overlaid with tinfoil. Dessert was lemon tart, the mains a choice of chicken or quiche. All there was to do when they got there was add whichever fresh element the plates needed – warm toast, crème fraîche – and bang it out the door. For Boyd it was an unforeseen but tremendously pleasing aspect of charity catering: he didn't feel obliged to give anyone a choice about anything. Eat it or leave it.

He got Helen, the youngest waitress, to lift the tinfoil lids from the trays while he added a garnishing sprig of dill to the poached pink strip on each plate. Helen had failed her exams, he remembered that much about her. Missed out on uni this year, was attending a crammer to get her grades up. She laid the tinfoil back down like a stage assistant covering a watch, smiling as Boyd played the part of the magician:

'Now you see it. Now you don't.'

Helen was quite attractive, slim and dark with big eyes, but she had a confident look about her. She looked as if she'd gossip if you asked her where to buy coke.

He could see another girl in the kitchen, Katie, decanting tubs of crème fraîche into enormous earthenware jugs. Katie was mousy though. She wouldn't know. He should just wait and see Tommy Farmer.

Since it was a blowout night, Boyd allowed himself the luxury of a little sexual speculation about the two girls and fixed on

Helen: Helen shy, Helen naked, Helen bending over a bed.

'What can I do for you?' Miss Grierson slid into his line of vision, expressionless. She was talking about the catering job but the overlap of thoughts made him uneasy.

'Right.' Boyd raised his voice so everyone could hear him. 'Susan will organise a trail of people to carry the starters to the hall. We'll need tray carriers and a couple of escorts in case they lose their grip or the tinfoil comes off while they're walking.'

Miss Grierson gave a curt little nod and went into the kitchen. A moment later she was out again, had all the girls with her, even the lazy part-timer Simone, who would hide out by the bins when it got busy. They each took a tray from Miss Grierson and Helen. Grierson held the door open, Helen followed at the rear and they stepped out into the soft evening air with poached salmon for a hundred people. Boyd watched the single file pass the window in neat procession.

She was good, Miss Grierson. Able. He felt quite calm about the challenge of the night. They only had to go two blocks, uphill, to the Victoria Halls. Boyd stepped out of the door, watching them go.

His congregation walked, heads up, arms laden, towards the promise of a public obligation honourably fulfilled. Boyd felt the rightness of the thing, the timelessness of it. In this ordered place, this event must occur.

Tommy was puttering about the living room, pocketing fags and bits of change into his dress jacket. Elaine hurried in with a cup of tea and a packet of biscuits. She set them on a side table, put the telly on to *Cowboy Builders* and jumped into the recliner. Using the armrests to lift her weight off the chair, she pushed the footrest out and settled in for the night. Tommy watched as she pulled her lap blanket over her knees, checked her tea and biscuits were within reach, that she had the remote – a pilot conducting final safety checks. 'You'll be late if you don't go now.

And mind you tell them it was me sold the raffle tickets.'

'I'll *tell* them, I'll *tell* them.' He was too adamant. Elaine gave him a look.

Tommy smiled. 'OK, I *will* tell them.'

'Aye,' she went back to watching telly, 'I'll be checking on that, son.'

Smirking because he'd been caught out, Tommy went out to the hall to see himself in the mirror. He kept his eyes to the details. Polo shirt collar straight. Hair flat. He avoided looking himself in the eye.

He opened the front door. 'Bye, Lainey.' And he stepped out into the stone close.

Lainey sing-songed 'Bye-ya,' after him and he shut the door.

Damp cold clung to the walls. Tommy checked for passing neighbours, back and front. No one. He walked up to the close door and shut it loudly, making a soundscape for Lainey. He opened it again, silently, and slipped out to the street, jamming the door with a bit of brick. Then he tucked his hands into his pockets and head up, face forward, walked past the living room window, letting Lainey witness him go.

Past the window, he ducked and doubled back to the close, staying under the sill. He toed the brick out of the way and snuck through the door to the back court.

The grass was thin and the ground uneven but he stayed off the well-lit path to the bin sheds. The fence was made of chicken wire, peeled back into the muddy back lane. He sidled through, careful not to catch his good trousers on the ragged wires, and made his way down to the dark end of the road and the abandoned lock-ups.

The second-to-last garage had a flip-up door, peeling red paint. No one used the lock-ups now, not since one of them fell in, but Tommy occasionally parked things in this garage. He knew they were safe. The door didn't open beyond knee height. He bent down now and lifted the door, crouching to feel into the dark, fingers wiggling in until they found the soft plastic handle.

He pulled the petrol can out and stood up, thinking his way through the job. He cautioned himself not to get any on his clothes. It smelled distinctive and he'd be flammable if he did. Also, fumes could stick on your clothes if you poured it in a confined space. So just use the spout, pour it through a window, leave the jacket nearby, roll the sleeves up. Stay out of the fumes. Keep the wind at your back. He was concerned that the fire would be spotted before it got going and look petty, not serious. It needed to be the right window to go well.

He couldn't turn up at the dinner with mud on his good shoes so, rather than heading down the dirt lane to the street, he slid back through the hole in the fence and cut across the back court again.

In his head he was already at the Sailors', with the wind at his back and his jacket rolled up, already striking the match, so he didn't see Elaine until it was too late. She was at the kitchen sink, looking out of the window straight at him.

Tommy stopped in the pool of light from their kitchen. For a startling moment their eyes met.

Elaine caught herself before he did, looking down quickly into the sink. She was pretended that she hadn't seen him but she'd looked straight at him, standing in the back court in his smart jacket, holding a red can of petrol. She blushed with the effort of evasion. Lies weren't Lainey's style.

Lies were Tommy's style, but not with his mum. Embarrassed, he kept his head down and walked out through the close to the street.

The bright white overhead lights in the Victoria Halls had to be left on for safety reasons. It was a very old building and the softer side lights hadn't been safety checked recently. It didn't matter how nicely the tables were dressed or how the food looked in the back room, it didn't matter how much dill or cress or how artfully arranged a drizzle of jus was, it looked like the canteen deck on a ferry.

The big hall was vaulted, the high ceiling painted peach with a white trim. For reasons, possibly of Victorian authenticity, possibly an aesthetic oversight, the vibrant peach had been twinned with mint green and pink walls. Long burgundy curtains were draped on the stage and windows. Ropes of red balloons hung around the balcony. Tickets had sold very well and tables jostled around the perimeter of the dance floor.

The top table sat up on the stage, a last-supperish affair of local nabobs and charity officials sitting in a row, chewing bread rolls as though they were setting an example for the lower orders on the floor.

The charity had contributed two big posters to flank the top table. A big-eyed girl with a shaved head and a nasal feeding tube taped to her cheek smiled wanly, twice, and watched the assembly eat.

Every demographic of the town was represented, the rich and old, the poor and almost young, all joined together to raise money for a worthy cause. Some of the women were more used to nightclubs than dinner dances and were fake-tanned orange and tottering about in platform high heels and minidresses. The sedate, older women of the town, more familiar with the conventions of the dinner dance, had their hair set and were dressed in long skirts and heels they could dance in. Men wore sports jackets and slacks, or else kilts, which were expensive and bought for significant weddings, and they were damn well going to get the wear out of them.

The starters had gone down well, though most of the fresh dill returned on the plates. Boyd was watching through the side door for the last empties and bread baskets to come back. The staff gradually assembled in the side room, ready to begin serving the main meal.

He turned to Miss Grierson. 'How long since the top table's starters came back?'

She checked her clipboard and watch. 'Eleven minutes.'

He nodded, watching the last set of plates weaving their way back through the hall. Four minutes and they would be late. Looking over the bald and grey heads in the hall, Boyd knew that most of them had children and most of the children would get married. The Victoria Halls was a prime wedding venue. When the day was chosen and the dinner was being booked these people would think of him. This was his chance to glean a lot of custom. All he had to do was serve good-sized portions of decent food at reasonable intervals.

Boyd ducked into the side room where the plates were laid out. From a bain-marie plugged into the wall he spooned mash and chicken onto five plates. One top-tabler had requested quiche. He sent the girls out.

For the next twenty-five minutes he spooned and served, looking hard at each plate to check for imperfections, envisioning the fresh eyes of diners landing on the food for the first time. He lost himself in the meditative task, enjoying the rolling rhythm of spoon to spoon as he shaped the mash, drizzled gravy over chicken. His face was damp, whether with sweat or the condensation of the bain-marie he didn't know, but he dabbed it with the tea towel at his apron and carried on. In the background he heard Miss Grierson call the tables.

'Two quiche on sixteen.'

'One chicken, no mash on eighteen.'

Interchangeable girls in black aprons, gliding in and out of the room with arms empty, arms full, never stopping to drink or talk.

Boyd had run out of plates to fill. He looked up.

'Service done,' said Miss Grierson.

Boyd nodded to the hall. 'Can you check?'

She went off to look through the door leaving Boyd alone in the carpeted side room. He had eight chicken portions left over and a full twelve-portion organic quiche. He could sell it in the café tomorrow.

Miss Grierson came back, smiling. 'Service done.'

'Going down well?'

'Come and see.'

Dabbing his damp face, he stepped out to look through the glass doors. A hundred heads were bent over plates, the room full of the discordant jangle of cutlery hitting crockery.

The waitresses were all locals and had stayed in the hall, chatting to diners they knew. The top table were eating, talking, looking at their plates as if they might be saying something complimentary about the food. Everyone was happy and Boyd was pleased.

He spotted Tommy Farmer, sitting at a table near the stage, smiling, leaning low over his plate to scoop mash into his mouth. His jacket was on the back of his chair and Boyd's heart swelled, as if he'd spotted a girl he had a crush on.

'That's really gone well,' he said.

'Yeah,' said Miss Grierson.

Could he just go over and talk to Tommy? A hand on the back of his chair, a whisper in his ear – All right, Tommy? Just wondered . . . But he was a bit sweaty and everyone was still sitting down, he'd be obvious. Wait until after the puddings.

Boyd meant to air-pat Miss Grierson's back in a congratulatory way, but his eyes were on Tommy and he didn't notice when she stepped back into his cupped hand. Boyd's palm landed on her waist, just too low. He was touching her buttocks.

Miss Grierson looked at him, eyebrows high with surprise.

Reeling away, Boyd scurried off to the back room. He was cringing, half laughing with embarrassment. He glanced back, hoping to find her embarrassed and laughing too.

She wasn't.

Miss Grierson was looking at him, expressionless, but the steadiness of her stare said yes.

*

Iain was at a corner table in the hall, in the shadow of the balcony, having been swept there on a wave as they were let into the room.

He didn't see anyone he knew very well while he was waiting, ticket in hand, at the doors. Murray was late, Wee Paul and the other guys were yet in the pub and Tommy didn't seem to be there either. He wanted to talk to Tommy, preferably in front of Wee Paul, but he'd have to wait.

He ended up sitting next to a couple he knew from years ago. They'd brought a gangly nephew with them. The boy stared at the table throughout and finished everyone else's food.

Iain sat quietly and let them talk among themselves. People came to the table and left, hands on Iain's shoulders, hands gone. Iain ate, savouring the hot food, realising he hadn't eaten for twenty-four hours and that was partly why he felt so bad.

The night fizzed around him; it peaked, it troughed. Then he spotted Tommy sitting across the room, near the stage, but they were eating their mains by then and Iain would have drawn every eye if he walked over to him.

He thought he saw the back of Murray, heading out to the toilet, but wasn't sure.

He saw Granny Eunice and she gave him a wee wave. She had her leg up on a chair and gave him an exaggerated wince across the room, to show him it was still sore.

Susan Grierson came in during the puddings, dressed formally in black clothes, holding a clipboard as if she was working with the caterers but not carrying plates. She walked over to speak to a waitress and passed quite close by but pointedly ignored him. He was pleased enough about that.

A man from the charity came around as the puddings were being finished, thanking them for coming, mentioning the sick kiddies, talking about dying, and how that was a shame.

Full of food, Iain felt very calm and tired. It had been a busy few days. All he had left to do was chin Tommy about taking credit for the lassie and he could go home and sleep. That was all he wanted in the world right now. To sleep, face down, unmoving, and wake up tomorrow morning, aching and groggy. He sat back with his hand on his stomach, looking around the hall. Smokers were getting up and moving to the exit. Tommy was over by the doors, texting and laughing at a joke Hank Murphy was busy telling. Iain might as well go and speak to him now.

Boyd had been cowering in the service room. Miss Grierson slid into the doorway and smiled softly. 'OK, Boyd?'

'Oh – yup.' He picked up a spoon and wiped crème fraîche off it nervously.

Miss Grierson stayed there, staring at him, until the girls started coming back in with the pudding plates.

Boyd busied himself, helping Helen to stack up the final load of plates from the mains. A few pernickety diners had eaten around the chicken or the mash or the salad. Mostly the salad. It had flowers in it. Wrong crowd. Boyd kept his head down as all the plates came back. He and Helen and Kate took the final load of plates out of the side door and put them on a metal catering trolley that was already half full. Take it back to the café, he told them, leave it in the kitchen and get your coats and bags and go home. They could do the washing up in the morning. They were getting time and a half for the evening, he didn't want the shift to go later than it needed to. He watched them trundle the heavy trolley off onto the street and went back to look into the hall again.

Coffee-making had been delegated to the people who ran the hall but Boyd had sent the girls out with a small plate of chocolates for each table, a *Compliments of the Paddle Café* card set prominently in the middle. Miss Grierson took the last few out herself.

Hungry for a sight of Tommy, Boyd dropped his tea towel and went to the hall doors, peering through the bevelled glass. The tables were breaking up. They'd have a smoking break before the charity auction and then the dancing would begin. He saw Miss Grierson in the hall, mingling, asking people if they enjoyed their meal and being reintroduced to a lot of the upper-middle-class diners who might remember her. She stood by comfortably, hands clutched in front of her, allowing herself to be explained. An occasional flash of sadness in her eyes, probably when her mother's death came up. Then a gracious smile and a promise to meet up again soon, have a good night, enjoy the dancing. She slid between tables, her pleasant smile unwavering.

She wasn't actually old, he realised. She could only be fifty, early fifties. He supposed her old because she was older than him when it mattered. Maybe it didn't really matter any more.

Suddenly tired, Boyd took a deep breath, tilting his head back and looking down a cheek at the hall. His half-shut eyes turned the people into a blur, melting them into a solid mass of hairspray and jackets.

Smokers were coming to the door, bringing hats and bags, gleeful at being free to go outside. Tommy Farmer was standing by his seat, pulling his jacket on, about to leave, and Boyd thought he could go in and approach him now. He opened the door just as a fat man in full kilt outfit came through the door.

'Ahh!' He threw his arms out and grabbed Boyd. 'Brilliant!' He was sweating wildly. 'Fantastic food, Boyd.'

Tommy drifted past them as the man dragged Boyd into the hall. Everyone turned to look at him. A smattering of applause rolled round the room, not quite enough in Boyd's opinion but a round of applause nonetheless. They'd thank him during the speeches, maybe people were saving their appreciation for later. Then he was in the hall, out on the choppy waters of society, bobbing from table to table. Hands reached for him, congregation members and customers. He found himself sucked into eddies of conversation, compliments and introductions.

Now he was under the balcony being introduced to a small,

purple-faced pensioner who knew his father. The plum-faced man talked angrily about the Reverend Robert having died, how the church had gone downhill since, as though the death had been directed at him. His flustered wife took over the conversation. She was at school with someone who knew his mother, but they had died and that was a mercy and wasn't Boyd doing well? So nice he was back home. And how many children? Two boys? Well, that must be a handful!

Miss Grierson was suddenly behind him. She didn't wait for a break in the pensioners' ramble but whispered in his ear,

'I've got some white.'

She said it very casually, as if she was warning him about a gravy spill.

Boyd stood as still as if she had goosed him back. He nodded at the old woman in front of him. Someone's daughter had an illness of some kind but she didn't let that hold her back.

Miss Grierson murmured to him, her lips brushing his ear lobe, 'Give me the café keys and wait five minutes.'

Without breaking eye contact with the lady telling the story, Boyd took his keys out of his pocket and handed them to her.

From the corner of his eye he saw Miss Grierson coursing to the doors, tacking between tables and squally groups of people. Elated, he looked around for someone to waste the five minutes on.

With misplaced delight he smiled at an old woman sitting nearby. She gave him a pained smile, her hand rubbing circles on her swollen knee in an orthopaedic brace.

'Knee's giving me gyp,' she said, as if he had enquired.

'She's to keep it up, haven't ye, pet?' another old woman explained across the table. She was warmer, more likeable. 'You the Puddle Café man?'

'Paddle. Yes.'

'Oh, son, your prices are criminal.'

Boyd was irritated by that, but he was getting a sniff in a minute, so he shouldn't really let trivial slights worry him. Let it go.

'You're a Fraser, aren't you?' chimed the Martyr-to-her-knee.

'And tell me this,' the stupid cow called over, 'isn't your family the Lawnmore Frasers?'

It was the way she said it, the intonation of the odd girl he'd met on the seafront. Boyd realised that he was looking at the two grannies and he smiled.

'Yeah, the Lawnmore Frasers.'

The two grannies nodded, once to each other, once to him, running through the family history in their minds, finding him acceptable.

'Are you Granny Eunice and Granny Annie?'

'Oh! How would you know that?'

'I met Lea-Anne earlier, with her dad, down at the esplanade—'

'Coming out of the pub, likely.'

'Yeah,' said Boyd, 'coming out of the pub. Didn't she say one of you was babysitting tonight?'

The women looked at each other. The father didn't want to go out in the end, one said. He gave them the ticket, said the other, and they just came together.

Boyd started to tell them how he recognised the intonation of their speech in their granddaughter's, but someone who had a sister who had just had a stroke was standing by the table and no one was very interested in his phonetic observations. He shifted away and the Martyr called after him,

'And son? Listen: your gravy wants salt.'

He walked away feeling belittled and imagined Sanjay laughing at him. Your gravy wants salt.

Tommy Farmer crossed his path and glanced at him, but Boyd didn't give a fuck about him now. He walked straight out of the halls and down to the café.

*

Iain watched Tommy cross to the door and thought quite suddenly that it might be nice to get a breath of air himself. He stood up, lifting his jacket off the back of the chair and smiled suddenly. Fresh air, indeed. An addict's lie: he was going to beg a smoke off someone.

And then he was outside with the gaggle of smokers lined up along the disabled ramp. Everyone was there, all the good-looking women and guys, younger than him, most of them, but good guys. A young team were listening to Darren Oaky tell a story and snorting and laughing. Tommy took a fag out and watched Darren, a little jealous pinch between his eyebrows. Tommy couldn't tell a story.

Iain walked towards him and saw Tommy's face harden.

'Wee Paul says you says it was you,' muttered Iain.

Tommy snorted, 'So?'

They squared up to each other. No fighting though, Mark would not approve, so they looked at each other and neither said what they were thinking.

Tommy was thinking that it *was* him: he'd done all the organising, got the van, etc., so it *was* him, really.

Iain was thinking that he had raised his hand over the woman. He got Andrew Cole to loan them the boat and it was his hands that had killed her. Slowly, Tommy's eyes fell to Iain's fingertips.

'Your hands look fucking mental,' he said.

Iain looked at them. Lainey said that too. But Tommy was just distracting him. 'You leave off Murray Ray,' Iain said, dropping his hand, 'or I'll fucking swing for you.'

They looked at each other. Tommy decided something that Iain couldn't fathom. He smirked. And lit the cigarette. Iain looked at the packet. 'Gae us one.'

Tommy did. Iain still had his lighters, yellow yellow, but that didn't bother him as much any more. They smoked next to each other on the ramp, a peace pipe of sorts.

Darren was into another story and more people came out.

Some of the smoking women had men's dinner jackets draped over their shoulders for warmth. Tommy sloped off.

Iain begged another fag off a woman he knew. He'd done everything he needed to do. He felt quite good. He stayed outside, even when the cigarettes were done, keeping to the outskirts of the crowd, enjoying being part of it but still separate.

It got colder, darker. The smokers pulled their jackets and coats around them, huddling together for warmth. Darren and another young guy started telling the same story. They were speaking too loud, shouting different versions of the punchline over each other for the audience of women.

The drone was so faint it felt like a memory at first, a faraway whine coming over the roof tops from the east: fire engines. Chat around the door petered out. The night felt suddenly cold as the drone got louder. It was coming from the shore.

Red lights flashing at the bottom of Sinclair Street, filling Boots the chemists' window with a bloody, molten smear. Sirens cut dead in mid wail.

The crowd drifted out to the street, watching down to the water. A black cloud of smoke billowed taller than the town, rolling in like a monster stepping out of the sea.

A voice in the crowd: 'Oh, Christ, it's the Sailors'.'

A woman called to the doors – 'Somebody! GET MURRAY OUT HERE' and people in the hall took up the cry – 'Murray's place is on fire!' 'Get Murray out here!'

But Murray wasn't in the hall.

Hardly breathing, Iain watched as Eunice and Annie came to the door. They stood, backlit. They held each other, watching down to the water, as stone-faced as fishermen's wives in a storm. Iain froze: they were both there. Murray wasn't there and Lea-Anne was never left alone.

Iain was next to them, looming over them, breathless with terror and the little women didn't need to speak or tell him. They turned their horrified faces to the fire. 'WHERE ARE THEY?'

shouted Iain, but he knew where they'd be. 'YOU NEED TO
TELL! YOU NEED TO PHONE!'

But they didn't have phones with them. From the corner of his
eye he saw a bright rectangle of light, someone taking a picture
of the fire. He grabbed it, shoved the indignant photographer
away and held it out to Annie: *Emergency! Say they're in there!*
Annie fumbled the phone to Eunice and she stabbed at it three
times.

Glass exploded somewhere far away, the high snap carried
on the wind. Iain saw red flames lick above the rooftops, stark
against the black water. Thick black smoke curled up taller than
the town, billowing in from the west. The smoke was Mark's
proxy, the town cleaved to his will and Iain watched it coil around
the buildings on the seafront.

He was moving, heart hammering, not certain he was moving
because everyone around him was moving too, inexorable as a
mudslide, downhill, into the fire.

A gust of wind from the water blew the thick smoke up the
valley of the street towards them. The mob recoiled but not Iain.
He walked on into the benedicting smoke. Heat and a grainy
weight pressed on his chest. He hurried into it, breathing deep
the suffocating black.

The wind changed direction. Like a giant incense burner over
the town, it swung the smoke out of the narrow street and away,
up, out to sea.

Iain slowed to a stagger. As sudden as the grace of faith withdrawn, he found himself alone outside the Tesco Metro. Smoke
rose from his good jacket. He coughed and his spit was black.

He shuffled on, to the corner, stopping when he got across the
road from the burning pub.

The inside of the café looked bigger in the dark. It looked bigger
and braver and, like, just the smartest thing anyone had ever
done. Boyd was sweating and, as if seeing the half-lit room for

the first time, he knew, deep in his heart, that he had done a laudable thing here.

Really, when you thought about it, bringing seasonal, local, organic food to the town – genius. And he *had* brought it to the town, because there was nothing, literally *nothing*, like that here before him. And they complained that his gravy wanted salt.

He looked down at Miss Grierson's head, bobbing at his crotch. He'd momentarily forgotten what they were doing but abruptly, all the sensations flooded his mind and he was lost in it, the wetness and strangeness, that it was her, that it was here, in the dark, when his eyes were burning, his nose fizzing. The blinds were drawn on the windows. Lights flashing past, white noise outside, people in groups passing. The detritus of the evening's event was stacked all around the kitchen. He didn't need to come in tomorrowrowrow—

Flashes of light blossomed behind his lids as he bucked into her mouth, long-term tension pulsing out through his cock. He caught his breath and his work-obsessed mind finished the thought – he didn't need to come in tomorrow because the girls would do the washing up in the morning.

Fuck. He opened his eyes. Fuck. Even a blow job from a stranger was ruined by intrusive notes about the fucking staff rota. He was wired and angry again. A waste of a crime.

He looked down and saw Miss Grierson pull away. Then she did a very odd thing. It happened so quickly, just a second. Boyd instantly blinked, rerunning the action in his head, teasing the different movements apart because they didn't seem to fit together: first, she twisted away from him, turning the full three-sixty, fishing in her mouth for something. Then she turned back to face him and her hand was at her side, her face a picture of innocence. An air hostess smile, devoid of personal feeling, an obligation.

Boyd opened his eyes. It was odd because the movement was

so fluid. It seemed – he couldn't think of the word for a second but then it came to him – *professional.*

Time lag. Time slips. He hadn't taken cocaine for a long time but did remember time slips. This didn't feel like that though. Didn't have the guillotined sharpness in the middle.

Miss Grierson stood up and smiled at him. A silver trail across her cheek caught the light. She had a little snowy rim on her nostril.

'Let's go to my house,' she whispered. 'I've got plans for you.'

He glanced down and saw a baggy condom in her hand. She saw him looking at it. 'Dental dam,' she said. 'HIV.'

It wasn't a dental dam, though. It was a female condom, sort of. But shorter, sort of?

Boyd took his key out of the door shutter and stood up.

Now that, just there, that was a time slip. That did feel like a cut-out bit. He couldn't work out why that mattered really, until he turned and saw her smiling as she walked away uphill. Miss Grierson. For fuck's sake. Walking time lag.

Side by side, they took the wide road diagonally, each with their hands deep in their pockets, staying wide of each other in case they were spotted. Down a back road towards her house. Why had they gone uphill, he wondered, as they walked through moonshadows from overhanging trees. Her house was downhill from the café. Was it a short cut?

'Did you see someone down there?' he asked.

'What?'

'Why are we going this way?'

'Just . . . I like this.' She drew an arc over her head. 'The trees.' She smiled away from him, her eyes lingering on his face. Everything felt weird now. He was cold, she was odd. Was she a prostitute? What had she done for a living in America? In London?

'What did you do for a living in America?' He meant to ask her casually but it came out like a demand for payment.

'In America?'

'Yeah.'

They walked on for a bit.

'School teacher!' She sounded exclamatory herself, as if she was shouting a joke. But she wasn't smiling.

'Oh.'

They carried on, crossing so they were walking next to a high wall into someone's garden, on the grassy verge, even though the road was empty. They were keeping in the shadows, him following her. She did not want to be seen with him. That made him feel more comfortable. She was secretive. That was good.

He followed her across the road, down the side of her family grounds, through a garden gate at the side, which was fitted with a new padlock.

The gate shut behind him and Boyd found himself in the Grierson's massive garden. Everything was dead. Trellises of desiccated vine skeletons were nailed to the back wall. It looked like a vegetable torture chamber.

She saw him looking and dropped her hand to her side, the keys jangled in her hand.

'Lovely,' said Boyd of the midnight garden.

She looked at it and her lip curled distastefully.

'Don't you like it?'

She shrugged a shoulder. 'What's the point of it?'

'Making something.' He smiled. 'The point is a lovely garden.'

She nodded reluctantly. 'Yeah, I've never seen a gardener enjoy a garden, have you? It's never finished. They can't stop. It's work that makes work. Bit bloody pointless to me.'

He felt weird hearing her say that. It sounded so nihilistic, so contrary to all of the given values in this place.

They looked at each other in the dark, her face up to meet his, her eyes sad initially, becoming amused as the look lasted too long to mean nothing.

'What are we doing here?' asked Boyd.

'Having a dirty little fuck?' She laughed, self-mocking, sweet, and he realised the sinister overtone was just a mixture of coke and tiredness and worry because he'd never done this before. But he was enjoying it. And he'd done it now. And it wasn't going to get any better or worse if he left right away. And she had made him cum so he sort of owed her.

'Let's go inside,' he said.

She squinted down the garden. 'You sure? You're married. I'm not.'

'Is that an issue for you?'

She looked at the keys in her hand, separating them, laying them out on her palm. 'I've decided: I'm leaving. I don't belong here any more. I don't know where I do belong, but not here. Tonight I just want a bit of a high and a little fuck.' She looked at him, pleadingly. 'No bullshit afterwards. '

Something had happened to her, he could see it in her eyes. She'd had an affair and got burned. Boyd thought maybe the man told his wife. The wife would be angry. The wife would have blamed Susan and all she wanted was a fuck and a bit of tenderness and it was a damn shame.

Boyd bent down to kiss her on the lips. As he did, he felt a salt glaze of dried sweat crack on the back of his neck. His T-shirt, heavy with perspiration from the evening's work, peeled away from one of his underarms.

Boyd wanted more coke. He wanted a bit of tenderness and a nice, uncomplicated fuck that didn't have to be negotiated for with promises of time back for yoga practice. He wanted those things so much it didn't occur to him to wonder why Miss Grierson was moved to fuck a sweaty married guy, on the floor of her mother's conservatory, next to a hole in the floor that was shaped like an open grave.

Three fire engines were already addressing the blaze, but here came another. The fourth engine, heard in the distance, was coming from another station. The ear-splitting alarm came closer and closer until it was so loud Iain felt it in his eyes.

The Sailors' Rest was spewing smoke and flames out into the night. Firemen in beige jumpsuits unravelled hoses, adopting long-rehearsed formations around the engines. A warning call, lost in the howl of the fire, heralded the water and they fired it over the roof, controlling it.

Fresh water. It was useless.

Iain was wet. He didn't know if it was sea or spray from the hose. He leaned against the side of the building, facing the fire, his eyes smarting, his feet numb.

He watched, oblivious to the firemen shouting at him to get out of the street.

He ignored the police who arrived after the fire had been put out, when the smoke was thin and miserly and the street awash with blackened water.

He stayed as the ambulances arrived, two of them, and he watched them load the black body bags, one big, one small, and he watched them leave.

And by then it was three a.m. and he didn't know if he could stand any more. His feet were numb. His knees buckled. He slid onto his side on the cold wet pavement. She began to gnaw through his chest.

22

Morrow liked to get into the office ten minutes early to clear her head of shopping lists and resentments, politics and bullshit; to read reports and think. Reading and thinking were unquantifiable in budgetary terms so she had to do them in her own time. It was rare nowadays, with the boys up so early, but she'd managed it today. She tapped her computer out of sleep mode and opened her email. A Met report of yesterday's interview with Maria Arias.

Maria admitted meeting with Roxanna Fuentecilla the evening before. Roxanna came to her house, here, in Chesterfield Gardens, Mayfair. Roxanna was upset because she had argued with her partner, Robin. She missed her London friends and needed a chat with a girlfriend, *You know how girls are?* Morrow despised Arias's faux girlishness. She was kicking fifty up the arse, for Christ's sake. Ms Arias was at pains to point out to the officers that Mr Walker was much younger than her friend and probably just after her money. Arias knew that Roxanna Fuentecilla had no money of her own but the Met officers didn't know. They hadn't been briefed about Arias putting up the money for the business in Glasgow so they hadn't questioned her any further about it. They hadn't asked anything useful. They just listened to her excuses and left.

An addendum to the Met report was marked 'controlled access' and warned 'DI Alec Morrow' not to divulge the information in it to her crew or anyone not specifically notified by the investigation team. She had to type in her warrant card number and personal password to get it open. It informed her that the Fraud

Office were on the brink of seizing the Ariases' bank accounts, business and private. This department did know that Arias had put up the money for the Glasgow business and they wanted it all back. As soon as Fuentecilla was located, dead or alive, they were to be notified immediately.

Morrow read the addendum again. Police Scotland wouldn't be getting any of the proceeds. The money was being ring-fenced for either Fraud or the Met, she couldn't work out which.

On the last page of the same secret report there was a one-word response to Morrow's speculation about Fuentecilla's disappearance, the deliberate use of the seven-year sleeping period and the transfer of property back after the Declaration of Death under Scots law: *unlikely*. They hadn't even bothered to capitalise it.

She googled the book from Delahunt's desk the day before – *Property Trusts and Succession* – and followed a link to the Presumption of Death (Scotland) Act 1977. A summary of the legislation said that the person had to be missing for seven years with no sightings. The declaration could be raised earlier, but there had to be good reason to assume they had died. The action could only be raised by someone who had been resident in Scotland for a year. She couldn't see Robin Walker staying on if Roxanna was missing long-term. Morrow's guess was that they'd be counting on Delahunt, which meant he was in it up to his ears.

They had set it up perfectly. Roxanna had to disappear under suspicious circumstances so they could argue later that she had died, but not suspicious enough to prompt an investigation. Serious crime wouldn't normally be investigating an abandoned car. They were only involved because of the proceeds trail. She felt she had stumbled on an as-yet uncharted scam, but the Met had deemed it *unlikely*. She shut the file, as requested, and watched as the system locked it.

She had three minutes of thinking time left before the start of her shift. She sat with her face in her hands and tried to imagine a timeline for Roxanna's disappearance. Roxanna got up and got the kids ready Danny. Shit. Roxanna got up and Danny. Shit. Danny got up and got the kids ready and. Morrow looked up. Do it now.

She phoned the Southern General and asked for his ward. A nurse told her that Danny was stable. He'd had 'a good night'. She carried on describing the nature of his 'good night': good respiration, no complications from surgery, but Morrow was lost in the familiar phrase. Her oldest son had died when he was two and a half. A 'good night' was her fondest hope at one time. Just for one nurse or a doctor to smile at her when she came in to take over from Brian, for someone to say Gerald had a good night instead of 'unfortunately' and 'I'm afraid'. Danny McGrath didn't deserve good nights, but Morrow reminded herself that health was nothing to do with justice. The nurse said she could visit her brother but would need security clearance and would have to 'stand outside a physical barrier'.

Morrow thanked him and asked what had happened. Danny had been stabbed with a chair leg. His spleen had been removed. No, it wasn't an essential organ.

Morrow hung up, feeling slightly less guilty than before.

Three days ago Roxanna got up and got the kids ready and drove them to school. She fought with the kids in the car: was their father having an affair? Maria was attractive. Roxanna dropped the kids and drove to London to confront Maria. She came back late, overnight, but didn't go home to see her kids or phone to reassure them. She went to an empty field in Helensburgh and evaporated.

Morrow moved on to the file on the body in the loch yesterday. She ran and reran the footage from the golf course security camera for the morning. It told an interesting story. The forensics on Mr Cole's boat had found clumps of the dead woman's hair trapped in a cleat on the deck. They were testing for blood residue but the boat had been hosed down.

Gruesome photographs of the body in situ, on the dock, then

lying on a slab. She was mumsy, Glaswegian. She looked like every dumpy woman in every queue in every supermarket in the city. The night shift had checked: her fingerprints were not on file and no one fitting her description had been reported missing.

Morrow pulled up the effects photographs. She looked again at a thumbnail of the Injury Claims 4 U lanyard. Another scaled photograph was a close-up of a necklace she had been wearing. It was a gold chain, nothing special, with a crucifix and a Star of David threaded together. Mixed marriage or hedging her bets on the afterlife, maybe.

The report on Fuentecilla's car was more interesting. The food bag from the glovebox had nearly two grams of what, superficially, was cocaine. It was enough for a fairly extravagant night, or a long drive back from London, but it was a personal-use amount. It wasn't enough for a dealer. There were a couple of good prints on the outside of the bag and they had been lifted and were being run this morning. Morrow was right about one thing: the car had been cleaned with alcohol wipes.

Morrow sat back and closed her eyes: wipes were professional, but only quite professional. It would have been less clumsy to leave no trace, no alcohol residue. The clumsiness could be deliberate, so that Delahunt had 'suspicious circumstance' to support an early Declaration of Death. But maybe she was giving them too much credit. Maybe it was *unlikely*.

She dialled Simmons' office number, realising after the first ring that it was seven a.m. and Simmons probably wouldn't be in. But Simmons did answer, helloing with a resigned sigh.

'Simmons? I was going to leave a message. I didn't think you'd be in yet.'

'I'm not "in yet". I haven't been home *yet*. We had a fire in the town. Two dead, father and young daughter.'

'Oh, God, I'm sorry.'

'Yeah,' said Simmons.

'Domestic?'

'Commercial property.'

'Insurance claim?' Morrow asked hopefully.

'Unlikely. The owner had remortgaged his house to pay for building work, they were nearly finished. He was inside with his daughter and they died in the fire.'

'Accelerant?'

'Lots. Fire service say there were petrol fumes everywhere but we'll have to wait for chemical analysis to be sure. Anyway, what did you call for? Is it urgent because I'd like to get back.'

'Sure.' Morrow sat back. 'The golf course body traces back to our case. We'll be taking it.'

Simmons was so relieved that she sounded almost pleasant, but not quite. When Morrow told her she was about to interview Andrew Cole, Simmons grunted OK and hung up.

Morrow walked briskly through the front lobby, down past the locker rooms to the back bar and the holding cells.

The desk sergeant was at his post, bright and perky despite being at the end of a long night shift.

'Ma'am.'

'Is Andrew Cole awake yet?'

He glanced at a computer screen below the lip of the desk. 'There he is, having a wee cup of tea.'

Morrow slipped around the back of the desk and looked at the screen. Andrew Cole was sitting on a bare plastic mattress, sipping from a large tin mug.

'What happened to his bed sheets?'

'Had to take them out.' George looked at the night log on another screen, running his finger down to the right entry: 'At . . . five oh eight a.m., when "Mr Cole became very disturbed and there was some concern for his safety".' He smiled and looked up.

Morrow was surprised. 'Suicide watch?'

George gave a dismissive wave. '*Very* briefly. Probably the wrong call but better safe than sorry.'

Back on the screen Cole sipped from his mug. He seemed calm now. 'What was he doing to make you think that?'

George read again: 'A lot of "shouting" and "swearing", "banging on the cell door". Said he "couldn't stand it", "wanted his mum to die", mad stuff like that.' He shook his head. 'Wee bit of concern. It passed quickly. He's never slept since then.'

On the screen in a fog of grainy grey, Andrew Cole took another sip and looked into his mug of tea. If he was on suicide watch the tea would be lukewarm at best. Still he cupped it between two hands, trying to warm himself.

23

Iain hadn't slept. He didn't have an appointment. He had just turned up at Dr Neiman's early morning surgery. Dr Neiman. The name had rolled around and around his head all the way back to town. It became an anchor, a thing to think. Dr Neiman. He couldn't think those other names, her and him, the black bags. He couldn't.

He had spent the night walking, taking the Gareloch Road, following the water. He walked blindly for hours, through woods and towns, past marinas, inland to hillsides, always following the same road. His feet were numb. It rained. He was wet and then he was dry again. He didn't remember turning around but he was heading back towards the town as the sun came up.

He sat down in the surgery waiting room. For a moment it felt wonderful, as if his hips and thigh bones were melting into the seat, but then a spurt of adrenalin forced him to his feet again and made him pace. It wasn't easy to move around. There were a lot of people waiting, workers and navy staff, kids in school uniform, feet to step over. He did a couple of circuits of the central island of chairs until the receptionist called his name, waving him over to the doctor's office door.

He passed the receptionist and saw that he was scaring her. Was he moving too fast? No, he thought, no. Dr Neiman. Dr Neiman. She waved him down the corridor to the doctor's office. Iain was moving normally, but maybe he was a bit alarming. His manner was alarming because he was coming apart.

Dr Neiman stood up at his desk when Iain slid into the room. The doctor was scared too.

'Mr Fraser!' said Dr Neiman, his German accent lending a clipped, ordered tone to the name. 'Have you been burned?'

Iain stared at him, his mind blank, feeling behind himself for the wall. Conscious suddenly of the blackness of his hands smearing the woodchip behind him, he let go. Adrift, he reached for the chair, the patient's chair, at an angle to Dr Neiman's desk. Iain held the back of it and used it as a guide rope to pull himself in. He dropped onto the chair, feeling his hip bones melt again.

'Were you in the fire, Mr Fraser?'

'No. Near.'

'I can see that very clearly. You are covered in blackness, Mr Fraser.'

'Blackness?'

'Soot.' Dr Neiman stayed on his feet, talking over Iain. He was very tall and thin. Iain found it was easier to talk to his stomach. His eyes were hard to look into.

'Please. May I examine you?'

Iain sat limp while the doctor checked his forearms for burns, listened to this heart, took his blood pressure. He was used to this, allowing himself to be examined, sitting while prison doctors took bloods and checked his balls for lumps. Handing over responsibility for the chaotic tangle of threads to someone else was a relief, if only for a moment.

The doctor asked him to lift his polo shirt and he breathed on the metal disc of his stethoscope before placing it on Iain's chest. He said something about cold.

'Haven't got a cold,' said Iain.

'Mmm.' The doctor listened. Then he took the plugs out of his ears and asked Iain to lift his shirt at the back so he could listen. 'I said this was cold. I just breathe on it, like this . . .' he gave a little puff, Iain couldn't see him, he was behind him now, 'and it warms it a little bit.'

The metal disc was on his back.

Iain could feel her in there, no longer writhing and angry. She was bigger, grown, gnawing joylessly. Iain imagined the grind of her jaws, her face tight and tired.

'I hear just a very slight crackle, Mr Fraser, not low down. It could be a little smoke inhalation. How's your back?'

'Still sore. Here.' He reached up between his shoulder blades and drew the hand down his back. 'And now I've got pain here.' He touched his side.

The doctor nodded and frowned. 'How long for, the pain in the side?'

It sounded innocent but Dr Neiman was a ponderous man.

'Few days.'

'Are you coughing?'

'A bit. But I've been smoking again so—'

'Ah, no. You must stop. Promise me.'

Iain shrugged and muttered that he would.

Dr Neiman nodded, as if that was agreed, and sat down in his chair. He began to write something on the computer. Iain felt a burst of sudden pride, noticing for the first time that he had managed to bring himself here, to the doctor. The thing inside him would hate that. He'd had the presence of mind to do that. Iain realised then that the doctor was looking at him, had spoken to him, and he wasn't responding.

'Sorry?' said Iain.

'You are dishevelled and smell heavily of smoke,' said Dr Neiman, precise about his diction. 'You were at the fire last night?'

The doctor's eyes narrowed. He knew Iain's history. He knew he'd been in prison. He suspected him.

'I was at the dinner dance. I saw the smoke and went down.' The doctor nodded, encouraging him to say more, but Iain had no more to say. 'I went down,' he repeated. 'My best friend. Niece? In fire. Died.' He stopped talking, understood the impossibility of being heard, of articulating a loss so deep. And he knew it didn't matter anyway, explaining. And he sat for a bit, his blackened hands open on his knees like a beggar.

He looked up after a while and found the doctor still nodding and waiting. Everyone complained about doctor's appointments being short but this felt interminable.

Eventually the doctor said, 'So, what brought you here to see me today?'

Slug in my lungs. Snakes in lung. Iain didn't know how to express it: '. . . *upset*.'

'Would you say you are depressed, perhaps?'

Iain got stuck on the word *perhaps*. He meant to draw the doctor's attention to the word, how odd it sounded, but the doctor took it as confirmation.

'And you seem a little confused, also.' He raised his eyebrows in a question. 'Is that the case, would you say?'

He was right. Iain was confused. Iain nodded. 'I am.'

'Did you stay at the fire all night?'

'I was. I was there all night. I couldn't . . .' A wave rolled up from the base of his spine, engulfing him in sorrow, throwing him forward over his knees, cranking great dry sobs up from his balls. He waited for tears to come out of his face but none did. It was stuck in his throat. He sat up and found the doctor's hand on his. It was inappropriate, not the gesture of a doctor to a patient, but a kindness from one person to another and it was a comfort.

'I don't know,' burbled Iain, 'I don't know what.'

'You are overwhelmed.'

'I am.'

'I think you have had a very upsetting night.'

'I have.'

'You had one psychotic episode before, when you were in prison?'

Gripped with the sudden conviction that the doctor was going to put him in hospital Iain stood up and knocked the chair over. 'I'm OK.'

But the doctor didn't get up or try to wrestle him to the ground. He didn't call prison officers from outside the door to restrain him, or inject antipsychotics that made the world move slower and his feet heavy. The doctor just sat where he was and looked straight at Iain.

'This could be a recurrence. We have to be prepared for that. But it might not be. Everyone is very upset by this fire. Many patients . . . You have to know that you are not alone.' And then Iain saw, or thought he saw, a tear well up in the doctor's eye. But the doctor looked at his computer screen and blinked a lot and when he looked back it was gone.

'Mr Fraser, please, sit down on the chair.'

Following orders, Iain righted the chair, sat down, didn't know what to do with his legs, tried crossing them but got confused and gave up.

'I would like to write you a prescription for one day only, yes?'

Iain nodded dumbly.

The doctor pointed at the screen. 'Have you taken this medication before?'

Iain nodded. He'd had it before and it was a nice sleep you got with it. He didn't get it on prescription though.

'So, I want you to take,' the doctor was writing on his computer, tip tap tip tap, 'one pill three times today, again in the morning and come to see me tomorrow morning. We will see if the anxiety abates. Do you know what I mean by that?'

'Goes away,' said Iain, a little insulted.

'Yes, goes away. And I want you to be very careful with yourself. I want you to make sure that you sleep and eat regularly. OK?'

A pink prescription rolled out of the printer. The doctor took a silver fountain pen out of his top jacket pocket, wrote on the paper and handed it to Iain.

Iain went to take it but the doctor didn't let go of his end. He made Iain look at him. 'Go and get these from the chemist now. Take one and only one. Go home and wash and try to sleep. When you wake up take another one. Then a third pill, you will take it tonight. Do you understand?'

'Yes.'

'Tomorrow I would like you to take the last one and come back, first thing. Nine a.m., am I clear?'

'Yes.'

'Come back and see me.' He stood up, lifting a hand to the door. Iain looked at the hand, read it and oh! He understood. He was to get up also. He did.

Then the doctor shook his hand. 'You have witnessed a horrific thing, Mr Fraser. It has been a bad night for everyone. You must look after yourself today and be careful.'

Iain saw the doctor's eyes then, saw that Dr Neiman understood the horror of what Iain had seen and why he stayed at the fire. Iain felt heard and he felt better.

He left the surgery, walking through a backstreet that smelled of burnt paper and hair. The smell of the fire clung to the town, sticking to walls and streets despite the wind's best efforts.

Iain slunk downhill to a chemist, clutching a paper promise of succour. He kept his eyes down and passed a bank, a grocer's, a charity shop. He stopped at a newsagent's window. A poster for the local paper:

FIRE KILLS TWO:
HEL. MOURNS

24

Before the questioning began and the tapes had been installed, Andrew Cole said he definitely didn't want a lawyer. Now, when they asked him to say it again for the benefit of the tape, he didn't sound sure.

Morrow and Kerrigan sat across from him, waiting for the answer. Cole looked anxiously at the tape recorder, an ominous black plastic machine fitted to the wall. Morrow knew that a hesitant answer on the tape could make the court think the accused had been leaned on. Sometimes the sharper accused were deliberately ambivalent or upset at interview, knowing they might give themselves later grounds for appeal.

She didn't know Andrew Cole but suspected that he would have access to lawyers with the time and motivation to read the files before they came in for interviews.

'Mr Cole, if you've changed your mind, please feel free to tell us and we'll stop the interview right now.'

'No,' he said finally, 'sorry, I'm just, I don't want one.'

'OK. You sure now?'

'Yes.'

'Not too late to change your mind.'

He seemed to relax at that, as if all he had wanted was reassurance.

'Fine.' He gave Kerrigan a charming smile, sat back and opened his hands to Morrow. 'Ask me anything.'

Morrow glanced at her notes. An odd boyish wee man. He didn't seem to have a grasp on the shit storm about to engulf him but he had been in prison before. He couldn't be entirely naive.

'Mr Cole, you called the police yesterday—'

'And I *must*,' he interrupted her and turned to the tape machine on the wall. 'Sorry,' he told it, 'but I must apologise for yesterday and um, the, you know . . . ?' He looked back at Morrow, asking whether they might just keep this between them? And, perhaps, not tell the tape machine he'd been spliffed? Please?

'You called the police,' said Morrow patiently. 'From the boat. Can you tell me what happened there?'

Mr Cole smiled warmly and nodded, as if they had agreed to collude in covering up his parole violation. He launched into a prepared story about being told to go out and clear some dead wood floating in view of the course. Unsightly debris in the water. There had been a storm earlier in the week and some branches had come down. Andrew did as he was told. He was fishing some branches out when he saw a foot in the water, by the bank. Thinking it was a shop dummy, he went over to try to pull it out. He got closer and realised it was human and thought she was a suicide. But then he saw, you know . . . He ran a flat hand over the top of his head, cringing beneath it, looking sick. His body language was right for an accidental find. She wondered if he could have blacked out and killed her.

'What made you think of suicide?'

'Well, the south end of the loch is a terribly small place, really. If anyone goes missing everyone knows about it. We'd all be watching out for someone if there had been an accident of some kind . . .'

'Tell me a bit about yourself, Andrew. I understand you've been in prison?'

'Unfortunately, yes.' Mr Cole gave a solemn nod.

'What were you convicted of?'

'Well, *sadly*,' he said it as if it was a stage direction for his performance, 'possession of cocaine.'

Morrow grinned at his expression. 'That is very "sadly".'

'Yes, it is.' He made himself look sadder yet, unaware that he was being mocked. 'A very great shame.'

'A shame that you got caught?' asked Kerrigan sharply. She was less charmed by him than Morrow.

'No, officer, it's a shame that I did that. I had every chance, you know? Great school, great family.' He held his hands up helplessly. 'Threw it all away.'

Morrow was enjoying Mr Cole's performance, not because his act was particularly credible, more that it was a refreshing change from cursing and silence or threats of violence. She wanted to prompt him into saying other daft things but they didn't really have the time.

'So, you did three years of a six-year sentence – that's a lot of time.'

'But I got out early. Exemplary behaviour.'

'Three years, though. Serious offence.'

He wobbled his head ambivalently. 'There were a lot of extra-judicial factors in the sentence being so harsh.'

Kerrigan was exasperated. 'Did you resist arrest?'

'No, I mean *political* factors. Reasons why my sentence was so long. My family know a lot of people in the judiciary. Bad blood.'

Kerrigan sucked her pointy little teeth with annoyance. Morrow watched his eyes flick around the table as he theorised. The truth was that Cole got a stiff six years because he'd had so much cocaine on him. All sentencing was carefully monitored for parity. Judges couldn't make it up on whim. Cole really believed though, that it was about who knew who and what they thought about him and his family. He was in an odd little world of his own, a charming one, compelling because it was so jarring, like stumbling across a bizarre foreign language soap opera.

'Mr Cole, what I'm wondering about is who let them in?'

He smiled and shook his head. 'Who let, sorry, *what?*'

Morrow spoke slowly: 'Who let them in? To the golf course. Who gave them the code to get into the grounds?'

A titter of polite confusion. 'So sorry . . . ?'

Morrow sighed and stared him out. 'You trashed your cell this morning.'

Another titter. 'Sadly—'

'Sadly, the golf course don't let anyone in without the code or a visual ID from security staff. They've got CCTV film of a blue van with the plates covered up stopping at the service gates that morning. An arm comes out of the window and types the security code into the keypad.'

Mr Cole looked confused. He opened his mouth to speak but thought better of it.

'We checked with estates management. They didn't ask you to go out and clear debris from the water.'

'Well,' very quietly now, 'it *is* part of my job.'

'You said you'd been "sent out to clear debris". You weren't. You went out because you knew something was out there.'

'I did not.'

'You knew she was there. Did you kill her?'

'No! God, no!'

'Take her out on the boat and kill her?'

'No! I'm not *capable*.'

'OK. If you just tootled out yesterday to do a wee job there'd be no traces of her on your boat. But Forensics found her hair trapped under a cleat. They're looking for traces of blood now but they said the deck had been hosed down. If she was anywhere near your boat before she died they'll find out.'

Cole was badly shaken and Morrow felt that now was a good time to draw his eye to a way out.

'Look, Andrew, when someone unaccustomed goes to prison they're befriended by people they wouldn't normally be friends with. Sometimes, after the sentence is over, those relationships are used to make them do things.'

177

He looked wary.

'People,' she prompted again. 'Nice people like yourself – and we see this *a lot* – get caught up in things.'

But Andrew was refusing to move towards the open door. He knew it was there, she could see that, but he had decided not to name and blame.

'It's a very prestigious golf course,' said Morrow. 'I'm quite surprised they'd give a job and a tithe cottage to someone with your record.'

'Well,' he shook his head, 'it was my mother . . .'

'She got you the job there?'

'She knows . . . everyone. It was a favour.'

'Have you been dealing cocaine to members of the club?'

'Fuck no!'

She knew he hadn't. The club wouldn't tolerate a stoner with a criminal record dealing on the premises. They would tolerate a dealer waiter or a groundsman dealing, as long as he was discreet and got the members what they wanted.

'See, this can be big or this can be small. Depends how willing you are to give us information. Who did you give the security code to?'

He wouldn't say a name.

'Mr Cole, we can just go through a list of names in Shotts Prison and see who you've been in touch with. My own guess is you texted the code to someone?'

He put a clenched fist over his mouth, elbow on the table, red-rimmed eyes staring furiously at the wall.

'You won't say a name. Maybe you're afraid?'

His eyes flashed up her, angry at the suggestion. She pretended not to have noticed.

'I see. Can we agree that you gave the code to someone? It'll save me calling up your phone records.'

He nodded. She made him say 'yes' for the tape, even though they were being filmed. It was good to get them to speak.

'Did you agree with this unnamed party that you'd go out on your boat and "accidentally" find the body?'

His face flushed pink suddenly and he shouted at the table, '*I didn't know what was going to happen!*'

She could picture him trashing his cell now, cornered and desperate and feeling he had nothing to lose. Cole couldn't cope with being held responsible for his actions. It was his weak spot.

She patted the table in front of him, rhythmically, as if it was his back. 'Andrew, it's OK. It's OK.'

He looked to her, saw that she was still framing him as an object of concern. His panic abated.

'It's OK,' she said again, giving him a tissue out of her pocket. He blew his nose with a comical little 'parp' that left him shuddering.

Everything about Cole was small and sweet and unthreatening. She thought about him ripping his cell apart this morning, doing a long sentence, cleaning his house of drug paraphernalia before going out to look for a dead body in the water.

Police interviews were intense. Like a job interview or a first date, people were profoundly self-conscious because a bad impression could have lifelong consequences. The pressure meant that they often presented themselves paradoxically and, instead of brushing over flaws, insisted the opposite. 'No one fucks with me' usually meant 'People have been fucking with me'. 'I don't care what anyone thinks' meant 'I care what everyone thinks'. Thinking about that made Morrow consider her own frantic insistence that she didn't care about her brother. The admission made her mood drop. She looked up again. Here was Mr Cole, telling and retelling the same story about himself in different ways: I'm a harmless little man, I'm Mr Mole. All my sins are crimes of omission and good faith, I'm not to blame and I am sorry.

'Are you going to name the person you gave the code to?'

He shook his head, remembered the tape and said, 'No.'

'Because you're afraid of them?'

He smiled. '*No.*'

There was no fear in there. Ridicule perhaps, but not for the person he'd given the code to. The ridicule was for Morrow.

'Why won't you tell me their name?'

He drew a parallel line back and forth on the table top with his finger. Mr Cole's paradox was that he was not chaotic. He was calculating. He was going back to prison and knew what it meant to go back as a grass. It meant a full sentence in segregation units. Years in the segs, with no one for company but child rapists and the nutters who wouldn't survive gen. pop. He wasn't chaotic and he wasn't going to budge.

'OK,' she said softly. 'Tell me what *you* did. You texted the code, let them in and, what, *met* them?'

'No.' He had worked this out in the night, a legalistic version of the story that would make him the hapless patsy. 'I texted someone the code. Lots of people on the estate do that. But I stayed in my house.'

'And? What did you think was going to happen?'

'I'd said they could come in and use my boat. I thought they were dropping something—' He broke off, lost in considerations of parole violations, admissible and inadmissible facts.

'I'm not interested in what you thought, Andrew,' said Morrow. 'What actually happened?'

When he spoke his voice was deeper and sadder, he sounded his age. 'I was in my house, in bed, and I heard a scream. It woke me. They'd asked me to leave the key on the boat. I thought they were going to drop something— But then I heard her scream. I knew. I stayed indoors. I heard the boat go out and heard it come back. I stayed in. I was in all day. I was hiding in the back room. I heard them leave but it took me a whole day to come out. I went to look at the boat. Blood, *everywhere.*'

'There doesn't seem to be blood there now.'

'Washed it. Hosed it.'

'Why?'

He shrugged one shoulder.

'Did you know her?'

He shook his head.

'Can you say that for the benefit of the tape, please, Andr—'

'*BITCH,* I DID NOT KNOW *HER.*' His eyes were so narrow they were watering. He caught himself, widened his eyes and acted as if he hadn't said it.

But she'd seen him now, the real Andrew Cole. A bitter angry little man who wasn't going to be told what to do by filth like her, or sympathised with by filth like her, or ordered around by filth like her.

She dropped the sympathetic mask and looked at him, cold. 'You're going back to prison.'

Morrow smiled warmly because they both knew what that meant: he would be ordered around by filth like her. He would be watched as he sat on the toilet by filth like her. He would have to beg filth like her for soap and shampoo and plastic forks. And he was going there for a long time.

They sat for a moment, she smiling, watching all the fight go out of him.

'Why did you stay indoors for a whole day?'

He took a deep breath.

'Andrew? You must have known. Otherwise, why'd you have to get off your face to go out looking for her?'

He looked despairingly at the ceiling, fat self-pitying tears rolled down his spoiled boyish face. 'I didn't. It was that scream. Wasn't a normal scream. Not a person scream. Like an animal. Like an animal in a trap.'

25

Shoppers stared at Iain in the busy chemist's shop. He was sitting in a chair beneath the high pharmacy counter, waiting for his prescription. He didn't care that they were staring. He looked a mess but he didn't care because the doctor had touched his hand and was upset too. He wasn't alone.

The doors to the street crashed open. A skinny guy, young, Iain didn't know him, stormed straight for the counter. He was limping, swinging his arms, and scattered the women looking at make-up.

Methadone!

Stamping from foot to foot, he leaned all his weight on the counter, lifting his feet off the floor, clucking. The pharmacist asked if he'd like to come to the cubicle but – just gaesit. 'M fucking ganting.

He necked the clear green liquid from the measuring cup. Iain watched the make-up-perusing women leave, muttering, gossiping. They'd know the boy's family, who he belonged to, the whole back story.

The boy was thin. Even his tongue looked thin as it rolled around inside of the plastic cup, licking the residue from the ridged bottom. He went to put it down but spotted another little green pool and lifted it to lick again. Then he dropped it on the counter, gave the pharmacist an angry glare and stormed out, slamming the door again as he left.

The pharmacist waited until the doors were shut and he'd passed the window. She looked at the measuring cup. Bending down, she lifted a small bin and used her elbow to knock the empty cup into it, catching Iain's eye.

'Saliva,' she explained, disgusted. She looked at him, hopeful, and said, 'Are you a fireman?'

Iain didn't answer. She decided he was and started to cry.

'Oh my God,' she said, hoarse, 'that Lea-Anne Ray. My God, she was a right wee ticket.'

They couldn't look at each other. They stayed still, an ocean of shop between them, until the door to the street opened and a woman came in. They each hid their faces.

Iain's prescription arrived in a neat paper bag. He wanted to take a pill in the shop but thought he might remind the pharmacist of the methadone addict. He liked being mistaken for a good guy. He thanked her and walked casually out of the shop.

Outside he ducked down a lane, around a corner, standing by the bins, ripped the paper bag open and took out the smoked glass bottle. He pressed down on the lid, felt the mechanical whirr, a clock being wound to work again. It was quite a big pill but he swallowed it dry. It lodged in his throat leaving a catch there, and then slid down. The ghost of the pill hurt his throat. He swallowed again. Was it down? Probably.

If it was any good it would take ten minutes. If it was no good after twenty minutes he could always take another one. He went out onto the street and started to walk slowly, watching his feet, gauging his mood with every step. A little better. A weak sun warmed the street. The smell was lifting. He felt a little better.

He felt calm enough to lift his head and look around. A cluster of women at a street corner looked tearfully down to the water front and talked in low voices, hands covering their mouths. Pensioners in the cafés looked sad and worn. Even 4x4 drivers looked upset and craned to see the fire brigade tape at the end of Sinclair Street.

He walked down towards the water. On the esplanade, a block away from the blackened Sailors' Rest, stood a mobile police unit with shiny aluminium stairs down into the street. A cop on guard outside looked expectantly around the street but no one would meet his eye. His hands were clasped behind his back, his feet splayed. He'd been there for a while. Iain saw a man steer his wife away, making her cross the street. No one would make a move until Mark Barratt got back. The town was waiting for orders.

Iain had no right to feel righteous. He wasn't doing anything either. He was no better than them. Annie and Eunice were all that was left. Iain couldn't believe he hadn't thought of them before now. The grannies would be distraught. He turned uphill and headed east, squeezing the pill bottle in his pocket, willing the medication to dull his perception.

Across the road, through a charity shop window display of crystal vases and dun pewter tankards, Susan Grierson watched him wish.

26

Cadogan Street was in the old commercial district of Glasgow city centre. Monumental Victorian office buildings in blood-red sandstone faced-off across narrow streets. They were tall, blank and imposing. Busy with early morning commuters, the street was a bland string of doorways into the bright lobbies of dull commercial enterprises, the tedium broken by occasional sandwich bars and coffee shops. Office windows above crackled with rancorous strip lights.

The Injury Claims 4 U office was through a glass door. The concierge had been told to expect them first thing and he let them in, directing them across a grey lobby.

'Early,' he said vaguely, nodding at his watch.

It was ten to eight in the morning. They needed to talk to the Injury office staff but two of them already had other jobs. They had agreed to come in before work.

The concierge led them to a cramped afterthought of a lift. 'Eighth floor. The only door on the landing.'

The doors slid shut and the lift rose slowly. The eighth floor made the grey lobby downstairs look glamorous. A chipped door sagged open. It was painted in battleship-grey emulsion and had a metal strip on it that read *I4U*.

They stepped into a reception area that looked and smelled as if someone had been chain-smoking in it for thirty years. Everything was tinged brown, the carpet, the desk, the chair. Even the pale blue hessian walls were overlaid with yellow.

'Didn't expect this,' said Morrow, quietly. 'Not at all.'

She had imaged sleek, handsome Roxanna in quite a different

workplace. Somewhere with glass partitions, designer furniture and other office luxuries, like breathable air.

'No wonder they don't like Glasgow,' said McGrain, his civic pride offended by the state of the place.

Looking at the office, it seemed obvious that Fuentecilla had always intended to shut it down. If she had been planning to stay she would have moved offices. She would have bought furniture. She would have had the place painted or, at the very least, opened a window.

'Hello?' called McGrain.

A sudden sound of bubbling water caught their attention. They followed the noise around the corner and found a small staffroom with a full kettle boiling on top of a small fridge. Three tea-stained cups were lined up by the kettle, each with a tea bag slumped forlornly in a finger of milk. Looking up at them guiltily from a round table were the three staff members they had called in, a woman and two men, all in their twenties. A half-eaten packet of Bourbon biscuits sat in front of them on the table.

Morrow and McGrain introduced themselves and showed their ID badges.

Maxine Bradford kept her hands clamped between her knees as if she didn't fully trust them. She had curly blond hair and far too much make-up for the hour, or indeed any hour, apart from dress-up night at a social club for clowns.

Lorrie Whittle held up a hand as he introduced himself, ducking his head, as if he was embarrassed. The other two were dressed for work but Lorrie was wearing grey trackie bottoms and a sweat shirt. He didn't have a job yet.

The third man stood up and straightened his suit jacket. 'Jim Moonie.' He held his hand out to shake and made you-can-trust-me eye contact, the convention of his profession. He shook hands with Morrow, then McGrain and capped it with a habitual, but inappropriate, 'Delighted you could come.' He knew it was wrong and sat back down, admonishing himself.

'OK.' Morrow took charge. 'Well, thanks very much for coming in so early, all of you. Very kind. We just need a general chat. Can we sit down somewhere?'

Moonie offered her his chair and then brought two more chairs in from a nearby office, setting them around the table. Tea was offered and refused. The biscuits were offered and McGrain took one.

'Did you find her?' asked Maxine, a little excited. 'Is she dead?'

McGrain shook his head. 'We haven't found Roxanna Fuentecilla.'

'We found someone, but not her.' Morrow put a photograph of the Star of David and the crucifix on the table. 'Do you recognise this?'

They stared at it for a moment.

'Is that Hettie's?' Maxine suggested.

Lorrie touched the picture. 'Loads of folk wear that sort of thing.' He picked up the photo and handed it back to Morrow, repeating: 'Loads of folk wear that sort of thing.' As if she hadn't heard him.

'Loads of folk who work here?'

They were shocked at the implication.

'The woman who was wearing this necklace was found dead. She had this in her pocket.' She put the photo of the lanyard on the table.

The effect was immediate. Maxine gave off a little scream and said 'Oh my God', once to Lorrie, once to Jim, once to Morrow and McGrain. Lorrie blinked back insistent tears and couldn't take his eyes off the picture.

Jim took an exact copy of the lanyard out of his pocket and put it on the table. It had an ID badge attached to it with his photo on one side and a magnetic strip for the door entry on the other. 'That's for a pass, to get in the front door. We've all got them.'

Morrow nodded. 'Is there a personnel file for Hettie?'

Lorrie Whittle muttered that he knew where they were. They

followed him in a back room, where the firm's records were kept. The forensic accountants had been through these files with a camera and sharp eye and found nothing very much at all. Whittle took a file from the grey personnel cabinet.

Hester Kirk had been made redundant as soon as Fuentecilla took over. She had worked out her contract and left three weeks ago. A small passport photo was attached at the top right-hand corner of the file. Morrow recognised her as the body in the water. She was chubby, heavy-chested, and wore the necklace in the photo. Her hair was dyed blonde and pulled back in a ponytail. She had the expression of someone caught off guard by an automated photo booth, her mouth loose, one eye slightly closed. Her home address was in Clydebank.

Back in the kitchen, Morrow asked who had been here for the longest. Jim said it was him, he'd been here for a year and a half.

An office was found. Jim Moonie sat in a stiff chair holding tight to the sides.

'Jim, what can you tell us about what's been going on here?'

Jim looked from Morrow to McGrain. 'How do you mean?'

'Just tell us the story of what's happened here. We'd be interested to know how it looks from your perspective.'

'OK. Hmm.' He considered the proposition for a moment. 'Well, the office is shut. That's all we know.'

'You were here before Roxanna?'

'Aye. Bob Ashe was the owner before her. Injury claims. That was the business. Not squeaky clean, always, but you probably know that already. It was low-level stuff, not organised insurance fraud. Not really.'

'We know. We're not really interested in that. We want to know what happened when Roxanna got here.'

'Well.' He smacked his lips. 'In they come, out he goes. He calls the office together, looking well-nervous, here's your new boss, cheerio. No warning nor nothing. Off he goes to live in Miami.'

'Did that seem like something he'd been planning?'

'No. But he's got grandweans there. He was back and forth. If he was going anywhere it was there.'

'No, I mean selling up and leaving?'

'Not at all. He hasn't even sold his house yet, I know it's still on the market. I see it in the listings in the papers every week.'

'Where did he live?'

'Helensburgh. Market's dead out there, until after the vote. No one knows what's going to happen, do they?'

Morrow got him to write the address down for her.

'Was the house for sale before he announced he was leaving?'

'No. You wouldn't sell out there just now. But it seemed like something he couldn't resist. Like he'd been given a big bung to fuck off, excuse me. Then she takes over. Knows nothing about the business except who's on the fiddle and she wants them out.'

'Hester Kirk?'

'Hettie was the Queen of the Scamsters. I'll be frank with ye, I loved it when Hettie got the boot. I liked her personally, but she was a robbing fucker, excuse me. I thought we were going straight. There's a good living in this game if you do it right. But if you're willing to do it wrong there's a killing in it. Hettie was always giving me earfuls about do this do that, bring your numbers up, you're dragging us down. But it's illegal, you know? Well, of course you know, you're the polis. I'm not religious or anything. I'm just not a robbing fuck, excuse me. I just don't do that sort of thing. So, I'd had a hard time but then Fuentecilla's come in, seemed to be cleaning up the business. Got rid of the robbing fucks, excuse me.'

'Like Hester?'

'Exactly, like Hettie. She was the first one out. We get paid on commission for claims, you know? Temptation is to pad it out. Hettie gave in to temptation. And backhanders.' He looked guilty suddenly. 'It's OK to tell you this, isn't it? Since she's, you know . . .'

'Dead?'

'Aye. Dead.'

'Did Fuentecilla tell you what she was doing? Was there a meeting or anything?'

'No. But it was obvious because of who got the boot. We all got the message.'

'Fuentecilla didn't say anything about income or the firm's sources of income or anything like that?'

'She wouldn't bother to tell us. She's quite snooty, isn't she? Anyway, it's her firm now so she can do what she likes. But they weren't cleaning it up, were they? Because then they told us all to fuck off, excuse me.'

'How did Hester Kirk react to being laid off?'

Jim said Hettie'd been there for, maybe, two years? She was kind of an angry woman anyway, you know? Divorced. Her ex was a junkie and tried to rob her a couple of times. Well, now she was furious. Said she'd never get another job like this. Her redundancy package was the legal minimum. Said she wasn't going to take that lying down. She knew all about the business and who was this Spanish cunt anyway, excuse him.

'Anyway, we all got our books last week. Rent's paid. Another firm's moving in next week.'

'Fuentecilla paid you all off?'

'Aye. Last week.' His lip curled. 'Never even bothered to tell us face to face. Just left letters and final payslips on everyone's desk. The rest of us stopped coming in. She's daft, really. I mean, it's a partnership. If the firm goes down with bags of debt she has to pay them out of her own pocket.'

'We checked for debts; I thought the firm was square?'

'Oh, it can't be.' Jim smiled. 'You don't know about her spending spree. All the purchases.'

Morrow looked around the poor office. 'What was she buying?'

'Land,' said Jim. 'And I only know because Hettie'd told me.

Broke into the filing cabinets one night, in the back office – she's double wide – found letters from estate agents, deeds of sale.'

Morrow stood up. 'Can you show me?'

The back office was across the reception area. Fuentecilla had put her own office as far away from the rest of the staff as possible. Jim opened the door tentatively, as though his Spanish beauty of a boss might still be in there. He reached in and turned the light on.

Clean. A glass desk with a purple Bang and Olufsen phone standing upright. A transparent chair. A wall of red filing cabinets with drawers of differing sizes, all with the same designer name on them in steel lettering.

The forensic accountants hadn't been in here. Hester had been. She was angry when she searched this office and had used a chisel to jimmy the cabinets open. Papers were scattered all over the floor. Morrow wouldn't have been able to look at them without a warrant but since it was a suspected break-in she could look at anything she liked.

Morrow and McGrain wandered from pile to pile, touching nothing. Purchase orders and title deeds, conveyancing reports. All for undeveloped land around Scotland's west coast. With the uncertainty in the market right now prices would have slumped. No one else was buying. Property speculation wasn't criminal but undeveloped land was one of the few assets that could easily sit untouched for seven years, accruing nothing but value, until a Declaration was applied for and the legal cogs ground into motion.

Morrow's phone rang. She answered it. It was DC Kerrigan. The fingerprints on the bag of cocaine in Fuentecilla's car had come up with a match: Iain Joseph Fraser, currently of Helensburgh, previously of Shotts Prison. They tested the cocaine and found traces of Jaffa Cakes in it. Odd.

Morrow nodded at McGrain, telling him to distract Jim Moonie.

McGrain did as he was told, turning Jim away to ask, 'When did you first notice that Hettie'd broken in here?'

Morrow went out into the corridor: 'What was he in for?'

'Assault to severe injury,' said Kerrigan. 'Pretty ugly attack. I've sent you his record.'

'Good. Take Thankless. Go to Helensburgh and see if you can pick Iain Fraser up. And while you're driving out call Mr Halliday at Lurbrax Farm. Ask him if he's sold any undeveloped land recently.'

She didn't want to ask him herself. She liked the idea of Halliday recklessly campaigning for the next generation at his own expense, but she knew too much about people.

27

Boyd peeled his sleep-sodden eyes apart just long enough to glance at the bedside clock. Ten past eight, but that was OK: Helen and Katie were coming in at nine to do the washing up, they would let the cleaner in and sign for deliveries. It was OK.

He dozed, savouring the luxury of an empty bed, of not having to get into work, of his throbbing head and aching muscles.

Physically, he felt like shit but a blowout was exactly what he'd needed. He reran the night backwards: tumbling into bed with Lucy cursing him in her sleep. Drinking malt in Miss Grierson's, to shave the edge off. Quite bad sex, really. Not actually worth it, now it was over. On a dirt floor. With a woman who wasn't half as nice as Lucy. She didn't feel old, but she was quite old.

Nausea propelled him upright, his brain sloshing hard against the inside of his skull. He shut his eyes and waited for the pain in them to subside.

The boys were screaming along to a high-pitched kids' TV show in the kitchen. He remembered, as he always did at this point, an article in the *Observer* about hangovers and how someone had proved that regret was a chemical reaction to alcohol ingestion. His calves were tingling, about to cramp. He made himself get out of bed and staggered into the bathroom to run a shower.

Standing under the water, soaping Susan's dried saliva off his thighs, he remembered the dental dam in her mouth and the odd, sneaky way she took it out. Had someone complained about it, about her using it, and she'd learned to hide it? No, that didn't seem right. Maybe she had HIV? Or thought that he did? No, because afterwards, at her house, she wasn't careful then. It was odd. The whole night was odd. He listened to the breakfast clatter of Lucy and the kids in the kitchen. They sounded very far away.

Boyd was distant from his family, in the same way that his father had been distant. He hadn't liked that about his father. When he was young he thought his father didn't like him; later he blamed the church for stealing his father's attention; later still he blamed his mother, somehow. He saw that coldness now in himself and wondered if Fraser fathers were destined to be glimpsed only, distant and God-like. He thought of all the family photographs. They went back decades. Presently they were in a cardboard suitcase in the attic. Generations of kids and aunties smiling, fathers reading newspapers in backgrounds, fathers smoking in the distance, fathers behind. He was like those Fraser fathers. Distracted. Disgruntled. Distant.

He remembered now why he liked to get arseholed sometimes: this was just the sort of epiphanic self-honesty a blowout prompted in Boyd.

He dried himself, holding hard to the realisation, feeling it slip from his mental grasp like the memory of a dream. He was distant, like his father. He didn't want to be. Trying to think of a way of phrasing it, a sentence that would capture the sense of it, he padded into the kitchen.

Lucy and the boys, even Jimbo, froze as he came through the door. They were wary of his mood. He smiled.

'Morning, all,' he said, sitting down at the table.

Lucy muttered 'Morning' nervously, and went back to pouring out cereal for the boys, shifting her weight so that Boyd couldn't quite see the orange and green box. Boyd didn't approve of that cereal: it was full of colourants and sugar and salt. It was a big box and it was half full. They'd already eaten a lot of it, on other days. She must be stashing the box.

They were hiding their lives from him, the way he had hidden his from his father, the way he and his mother conspired to keep the worst from the Reverend Robert. Tickets for rock concerts. Reeboks: 'Too much for sandshoes' his father had said.

A pang of chemical regret shot through Boyd. He didn't want this for himself and his boys. He stood up suddenly, making Lucy flinch. Reaching into the cupboard, he took down a bowl and held it out for Lucy to pour him a helping too. The boys were watching him, wary. Jimbo skulked out of the room. Boyd tried to catch Lucy's eye. She half smirked as she poured the cereal for him, pouring too much, spilling it over the side and onto the worktop and floor. Boyd picked up the extras from the worktop and held her eye as he put them in his mouth. She smiled, still uncertain, and watched him sit down with the boys.

'What happened to you last night?'

'I got ruined.' He poured the milk in and reached over to the drawer for a spoon.

The boys began to bicker silently about who had the most dried strawberries.

Lucy dropped her voice. 'You were late.'

He saw her left eye on the brink of a wince. This was the point where he would normally shout, though he couldn't remember why. Lucy was lovely. She deserved better.

'Bonding exercise with the staff.' He glanced at the kids. 'Tell you later.' And then he whispered. '*I got a deal.*'

Lucy laughed in disbelief but took in his sorry red eyes. It was obvious that he was telling the truth.

William was trying to steal a tiny red fleck from his brother's bowl but little Larry wasn't having it and pinched his wrist. William howled. Lucy reached into the box of cereal and picked out some withered red bits. She dropped them into the kids' bowls.

'Now eat what you've got or I'm taking it away and giving you cornflakes. With *no* sugar.'

They spooned it into their mouths, cautious of their mother and suspicious of each other.

She whispered to Boyd, 'Get me some next time.'

'I will,' said Boyd, relishing the impropriety of saying it in front of the boys. 'I'll try today.'

'Blinking flip!' Lucy's voice cracked with excitement and she went back to her work.

Boyd ate the disgusting cereal, making faces at the boys, pretending it was lovely.

Behind him Lucy moved around with unearthly grace, tidying away, wiping down, her movements balletic. Boyd, raw as he was, felt keenly how strange it was to everyone that he was eating with them, making eye contact, not being angry or mean. He felt like a divorced dad who had been forced to stay overnight because his car had broken down or something. He was trying too hard.

He stopped and let the boys get on with staring at the TV as they ate. Lucy looked at him and smiled. It was a long time since she had smiled at him like that. He thought about how it must be for her here in Helensburgh. She came from Devon. She had a big gang of friends there, all top girls, all sweet and pretty and fun and lovely. She must feel trapped in this house, his house, his town.

She carried on serving them, pouring, wiping, putting tiny vests on radiators so they were nice and warm to slip on. Caring. She came past and Boyd pushed his chair out from the table, wrapped an arm around her waist and pulled her onto his knee. Lucy melted into him and he held her, nuzzling into her neck as she kissed his hair.

He gave her waist a gentle, appreciative squeeze and she kissed him again, moving to get up but he held her there, playful, trying to eat his cereal across her lap, dripping milk onto her pyjama trousers and making her laugh her throaty laugh. Grinning, she got up and poured him a coffee from the pot.

Boyd and his boys ate and then he dressed them in their little warm vests and jumpers and dungarees. Then he put their socks and wellies on and opened the door to let them bomb around the garden with Jimbo. It was a clear day. From the front porch he could see straight down to the glittering water.

Lucy came out to join him, sitting in one of the faded blue wicker chairs they had found in the attic. Boyd pulled up the matching chair and sat next to her. He took her hand and they watched their lovely boys in their lovely garden on a lovely morning.

'Did you hear about the fire?' Her voice was low, her lips hardly moving. She kept her eyes on the boys, making sure they couldn't hear.

'What fire?'

'The Sailors' Rest. Burnt down. Two inside.'

'Oh God,' he said, but he was thinking about Lucy and how she was, he was thinking about the boys and how everything was going to be better now. He didn't take it in until she said, 'The man who owned it and his daughter were inside. They died. Smoke inhalation.'

'Fucking hell.' He remembered then Murray and Lea-Anne. He remembered the odd conversation, everyone at odds and Tommy Farmer radiating threats.

Lucy looked tearfully across the lawn. 'I think they say "smoke inhalation" because they don't want to say "burnt to death", you know, because that sounds so brutal.'

'I *met* them yesterday.'

'Who?'

'The owner and his daughter. I met them. They *died*?'

'Yeah.'

'There was a bloke, a kind of scary bloke, Tommy Farmer. He was sort of menacing them.' Boyd was glad he hadn't bought anything off him. If Farmer was involved in a fire setting then he didn't want anything to do with him.

'They must have had debts.' Said Lucy, 'Maybe they tried to burn it down themselves and got stuck, you know? For the insurance?'

197

'Maybe.'

Lucy carried on talking but Boyd was back at the dinner with the two grannies. One of them was supposed to be babysitting Lea-Anne but Murray had dropped out and given her his ticket.

'At the dinner,' he said, 'she was supposed to be babysitting, the granny, one with the sore leg, but she was there at the dinner dance, both grannies were there . . .'

'What?' Lucy was looking out over the lawn, watching the boys didn't go too far down to the end of the grass and the steep escarpment between the lawn and the garden wall.

He explained about the granny, about how she was supposed to be at home with a bad leg or a bladder, but how he met them both there. Fuck! How awful. And God, imagine!

They looked down the grass to their boys, squatting in front of a fuchsia bush, watching something in the grass.

'Awful,' said Lucy.

'God, this town,' said Boyd, standing up too quickly, his calves tingling as he tried to straighten his legs. He'd meant to go down to the kids but he could hardly walk.

Lucy laughed as he hobbled down the steps to the lawn. 'You had a faceful last night, didn't you?'

'Christ on a bike,' he said, trying to make light of it. 'I need more coffee.'

The boys were running back in anyway, a fight breaking out between them. They clambered onto the porch and plopped down on their bottoms to pull their wellies off. Boyd watched Lucy help them out of their outdoor clothes. Sternly, she promised them ten minutes of cartoons in the kitchen if they both went to the toilet on their own.

Back in the kitchen, Boyd poured himself another cup, drank it in four gulps and slid his arm around Lucy's waist.

'Fucking love you.'

'You talking to me or the coffee?'

'The coffee.'

She laughed as he held her and he felt vibrations from her rumble through him into his belly. 'Who did you get the deal off, that fat waitress?'

'No.' He let go and hid his face in his coffee. 'It was Susan Grierson. She came into the café and asked for work.'

'Grierson? From that big house on Sutherland Crescent?'

'Yeah. Very old Helensburgh family.'

'She's back?'

'Her mother just died,' said Boyd and sipped again, keen to move the conversation on.

'Not recently, she didn't,' said Lucy. 'Sara Haughton inquired about that house a year and a half ago, wanted to buy it for the garden. The owner was already dead but the estate wasn't settled or something.'

It was a slightly too detailed statement for Boyd to take in. He didn't like Sara Haughton. She was snobby about him being a 'cook'. Lucy could tell he wasn't listening.

'Boyd, old Mrs Grierson died two years ago.'

'Well, she's just getting around to it now.'

'Settling the estate? I'll tell Sara then, if she's selling. She loves that garden.'

He held his wife and kissed her softly. 'Lucy,' he whispered, 'I've been a moody cow recently and I'm sorry. I don't want to be like that.'

'You're not *always* like that.' She patted his back and tried to pull away but he held onto her.

'I don't want you to flinch when I come home.'

She changed then, gave him a warning look and shrugged his arm off. 'Well, don't come home in a flipping mood every day, then.'

'You're right,' he said, as she walked past him. 'I'm sorry.'

It was a real change of tone for him, they both knew it. She stopped and looked at him.

'You should get wasted more often, Boyd. Regret suits you.'

Because Lucy read the *Observer* too.

28

They were sitting in the warm car outside Fuentecilla's house until Morrow finished her calls. It was still early and it felt like a good day, a day when things would get done.

Kerrigan answered the phone. She was in the car with Thankless, driving to Helensburgh. Mr Halliday was reluctant at first but he'd finally admitted to selling the field next to his farm a few weeks ago. He needed to, for his retirement, he said. It had planning permission that he'd been working on for years. Increased the value by a factor of ten, he said. The company he'd sold it to were called Claims4U. Delahunt handled the purchase, Mr Halliday had recognised his name.

Kerrigan said DI Simmons had called about the fingerprints on the bag from the Alfa Romeo. Iain Joseph Fraser was known in Helensburgh. He had a long record and was now a known associate of Mark Barratt. He'd done a series of sentences for crimes of violence against the person. He always came back to the town after prison. Simmons had given them a list of known addresses to check for him.

Morrow hung up and looked at her phone. Halliday didn't give a shit about property prices because he'd already sold up. She was disappointed in him. She hoped they didn't meet again. She didn't want to listen to his excuses.

It was clear to her that Delahunt was the author of the scam. It was his style, but the money came from the Arias couple. There had to be a connection between them. Bob Ashe, the retired owner who had unexpectedly gone to Miami, was from Helensburgh. He might well know Delahunt. It was beginning to make sense until Roxanna's disappearance. Then it all got messy, looked improvised, as if something had gone unexpectedly wrong. The catalyst was the phone call from Vicente and the mention of Maria Arias and Roxanna's desperate drive to London.

'Ready?' asked McGrain.

Morrow pocketed her phone. 'Yeah. Let's go.'

They got out of the car and walked up to the entrance of Walker and Fuentecilla's building. A female neighbour, struggling to get two toddlers and a double buggy out of the door, let them in.

The bright morning light did the place no favours. Yellow sunshine filtered in. Lazy flecks of yesterday floated in the warm stairwell, rising on the current, settling on the banister.

Morrow knocked and Robin Walker opened the door.

'Have you found *anything*?' His anger was tinged with reproach today. Morrow blanked his mood.

'Can we come in, Mr Walker?'

'I'm getting the kids off to school. They're late already.'

'I understand. Can we come in?'

Mistaking her unwillingness to fight as a foreboding of terrible news, Walker paled.

'No,' she reached out to him, 'nothing like that. We just want to ask you about some details that have come up, that's all.'

He'd thought Roxanna was dead. Relieved, he rubbed his face with an open hand and then got angry again. It was pretty intense for a stairwell conversation. His moods were swinging wildly. Morrow wondered if he was medicated or drunk.

'Can we talk inside?'

'I'm sorry, come in. I thought, she'd . . .' He looked at McGrain. 'You know what I thought.'

'We're just here to ask some questions, that's all.'

They went into the living room and Robin waved them onto the settee. 'Please . . .'

He sat down himself, suddenly keen to help. Now they were

in the bright living room she realised that Walker wasn't on anything but he didn't look as if he had slept.

'Robin, we've found a woman who used to work for your wife murdered and left in Loch Lomond. Her name was Hester Kirk. Do you know her?'

He seemed to have stopped breathing.

'Mr Walker: *Hester Kirk*. Have you heard that name or do you know her personally?'

'I know *of* her. I think.'

'What do you "know of her"?'

'We let her go, I think. Did we?'

'"We"?'

'Roxanna did. Let her go.'

Morrow held his eye and nodded. 'She got her books?'

'Yes,' he affirmed.

'Why did Roxanna make her redundant?'

'Hmm, well ...' He was too tired to think of a fast lie so Morrow interrupted.

'Look, Mr Walker, please be straight with us. You need to understand what's going on here: a woman has been murdered and your partner is missing. We've found Roxanna's car abandoned out in Helensburgh. We're very much afraid for her safety.'

Martina suddenly strolled diagonally across the room as if she had walked out of a wall. She was holding a plate of toast and ignoring them. Dressed in her school uniform, she must have been making breakfast when they came in and got trapped in the kitchen. She didn't want to talk to them and veiled her face with her loose blond hair. Aware that every eye was on her, she hurried to the door, anxious to get away.

'Martina?' said Morrow, half expecting to see a black eye when she looked up.

Martina stopped, acting surprised, as if she had just found them hiding under a piano.

'I'd like to talk to you,' said Morrow.

Martina fingered her toast while she considered the request. 'All right. I'll be in my bedroom.' She started across the room again.

Morrow waited until she was gone. 'She seems a bit cheerier than she was yesterday.'

Walker watched her leave. He looked confused.

'How's Hector taking it?'

'Badly. He's in his room. Anyway, Hester Kirk was one of the old guard. She'd been submitting and passing questionable claims, sort of grey-area illegal. That's why Rox got rid of her.' He watched their faces to see if they believed him.

'Hester Kirk broke into the office a few nights ago to go through the files. Did you know that?'

Clearly, he didn't. He said, 'What?' to buy himself some time.

'We know Roxanna was shutting the office down. Closing up this Friday.'

'Well, I don't know anything about her business.' He had said the line before.

'See,' said Morrow, sounding reluctant, 'that strikes me as a lie, Mr Walker. You're alone in a city neither of you know. She's shutting down a business and you don't talk to each other about it? It's unlikely, isn't it? You're her boyfriend, not the au pair. I look at those photos you took, at how she looks at you in those photos, and she's clearly in love with you. I can't believe she'd tell you nothing.'

He tried to smile.

'Why didn't you tell us that the office was winding up?'

'We were never here permanently.'

'Are you leaving?'

Walker shook his head. 'Not, um. I don't know.' But he did know. He knew the plan and he wasn't going to tell them.

'Why was she buying undeveloped land?'

He flashed a nervous smile.

Morrow tutted. 'Robin, d'you want me to guess what's going on?'

He tried to smile again.

'Money laundering?'

'Sorry? Money? *What?*' Wherever else Robin Walker's good looks might take him, they would not take him onto the stage.

'When we looked through the firm's papers we didn't find any debts, but we know you've been buying up land. We found that quite odd, for an insurance company.'

'It's not an insurance company. It's a trading partnership. That's a very flexible trading structure. They don't have any shareholders to notify if they change their trading practice, you see.'

She could hear another person's intonation in his voice, Delahunt's probably.

'Delahunt told you that?'

His eyes widened. 'Sorry?'

'Your lawyer,' she said calmly. 'I'm guessing you're not a Scots law graduate.'

'No, no, I'm not.' He didn't blink.

'So, you bought the company outright and are funding fairly substantial land purchases. Can you tell me where the money for that comes from?'

'I don't know.'

Morrow hummed non-committally and held his eye. 'Roxanna drove to London the day she disappeared. Then she drove back up, overnight, past here, and on to Helensburgh. The only reason I can think that she would do that is that she felt she was in danger. She didn't want to put you in danger by coming back to the house.'

He was listening intently. 'What was she doing in London?'

'She went to see Maria Arias.'

'*Maria?* I called her three times. And I called her yesterday. She said Rox hadn't been in touch, she hadn't seen her – she said she'd call me if Rox contacted her. Why would Rox go there?'

'Hasn't Martina told you this?'

'Told me what?'

'They had a fight in the car on the morning Roxanna disappeared. Martina mentioned that Vicente Miguel called. He casually said something about Maria Arias. For some reason it made your wife very angry—'

It made him very angry too: Robin stood up and shouted, 'That's . . . interfering little bitch . . . she's talking SHIT!'

'Why is it shit?'

'Maria and Vicente don't *know* each other. They can't fucking know each other, for fuck's sake.' Winded, he sank back onto the couch.

'What if they did?'

He looked terrified.

'*If* they did know each other,' continued Morrow quietly, 'If they did, then Roxanna has been set up in a dodgy money-laundering scam by friends of her spiteful ex-partner. What was the exit strategy?'

Walker stared blankly at the carpet.

'Roxanna was going to put the company to sleep and what?'

She could see that he did want to speak. He wanted to tell her so much that he covered his mouth with his hand, afraid he'd blurt it out.

'You were all going to disappear? Get flown somewhere in their private plane and start afresh? With a big bag of money for your troubles?'

He looked at her, pleading for compassion. 'They've done it before.'

'You have to trust them for that to work, though, don't you?'

He nodded softly and dropped his hand.

'Because the alternative,' she continued, 'if you can't trust them, is that they get rid of Roxanna some other way. If she's arrested the company goes dormant too and they save on the pay-out. The property reverts back to the investors in just the same way. Same if she's killed.'

'Vicente and Maria don't know each other,' he insisted. 'They don't *know* each other.'

But they both knew they could. And if they did then Roxanna was in a nastier game then she'd realised.

'How did you meet Juan and Maria?'

'At the kids' school.'

'Roxanna and Maria became friends?'

'Good friends.' He stalled and thought about it. 'Very good friends.' He glanced at the Larkin & Sons cabinet. 'They bought us that.'

'That wall unit?'

He didn't like that term. 'It's actually a free-standing display cabinet.'

'Quite an odd present, isn't it?'

Robin waved a hand. 'We were at an auction, a charity dinner thing. They invited us, we didn't really know them. We were looking at the catalogue and saying, you know, how nice it looked and they got a friend at the table to bid in our names.' He was still impressed. 'They paid in *cash*.'

Morrow didn't look impressed enough apparently so he added, 'Sixty-four grand.'

She did act impressed then and so did McGrain, but she was thinking about the cynical couple. They must have been setting Robin and Roxanna up right from the beginning. They probably knew that they were being watched at the auction because the Met were famously leaky. It was so obvious, so public. It drew the police's attention completely and exclusively to Roxanna and Robin. The disappearance strategy depended on Roxanna being invisible. They'd been setting her up for an arrest from the start.

'We have to consider every possibility, Robin.'

'Rox and Vicente are in dispute about custody of the kids. He's a total fucking bastard.'

She wanted to warn Robin, hint and give him a chance to mitigate his sentence by opening up. She wasn't allowed to. The Met report had warned her. She shouldn't even have mentioned Maria Arias because Walker might phone her and give them advanced warning. Compassion was in no one's interest, because of the proceeds.

'Would Vicente conspire to harm her?'

Walker was too distracted to answer.

'Let's take it back a bit more: would Vicente collude in setting her up in a criminal enterprise, one that could result in her imprisonment?'

Walker looked straight at her, eyes wide, and gave a terrified little nod.

'At the moment we're working on the assumption that Roxanna heard about the connection between them. That she panicked and went to London to confront Maria. We need to find her to keep her safe. Her mobile phone was traced to a field on the outskirts of Helensburgh the morning after she went missing. We went there and found her Alfa Romeo, unlocked, parked by a field.'

He sat forward hopefully. 'Delahunt, our lawyer, lives in Helensburgh.'

'We've already interviewed Mr Delahunt, he hasn't seen her. Did she know anyone else out there?'

'No. No one.'

'We found a bag of cocaine in the car.'

'That's not hers.'

'Why?'

'Roxanna doesn't use cocaine.'

'Robin, she drove all the way up from London overnight, maybe she was using it a little bit?'

'No,' he said, certain. 'Rox has a heart murmur. She doesn't even drink coffee. If it was in the car and it's definitely her car then someone else left it there. They're trying to get her arrested, aren't they?'

She nodded, lying to comfort him. The motive seemed a bit more sinister to her now. Iain Joseph Fraser, a known local criminal, had left clean prints on it but that was unprofessional, inconsistent with the wipes and the vacuumed floor. It looked like a misdirect, a magician pointing at a dove while an assistant scrambled out of the back of the box. There had never been any suggestion of drug misuse or dealing in the family. They kept regular hours, both parents exercised regularly, they had very little company. It was a clumsy plant but Morrow couldn't fathom what she was being directed away from seeing.

She stood up. 'OK. I want you to think about where she might have gone. In the meantime, I'm going to go and talk to Martina.'

McGrain stood up with her, nodded his sympathies to Walker and followed her to Martina's room.

They knocked. They waited. Morrow was about to knock again when Martina came to the door, blocking the room with her body.

'What?'

Morrow pushed the door open and walked in, looking around like a suspicious mother. Martina had been packing her school bag, it bulged on the bed.

She was indignant. 'Excuse me! You can't just barge into my room.'

Morrow sat down on the desk chair. 'Sit down, Martina.'

Reluctantly, Martina sat on the edge of the bed and Morrow examined her. 'We are police officers, Martina, do you understand what that means? I'm not your mum or your stepdad or a teacher. Something has changed. What's happened?'

Martina feigned confusion.

'Since yesterday? You were so worried about your mum that you phoned the police. Aren't you worried any more?'

She welled up and nodded. 'No, I'm still . . . my mum . . .'

'Has she phoned you?'

'No.' It seemed sincere but Morrow made a note to check her

phone records. 'If you hear anything I want you to call me.' She gave Martina a card. 'Will you?'

'Of course.'

They left and shut the door, knocking lightly on Hector's. He called 'Come in' and they found him lying on his side on the bed, red-eyed and dressed for school. The curtains were shut, the room gloomy. His mobile, a round-edged early model iPhone, a parental cast-off, sat on the pillow. It was next to his face, as if they'd been whispering secrets to each other.

'Can we talk to you for a minute?'

He nodded. He must have heard them, knew they were there.

'Aren't you going to school today?'

'Yeah.' He looked teary. 'I'm going.'

Morrow sat on his desk chair and McGrain stood at her shoulder. 'Have you heard from your mum, son?'

He shook his head.

The iPhone lit up, bright in the gloom. Morrow glanced at it. It was a text from *Mart*. One word: *Callate*. Hector saw it, startled, and turned the phone on its face.

'What's *callate*?'

Hector pulled the covers up over his mouth as if he was afraid. 'Don't know.'

'Why's she texting you from across the hall?'

'I asked her not to come in. I don't know anything about it,' he said and began to cry again.

Back in the car Morrow looked up the word *callate* on her phone. It was Spanish for 'shut up'.

She had a voicemail: Hester Kirk's family had been shown a picture of the dead woman's face and confirmed it was her. Family Liaison was there now. Three daughters remaining in the domicile, ages fourteen, sixteen and eighteen. No father.

The woman had been missing for four days. Morrow counted back. That meant she had been missing for two days before she was killed. If the same people had taken her, Roxanna might still be alive.

They drove onto Clydebank and she called the office as they were pulling into Hester Kirk's estate. She got a male DC she hardly knew and whose name she didn't catch.

'PINAD: did we ask for a trace on the Fuentecilla kids' phones?'

'We did, yeah.'

'Can you open it and see if the children have received any calls from their mother?'

'Open, ma'am.' He hummed as he read down. 'Ah! Martina: no calls from her mum. But has been getting calls from an unlisted number over the last two days. The phone is turned off now but the last location was in Helensburgh.'

'Frank Delahunt?'

'Let me see.' He clacked his tongue as a filler while he looked. 'Nope. Triangulated to number seven Sutherland Crescent, Helensburgh.'

Morrow said they were going to question Hester Kirk's family and would head out there afterwards. Notify Kerrigan and Thankless that they were on their way.

29

Iain walked the town, uphill, downhill, while he waited for the medicine to kick in. He didn't want to go and see the grannies until he was calm. He was scary. He didn't want to scare them. People shopping, people visiting, people walking dogs. On the esplanade the mobile police unit had emptied the street of its usual traffic. Even the cars were avoiding the road in front of it.

Crossing Colquhoun Square, Iain stopped: coming uphill in a clean car were two mismatched people, man and woman. They were driving too slowly, paying close attention to the faces in the street, and they weren't from here. They were police and they were looking for someone. Iain ducked down a lane, towards wee Asda, around the corner to the big bins where a car couldn't see.

'Hello.'

He looked up.

'Susan.'

'You're very dirty, Iain.'

'Fire,' he said.

She tipped her head like a seagull eyeing a chip. 'Are you upset?'

He didn't like her at all today. She must have followed him in here from the street. 'The fuck is it to you?' It was too much. He should have toned it down.

But she didn't react. He wondered if he had actually said it, she was so unperturbed. She was holding something out to him. Something white. An envelope. She had gloves on. It was a warm day. He didn't know what was going on.

She waved the other hand, with no glove, at the wall of the alley. 'Upset because of that fire? Dreadful.'

Iain's eyes were blurry. He waited for them to clear. But he could feel the medication pumping around his body. Now he was holding an envelope. He felt so sleepy so suddenly he thought he could lie down and sleep right here, next to the bins. God, it was lovely. He waited for a minute, savouring it. Susan waited with him.

When the calm paralysis was past he found Susan smiling at him. She hooked her arm through his, comradely now, leading him out of the lane and into a newsagent's.

She left him inside the door, went over to the counter and bought a chocolate bar. Iain didn't think she really wanted it. She seemed to pick it at random, pay and then drop it thoughtlessly in her bag.

'Tobacco?' she said, as if they'd had a conversation about it in the alley. Maybe they had. He stepped forwards anyway and seemed to be buying some. He tucked the envelope in his back pocket to free his hands so he could get his money.

Now he had papers and tobacco and was paying when the shopkeeper asked Susan if she'd heard about the fire at the Sailors' Rest. Wasn't it awful? His wee granddaughter was at school with that girl who died.

Susan agreed that it was terrible.

'Aye,' said the shopkeeper, snarling at Iain. 'And every bastard in this town knows who did it, but no one'll say.'

'Why?' Susan looked innocently from one to the other.

Iain was picking the right change out of his cupped palm slowly so that he didn't have to look up.

The shopkeeper hissed at Iain, 'Well, why don't they?'

'Why don't you?' Susan was talking to the man.

He blushed. 'It's not *for* me to say—'

'You're reproaching him for something you won't do yourself?'

The shopkeeper huffed.

'Do you know what I find revolting about this country?' said Susan, her accent rolling into something else, 'All the fucking cant.'

The shopkeeper was out of his depth. 'What? Like "we can't"?'

'Cant. Self-righteousness.' Her accent sounded much more American now. Iain was in a medicated fog but even he could hear it. 'It's *repugnant*.'

Iain knew that she had let her mask slip. This was the real Susan and she had only let them see her because she was leaving. She was smart. She was disgusted. And she was leaving.

The shopkeeper was determined not to admit he was wrong. He shrugged. 'That's just people, isn't it?'

'No,' said real Susan. 'It's *here*.'

Iain was having trouble counting the money. Susan leaned over and pecked a five pence piece from his hand and dropped it on the pile on the counter.

Iain didn't want to be here any more. He kept his head down and picked up the pouch, heading for the door.

They walked back out into the street. Iain thought how little Susan understood the town. It wasn't about being sanctimonious. Nobody would tell on Mark or Tommy because they all got a wee dip here or there, all got a bit of work or had a cousin who did. They were all involved with each other, wrapped up and tangled, because it was such a small place.

'You're leaving, aren't you?' He said.

Susan looked surprised. She squeezed his forearm. 'The envelope.' She nodded to his pocket. 'Andrew Cole has been arrested for murder.'

He looked at her. He must have misheard. He nodded an urgent prompt at her mouth and she said it again: 'Andrew Cole. Got arrested. For murder. Golf course.'

'The fuck?' he asked her lips.

'The police. Will let him go. If you. Give them the envelope.'

'Why?'

'It's from his mother but you mustn't tell them. They know how protective she is. Give it to the police. Tell them Tommy Farmer gave it to you.'

'Tommy?'

'Tommy, yes. Tommy doesn't know Andrew's mother.'

'How do you know Tommy?' Actually, how did she know Andrew? 'How do you know Andrew?'

'I don't. I know his mother.'

Iain looked at her perfectly composed face. She gave him a smile. Warm and motherly, a good friend, a reliable neighbour. Not-real Susan again.

'Who are you?'

'Susan.' She gave a patient smile. 'Remember? Akela in the Scouts.'

'No,' said Iain, for once not doubting himself, 'no you're not.'

She smiled again, waiting for the moment to pass.

'The widow Grierson died two years ago. That's not why you're here and who are you?'

Hand forward, elbow cupped, warm hand, head tilt. 'I'm so sorry. You're having a hard time, Iain. I want to help.'

Her mask was very good. She had a banal gesture rehearsed for every eventuality but he knew he was right about this. 'You're no better than me.'

'Quite so.'

'Who are you?'

She muttered something pleasant to him, her face blank, and turned, walking away. *Shunt?* Was that what she had said? She didn't call him a cunt, did she?

She was walking casually away down the street now, glancing into shop windows, skirt swishing at the ankles, rich-woman hair catching the wind. He felt the paper of the envelope crinkle in his back pocket as he shifted his weight.

He blinked hard. Susan Grierson was a broken jigsaw. It made no sense.

Annie and Eunice. They were what was left. This he had to do. He turned and headed east, to their house. He could feel the energy going from his feet, the need to move leaving them and the pain from the night's walk. Baffled momentum took him up to Hardy Hill.

Small grey box houses with mean high windows and nowhere to keep the smelly wheelie bins but right outside the front door.

Iain banged and leaned against the cold concrete and waited. The door was PVC plastic but still the skin on his knuckles sang a tender reprise of the knock. He half wondered if his hand was burned but didn't care enough to look. He was concentrating on getting in, seeing them, because then he would feel better. They always made sense.

A bus passed by in the street, the engine growl reverberating against the concrete façades of the houses. Passengers looked out at him, slack-mouthed, faces indistinct.

The front door opened and there stood Annie, eyes as raw as fresh oysters. At the sight of Iain she retreated back into the dark hall. But then her hand came out, calling him in. Iain tripped across the step.

She shut the door but didn't look at him. Iain knew then that she half blamed him for the fire. He went after her, didn't know what to say and held his hands out and hugged her. Annie wasn't used to a lot of touching, neither was Iain. It was awkward. She hugged and patted his back, as if she was winding him, and she called him son. She wanted him to let her go, but he couldn't. He had come here for comfort, to see her from before, but it wasn't before and he didn't want to see her face.

He released her, averting his eyes, and saw Lea-Anne's pink coat hanging on a banister. A photo of Lea-Anne smiling in her school uniform. Lee-Anne's jazzy trainers. A One Direction school bag.

What little light there was in the hall was suddenly sucked away. Eunice stood in the kitchen doorway. She nodded, turned and hirpled into the kitchen. Annie tugged at Iain's sleeve, bringing him in with her.

Small table, wood-pattern veneer, pushed up against the wall.

A place mat in nuclear pink embroidered with flowers. Three chairs, one for each granny and a third with a One Direction cushion on it. The boy band were pictured hugging each other, smiling cheerfully up at whichever bottom was coming towards them. It was pushed out from the table, as if Lea-Anne had just gone to the toilet. They all three stepped carefully around it.

Eunice was looking at Iain, cold, lips tight to her teeth. She turned away. 'Tea.'

Iain leaned against the wall. He felt gigantic, looking down on the shrunken old women and the vacuum left by the child.

Eunice, Our Lady of the Bad Leg, spun and swooped, rolling her hip as she moved around the kitchen, bringing and taking and boiling. Her jowls were puffy, a map of thread veins over her cheeks. A small plate of biscuits was put on the table, three saucers, sugar, a carton of milk. Annie fingered the embroidery on the place mat in front of her. The sun outside went behind a cloud and the room darkened. Everything was on the worktops. Biscuits, milk, tea bags, sugar, boxes of crackers. Details crowded noisily in on Iain. No one looked at anyone else.

Annie reached up to him, her hand was in his hand, fingertips to his fingertips.

'Son,' she said, 'your hands is swole.'

He looked down. The bottom half of her face was crying, chin crumpled, breathing jagged and irregular. The top half of her face was looking at his hands, his dirty hands, as if she could see what they had done, what had been on them.

'Salt water,' said Iain, because women knew.

'You're mockit,' she said, releasing his fingers, letting him drift out.

Dirty. He was. From four miles out he looked at the two old mourners, bodies sagging around crumbling bones.

Eunice poured the hot water into three cups. She put three sugars into each and milk. Lea-Anne took three sugars. The women stirred their cups, taking turns with the spoon, stirring for Lea-Anne. They sipped their hollow communion. They didn't offer Iain any. The third cup was left sitting in front of the empty chair.

Iain turned to leave.

'Polis was here,' Eunice announced. 'Was looking for ye, son.'

Iain looked back. She wasn't looking at him. They were both hunched over their cups, concentrating on the ritual. They blamed him for the fire.

Annie spoke: 'Best take the back lanes.' She told her tea.

He passed a mirror in the dim hallway. He didn't recognise himself. The smoke had worked its way into every crevice of his face, tingeing his hair brown. They blamed him.

Out on the street a bus grumbled by, a woman pushed a buggy, a man made a phone call. The smell of smoke didn't cling up here in the high scheme but it clung to Iain. He was the smell now.

One more. He took the pill bottle out and took another one, swallowing it dry again, glad it hurt.

Their names came into his head. Lea-Anne. Murray. Murray and Lea-Anne. He saw their faces. Lea-Anne and Murray. Murray hiding by a burn when they were young, back in the days when Annie took a drink and the house was party central. Murray sitting on Iain's bed – *don't smoke*. Murray working sixteen-hour days in the kitchen at the hotel to raise the deposit to buy the Sailors' at auction. The excitement when he got it. Gone. Murray and baby Lea-Anne sitting at a low table in a visiting room, Iain walking in and seeing them turn their faces to his. They were waiting for him.

They blamed him. Andrew Cole had been arrested? For what? He didn't do anything. Everything was jumbled and broken.

He knew then that he could be free for the rest of his life, or he could be in a cell. It didn't matter. If he didn't do something, grab hold of something, he would be lost. Police.

He walked purposefully for three blocks, rolling and smoking cigarettes on the way.

With the sun in his eyes and a cigarette on his lip, he climbed up the four steps to the doors of the police station. He rattled the handle. It was locked. He rang the bell. Nothing.

Then he saw a laminated note on the door, written in small letters. It told him to call this number and leave a message. He looked for the car with the mismatched couple, the cops on the lookout, but it wasn't there. He thought of the mobile police unit but Mark would hear if he walked down there because someone, someone would be watching.

Someone.

The thought of a sinister, faceless presence made him think of Susan. That's what she was. A dark nobody.

He stood on the steps, looking down into the street. Nicotine coursed through the channels, speeding up his brain. The pills dampened his feelings. It was a good combination. Susan was something he couldn't understand but he knew she was working him. He'd be stupid to do what she told him. The envelope. She wanted him to give it to the cops. So don't. Do something else with it. Do whatever she didn't want. Give it back.

Glad the police station was shut – he could have done something really stupid there – he tripped down the stairs to the street.

30

The yellow-brick estate was new and pleasant. It had yet to wear and show its weaknesses. The houses were small but well proportioned, laid out in winding streets with wide pavements for the children to cycle on, safe from passing cars. The streets were midday quiet, empty driveways, children at school. A small dog watched them from a neighbour's window.

Though it was daytime, a blinding bright spotlight shone straight down on the step outside the Kirks' front door. McGrain pressed the bell and an elaborate electronic jingle sounded inside. The door was opened by a uniformed Liaison officer who was pulling her coat on.

'I need to go,' she said quickly, sliding past them.

'Something wrong?' Morrow stepped into the hall.

'No,' said the officer. 'Just, got another house – busy morning.' She called back into the kitchen, 'Girls! I'll be in touch this afternoon if you don't phone me before then.'

She shut the door as the girls called their goodbyes in a ragged chorus.

Morrow walked across the hall to the kitchen and found three scantily dressed girls in there, standing, drinking from pint-sized mugs of tea. Eighteen, sixteen and fourteen. The girls were fat and no wonder: the kitchen was a private chapel dedicated to sugar. Every spare surface was stacked with catering boxes of biscuits, chocolate bars, sweets. Two packets of crisps were open on the worktop next to the kettle, a suggested accompaniment to a cup of tea. Even the window sill behind the sink was lined with bottles of red fizzy juice.

Morrow introduced herself and McGrain. The girls stood up and shook their hands in turn. Scarlet, the sensible oldest, was very dark and pretty. Marnie, the middle child, had her head shaved at the side, green eyes and a slightly manic giggle. Debbie had shocking pink hair and raw red stretch marks down the backs of her chunky arms. No one was angry, Morrow noted, and no one was crying.

With the front door shut Morrow realised suddenly that the house was unbelievably warm, which explained why the girls were all wearing as little as possible.

'I know!' said Marnie. 'Boiling! We don't know how to work the central heating.'

McGrain nodded at the boiler cabinet on the wall. 'Is it a combi?'

They didn't know.

'Let me have a look.' He opened the cabinet door. 'I've got one like this. See the dial there? Looks like a volume control?'

The girls were standing up, watching him turn it down.

'There.' He shut the door. 'That should be all right now.'

'Thank almighty fuck for that,' said Debbie. 'We've been sweating bullets in here.'

The girls all smiled at each other, because they'd solved a problem and because of the funny image.

Scarlet saw that there wasn't enough room in the kitchen and suggested moving into the living room so they could all sit down. Debbie and Marnie pressed them with offers of cups of tea? Coffee? Glass of ginger, then? Want a wee biscuit? Sure? Crisps? Are ye sure? They told McGrain to take his coat off anyway, and clucked and fussed them into the cluttered living room.

Two outsized beige leather sofas faced each other, backs pressed tight to opposing walls. In the middle, a gigantic television dominated the room. Scattered around the base like votive offerings were flexes and wires and handsets and gaming consoles, some still in the boxes.

The girls all sat on one sofa, squashed up tight on a two-seater, giggling. Morrow and McGrain took the facing settee.

Morrow, observing protocol, told the girls she was sorry for their loss. The girls gave yelps of regret and shut their eyes, as if they'd just heard of something terrible happening a long way away.

'God!' said Marnie. 'What a thing to happen! The poor woman.'

Morrow wasn't sure it had sunk in yet. She said she had some questions but she could give them a little time if they felt they needed it—

'No,' Scarlet said firmly. Her sisters nodded in agreement. 'You know, it's complicated with my mum. We're not . . . well, just you fire away.'

'You're eighteen, Scarlet, are you?'

'Yeah. Ask away.'

'And you're prepared to explain what's going on to your sisters, that they don't need to answer anything they don't want to . . .'

Scarlet turned and looked at her sisters with theatrical suspicion. They grinned back to show they got the joke. Morrow thought maybe they should wait for a social worker. They weren't taking it very seriously.

'Where's your dad? Does he live with you?'

Marnie tutted. 'Noonan's a junkie fuck.'

'Will I get put into care?' Debbie fretted. 'Because I am *not* staying with that psycho. I'm not.'

'You'll be appointed a social worker,' said Morrow. 'They'll tell you more about what might happen.'

'I can adopt you.' Scarlet turned to Morrow. 'Can't I? I'm eighteen. 'Cause Noonan's a junkie. He's up at this door once a week looking for fucking money or anything he can sell, banging on the door like a zombie trying to get in. He nicked the plants out the front to sell. Sold them in a pub, can you imagine that? *Twat.* He's looking in this window and he can see all this shit my mum bought.' She pointed at the gaming consoles and the TV. 'Junkie bait, all of it.'

McGrain looked covetously at the pile. 'You not gamers, girls?'

'No,' said Debbie. 'She's bought it and says "that's for yous" but it wasn't for us at all.'

'That's right,' Marnie interrupted. 'It's for Noonan to see through the window.'

'He left her,' explained Scarlet calmly. 'Went off with some skinny bird and then she's buying all this stuff so's he can see it and it's driving him mental. We can't leave the house empty. Anyway, come on: ask us your wee questions.'

'When did you last see your mum?'

Marnie answered, 'Sunday night.' It was four days ago and they hadn't reported her missing.

'What time?'

'She went out. We were watching that Doctor Who documentary. Boring. It was about ten thirty. Remember it was boring?'

The other girls nodded.

'Where did she go?'

They looked at each other and Marnie shrugged. 'Two men came for her. She's went off with them.'

'Did you know the men?'

'Never seen them.' Scarlet looked regretful. 'She just went with them.'

'How do you know there were two men, then?'

Scarlet said, 'She's come in and says "That's me offski." We were watching the Doctor Who thing.'

It didn't answer the question. Morrow looked at the other two. 'Either of you see them?'

Debbie shook her head but Marnie said, 'I saw two guys outside the front door but there's a porch light above the door. It got knocked by a football and now it's like . . .' She flattened a hand over her head and cowered under it, making a high drone. 'And they were outside it and I didn't see their faces.' She looked at her sisters. 'They were just, kind of, I dunno, *guys.*' The other two nodded.

'What were they wearing?'

'Hoodies, jeans and that.'

'What colour were their hoodies?'

'Dunno. But she went out and one of them turned away and I saw he had those, know those jeans from Markies, know the ones with the white wiggle on the arse pocket?' Morrow nodded. 'Except he would have bought them second-hand because he didn't look like he shopped at Markies. He looked kind of prisony.'

'How did he look "prisony"?'

Scarlet shrugged. 'Pale. Poor-looking. Blond hair and tall. Broad across the chest.' She drew a hand from shoulder to shoulder. 'Handsomey, but also, kind of *prisony.*'

'What about the other one?'

'Never seen him.'

'Did your mum know them?'

'Don't think so.'

'Did they threaten her?'

'No.'

'Why did she go with them, then?'

The girls looked at each other. Marnie muttered at Debbie, 'You say . . .' They seemed to have discussed this already and Debbie had been appointed the storyteller. The other two sat back as she began:

'See all this gaming stuff? Ready money. Mum's been ripping off the company she worked for. Well—'

'Not "ripping them off",' corrected Marnie.

Scarlet slapped Marnie's arm behind her sister's head. 'Let her tell it, Marnie.'

'OK,' Debbie conceded with a nod at her sister, '*fiddling.* Getting cash she shouldn't have. So she had to spend it all on like . . .' she opened her hand to the tumble of electrical goods on the floor, '*crap*. Because she had to get rid. You can't bank fuck all now—'

'It's not "crap",' Marnie told McGrain. 'Ye can sell that stuff.'

Scarlet told Debbie, 'It has got resale value, right enough.'

'*Fuck's sake*,' lamented Debbie, 'I'm trying to tell the story.'

'Well, tell it right.' Marnie grinned at Morrow.

'Shut it!' Debbie had a hand up to still her sisters. 'Right?'

'OK.' Scarlet nodded, looking at Morrow. 'SILENCE!'

Marnie laughed. 'Yeah! SILENCE!'

Debbie was indignant. 'But you said for me to say!'

'SILENCE!' reprised Scarlet.

Morrow was an only child but she remembered the frantic atmosphere of crowds of girls at school, tumultuous emotional storms that were forgotten as soon as they passed.

They were a nice family, kind to each other in their confusion and sadness. They weren't just a pool of genetics and mutual misfortune. They were so likeable, the three of them. The fondness in the way they spoke and moved as a single entity, their prompting and corrections, gamely slapping each other, looking to her only to witness what they had between them.

Debbie started again. "K. She's doing – I dunno, *whatever*. She's getting money. She's spending it on resellables. Storing them up. The house is heaving. Then some Spanish woman takes over and – boom – she gets the bump.' She paused for dramatic effect. '*Not chuffed*.'

'What did she do?'

Scarlet took over. 'Kept just going into the office. I don't think she believed it. Then, when she's finished working her time, she got drunk for a few days. Up there, in her pit, smashing about.'

They all glanced at the ceiling as if Hester was still up there, still angry.

Marnie whispered, 'Fucking *furious*.'

'Bealing,' nodded Debbie.

Scarlet sat forward to be heard. 'And then she appears in the kitchen one day, cooking food an' that—'

'Mince and potatoes,' reported Debbie ominously.

'Creepy as *fuck*,' said Scarlet. 'Well creepy.'

'It *was*,' Marnie agreed, 'Like, *really* creepy. She's like "HELLO DEAR!"' She said it in a shrill falsetto and made the other girls jump and laugh. 'And all that, like *normal*.'

'Debbie's like that . . .'

They watched as Debbie gave the police a pantomime rerun: mouthing 'OH MY GOD', waving her hands wildly by her head. They laughed and Morrow laughed along with them.

'Anyway, anyway.' Marnie batted a hand to calm the laughter down. 'Hettie had a plan, she told us later. They weren't going to "get rid of her that easy", 'cause that's how she talked, wunnit?'

Scarlet gave her sister a rueful smile. 'That's right, clichés. Talked in clichés, thought in clichés.'

'"Hunners o' gear",' said Debbie, wiggling her shoulders, mimicking her mum. '"Hunky guys", like that.' Suddenly self-conscious about taking the piss out of her dead mum, she gave Morrow a guilty look and stopped. 'Anyway. She was going to get even. She said they were at it. This new woman wouldn't want an investigation into whatever they were doing now. She's told the Spanish woman she'd get the cops in to investigate if she didn't pay her off. That's what the two guys were here for, taking her for the pay-off. She's hung in the door and she's like "That's me offski for the big bag."'

'"Big bag of readies",' said Marnie. 'That's what she's called the pay-off.'

'She was blackmailing them?'

'Aye. Pay me or I'll get the polis in, sort of thing.'

Hettie would have gone quite happily, thought Morrow, imagining her climbing into a car or a van, a small greedy smile on her face.

'Anyway, I'm not fucking living with Noonan,' said Marnie.

'They'll never ask us to live with him,' said Debbie. 'They won't, will they, Scar?'

'Can I adopt them?' said Scarlet, thumbing at her sisters.

'Social work'll do whatever they can to keep you out of care. How come you didn't report your mum missing?'

The girls looked at each other.

'She went missing a lot. Went on holidays and that. Didn't always tell us. Ye didn't know when she'd be here, really. And we've got food . . .'

Morrow could see the girls and their mum, the trust between them damaged early on. The girls were too young to feel they should lie about their feelings for her. They'd formed their own family without her and their sadness was for Hester's loss, not their own. They didn't seem to feel they had lost that much. It made her think of Danny. She wished she could be as honest as them.

Marnie interrupted Morrow's train of thought: 'What would you do with all of this stuff?'

Morrow looked at it, pricing the consoles and the telly, at a big Buddha's head on a table in the corner. They should confiscate it for proceeds of crime. 'EBay it.'

Marnie nodded seriously. 'Reckon?'

'Quickly. Get all the money and put it in a bank account. Show the social worker you're able to support yourselves. Your dad won't stand a chance then.'

She was lying to them. Noonan wouldn't get custody of the girls if they objected but he might burgle them and then they would have nothing. It was pretty good advice. She felt that she had finally managed to do something useful.

'Is there any more of it?'

'Serious? Come 'ere.' Marnie was on her feet, leading the way out to the hall. Morrow and McGrain followed her up a steep set of stairs to the landing. The other girls came too.

On the landing Marnie stopped outside the first bedroom and

reached for the handle. She turned it, throwing wide the door to her mother's inner sanctum, and stepped back quickly, chin down, wary, as if the God of Avarice might fly out of the dark and eat her.

The room was dim, the curtains drawn. For a moment Morrow couldn't make visual sense of it. She stepped into the room. A double bed in the middle, lit by the light from the hall. It was unmade. The indent from Hettie's head still on the pillow.

From the corner of her eye Morrow saw what she assumed was a narrow black wardrobe. It was actually a TV the size of a single bed, still shrink-wrapped, propped against the wall. Her eyes adjusted to the dark and she saw, suddenly, all around the walls, on the floor, stacked up, boxes and bags and suit bags and unopened internet packages. A tumble drier, still packed in plastic, against the wall. On top of it was another TV, in the box, and two Blu-ray DVD players. A narrow valley led from the door to bed.

Debbie looked at it and spat, '*Stuff.* Fucking . . . *stuff* and more *stuff.*'

'Clothes?' asked Morrow.

'Bags and clothes and shoes and jerseys and designer shit she was too fucking fat to even wear.'

Morrow looked at Marnie's clothes. 'Nah,' said Marnie, looking down at her cheap Primark vest and shorts. 'Never bought us nothing if she could help it.'

'*Stuff,*' said Debbie again, looking into the room. 'Couldn't stop herself. Couldn't wear half of it or they'd know she was at it. Just. Mental.'

They stared into the room, reluctant to cross the threshold into their mum's cave. Then Debbie did. She stepped very pointedly over the metal edging strip on the carpet. Her sisters followed her. Debbie snapped the light on and broke the spell. They looked around as if they were in a warehouse sale, touching and toeing individual items.

Debbie's voice had dropped reverently, as if she was in church. 'Sure the polis won't take it away?'

'Well,' said Morrow, aware she was polis, that they were desperately in need of funds and she should be taking it away. 'We're investigating your mum's death. It doesn't look right if we start emptying your house.' She looked at McGrain and he nodded. 'I wouldn't make a big noise about it though.'

'Poor Mum,' said Debbie. 'What a fanny. The fuck did she want? More and more and more. She had enough.'

'Fucking stupid.' Marnie was looking down at a stack of three identical DAB radios still in their boxes.

Scarlet put her arm around Debbie's chubby shoulders and they cried a little. Marnie moved near them, squeezed her little sister's wrist and shook her head mournfully at a stack of shoeboxes.

Morrow didn't think they were crying for their dead mother but mourning Hester's mistake – more and more and more at the price of enough.

They were right to cry. It was tragic.

31

Morrow and McGrain looked out at Sutherland Crescent. It was a neat semicircle of immaculate properties behind well-tended hedges. Except for number seven where the hedges erupted exuberantly over the grass verge. A vigilante gardener had hacked angrily at the branches from the street but the hedge was growing back, serene and green and wild again.

The Helensburgh houses they had seen so far were on the hillside, facing forwards, each insisting on a personal relationship with the sea. But a different set of fictions was playing out here. This area was flat and the crescent looked out over a faux grassy common, as if it was deep in the heart of the bucolic countryside.

McGrain pulled on the handbrake and they got out. The houses were modest by comparison to the big gardens.

The Vicente children had been calling someone located here, possibly their mother. Roxanna might be captive here, or she might have run off, Morrow didn't know what she was dealing with any more. She could be hiding in there. Morrow considered how Roxanna could know it was empty. No estate agent's sign outside advertised it for sale, but she might have viewed it and taken a sign down. She might even have bought it.

The thick hedge hid the house. Morrow and McGrain found a high wooden gate to a driveway, rotting on its hinges, the nose ploughed deep into the muddy ground.

Together they lifted it up and managed to swing it inwards through a thick tangle of nettles. They left it there, lolling drunkenly on one good hinge.

It was a forlorn little house. Someone had loved it very much, but that was a long time ago. Glazed blue patio pots under the window were choked with dead weeds. The roof sagged in the middle. Paint was peeling from the window frames and a glass pane was cracked on the attic.

They waded through the grass and nettles of the driveway towards it. It was only when they got to the front door that they noticed a garden path covered with flattened weeds, leading over to an obscured break in the hedge: someone had been here very recently.

She ordered McGrain around the back of the house, waiting for him to get there before knocking gently on the door. She watched through the frosted side window, alert to any changes in the light inside. She waited, knocked again and saw nothing.

Taking the other side of the house, she was walking around to join McGrain at the back but found her way blocked by a car under a mouldy green tarp. Slipping on a glove she lifted the edge and saw the bonnet of a silver Ford Fiesta. She walked around it. An overgrown driveway led into the back lane. The grass and weeds were flattened.

Morrow slipped past the car around to a vast back garden enclosed with a high brick wall. It was a mess. Plucky sycamore saplings and weeds had grown tall along the top of the wall, setting the garden in perpetual twilight. Wooden sides on raised beds had crumbled and rotted, dead plants were nailed to the wall. A slice of bright day caught Morrow's eye.

It was coming from a door in the garden wall. It was hanging open, framed in a brick arch. Morrow walked over and teased it wide with her finger. The fastening on the outside was rusted but the rust was worn and uneven. Something had been rubbing it. She ran her finger over the top of the hasp. The loose rust had been rubbed smooth in the middle, and recently. A padlock had been hanging on it but was gone now.

She turned back to look at the house. An old-fashioned con-servatory, attached to the back of the building, listed softly to one side. The kitchen door was open.

As per protocol, she phoned Kerrigan, notifying her of the lo-cation and the time. If she didn't phone back in twenty minutes they were dead at this address. Kerrigan said, oh no, hang on, Thankless was driving them to that address anyway: Fraser had been spotted talking to the listed householder in the town this morning.

Morrow looked up at the derelict house. 'A householder? For this address?'

'Yep. Susan Grierson. Tall, fiftyish. Slim.'

Morrow hung up and took a step towards the kitchen door when she heard a voice behind her.

'The fuck?'

Framed in the open garden gate stood a man, backlit in the bright contrasting day. Like a stained glass window, his hands were open at his sides and black soot outlined the contours of his face. He was tall and broad across the chest. Handsomey, but also kind of prisony.

McGrain had recognised him too. 'Sir—'

It was meant as a preamble but Iain Joseph Fraser had been arrested often enough to know police patter. Startled, he fell back a step as if he was going to run. But then he didn't. Conflicted, he twisted back and away, his feet planted. McGrain took his wrist and he didn't resist. Gently, McGrain levered the man's hand up his back.

'OK,' said Fraser, nodding. 'Aye, it's OK.'

Morrow was at his side. 'Are you Iain Joseph Fraser?'

He nodded, too slowly, looking out into the street, remind-ing her of Andrew Cole. 'Are you on drugs, Mr Fraser? You're moving quite slowly.'

His breathing was laboured. 'Pills,' he said. '"Scription.'

'What sort of medication, sir?'

'In my pocket.'

'I'm just going to check for you, sir, OK?'

Fraser nodded his consent.

'Have you got any needles or sharp objects on your person that I should know about?'

'No.'

Morrow reached gingerly into his hoodie pocket, nothing. Other pocket, a dry tissue. Back pocket of his jeans, an envelope, unsealed. Unsure whether she was looking for actual medication or a script for medication she opened the envelope and pulled out a photograph. It was taken several years ago and was poor quality but still clear.

Roxanna was standing in a street with two men. She wore a raincoat and carried an umbrella. The road was wet but the men were in shorts and T-shirts.

Morrow held it up at Fraser. 'Who is this?'

He shrugged.

'Is this the picture you used to find her?'

Iain Fraser looked at it again. He shook his head.

'Why have you got this photograph?'

Shrug. 'Someone gave it to me.'

'Who gave it to you?'

He didn't answer.

She pointed at Roxanna. 'Did she give it to you?'

He looked at it again, seemed hurt and then frowned. He was looking at one of the men in shorts. 'Him?'

She followed his eyeline and pointed at a face. 'Him? This man gave you this photo?'

'Know *him*. I've seen him. Where's Andrew?'

'Do you know his name?'

He shook his head. His breathing was ragged, as if he'd run a long way. She reached into his front jeans pocket and took out a small bottle with two pills rattling at the bottom. She read the label. There had only been four pills in there and the label dated them this morning. He hadn't taken an overdose, but it was a high dose of antipsychotics.

'Where did you get this photograph, Mr Fraser?'

He looked up and nodded at the house, at the door lying ajar. 'From her.'

'The person in this house gave it to you?'

'Yeah.'

'This woman?' She pointed at Roxanna.

'No. Susan,' he said. 'Look: it was me. I killed a lassie at the loch. Not . . . It was just me.' Fraser's knee buckled and he looked as if he might fall over. They took an arm each and sat him down on the ground. Fraser's shallow pallor wasn't just a prison tan. The man wasn't well.

She told him his rights, speaking carefully. She knelt down and showed him the picture again. 'Susan Grierson gave you this?'

'She's not Susan.'

'Susan is not Susan?'

'She says she's Susan but she's not Susan.'

'Why did she give it to you?'

'For Andrew Cole.'

Morrow stood up. She didn't want him to say any more about that until she got a tape recorder working in a station.

'Everyone here seems to know everyone else,' she said, for something to say.

Fraser lifted his face to look at her. His eyes were bloodshot. 'No one here knows *anyone*.'

Thankless and Kerrigan arrived at the back gate. Morrow told them to take Fraser to Simmons' office. 'And get him checked out by the police surgeon. The prescription seems to be a new one. He might be having an adverse reaction.'

She watched as they walked Fraser to the car, telling him what was going to happen next. Fraser was relieved to be taken in. He was compliant the way habitual prison hands often were on rearrest.

As she watched Thankless cup Fraser's head to bundle him into the back seat of the car she felt a pang of tenderness. Hard-core jail fodder like Fraser might be perpetrators of horrors, but most of them were victims too. It was a hard story to hold in your head, hard to tell and harder to hear. She thought of him in Shotts. He'd been there until recently. He'd have been in there with Danny.

The car drove away and Morrow and McGrain turned back to the house. If anyone had been hiding in there they'd had a good long time to get out now. She felt a bit of relief about that.

The kitchen door opened silently. A smear of fresh oil glinted on the hinge. It was a big kitchen, bright if the windows had been washed, but they hadn't. Warm currents rolling in from the glass conservatory invigorated the dusty air, making it almost viscous. A large table in the middle of the room. Old units from the fifties, a modern electrical hob cut into the work-top. The ceiling had collapsed in a corner. They checked double doors opposite and found they led into a damp and empty cupboard.

The hallway was sticky, long-term cold. A big dirty window on the stairwell lit the space. A neat quarter-circle combed through the hall carpet showed that the front door had been opened re-cently. Two rooms led off the hall, one door open, one door firmly shut.

She knew.

Through the open door, a dining room. Polished dark-wood table. Sideboard cabinet. A glass display case, empty.

Morrow knew. Before she opened the second door in the hall-way. She could smell the sweet, heavy odour of bad meat wafting up from behind it.

McGrain knew too. He groaned 'Oh shit' and reflexively pulled a police-issue taser from his pocket, turned it on. The battery was flat.

Morrow and McGrain snorted, laughing because it was stupid

and futile: you couldn't taser a dead body away.

Morrow groaned and reached forwards, opening the firmly shut door.

Dark room. Curtains drawn. A nest of occasional tables next to the fireplace. A couch. A chair. Behind the couch, on its side, a zipped up sleeping bag. Bulky. Leaking. The source of the smell.

32

Morrow stood in the doorway of the room. The menthol petroleum jelly on her top lip made her eyes water but mercifully masked the smell. She watched the sleeping bag being unzipped under the white lights and recognised the tumble of blond hair around a bloated red face. She wasn't sure until she saw the plain rose gold hoops in an earlobe. Roxanna wore them, always.

Superficially, the senior Scene of Crime officer said Roxanna had been strangled with a length of wire. He could tell because it was still lodged in her neck. She'd been dead for at least two days. The officer explained that the impact bruising on her knuckles, very pronounced with post-mortem lividity, showed extensive defensive wounds on her arms and hands. A struggle. Defensive wounds from wire cuts through her forearms. She'd been punched on the side of the head behind her ear. Probably attacked from behind.

Morrow gave a nod and they zipped Roxanna back into the sleeping bag. They would keep it intact while they transported her to the path lab.

She moved out to the hallway and found Thankless waiting for her.

'Got the info on the owner of the house.' Thankless stood behind her, too close, smiling annoyingly. She knew that everything he did was wrong and the fault was hers. He pulled his notebook out of his pocket, stupidly.

'A Susan Grierson owns the house. She moved to America decades ago but her mother died . . .' he peered at his own writing, 'nineteen months, does that say? Nineteen months ago and she inherited the house. Well, it went into a trust in her name so . . .'

'A trust in her name?'

'Americans?'Thankless shrugged. 'Tax. They're wily.' He looked at his shoes. 'Like the coyote.'

That was quite funny, she knew that, technically. 'Has she come back, then?'

'Well, Iain Fraser is quite insistent that he's met her. He came here looking for her. A shop owner in the town said he saw Fraser with her and he knew her as Susan Grierson. He was at a charity dinner last night, a hundred people there and she was being introduced to people. She was working for the caterers, apparently.'

'Who did the food?' A sharp blue light lit the living room.

Morrow wondered why the hell they would test for that.

'I'll find out,' said Thankless.

Morrow heard the photographer mumble in the living room and take some pictures. She couldn't bring herself to look back in. She shouted into the room, 'Please, for God's sake, tell me it's not?'

'Sorry,' shouted the SOCO back, 'but it is.'

Morrow cringed. Some scenes were just too grim.

'What is it?' asked Thankless.

'They've found semen.'

'Oh.' He grimaced. 'Oh! Jesus!'

'But it's in a weird pattern,' called the SOCO. 'It's not ejaculatory. Looks like it's been poured in there.'

The whole scenario was off. A house held in trust by a woman who didn't live there. Iain Fraser said she was an imposter and now this. Morrow remembered the alcohol wipe marks on Roxanna's car and the clear set of Fraser's prints. Professional, but not very.

They heard the plastic flap of the body bag as it was opened wide to swallow the sleeping bag. They'd roll her into it and when they did Morrow and Thankless both knew a rancid haar would roll through the house.

They covered their mouths and noses and walked back out through the evidence path, through the door, to the front garden. Kerrigan and McGrain were standing there, chatting.

'Did the people who met Susan Grierson recognise her from before?'

'Why are you asking that?' Thankless was squinting at her.

It was an astute question. She thought of the alcohol wipes and the clean floor in Fuentecilla's Alfa Romeo. 'Professional,' she said. 'Seems professional to me. But then to leave her in your house, that's just the opposite.'

'Careless?' suggested McGrain.

'That's the most likely answer. *Semen*, though? Christ. Thankless, phone London Road, tell them we think we've found Roxanna. Get them to put out a call to stop Susan Grierson leaving the country. Airports, ferries, all that. You and Kerrigan drive around the town, see if you can dig up a photo from last night, check phones. McGrain and I'll be at the local station with Fraser. Get Family Liaison over to Robin Walker and give him an update.'

Morrow covered her nose and went back into the house.

She caught the chief SOCO. 'Keep it discreet here, would you? Small town. We don't want the neighbours knowing what we've found.'

'Always,' said the officer.

The police surgeon was German. A kind man who knew Iain Fraser and had actually prescribed the medication to him this morning. Mr Fraser, he told them, had suffered a psychotic episode before, while incarcerated, and he had also suffered a very terrible shock last night: he had witnessed two people killed in a fire. He was incredibly upset and the medication could potentially make him suggestible but he was fit for questioning.

'If I may give you some advice?' said Dr Neiman.

'Sure,' said Morrow.

'My understanding of Mr Fraser's last day is that he has not yet slept. I would, perhaps, leave the questioning of this man until he has at least had some sleep and eaten.'

Morrow didn't exactly tell him to fuck off but she strongly implied it between thank yous and goodbyes.

They took Iain Fraser into Simmons' interview room on the second floor. The flood from the burst pipe was marked down the wall, a mould-speckled river of black. The room was small and smelled of sweet mildew. Their giant suspect sat very still, his mouth open, his hands loose on the table.

Iain Fraser did not want a lawyer. His eyes were very red and he spoke slowly but he was clear about this: He didn't know a woman called Roxanna Fuentecilla and he didn't recognise her in any photographs. Susan Grierson had given him the enve- lope with the picture in it at the bins by the wee Asda. He was at great pains to tell them that he had killed Hester Kirk. He, and he alone, had killed her. She didn't *deserve* it. And she was a nice lassie. She was nice. So nice she let him take her. He, and he alone, took her to the golf course and killed her on the dock and it was him. Just him. And yes, he would repeat it for the tape and no, he didn't want a lawyer. Let that be an end to it.

'Can you drive, Iain?'

He couldn't.

'Did you walk her there?'

No, he didn't.

'D'ye get a minicab?'

He didn't know how to answer that.

'Who gave you the code to get in?'

He looked up at that.

'A what?'

'Who texted you the security code so you could get through the gates and onto the golf course?'

'Text?' He spent a while looking at the table and then looked up at Morrow's throat and told her he didn't get texts. He didn't have a phone.

She told him: There's someone missing from this story. Someone drove Hester Kirk to the boat. Andrew Cole texted someone the security code to get into the golf course in a van. So there's someone missing from your story. Can you tell us who it is?

He shook his head, frowning at the table. Andrew? he said. Andrew texted it?

'Do you know Andrew?'

Andrew Cole. Andrew Cole was in Shotts. *Andrew* texted someone the security code?

'We're quite sure he did. Why?'

Fraser was hurt by that, for some reason. He said he'd thought Andrew Cole was like a kid or something.

'Mr Cole likes to come over as quite helpless, doesn't he?'

Fraser looked up at Morrow, suddenly coherent and clear-eyed, but he didn't speak.

'I'm not convinced Mr Cole is an innocent.'

He flashed her a wry smile. 'Who *is*?'

She smiled back. 'We found your fingerprints on a bag of cocaine in Roxanna Fuentecilla's car, Mr Fraser.'

He wasn't even agitated by that but shrugged lazily, as if it wasn't true but he couldn't be bothered arguing. Morrow wanted to shout over the table at him, order him to give a fuck. But he didn't. She could see he didn't. And it wasn't just the medication.

'We found a body in Susan Grierson's house. A woman. Can you tell me anything about that?'

He didn't react beyond lifting an eyebrow. She wasn't sure he'd heard her. 'Mr Fraser? We found another woman, dead, zipped up in a sleeping bag, in that house you were at today. Did you kill her too?'

'No.'

'Who do you think did?'

'Susan.'

'Why do you think that, Mr Fraser?'

'I don't think she's Susan.'

'Who do you think she is?'

He shrugged. 'Thinking back ... dunno. She said she was Susan, but I dunno ...'

'Why would you doubt it?'

'She's different.'

'In what way?'

He thought about that for a long moment. 'Exploiting.' He rolled a hand slowly, as if he was hoping more words would come, but they didn't.

'Were you in Roxanna's car? An Alfa Romeo car, black?'

He shook his head.

'Did you touch a Waitrose freezer bag of cocaine?'

He frowned at her, asked her to say it again.

'A blue Waitrose freezer bag full of cocaine. It had bits of Jaffa Cakes in it. Did you touch one of those?'

He thought about it for a moment, staring at the table, and then, as if he'd never heard a funnier joke in his life, he huffed small laughs to himself. 'Jaffas ...' He laughed. 'The fucking ... Waitrose.'

He couldn't be brought back to the conversation then. He kept saying the supermarket name over and over, snorting sleepily to himself. Whatever she asked him, he kept coming back to Jaffa Cakes and Waitrose.

Morrow called Thankless and Kerrigan in: take him to Glasgow. Keep a close eye, I don't know if Mr Fraser's very well. She was turning to leave when he sat upright and spoke to her.

'Barratt,' he said.

Morrow turned to him. 'Mark Barratt?'

'Coming home. Tomorrow. Seven fifteen a.m. from Barcelona. Into Prestwick. He'll tell them. About the fire. Tell them who.'

'He'll tell what?'

'The fire. Murray and . . .' He wilted, face down, into the cradle of his arms, muttering, 'It wasn't me. Make Barratt tell Annie. And Eunice.'

Morrow watched him for a moment, heard him snuffle, and realised that he was asleep.

Simmons was waiting outside the interview room. She was delighted when Morrow told her that there was a connection between the dead woman in the loch and the fire at the Sailors' Rest.

'You'll be working with us, then?' she said. 'Because I am seriously stretched here.'

It would have been better manners to pretend she was pleased for another reason, glad of the insight and skills Morrow's team would bring or anything other than having less to do herself.

'Do you know a woman called Susan Grierson?'

'No.'

'Lives up at Sutherland Crescent.'

'I don't know many people who live in Sutherland Crescent, DI Morrow. Is it her house the body was found in?'

'Yeah. We're looking for her but there's no sign. She worked for the company that did the cooking for the charity dinner last night.'

'The Paddle Café? I know them, they'll tell us where she is if they know.'

'Iain says she gave him this photo.' Morrow showed her the picture of Roxanna.

Simmons looked at it. 'Oh, yeah, there he is.'

'Who?'

'Him.' Simmons touched the man in shorts in the photo. 'He owns the Paddle Café. This was taken a while ago though.'

The man on the left was holding up a medal on a ribbon that hung around his neck. Morrow looked closer at it. It was a medal for the London Marathon.

33

Boyd hadn't come in until after the lunchtime rush and it was fine. They had done the washing up, taken the deliveries, served lunch and the leftover quiche from last night had sold. He couldn't have been more pleased. He promised them an extra twenty quid in their wage packets and sent them both home an hour early.

He was wiping the counter top with a cloth, smiling at a four-toothed toddler hanging over his mother's shoulder, when he heard:

'Boyd Fraser?'

They looked like debt collectors, the man and woman blocking his exit by standing at the break in the counter.

'Are you Boyd Fraser?'

'I am. Can I help you?'

'We're from Police Scotland. Can we talk to you through the back for a moment?'

'Can't you talk to me here?'

'It's quite a serious matter . . .'

Shit shit. The sniff. It was the fucking sniff.

'Of course, please do come through.'

He took them through the kitchen to the back office but when they got to the door he realised that they wouldn't fit. They had to shuffle back in single file, to the kitchen.

'We can sit here.' He patted the edge of the steel kitchen table, asking the part-time cook, Moira, 'Will we be in your way?'

He was never that polite but he was trying to come over as a good bloke. Moira went along with it.

'Oh, you're lovely there!' she said warmly, though they never really spoke to each other like that, it was just for the benefit of the strangers.

Boyd dragged the office chair into the kitchen and was asking Moira about the fold-away sents they kept in the lock-up but the blonde woman stopped him. 'We don't really need to sit down. This is quite urgent. Could you stop . . .'

Fussing, she'd been going to say. He was fussing.

'Sorry.' He stood still, nodding Moira away into the café. She was only waiting for trays of brownies to come out of the oven anyway.

'OK, Mr Fraser. Do you know a woman called Susan Grierson?'

Shit. Susan! She was a dealer or something. Prostitute dealer or something. Worse than he could have imagined, the way this was going. Lucy would fucking kill him. She would leave him and kill him.

'You don't seem sure.'

'Yeah, no, I do, I do know her, yeah.'

He was holding the edge of the table and noticed, at the same time as the woman cop, that his hand was shaking. He put it in his pocket and gave a ridiculous high-pitched giggle. It sounded suspicious. So suspicious that he began to sweat a bit.

'How do you know her?'

'She's, um, she worked for me last night. At a charity dinner. She's from here.'

'Have you known her a long time?'

He nodded.

'Did you know her in the States?'

'No! She went there to live when I was young. She came back because her mum died . . .' But then he remembered that, no, she hadn't come back because of that. Her mum was dead but that was . . . Lucy said it was a while ago. 'She . . . No – her mum – ah, she came back.'

'When did you meet her again?'

'Two days ago.'

'Did she say why she was back?'

'She told me her mum died and I sort of assumed that's why she was back. But actually, that wasn't why she was back. But I don't know if she said that to me.'

'How did you find out that it wasn't why she came back? Did she tell you some other reason?'

This was good, they were interested in Susan, not him. God knows what else she'd been up to. 'No, she didn't. She said she was back because her mum died, but my wife said that Mrs Grierson, old Mrs Grierson, died a couple of years ago. So, I suppose, that's not why she was back.'

'Two days ago. That was the first time you met her again?'

'Yes.'

'How did you meet her?'

So he told them the story, about her being in here, them seeing each other by accident . . .

'Did you recognise her immediately?'

'Yeah, she said she was Susan and I recognised her.'

'*She* said she was Susan?'

'Yeah, and I recognised her.'

'Did you recognise her before she said her name?'

Odd question. He cast his mind back. 'No.'

'Did she approach you?'

'Um, yes.'

'Have you been to her house in Sutherland Crescent?'

Lucy didn't know he had been there. Did it matter? She would have wanted to know about the inside of the house for Sara Haughton. But they were the police and lying to the police was stupid. He hadn't really done anything. 'I have. I did. Last night.'

'What for?'

Boyd licked his lips and looked through to the café. 'Just, you know, had a drink or something. It was after the charity dinner. We were celebrating. Drink and so on, you know.'

He was pleased with his answer. Honest, but giving nothing away, but the cop wasn't listening any more. She was looking around the kitchen, nosy and not hiding it the way a polite person would. The man caught his eye and smiled as if this was a normal thing.

'We'd like to ask you about a photograph, sir.'

The woman carried on nosing around, even bending her knees to look under a shelf of dry goods, for fuck's sake. The man held a photo up to him.

'Yeah! Me and Sanjay,' he said, enjoying seeing him again. 'What? Is this about Sanjay?'

The woman reached across and her finger landed, gentle as a fly, on Sanjay's girlfriend's face. 'Who's this?'

'Sanjay's girlfriend, at the time.'

The man asked, 'Who's Sanjay?'

'Sanjay Hassan. We worked together in London. He was a trainee solicitor then, he's qualified now. We worked for a catering company together. Events.'

The woman asked, 'How well do you know her?'

Relieved, he smiled. 'Oh, look, I don't know her. I met her at the end of the marathon with Sanjay. They split up after a few dates. She had two kids.'

The man said, 'Roxanna Fuentecilla.'

'Roxanna! That's right. I remember now. Roxy, he called her. What's going on?'

The policeman looked at the policewoman, as if he didn't know what else he should ask. She was staring at the row of plastic tubs on the dry goods shelf. She nudged the man and pointed at one of the tubs. The plastic on the lid was cloudy, scratched from being washed and reused. It had *Baking Soda* written on it in black felt pen.

'Is Sanjay OK?'

'Can I open that?' she asked.

'Of course!'

She put on latex gloves and peeled the lid back. On the flat white surface sat a bubble of blue. Someone had shoved a blue plastic bag in there.

'What is it?' he asked.

The police officers looked at each other and asked if Boyd had any tinfoil.

'Of course!' Trying to be helpful, Boyd reached under the sink and hoisted out a big tinfoil roll onto the table. 'What do you want me to do with it?'

They were quite insistent that they'd do it themselves and the man put on latex gloves as well. Then they rolled out a length of the foil on the table and she pinched the bubble and lifted it out of the baking soda. It was a mobile, a Samsung, quite new.

'What's that doing there?' asked Boyd and then realised it was a stupid question. It was his kitchen in his café.

The cops eyed a conversation at each other. Boyd could tell it wasn't favourable to him.

'That's not my phone.'

The woman flattened the freezer bag against the phone and turned it on. She went into her own pocket, took out a clunky work phone and called a number. The phone in the freezer bag lit up.

'Whose phone is it?'

The woman cop hung up her own phone. 'It belongs to the woman in the photograph of you and Sanjay.'

'Sanjay's ex-girlfriend?' He laughed again, not sounding like a dick this time, just incredulous. 'Sanjay's *ex*? *What*?'

'Mr Fraser, I'm afraid we'll have to ask you to come with us. And we're shutting the café down for a thorough search.'

'Why?'

'This woman has just been found dead. In Susan Grierson's house.'

*

They shut the café down. Moira ushered all the customers out with their lunches packed up to go. She took the tray of brownies out and set them on a mesh tray to cool. As a final dutiful gesture she phoned Lucy at the house, told her to come down because the police were here questioning Boyd. Then Moira left, glad to get out but rubbernecking through the window as she passed it.

The cops told him he had the right to remain silent and other things. Boyd didn't really listen because it was just a mix up.

Minutes later the double buggy came through the door. Boyd saw that William had just woken up and looked cross and startled. He looked up and Lucy caught his eye. She had the same look on her face. The cops wouldn't let them speak to each other. Then two other cops came, a bald man and snaggle-toothed woman, and they took Boyd away.

34

Morrow and McGrain looked through the café, in the cupboards, in the toilets, behind the counter displays. They stood on a chair to check the high-up shelves. Three yellow olive oil drums were lined up on a shelf. They were empty but brought a splash of vibrant yellow and green to the room. McGrain lifted each one in turn and shook. The third one had something in it. He brought it down and they lifted off the lid. A bag from Waitrose, blue, with white powder inside.

'Must've used a whole bloody roll of freezer bags,' muttered Morrow.

Lucy Fraser said, 'That's not his.'

She was sitting in the café with two small boys, one fighting to get out of the buggy. She had given them a brownie each from the pile on the counter and one of them had fallen asleep with a tiny chocolate bite still on his tongue. Morrow wanted to go home and see her own boys so much she could hardly look at them.

They lifted the tin down from the shelf carefully.

'I'll tell you why I know it isn't his,' said Lucy Fraser. 'Because he only got a deal last night and this morning he said that when he got another one he'd get some for me too. So, there's no way that's his. We've been here for two years and we've never had a deal. We've just set up a business and we've got two kids. Honestly, it's not his.'

She looked slumped, miserable and sad but Morrow could tell she had no idea that they were investigating a murder. Morrow should tell her. It wasn't a chore she was relishing.

'McGrain, go to the car and get one of the big production bags.'

He put the oil drum on the floor and left through the door to the street.

'Really,' said Lucy Fraser, staring miserably at the drum, 'that's not his.'

Morrow looked sceptical.

'I know,' said Lucy. '"Husband lies to wife." Hardly front page news, is it? But it isn't. He said he didn't have any . . .' Her voice trailed away at the end and when she spoke again it sounded very faint. 'I know I sound like an idiot – here with my kids, looking absolutely knackered. But I know what sort of shit he is, and he isn't a hold-out shit.'

Lucy and Morrow smiled at each other, not warmly, just an acknowledgement that they were both there and both human.

'Lucy, I think I should tell you—'

'Look,' Lucy steeled herself, 'Boyd didn't come home last night. He didn't get in until very late. We used to take sniff a lot, in London, just for fun, but we haven't done it for ages and I know the signs and I know when he has and he hasn't.'

'What time did he get in?'

'About four thirty.'

'Where was he?'

McGrain was passing by outside the window, reaching for the door.

'I think he was out fucking some waitress.' Lucy Fraser's chin buckled. 'He's pretty restless at the moment.'

The door opened, McGrain came in and the moment was gone. Lucy went back to tend to the boys in the buggy.

McGrain opened the production bag and held it wide. Morrow lifted the tin very carefully and put it inside the bag.

'Fill the label out and put it in the car, would you?' McGrain took the production bag out and Morrow waited for the door to fall shut.

'Lucy, you need to know that this investigation isn't about a deal. Two women have been killed. We don't think Boyd did it but there are a lot of confusing coincidences. Too many coincidences for it to be chance.'

Lucy's face had turned grey. She stood up, her mouth slack, eyes open wide. 'What can I do?' she murmured.

'Tell me the truth?'

Lucy nodded at Morrow's stomach.

'Which waitress do you think it was?'

'Susan Grierson, I think. This morning, he flinched when her name came up. He was coming down this morning so he was all sort of twitchy and exaggerated. He was trying to be nice.' She smiled miserably. 'Out of character . . .'

Morrow nodded. 'Other than last night, has he been out late?'

'No. The most he does alone is go for a run but that's usually teatime or lunchtime and only for half an hour. Other than that he's here or home.'

'Two days ago, Tuesday morning at five thirty, where was he?'

'Asleep next to me,' said Lucy.

Morrow believed her.

No one by the name of Susan Grierson had tried to leave the country. Thankless had found a photograph of the woman. He had been asking in a butcher's shop on the square and a customer behind him volunteered the series of photos of the dinner dance that she had taken on her phone. She'd let him skim through until they found one with a woman in the background that everyone agreed was Susan Grierson. Thankless got her to text it to him.

They stood in Simmons' office and looked at it. Susan Grierson was tall, she was slim, she had a long nose and grey hair cut in a sharp bob.

'Print that,' said Morrow and went off to use the phone.

The fire investigation team had set up camp at one of the desks and were swanning about with great purpose.

Boyd Fraser had given her Sanjay Hassan's mobile number. He picked up at the third ring. Hassan was walking in a very noisy street. When he heard that his friend Boyd was in custody he did them the favour of not going down into Holborn Tube station but staying on the phone.

Morrow messaged him the photo from the envelope in Iain Fraser's back pocket and he called her back. That was the day of the London Marathon, he shouted over the noise of buses rumbling past. He had run it for the last three years as well and beat that time. Morrow thought he had been cut off.

'Sorry, "beat that time . . ."?'

'My TIME,' he shouted. 'My *time* is better now. On the marathon.'

'Oh, your marathon time?'

'Yes, *my* time.'

She asked him if he could possibly keep speaking to her but go somewhere quiet so that she could hear him properly. He said he could. An abrupt change in atmosphere and soft background music told her he was in a shop.

'I'm in a *shop*,' he shouted.

'OK, Mr Hassan, the woman in the photo, what can you tell me about her?'

'That's an ex of mine, Roxanna Fuentecilla. She had kids.'

'Where did you meet her?'

'Oh, God, I don't know. Brown's, maybe? I worked as a waiter then, part-time, for money while I was training. I think it was Brown's. We only went out a couple of times. She was Spanish.'

'Did Boyd know her?'

'No.' He seemed quite sure.

'Who would be able to get a copy of that photo?'

'Didn't Boyd have that on his café's website or something?'

'Did he?'

'Still does, I think, doesn't he? He asked me what I thought of his website and, well, I don't really like that picture. He beat me that year and he looks really smug. I'm sure he put it up to piss me off. My time's better now. I don't think Boyd even runs any more.'

Morrow could hear a shop assistant whispering to ask if he wanted to try that on?

'Have you seen her since?'

'What do you mean?'

'You haven't bumped into each other or been at the same parties or anything?'

He didn't know what to say to her. 'Have you ever been to London? It's pretty big.'

35

Boyd had been sitting on the concrete bench for forty minutes. Each time he shut his eyes to blink, he expected the world to be different when he opened them. It never was. A dead woman found at Susan's.

Boyd only met Roxanna once. Sanjay didn't talk about her much and then she was history. She had kids. They were young blokes. Boyd was honestly more startled to hear that Sanjay's ex had been in Helensburgh than that she was found dead in Susan's house. His time in London and Helensburgh felt so separate. It was like finding a character in the wrong movie.

A grey wall opposite him. A grey floor in front of him. Heat-sapping cold under his buttocks. He leaned forward again, folding the thin mattress under his bum and sitting on that. He had been alternating for thirty minutes between sweating into the rubberised plastic and freezing his balls off on the bare concrete.

He shut his eyes. Question him. They needed to question him about a murdered woman? Lucy didn't know how serious it was when they took him away. She thought Boyd got caught for getting a deal. He could see she blamed him.

His mother's angry voice came into his head: Speak clearly, don't mumble, stay calm, don't lie. Fucking useless advice in this context.

He kept shutting his eyes and thinking about Miss Grierson. They said two women had been killed. She was the only woman he could imagine might be missing, the only woman he felt guilty about. She said she was leaving, that she didn't belong here and he should tell them. That should be the first thing he told them. Less than twelve hours ago she stood in the doorway to her garden, watching him leave, a reassuring lack of affection and warmth in her expression as she said goodnight, see you later, formulaic phrases that promised nothing and asked for nothing.

If she was dead they would find traces of him all over her. Even if she'd taken a bath as soon as he left, bits of Boyd would be all over the kitchen and on the floor of the conservatory. He felt sick at the memory of the conservatory. Why did they do that there, on a dirty floor? The house had bedrooms. But he knew why. They did it there because it wasn't a bedroom. Neither of them wanted intimacy. They were looking for the opposite of intimacy.

Footsteps outside the door. Locks scraping open. A stern woman. Come with me, please, sir.

They took him out of the building onto the Helensburgh street and put him in the back of a car, a shitty car. Then two uniformed police got in the front and they drove all the way to Glasgow in silence. It was horrible.

They pulled up in a shit area of that shit city. Why would anyone live there? It was so ugly. Around the back of a big building and into a walled car park topped with razor wire and cameras.

They got Boyd out and walked him up a concrete ramp, through a security door and to a sort of check-in desk. Then they handed him over to the cops there, gave them a padded brown envelope with all of Boyd's personal belongings in and left, saying they had to go back to Helensburgh and get someone else. Who else? Susan Grierson?

A very tall female officer came and stood by him. The man behind the desk took his details and they moved him over to a big machine that photographed his fingerprints. The man looked at Boyd's cashmere sweater and told the giantess to be careful with this one.

A joke. She was built like a tank.

Boyd only realised it was a gentle joke, not nasty, when they were around the corner on the way out to the interview rooms. Boyd wanted to go back and smile at the man, show he got it. But he couldn't. He followed the giant sheepishly, through a stairwell, into a room with a wire mesh window on the door and a table in the middle with four chairs.

They wouldn't be long, she said and then she left him alone. A sarcastic camera winked high in the corner of the room.

Now she was missing too.

The door flew open behind him. The people who had come to the café marched in. They introduced themselves as DI Alex Morrow (the woman) and DC Howard McGrain (the man).

'Right, Boyd, we want to ask you about Roxanna Fuentecilla: when did you meet her?'

Boyd hesitated. 'After the London Marathon. Three years ago.'

'And the next time?'

'There wasn't a next time. That was it.'

'Did you go for something to eat afterwards?'

'No.' Obviously she had never run a marathon. He wanted to tell her that you didn't exactly feel like nipping into a Nando's afterwards but he was scared of her.

'When Fuentecilla came to Helensburgh, did she come to the café?'

'You know, honestly? She might have. But if she did I didn't recognise her. I met her that one time and I'd just run a marathon. That was it. If it wasn't for that photo I probably wouldn't even remember. Sanjay split up with her afterwards. She had kids and I think all he liked about her was her house. She lived in Belgravia. He thought she was rich.'

'Was she?'

'I guess not. I think he could have overlooked the children if she had been.'

'Have you sold any land recently?'

'Land?'

'Have you?'

'No.'

'Do you know Frank Delahunt?'

'No.'

'Tell me what happened with Susan Grierson.'

He baulked at that, but he told them: I knew her growing up. She moved away for a very long time. I met her again recently. She asked for a job and worked for me for one night. After the dinner she approached me. She said she had some cocaine. She went to the café and waited for me. In the café, after, well, sort of . . .

Boyd was blushing furiously. It was one thing to do things but telling was different.

The woman seemed to have been through this before. 'Just look at the table and say it. You'll not be telling us anything we haven't heard a hundred times.'

He looked at the table and said it: She gave me a blow job. Weird. How was it weird? She had a kind of bag in her mouth. She sort of hid it from me by doing that – he showed them the mouth movement and the way she swung her head away, covering her mouth with her flat hand. So that was, kind of, odd. We went back to her house. We took more coke—

'Where was the coke, was it in a packet or an envelope of some kind?'

'Yeah, a Waitrose bag. Freezer bag. Small size. Like that one the phone was in. I noticed it because it made me think of work. Waitrose take a lot of our custom.'

'Then what happened?'

'Well, we went to her house and you know . . .'

'Had sex?'

'Yes.'

'Where?'

'In the kitchen area, sort of. Please don't tell my wife.'

The woman looked at him for a moment, as if she was deliberating. 'Your wife knows. She told me. She said, "I think he was out fucking some waitress." Where is Susan Grierson now?'

He was too startled to speak. All he could think about was Lucy in the kitchen with the boys this morning, crying, hiding it from them, and how sad she must feel. He had done that. And she had known, this morning, when he stomped into the kitchen and hugged her and pulled her onto his knee. She had known. He was an arsehole.

'Mr Fraser? Where is Susan Grierson now?'

Boyd forced himself to speak. 'Told me she was leaving. Again. Said she didn't belong here.'

They pushed a different photo over at him, a picture of a family in a botanical glasshouse. Roxanna was in the foreground. He hadn't seen her for a long time, barely remembered her from then, but she was still fantastically good-looking.

'Do you know this man?'

They pointed to a man in the background, red-trousered. The husband? Boyd looked at him for a moment. 'I think he comes into the café. He looks like a customer. Maybe.'

'And the woman?'

'Well,' he felt they were trying to trick him, 'isn't it Roxanna? The woman from the photo with Sanjay?'

'Yes.' They put it away. It felt like a dumb test of something. He was pissed off by that. The regret was ebbing away and he felt himself getting angry.

'Look, how did you even get the photo of me and Sanjay? Did Sanjay give it to you?'

'You put that photo up on the café website, didn't you?'

Oh, God. They were right. He had put it up there, as a finger to Sanjay; well not really a finger but more of a goading gesture. When it was obvious he was never coming up to visit.

'The picture we found is very low res,' said the man. 'We think it's a print from the website image.'

The woman was looking at her notes and Boyd suddenly thought, Fuck this. 'Can I go home?'

They ignored him.

She looked up. 'What's your relationship to Iain Fraser?'

Boyd shook his head. 'Sorry, who?'

'Iain Fraser. A man from Helensburgh.'

'I don't know him.'

'He has the same surname as you and he lives in Helensburgh.'

She didn't know the town. Boyd explained patiently that there were two different Fraser families in Helensburgh. There had been a spit in the family a generation back. His father's sister converted to Catholicism. Their father was a minister and Boyd's father was a minister, and the two sides didn't really talk to each other. Colquin and Lawnmore Frasers, they were known as. It felt odd explaining small-town family politics to a stranger in a Glasgow police station. It was more of a tea and scones conversation piece.

'So, Iain Fraser's your cousin?'

Cold crept over Boyd's shoulders. He had the sensation of the ground moving under him. 'I suppose. Technically.'

The woman's phone buzzed in her pocket and she took it out, looked at it and left the room to take the call. They were so fucking rude! When she came back in she was agitated and in a hurry to get away.

'That'll be all for now, Mr Fraser. We're going to go and talk to some people but we'd like you to stay here with us. We'll come back to you in an hour or so. OK?'

'Anything,' he said, not feeling gracious at all, wanting to cause a fuss and get out. 'Really. Anything that helps.'

They escorted him downstairs to the check-in desk and the man in the shirtsleeves. Boyd tried a smile at him, the smile he meant to give when he made the joke about the big woman being wary of him. The man smiled back pleasantly but Boyd didn't think he remembered.

A buzzer rang behind the desk, chiming with a bell in a distant concrete corridor. The shirt-sleeved man leaned down and spoke into an intercom. What is it? Cup of tea? Sugar? Sit tight, mate, and we'll get that to you.

It was the cousin. They'd gone back to Helensburgh for him. The Colquin Frasers, tainted by Rome, the non-elect.

36

Robin Walker had phoned Morrow: the kids were missing.

They set off for school after Morrow and McGrain left the house this morning. Robin had been waiting for them to come home at the usual time, ready to tell them the terrible news about their mother. But they didn't come home. He called their phones but they were switched off. He called one of Martina's friends and she said Martina hadn't been at school today. He called the school and was told by the secretary that a phone call in the morning notified them that the kids wouldn't be in today. As far as she could recall, the secretary said, it was a woman's voice.

Morrow had barely lifted her hand to knock when Robin opened his front door wide. He glared at her with blood-shot eyes and staggered off into the living room. They followed him in.

She found him slumped on the couch, in front of what looked like a half pint of vodka with a tinge of orange mixer and a brown-edged quarter of lime. He was drunk.

'Mr Walker?'

'Fucking fucks, those fucks.'

She sat down next to him. 'I'm sorry.'

'Well, now we know, don't we?' He slurred and lifted the drink to take a gulp. He looked at Morrow. 'We know where they've gone, anyway.'

'Who?'

'Fucking kids.' His breath reeked sour. He smelled as if he was sweating venom.

'When did this happen?'

'They set off for school. I went out for a run. Then one of *you* came, told me about . . .' He couldn't say it. He rolled a hand, easing himself over the bump. When he spoke again he sounded broken. 'Waited for them, from school. I didn't go in, too upset, I just thought – *Those kids, God, those poor kids.* And all the time I'm not thinking *my* Roxanna, you know, I'm thinking *their* mum. Their *mum.* You know?' He'd become a stepfather just too late. He took another drink, cringing as he swallowed, not enjoying it. 'They hadn't been in. I checked their rooms – everything gone. Their stuff gone and their passports. Every fucking thing. Gone. Set up to look as if - fucking *arseholes.*'

'They could have been kidnapped?'

'Bollocks.' He stood up unsteadily, staggered sideways two steps, corrected himself and fell forwards through the door to the hall. 'COME!' He roared, bouncing off a wall.

By the time they got down to Martina's room, a matter of seconds, Robin's mood had changed entirely and he was sitting on her bed, sobbing. All of the cupboards were open, all of the cupboards were empty. Martina had done a good job of not attracting attention though. Her sparse ornaments were untouched. Her bed was made as if she was coming back. She had even left her laptop on the desk.

Morrow looked at it. 'Robin, what do you think happened?'

He looked at her. She could feel him trying, through sheer force of will, to sober up. He couldn't though, because he didn't drink often, she thought. So now he was very drunk and very shocked. 'Vicente set her up. Murdered her. Now he's taken the kids.'

He rubbed his nose with the back of his hand.

'Would he do that to their mother?'

He snorted. 'You don't know him.'

Morrow sat next to him on the bed. 'Neither do you.'

He thought about that. He wept and scratched his arm. He looked around the empty cupboards and the room. 'I had a life . . .'

Thankless held up his phone. He had a call coming through

on silent. Morrow nodded that he could take it and he went out to the corridor.

Walker sniffed, 'I haven't got the rent for this month. I'm going back to London with nothing. Gave up my job and everything to come here. Except that bookcase.'

'A design icon,' said Morrow.

He smiled pathetically. 'Maria Arias set her up, didn't she?'

Morrow half nodded. 'But something went wrong, I think.'

'She knew Vicente from before . . .' He looked around the room once more and stood up. 'I'm going to get fucking hammered.'

She stood up too. 'Good idea.'

In the hall Thankless nodded her away from Walker. They watched him stagger off into the living room.

Thankless muttered, 'A woman fitting Grierson's picture was at Glasgow airport this morning. Private plane. Had two kids with her. She was travelling in the name of Abigail Gomez.

37

Glasgow International was a hard place to stroll into. After a failed terrorist attack, bollards and traffic-calming measures had been introduced on all the roads. Traffic was streamed within touching distance of the terminal but then drawn suddenly away again to the back of a high-rise car park. The boarding area for private planes seemed to be exempt from the general air of caution. A mess of bad signage and pot-holed roundabouts was deemed sufficiently stringent security. It was very hard to find.

Morrow and Thankless had shown their ID to the camera at the car park barrier and then were made to show it again outside the door to the small smoked-glass building sitting on the edge of the runway.

The doors slid open to a shallow lobby with plastic plants, double doors and a two-way mirror on the back wall. A young man with a long hipster beard and grey suit slid out from a side door, smiling and pulling his suit jacket straight. He was panting.

'DI Morrow? Come in here, please.' He held the door behind him open to them and followed Morrow and Thankless into the narrow corridor, excuse me-ing until he was ahead of them. Bit of a squeeze, he said, so sorry. He led them to an office at the far end of the building. A small window faced onto the runway. A desk below it held a bank of security monitors. On their left, a smoked-glass wall faced into the departure lounge.

Once inside the office he shut the door behind them, stepped over until he was between them and the monitors, straightened his jacket again and smiled as if they were just meeting now. There didn't seem to be anyone else in the building.

He introduced himself as the manager and asked for the flight number. As Morrow handed it over for scrutiny she realised that the small room was cold and the computer wasn't switched on. The manager was the only person here and he'd just arrived. In all probability, A7432 was the only private airplane to have left in the past few days.

He turned on the computer and they all watched the monitor as it booted up. It seemed to take a long time to churn on. The manager kept catching their eyes, giving a service smile and looking back at the screen, willing it faster. Morrow left Thankless to catch the smiles and eye contact and looked through the smoked-glass window into the departure area.

Square chairs in black leatherette sat neatly side by side, facing floor-length windows onto the runway. Attempts had been made to dress the lounge as something more than a waiting room, but they had failed. A coffee machine sat on a side table next to a platter of individually wrapped biscuits. A small fridge with individual bottles of wine was locked.

'Here we go,' said the manager, bending down to use the mouse. He called up the latest file and double-clicked.

They watched expectantly. A split screen view: the empty departure lounge next to a small hand luggage X-ray machine elsewhere in the building. They watched for a full minute. Nothing happened. The manager smiled an apology.

'Let me put that on fast forward for you,' he said and did. They watched again. On screen, in fast forward, the bearded manager and another man in a customs uniform scurried into view and turned on the X-ray machine. They chatted manically, then ignored each other as they form-filled and checked their watches. The customs man gave a speedy yawn.

The manager pressed play and there, languorous by contrast, Martina Fuentecilla and Hector sauntered in to the X-ray shot. Both were dressed in school uniforms. They waited by a high desk. The time was ten a.m. Morrow had just arrived at Hettie's house in Clydebank.

Seen from a high angle on the wall, as a god might see them, the children stood close to each other in the empty room. The manager looked at them and smiled warmly. In the small, cold room Morrow saw him watch himself on the monitor. She saw a small echoing smile flit across his face. On the footage neither child reciprocated his warmth. The manager on screen was embarrassed by that and turned his smile to the clipboard in his hand. He checked their passports, wrote something down and smiled more formally as he handed them back.

'What is that you're writing there?' asked Morrow.

'Passport numbers.'

They watched on. Martina and Hector put their backpacks on the conveyor, separating out their phones into plastic trays and sending them through the X-ray machine.

A third person in their party arrived on screen. She handed over her passport. She was wearing a long grey skirt, a blue cardigan that reached the back of her knees and a black beret. Seen from the back she could have been anyone. The screen manager smiled and pointed at the hat, asking her to remove it. He held up the passport, checked her face against her photo and handed it back. The woman put her bag on the conveyor belt and twisted towards the camera as she moved on. They could see her face.

He paused it. 'There?' he said. 'Is that the photo lady?'

She woman was in her fifties maybe, had grey hair, cut in a bob, and a long, straight nose. Susan Grierson.

'It is,' said Morrow, aware that he was looking for an acknowledgement. 'Well spotted.'

Satiated, he nodded. 'She's using a different name.'

'Seems to be. Can we see your passenger records for these people?'

'Of course.' He minimised the footage file and opened the passenger record. Theirs was the only plane to leave that day and there were three people on board: Martina and Hector Fuent-ecilla and a woman called Abigail Gomez. Gomez was travelling on a US passport but was resident in Ecuador.

'Can you check for this passport number coming in during the past week or so?'

He said he would but she didn't think he would find it. Gomez would have needed a visa to get into the country. She would have come in as someone else.

The private plane's flight record showed that the party had already landed in London City Airport. They had a connection booked on a commercial flight to Miami from City. They were travelling first-class and had an onward connection to Guayaquil in Ecuador.

'Did they make that connection?'

The manager checked a further file. They were presently on their way to Miami.

'What time do they land in Miami?'

'Just under an hour.'

38

She emphasised that it was urgent but had been waiting on hold for eight minutes. Now DCC Hughes was asking her for information that was available in the notes he had in front of him. Look, sir, she said, we need the warrant right *now* or they can't detain her at Miami.

Where was Fuentecilla found? In the house of a woman called Susan Grierson. The woman who passed herself off as Susan Grierson is travelling as Abigail Gomez and lands in Miami in twenty minutes. She's taking a connection to Ecuador with the children and this is our last chance to detain her.

Is Susan Grierson from Helensburgh?

Yes, sir, but Abigail Gomez is not Susan Grierson.

But Susan Grierson is from Helensburgh?

Morrow hesitated. Yes, Susan Grierson is, but this isn't Susan Grierson.

Did she call herself Susan Grierson? Yes.

Did she live in Susan Grierson's house? Yes.

In your notes you've said several people identified her as Susan Grierson and she seems to have detailed information about the local area.

Morrow had put that in to draw Hughes' attention to how well briefed Grierson/Gomez was, how professional she was. She'd meant him to realise that these were serious professional people, that they should move urgently to detain them.

So, DCC Hughes continued, voice close to the receiver, his breath buffeting her ear, realistically, she could be local?

Morrow shut her eyes. She bit her tongue. In desperation she began to tap her knee with her forefinger, because she understood then. If the case was local, Police Scotland would get the Injury Claims 4 U money. But all of the money would go to the Met if a connection was made with the London case through Miami, through Abigail and Vicente and Maria Arias.

Morrow had thought that the set up was shoddy. The body was dumped in the house, the alcohol wipes left a residue, even the semen sample was badly applied to the body. But it seemed to her now that it was less slapdash than cynical. Whoever she was, Gomez hadn't just killed Roxanna, got the kids out and implicated some hapless locals. She'd written a script for the police, constructing a pursuable case against the Fraser cousins. Gomez understood that the police needed an excuse not to spend money chasing her halfway across the world. If they let her go and charged the local boys instead they'd get a case cleared up and a slice of the seven million pounds. A wrongful conviction was in their interests.

'Sir, this is urgent. We need you to authorise the warrant within the next twenty minutes.'

There was a pause on the line and then Hughes spoke:

'Look, the Ariases' assets have been frozen. The Fraud are clawing back all their accounts and deposits.' His voice dropped to a shamed murmur. 'Have you got enough evidence to charge either of the Frasers?'

Morrow stopped tapping her knee. She was so angry that she felt her heart rate slow down.

'Sir,' she said very carefully, 'this is exactly what she wants us to do.'

He drew a breath but didn't speak.

'OK,' she said. 'Just to clarify my position here, Sir: there is insufficient evidence to charge either of the Frasers with this offence. If a case goes against them I'll be forced to resign and offer my evidence to the defence.'

It was a threat but Hughes knew she was lying. She heard him suck his teeth and then he lied back: 'I'll attend to that warrant as a matter of urgency.'

He hung up.

39

Iain Fraser had fallen into a delicious Largactil sleep in the car on the way to Glasgow. They managed to walk him part of the way to the cells but had to help him beyond the desk when he lost his balance.

They drove him to Glasgow in a police car, took him to a police station in Bridgeton and then took his pills and money and tobacco off him and put him in the cells. He slept on his back. Iain had been thinking about Andrew Cole, about the fire, about the heat in his fingers as he fell asleep. But he didn't dream of those things. He dreamed of the high-pitched sound of snapping glass.

He slept with his hands on his belly and when he woke up they were numb because he hadn't moved and it had been maybe two hours. He lifted them up, these dumb blackened fleshy things, and looked at them through sleep-puffed eyes. They were swollen. They looked like cartoon fingers.

He rang for a cup of tea and asked for sugar. He didn't usually take it but he was hungry now. They didn't let you smoke in cells any more. It was torture. He should have asked for a patch.

He waited and waited. He could hear people outside being attended to and processed.

He could feel her, sitting in his chest, heavy. She was waiting inside him. A solid heavy lump of a thing but they were at peace now. They weren't fighting each other any more. They were just looking for a way out of this together.

A door opened. A man gave him a plastic yellow plate, Ikea stamped underneath and a cheese sandwich on it. Iain ate the sandwich and drank tea, not hot tea, but strong. He was used to taking what he was given. Prison made you used to that.

A man, the same man, came for him and brought him out of the cells into the lobby of the holding cells and two cops he hadn't seen before took him upstairs. They sat him down and asked him if he was all right. Maybe he wanted to wash his face, he was awful dirty.

Nah, Iain breathed the word out as if it was his last *shee-laah*, I'm all right.

The lady cop and the man, the ones from Susan's house, sat down. No, thanks. He didn't want a lawyer. Iain rubbed his face hard. It felt grainy. He said the word, 'grainy' and looked at his massive black hands. They had a packet of baby wipes, would he like one?

Did he answer? He was holding a baby wipe and rubbing the moist cloth on his face. It smelled of perfume and felt oily on his skin. He rubbed his hands with it, like those flannels they gave out in the curry shops. It was black and ragged now. He put it at the side of the table.

Tell us about the woman from the loch.

He picked her up at her house in Clydebank and she went with him. She seemed quite happy to come. Who sent you to get her? No one. Did you know her? No. Where did you get her address? Don't know. He felt her nuzzle in his chest, listening to him tell her story. She approved and he was pleased because he didn't want to make her angry again. Above all, not that.

Where did you get that photograph in the envelope from? Susan Grierson gave it to me. In the envelope? Yes, in the envelope. Who is in the photograph? I don't know. Why did she give it to you? To get Andrew Cole out. She told me to tell you it came from Tommy Farmer but it didn't. Who is Tommy Farmer? Works for Mark Barratt. Small time. Never done time. Who is Boyd Fraser? I don't know. He's from Helensburgh, isn't he? I don't know. Who is Mark Barratt? Mark Barratt gets in tomorrow at seven fifteen. Prestwick.

Do you know Frank Delahunt? Iain didn't know anybody by that name but it was an odd name. He mouthed it back to them. Frank Delahunt. Half fancy, half Irish. No. I don't know anyone by that name.

Then he looked up.

She was the absolute double of Danny McGrath. The police woman, staring at him across the table, talking, he saw her mouth moving, grinned that she was Danny McGrath as a woman. Dimples, blond hair, thinner face but the same mannerisms, the same blank face and undertone of fury. She saw him looking at her.

I know you, Iain said, your face.

She said, Really?

And he grinned and said, You look exactly like Danny McGrath.

Do I? Do I look like Danny McGrath?

Yes, you do. His total double and you know what is most like Danny McGrath about you? Your stony face. The way you sit and move your hands. You're cold.

And who exactly is Danny McGrath?

So Iain told her: I knew him in Shotts. No, I didn't know him. I've seen him but I don't know him. He's a gangster in Shotts Prison and he's a bad man. He's a blank-faced hard nut and you wouldn't know he was coming at you until he was on you. And you look just like him.

And she said, Well, you've got a good eye for a man who can't even wash his own face, Mr Fraser, because Danny McGrath is my half-brother.

A slow smile rippled out from Iain's nose, crossing his face and warming him behind the ears. You, he said. You're that cop who put her own brother in prison.

He's not in prison because of me. He's in prison because he was convicted of conspiracy to murder.

She was as cold as her brother. Her voice never even wavered as she said it.

You've no loyalty, said Iain. You don't know who you are belonging to.

She looked him in the eye then, and she was smiling but angry with it. She said, No, Mr Fraser, I know *exactly* who I am belonging to. And I know who I am: I'm the person who tells the truth even when it doesn't suit me. Even if it hurts me.

The talk went on. Questions went on. Eyebrows rose, asking questions of him, but all Iain could see was this woman in front of him who looked like Danny McGrath but tried to tell the truth. All he could think was what a sublime thing it would be, to stop lying. He saw her standing in front of fires in pubs, standing in Lainey's hall, taking orders from Barratt. She was staring at him, at Iain. She asked another question.

Iain opened his mouth and out came the truth: Mark Barratt gave the orders. I killed her at the loch and I'm sorry. Andrew Cole lent us his boat. Tommy drove the van and Tommy started the fire at the Sailors' Rest that killed Lea-Anne and Murray.

No, I don't need a lawyer.

His mouth opened wider and more came out, yellow came out, and the woman told the truth too: I was killed on the dockside, in sand dunes on the dockside. I trusted bad men. That's why I came willingly. These are bad men.

'No, Iain,' the honest woman said, leaning close to him, 'Hester Kirk came with you because she was blackmailing someone. She thought you were going to give her a pay-off. That's why she came with you.'

'A pay-off?'

'It was about money. She thought you were going to give her money.'

A pay-off. That was why she waited so patiently. That was why she didn't try to run or talk them out of it. That was why she walked with them, from the van, through the high dunes of yellow yellow sand. She wasn't a martyr. She didn't say Sheila. She didn't go into his chest to teach him anything.

Iain felt his chest, but she was gone.

Iain spoke to her but heard nothing. She had never been there. There was nothing in him.

He knew something was coming. His vision was framed with a jagged bright white light. With a terrible sense of urgency he pleaded with her: tell them, will you? Annie and Eunice tell them that it wasn't me. Please? It wasn't me. But his lips were sliding across his teeth and his tongue was swelling and the light got suddenly brighter and the world was gone.

A slow wave, as high as a hill, washed over him, the cold of it touching his forehead, the point of the third eye, folding over him, a white wave, a cold wave, a salt wave.

40

Late in the evening, in her car, Alex Morrow sat looking up at the Southern General Hospital, at small windows burning into the night. Members of the public came and went. Nurses pushed patients out to a smoking shelter in the car park and then went back for them. Minicabs arrived, picking up or dropping off and then they drove away again. Danny was up there, behind one of those windows.

It was nearly midnight. She wanted to go home but sat in the car, so sad she felt paralysed.

Iain Fraser was dead. She had watched them lift his body onto a stretcher in the interview room. A massive heart attack, they said. They hadn't brought a body bag upstairs with them. The lead paramedic hoped that was OK? He could go and get one if she wanted? Morrow said no, it was fine. They could carry him downstairs and through the lobby and not pass anyone. No one came into police stations any more.

She was glad that there were cameras everywhere in the station, glad the surgeon who examined him was his own doctor, glad she had double-checked his medication. But still, when she watched the footage back and saw him half collapse on his way into the holding cell, she knew it would look bad. That was why she went to the hospital with the body. She needed to know it was a heart attack. She needed to know she wasn't going to be on a death-in-custody charge first thing in the morning.

Superficially, Iain Fraser had died of a heart attack, the lab told her, but actually, look. Look at the fingers here, see that? On his fingernails?

She couldn't see it but they were clubbed. She thought they said stubbed, but he repeated himself: *clubbed*. The tips of the fingernails were squared and swollen. Lung cancer. Untreated, advanced, his heart probably just gave out. He must have been in terrible pain.

Fraser was a lowlife, a career thug. She shouldn't feel sad for him but she did and it bothered her. She shouldn't have any feelings about him.

The arrest warrant for Abigail Gomez had gone through an hour too late. The party of three had made their connecting flight to Ecuador. She tried to rationalise the failure: international arrest warrants did take time. They did take time. She knew they did. But they didn't have to. They didn't always.

Whoever Abigail Gomez really was, she had a talent for identifying weakness. She had arrived in a tiny west coast Scottish town, swooping in like an omniscient being, posing as a returner with just enough information to make it work. She had found Police Scotland's weakness too. But lack of funds was universal. It wasn't a hard weakness to identify.

She had seen Iain Fraser's weakness too. He was determined to take responsibility but he was just a cog. She'd seen that many times before. It was a belief often borne of a traumatic childhood, it was so much more manageable to believe himself bad than the world. It was people like Danny she had trouble with. People who blamed everyone else or thought injustice was the natural order of things.

Iain Fraser died begging. He slumped over the table, mumbling, rambling. Morrow didn't know what he was begging for. He was pleading with her, Annie and her niece, tell them he did something, or didn't do something. But then he was gone. She could watch the tapes back but didn't think it would make it any clearer. She'd check his records in the morning and try to find Annie or the niece. She didn't know what she could tell them though.

Morrow sighed. She should go home but she didn't. She stayed there, looking up at the windows of Danny's ward, asking herself questions that were far too big for midnight in a rainy hospital car park.

Danny was up there, in a bed with a respirator hissing next to him, having a good night. He'd felt no compunction about letting a civil war break out to make a point. She cursed him and phoned the ward.

A female nurse answered. She dropped the phone when Alex gave Danny's name. Picking it up again, she sounded nervous and breathless, and said she would just get someone to talk to Alex, can you wait a wee minute? Would that be all right, pet? Morrow was crying before the doctor even picked up the receiver. He was very sorry. Alex said she was too, but she was lying. She hung up.

Iain Fraser was wrong. They didn't make the world. They didn't make all the lies and the crap in it. She shouldn't lie about Danny: she wasn't sad. She was crying with relief.

Weeping and exhausted, she turned on her headlights, let the handbrake off and drove the cherished journey home, to her warm house, to her good man, to her lovely children who were breathing and thriving.

41

In the bright early morning a two-car convoy crested a high hill. The sudden sight of the Irish Sea was broken only by Ailsa Craig, a bare stone island as round as a baby's buttock, sticking out of the water.

Morrow had not been to bed. Arriving home three and a half hours before she had to leave again, she made a pint of coffee and sat in the dark kitchen with a packet of biscuits, holding a solitary wake for her brother. She sat in the gloom for three hours, inviting the sorrow to hit her. Nothing came. So she dredged up memories, tender moments they had shared, kindnesses, sadnesses. Nothing came. She couldn't command grief any more than she could command the sea.

Prestwick Airport was a hangover from the Second World War. It was a cheap-flights airport and dressed the part. An advertising hoarding on the roundabout ordered drivers to fly to Rome for £9. The footbridges and outside wall of the train station advertised discounted airfares, car hire and hotels. Everything had a discount price on it. Prestwick Airport knew what it was selling.

They parked in short stay, a hundred yards from the entrance, and walked, hunched against a bitter wind, into the lobby. It was wide and tall and white and empty. Most of the flights came in or left early. It was part of the discount deal: holiday flights at business times, business flights on a holiday schedule. The arrivals board announced that the flight from Barcelona was expected at 7.15.

They had ten minutes to waste. Morrow ordered the DCs to sit down on the chairs and they did. McGrain sat with her. She had come team-handed in case Barratt had heavies with him.

It was quiet in the lobby. No one lingered. Most passengers hurried straight to security to meet their early morning flights.

Across the road a train arrived from Glasgow. The passengers crossed the footbridge and took the long escalator down, deposited luggage at the airline desk and scurried to the ordered queue for security. Within a few minutes, check-in printouts read, passports checked, they were swallowed by the security door and the lobby was clear again.

Morrow gradually became aware of a man in her peripheral vision. He was reading a copy of *The Times*, notable for not taking one of the plentiful empty chairs. She imagined he would be picking up a daughter, she guessed, back from gap year travels, playing at poverty but always with a nice house and her benign father's credit card to fall back on if it didn't work out. But then she noticed his red trousers. It was Frank Delahunt. McGrain had noticed them too.

'Ma'am?'

'Yeah, I know,' she muttered. 'Sit back.'

They waited, sitting still, doing nothing but sweating. Delahunt was behind them, he could spot them at any time. She thought he was there for Barratt but couldn't be sure until she saw them together.

The arrivals board announced that the Barcelona flight had landed. Delahunt saw the announcement too and folded his paper carefully, tucking it under his arm. He wandered across their path to the double doors marked *No Entry or Re-entry*. He was tense.

They waited. Finally, the double doors opened and a lone woman came through. Dressed in peach cotton and silver strappy sandals, she was ready for dinner on a Spanish beach and looked tired and pissed off to be back. Behind her, through the closing swing doors, a throng of people gathered around the luggage carousel, adjusting their dress after a cramped two-hour flight.

Delahunt shifted his weight to see through the crack in the doors. He was nervous. He wasn't expected and had come on his own initiative.

'Let's move,' she muttered, waving her officers up and over to the building exit so that Barratt wouldn't see them the moment he stepped through the doors. A man with his history would have an eye for polis, not that he'd need second sight to place the guys she had with her: even in plain clothes they all looked police. Too neat. Notably conformist.

They stood in a clump between the exits to the car park and the check-in desks. Morrow told two of them to face away and pretend they were checking their phones while she watched over their shoulders.

The Barcelona passengers began to trickle through the doors. Delahunt moved out of the way of the trolleys and the crowds.

And there he was. Mark Barratt came through the doors, small and broad-shouldered. His skin was white as dough, making him look as if he'd never left Scotland in his life. She realised that she'd half expected to see Danny, because Barratt had the same shaved head and tracksuit, but she felt nothing when it wasn't him.

Barratt was pulling a small, wheeled suitcase. It was incongruously feminine, had a tapestry pattern of an Alsatian dog on the front.

He spotted Delahunt and stopped. Surprised and angry to see him, he walked over.

Delahunt spoke to Barratt's shoulder. Barratt said two forceful words and walked away. Flustered, Delahunt pretended to look for someone else coming out of the doors.

Barratt thundered towards the exit, one of the wheels on his suitcase giving an intermittent shriek.

Morrow nodded the two DCs over to pick up Delahunt and she and McGrain walked over to the doors. 'Mark Barratt?'

Barratt stopped. He looked at them and knew what they were. He said nothing.

'Mr Barratt, we'd like to talk to you about events which occurred in your absence. Will you come with us, please, sir?'

'Giving us a choice?' His voice was a low rumble, a premonition of thunder.

'I think we both know I'm not, Mr Barratt.'

Delahunt was brought over and protested his confusion. Barratt shut him up with a threatening scowl.

'OK,' said Morrow, 'let's get these two winners in the motors.'

Delahunt was in her car as they drove back to London Road. He would talk. Morrow could tell from the unevenness of his breathing, the way he'd pull a sharp intake and let it out. She didn't speak to him. If he had anything to say she wanted it on tape.

At London Road, McGrain pulled the car through the back gate of the station. Delahunt sat, upright as an Irish setter, looking at everything, taking it in. The other car arrived and Barratt slid past in profile, expressionless.

They took them in through the back bar, left the desk sergeant, Mike, to do the paperwork, and took Delahunt straight upstairs to an interview room. Barratt's lawyer was called and on his way. They booked him into another interview room but told him they would have to book his suitcase because it was too big.

As he was led away, Morrow watched Barratt's eyes linger on the roll-on standing on its end behind the desk. She waited until Mike came back.

'That,' she said to the suitcase, 'has got something in it.'

Mike stared at it. They couldn't get into it without a warrant. To get a warrant they needed cause. To get cause they needed Barratt to say something, but he wouldn't. They weren't going to get into the suitcase. Mike looked at her.

'I could do with a hand, ma'am. If you could put that in the storage area for me?'

Morrow didn't know what he meant.

'I mean you can give it a good *feel*, you know, like a Christmas present.'

He was clever, Mike, always had an eye for the limits of regulations.

Morrow crouched down and felt the outside of the suitcase. It was cloth-covered. The tapestry on the front was raised, green and yellow on a black background, but it was solid at the front and back. She tapped it with a knuckle. It felt as if it had been reinforced with solid plastic. The front sank, the tapestry became slightly flaccid. On the back it felt heavier, moved differently and there seemed to be a solidity to the base, as if there was a false bottom inside.

Mike lay the case on its back and tapped the bottom. Again, a heaviness that was too uniform to be explained by shampoo and sandals. They stood up and looked at it.

'Where's he coming from, ma'am?'

'Just arrived from Barcelona.'

'Cocaine?'

'Dunno.'

'He's put his job down as "upholsterer". Said he's done an apprenticeship and everything. But would he bring it in himself?'

'It's the weakest point in the process, isn't it? Risk averse and you get someone else, but that really creates more risk.'

They looked at the suitcase. Even if it was packed with coke they weren't getting in.

'Store it,' said Morrow, pissed off, and went upstairs to interview Delahunt.

42

Delahunt was delighted to see her. He stood to shake her hand, his mouth hanging open, keen as chips to tell her the story he had made up in the car. She fitted the tapes, holding a hand up to stay Delahunt's gallop before the tapes were notified of who was here and what was afoot.

'OK, now, Francis Delahunt, can you tell me, in your own words, what you were doing at Prestwick airport this morning?' She spoke slowly, trying to counter his excitement and make him slow down.

'So, yes,' he began, holding his breath and looking at the floor. 'I was at the airport to wait for a friend when I happened to see Mark Barratt—'

'Name?'

'Name?'

'Of your friend. We'll check flight records for your friend.'

'Ah,' thinking on his feet, 'see the thing is—'

'FRANK.'

Delahunt looked at the table.

'Frank,' she said quietly, 'we found Roxanna Fuentecilla dead. We found another dead woman in Loch Lomond. She was an ex-employee at Injury Claims. The man who killed her worked for Mark Barratt. This is really serious now. Do you understand?'

Shocked, he jerked a nod. 'She's dead?'

'This is really serious. You're looking at serious jail time here.'

'Roxanna's dead?'

'Strangled with wire.'

He slumped in his chair, 'Oh, God.'

'I need you to tell me the truth.'

He nodded and his eyes pleaded with her to help him.

'I can help you, but I need you to help me. It can't all be one way. We need to help each other.'

He nodded still, he got that, he understood and whispered at both of them, 'I'm just her contact in the town.'

'For who?'

'Roxanna. I'm just a conduit. I'm not doing anything *illegal* per se. I'm giving advice and putting people in contact with one another.'

'What was Roxanna here for?'

Delahunt took a deep breath. 'OK. It's a system.' He sucked his molars, thinking, possibly excising himself from the story. 'Assets in a trading partnership. Partnership goes dormant,' he looked up, 'for *whatever* reason.'

'Because she's dead?'

'No!'

'Disappeared? Later declared—'

'No! Arrested! Arrested. They wanted her to get arrested. That was *all*. The man, the father, he wanted the children back. They weren't supposed to kill her. It shouldn't have happened that way. No one wanted that but she realised.' He shut his eyes, exasperated.

'She realised what?'

Delahunt sighed. 'One of the children told her that her father had called. He mentioned Maria Arias, so she realised that they knew each other.'

'She went to London to confront her?'

'Well,' he shook his head in disbelief, 'that was so stupid. These are not people you threaten, I told her that.'

'Did you warn her when she called you from the field?'

As she watched him recall that morning he seemed to age. 'I did. She said she'd been to see Maria. I told her to run. She wouldn't because of the children. And I decided to go, to convince her.' Delahunt blinked hard, as if he was trying to wipe something from his mind.

'Was that all you did? Get dressed and drive out to "convince" her?'

He was ashamed. He couldn't look at her.

'Or did you call Maria Arias first and tell her where Roxanna was?'

He sat defensively straight. 'Maria said I was not to go to the field. She'd told Roxanna to come back to Scotland, sit tight, it would be all right. She said I should just go back to sleep.'

'But you went?'

'I went and Roxanna was gone. And I hoped she had run. I kept hoping that.'

He looked up, needful of approval or at least understanding.

'Well,' said Morrow coldly, 'she didn't run. Who killed her?'

'I don't know. I don't know anything about it.'

'You've been running this dormant company con up here for a while, haven't you?'

He shrugged, 'It's not a "con"—'

'Did you pitch the idea to the Arias couple?'

'I don't know them. Bob Ashe and I *discussed* it. We know each other from the Helensburgh Yacht Club. We just discussed it, that was all. You can't charge people with discussing things.'

It was a lawyer's excuse. 'Who *paid* you? Mr Ashe?'

Delahunt smirked. 'I wasn't paid anything.'

'Did Roxanna pay you?'

'I told you, I wasn't paid.' He was pleased with himself. Morrow could feel a knee tap coming on.

'They hadn't paid you *yet*?'

'No.'

They stared at each other for a moment.

'Were you given,' she spoke very carefully, 'some consideration, in kind, for the services you provided?'

Delahunt smiled warmly. 'No! You see, they didn't pay me. The deal was that Injury Claims gave me a very favourable mortgage.'

'On your house? I thought the housing market was about to collapse out there?'

'The polls all predict a "no" vote. It'll pick up again and my house has been in my family for four generations. The upkeep is very expensive and with the crash, I'm afraid I invested rather—'

'And the mortgage came from Injury Claims 4 U?'

'Yes,' he said smugly. 'It was just a straightforward mortgage on the house. And a condition of the contract was that when the partnership became dormant the mortgage would be vitiated.'

The Fraud would claw every penny back and that would include Delahunt's house. Morrow didn't tell him. She wanted to savour it.

'OK. Frank, do you know Susan Grierson?'

His smile faded. 'What?' He couldn't seem to follow what was going on suddenly.

'Susan Grierson. Do you know her?'

He shook his head. 'I *knew* her.'

'When?'

He shook his head at the table. 'When she was alive I knew her. Why are you asking me about *that*?'

'Is Susan Grierson not alive?'

'Susan died a year ago. She lived in America. She hadn't been in Helensburgh for decades. Why *on earth* are you asking about Susan?'

'How did she die?'

'Breast cancer. She'd lived on Long Island for years, she married Walter Ashe, Bob's son. They've got kids. When the cancer ... They moved to Miami, for treatment. Walter and the kids are still there.'

'Bob Ashe, who owned Injury Claims 4 U? Susan Grierson was his daughter-in-law?'

'Yes, he retired there, actually. Did Susan's name come up on something? A contract or something? What's going on here?'

She thought of Susan Grierson's husband and father-in-law, all the way across the ocean in balmy Miami, hurriedly briefing Abigail Gomez on the small town history, letting her pick her a patsy, describing his dead wife's past to give her the perfect cover. He would have given her the keys to the house in Sutherland Crescent, Susan's passport to get into the country. He'd have told her just enough about everyone so that she wasn't a stranger in a small community, but a native daughter, coming back.

'Why are you asking about Susan?'

'Roxanna's body was found in Susan Grierson's house.'

'Sutherland Crescent? Oh dear! That lovely house!'

It was so odd, his obsession with houses, that Morrow stumbled, 'Yeah, well, it's not a lovely house any more. It's derelict.'

'Yes, it's been empty for years. Her mother hated Walter Ashe. She left Sutherland Crescent in trust to Susan and Walter's children. She didn't want Walter to have it.'

Morrow took the phone picture of Susan Grierson out of her folder and showed it to him. He shook his head. 'Susan was short and fat, until the cancer. . .'

He watched her put the picture away. 'Was that taken in the Victoria Halls? Who actually is that?'

'Why did you go to meet Barratt at Prestwick?'

'To warn him.' He stopped himself, thinking perhaps he could have chosen a better word. 'To tell him that Roxanna had disappeared. And about the—' He caught himself. 'Some other things.'

'Other things being what?'

'There was a fire. I thought he might not know what had happened . . .'

'I'm guessing he knew all about it. How do you know Mark Barratt?'

His eyes lingered on the file. 'It's very small, Helensburgh. Everybody knows everybody.'

'Does everybody come to meet everybody off the plane?' He didn't answer. He was looking at the file and wondering.

'Did Roxanna tell you she was having trouble with an ex-employee?'

Delahunt started a defensive lie but stalled. Morrow patted the file, implying that she would tell him who the woman in the picture was if he co-operated. She wouldn't. He took a deep breath and stalled again, looking at the folder.

'She either did tell you or she didn't, Frank, it's not a complicated question.'

'She may have mentioned it.'

'And you told Mark Barratt?'

'I didn't tell him. I merely *mentioned* that an employee had been difficult.'

'Did you merely mention her home address in Clydebank?'

'Look, I'm just a conduit—'

Morrow got up and left before she gave her superiors cause to send her on another anger management course.

Barratt's lawyer was well briefed. He arrived at the station and immediately asked for the suitcase back. He put it in his car before he went to see his client in the interview room. They would not be allowed to question him. Barratt had been out of the country when Hettie was killed, when the fire killed two people, and they couldn't prove a link to Roxanna. They had no cause to hold him any longer.

They watched from the office window as Barratt climbed into his lawyer's silver Merc. The lawyer was smoking, sucking the smoke in so hard he looked as if he might swallow his own lips.

43

Morrow and McGrain pulled a couple of chairs away from the back row in the Victoria Hall. They sat next to the wall, in the shadow of the overhanging balcony. They weren't there to participate in the public meeting. They were there to watch the crowd.

The appeal for information was being filmed and would be shown on both the local news and a national TV crime show. A huge camera took up the centre of the room, facing the table on the stage. Banks of plastic chairs were arranged in front of it.

The Sailors' Rest fire was national news because of the tragic death of young Lea-Anne Ray. Helensburgh was appalled by her death, but none of the information the police received had been particularly useful. The feeling was that a lot of people knew but were too afraid to speak out.

Morrow crossed her arms and looked around the familiar hall. She knew almost every corner of it from the plethora of photographs they had collected of the dinner dance. They were collating information on 'Abigail Gomez'. The search would continue on both sides of the Atlantic but Morrow could already feel the energy ebbing from it. Police Scotland would get their slice of the proceeds from Injury Claims 4 U but they would forego a case clean-up. Gomez was a potentially costly collar and they couldn't afford her. So far all they had turned up was a tentative identification: a dead woman by the name of Elizabeth Marquez. Gomez's photos had been loosely matched by a US facial recognition programme. A Venezuelan 'freelance security consultant', Marquez had disappeared in Nigeria three years ago. She was presumed dead. They only had eight points of facial identification, not enough to action.

The TV camera was bigger and boxier than Morrow would have expected. It was manned by slim people with suntans and haircuts too sharp for the small town.

On stage a short table and four chairs had been laid out in front of a blue backdrop banner with the thistle and crown logo of Police Scotland: *Keeping People Safe,* it said.

The burghers of the town began to filter in. A janitor pointed them to the seats and the TV people began to rearrange the audience like flowers in a vase. They placed the early arrivals in the front row and aisles, checking the composition in their monitors and going back to move them again.

Morrow could see the monitor screen on the back of the camera, the boxy view of the room making the hall seem small and intimate. The view through the monitor was insistent. Her eye kept being drawn back to the bright little rectangle of ordered reality.

Simmons arrived with Chief Inspector Pittoch who was wearing his full ceremonial uniform. They toured the hall together, smiling and shaking hands with the television people, with journalists. CI Pittoch gave a radio interview into a small dictaphone. Then someone from the TV came over and fitted the two of them with collar mics, sliding the wire down the back of their jackets and putting the transmitters into their pockets. All the while townspeople filtered in and were directed into their chairs.

More chairs were brought in for more people. They were arriving all the time and the crowd began to creep towards Morrow and McGrain.

A commotion near the door. Elderly members of the audience stood up, reverently watching two old women coming in. One was in a wheelchair, a bad leg straight out in front of her, two hands clutching the handle of her handbag like a steering wheel. The other old lady leaned heavily on the chair. Both of the women were dressed in their best, clean blouses, smart cardigans.

At the side of the stage they were mic'd up and helped up the steep steps to the stage. The standing woman took it slowly and the seated woman was eased out of the chair by a couple of audience members. She made it up to the stage one shuffled step at a time. The wheelchair was folded, handed up, opened again and she sat down. She was wheeled behind the table and her companion sat down next to her. A man in the audience gave a couple of misplaced claps and was slapped on the arm for his trouble by the woman next to him.

Still the town was arriving. The pensioners had come good and early, but now the rest of the town were streaming through the doors. Men in work clothes, women hurrying in as if they had just shed children in the car park, a woman with an NHS badge nodding to almost everybody.

Three young men came in together, all wearing 'Yes' badges and carrying handfuls of referendum literature. A ripple of annoyance ran across the hall. They weren't going to, were they? Not here, for goodness' sake! But they weren't. They sat down by the door, just canvassers on a break.

Frank Delahunt arrived alone and was ignored by everyone. He sat down next to an elderly couple. They took his proffered hand and shook it but resented having to do so. He wasn't liked and Morrow knew he had been told that he was losing his house. Police Scotland were going to auction it.

Boyd Fraser came in, still wearing his chef whites. He must have come from next door. He'd been out of custody for four days but he looked shaken. His wife, Lucy, held his hand tightly, her jaw clenched, her attention on his every step. She was worried for him and he was grateful for her.

The room stiffened suddenly. A momentary hush fell and everyone looked to the door. Mark Barratt was in the doorway. He stood with his chest out, taking the opprobrium full on. Morrow had to bite her cheek to stop herself from crying. It was the way he stood, arms out to the sides, fists balled, defiant. For a fleeting moment he had looked so much like Danny that she was afraid she would be sick.

The moment passed, the chatter in the room rose again and Barratt walked into the body of the room. He wasn't alone. The two younger men were dressed like Barratt, in dark tracksuits and they all had shaved heads. They looked like Barratt's apostles. One of them had very heavy eyebrows.

'That's Tommy Farmer,' muttered McGrain, and Morrow nodded.

The trio walked around behind the camera, surveying the hall for seats. Tommy Farmer found three chairs together and stood by them, looking to Mark for approval, but the other guy had found a run of four seats and Mark nodded and headed over to him.

Tommy looked puzzled. He stayed where he was and watched Barratt sit down and look up to the door. A woman was standing there. Barratt beckoned her over. They seemed an unlikely couple. She was messy, shuffling as she made her way over. Her ankles were swollen and she had a rip on the hem of her skirt. Her thin blonde hair was tangled at the back. She smiled and nodded at Barratt and sat down next to him.

Tommy was agitated. He hurried over, looking at the woman, looking Barratt, moving quickly, looking for an explanation of something as he sat on the other side of his boss. Barratt blanked him but the woman made a point of giving Tommy a big grin. She looked like him. It was Tommy's mother.

The room was full. The doors were shut. The TV directors checked their monitors. The old women on the stage flattened their hair and collars and cardigans. Simmons and her boss moved to the wings of the stage, watching for a cue. Silence fell in the room.

The director looked away from the monitor and gave the police a nod.

CI Pittoch pulled his tunic straight with a firm tug at the hem, gave the audience a fleeting look of utter terror, walked to the table and sat down on the nearest chair. Simmons followed him on. She looked very comfortable. The press conference began.

Pittoch welcomed them and said that the devastating fire at the Sailors' Rest had been started deliberately. A local man, Murray Ray and his young daughter, well-loved in the local community, had died. Now: people knew who was responsible and this was the time to tell the truth. It was difficult sometimes, in such a close-knit community, to tell the truth but it was important.

Pittoch introduced Mrs Eunice Ray, the lady in the wheelchair, and Annie Kilpatrick. They were Lea-Anne's grandmothers and they wanted to read a statement.

Annie and Eunice. Morrow hadn't known their names. She hadn't even mentioned Iain Fraser's stilted last words to Simmons because they made no sense. Tell them. It wasn't me.

The room was silent and still. Annie Kilpatrick kept her eyes down, trembling, as Eunice lifted her statement. The microphone was turned up so high to catch her faint voice that the room was filled with her breathing, the sound of her clothes brushing against each other. In the monitor screen Morrow saw that she was holding the paper too high, obscuring her face from view. She read in a high voice. Her only son and her granddaughter, their princess, had been murdered in this fire. People in the town knew who had started it. They had a duty to come forward and tell the police. Please tell—

She stopped speaking. The paper in front of her face trembled. The room was so still, the mic so high, they could hear her tears drip on the paper.

Eunice lowered the sheet, making herself visible again. She was weeping, looking at Annie sitting next to her. Annie was crying openly at the table, her chin on her chest. She whispered deep into the collar mic, 'Our lives are over.'

Everyone waited for her to speak again but she didn't. Simmons looked to her boss. CI Pittoch hadn't expected to be called upon to speak so soon. He was startled but took over:

'So! We appeal. To anyone who knows anything. Come forward and help this family.'

In his confusion he looked straight at Mark Barratt.

Mark Barratt sat, unflinching, and looked back at him. Then he nodded, just a little.

'No! Mark! No!'

It was the woman next to him. She was on her feet, grabbing across Barratt, reaching for her son, Tommy.

Barratt lifted an arm up and blocked her, took her shoulder and pushed her back into her seat.

In the far corner of the hall a small man raised his hand, watching Barratt's impassive face as he did. He was wearing a track suit too. He wanted to speak and Mark Barratt gave him a nod. 'Tommy Farmer started the fire. I seen him.'

A solitary shriek of a chair filled the room. Tommy was standing, looking at the door out.

'Stay!' Simmons was across the stage and down the steps. 'Farmer! Stay there!'

Mark Barratt was up. He lifted the woman at his side to her feet, yanking her out of the room with him.

Farmer shouted after them. 'I never!'

But Simmons was at his side, taking his wrist, nodding a cop over to the man with his hand up. CI Pittoch sat still on the stage, trying hard to remain dignified for the camera. The audience were nodding, satisfied, agreeable.

But Morrow wasn't watching the arrest. She was transfixed by the old women on stage. Anek and her niece. Annie and Eunice. They weren't watching the arrest either. They were crying, holding hands, forehead pressed to forehead. Everything they said was amplified by both their mics, so loud it drowned the room.

Annie gasped for breath through her tears and Eunice sobbed, 'Thank God! Thank God! Thank God!'

The room was a maelstrom of action, Tommy resisting arrest, the small man with his hand up being questioned, Boyd Fraser and his wife hugged in a corner. Groups of people swirled and ebbed, lives were changed and cliffs swept away, but Morrow wasn't watching any of it. She was listening.

Through the big speakers on either side of the stage surged the sound of old women crying, reaching for each other, and the rasp of blouse against mic filled the room as surely as water.

Acknowledgments

I'd like to thank Nicola White for inviting me to Hel often, and explaining the referendum politics of the area, though we were on different shores at the time. I'd like to apologise to Ms White if I have inadvertently misrepresented any of the nuances around the whole gazebo controversy. Any overt or covert implications on the use of gazebos for political purposes are inadvertent. I had strong opinions on this at one time but now I no longer care. To be clear: I will still fight ye, but the fun has gone out it for me.

Also thanks to the people who advise and guide and patiently explain why this bit is rubbish and that character wasn't even in the story until page 274 and everyone in the book has glasses on: Jon Wood, Jemima Forrester, Peter Robinson. Also to Angela McMahon and Graeme Williams, and sorry about forgetting to go to things all the time. Also to Juliet Ewers and Susan Lamb. And the God-sent Susie Murray and Trudi Keir, both of whom wrangle with the chaos and leave me free to work.

You're all bloody lovely and I wake up every morning grateful for you.

About the Author

Denise Mina is the author of the novels *The Red Road, Gods and Beasts, The End of the Wasp Season, Still Midnight, Slip of the Knife, The Dead Hour, Field of Blood, Deception,* and the Garnethill trilogy, the first installment of which won the John Creasey Memorial Award for best first crime novel. Mina has twice received the Theakstons Old Peculier Crime Novel of the Year award. She lives in Glasgow.